Epstein's Pancake is as close to Le Carré as we've got on this side of the Atlantic. It's historical fiction in the form of a highly charged political thriller, set in the political and financial corruption of Iran-contra. Like Ricki Tarr in The Spy Who Came In From The Cold, Rob Price is a junior guy with a French mother who lets his private life get mixed up in his agency work. Then he knows too much, and his ethics kick in. The pace is relentless, friends die, and the climax is horrific. This is a harsh, driven tale by an unusual new writer.

— Michael Segedy, author of *A Lethal Partnership*, *Hampton Road*,

This is a very political and sometimes violent book about a straight arrow Navy vet who turns whistleblower on his agency. Rob Price is making it up as he goes along, and you wonder how long he can keep it up. Set in the murk of Iran-contra, it's infiltrated with black humor by smart people who know what they're doing. The characters are strong and clear, and enjoyable. There's also a subtext about intimate relations between the spy business, government drug-running, the arms industry, and dirty banks. **Epstein's Pancake** turns out to be a high stakes tech scam by well-connected people with big offices who can lobby their way out of a jam. It's a hard day's night for all parties, and more than a good read.

— Jill Yesko, author of *Murder in the Dog Park*

EPSTEIN'S PANCAKE

a political thriller

BY

BJARNE ROSTAING

St. Marks Press

ISBN: 978-0-9899902-4-0
ISBN: 978-0-9899902-5-7

Printed in the United States of America

Front cover by Frank Siciliano

www.bjarnerostaing.com

For Linda Simmons, wherever she may be

With special thanks to René Grayre for his thoughtful editing.

We'll know our disinformation program is complete
when everything the American public believes is false.
— William Casey, CIA Director 1981-87

Don't you think we need a woman's touch
To make you come alive?
— Keith Richards, Mick Jagger

BACKSTORY

The 1988 elections ended an era most Americans were comfortable with. Ronald Reagan was a genial, calming presence, and nobody's fool in a crisis. When terrorist explosions in Lebanon destroyed our embassy and CIA station, followed by the Marine barracks, he saw the handwriting on the Mid-East wall and cut our losses. He welcomed Gorbachev and his perestroika reforms, but kept his distance and stayed the course with his Tear Down This Wall speech.

Despite near-nuclear catastrophes that went unreported and the shooting down of a Korean airliner in Soviet air space in 1983, a de-escalation of the cold war seemed to be on the way. But defeat in Vietnam only hardened the Dulles brothers' anti-communist line, and the US was exploring the possibility of an anti-missile system that would break the balance of super-powers. SDI (Strategic Defense Initiative, a.k.a. "Star Wars") would replace MAD (Mutually Assured Destruction), and it was backed by Reagan. It was Pandora's Box, potentially ending nuclear parity and undermining what might have become genuine detente.

Bubbling under the surface were unresolved issues. Vietnam was our first-ever lost war, and it split the nation. New York's Bowery and other skid-rows across the country were filling up with demoralized veterans, many of them drug or alcohol dependent, alienated by lack of respect and the general desire to deny what had happened. The government was ignoring the near-epidemic spread of AIDS and failing to prioritize research. Saddam Hussein was fighting a proxy war with Iran for us and killing Kurds with chemical weapons supplied by the U.S. Recreational drugs were a fact of American life and drug running was a major industry with multi-billion dollar cartels destabilizing Latin American governments.

Out of this came the War On Drugs, a costly failure much like Prohibition. But drugs were also funding the "Contras," a group of disgruntled Nicaraguans attempting to depose the leftist and legitimately elected Sandinista government. The CIA supported the

Contras, but they lacked arms, and the Sandinistas were holding their own. It was a stalemate, and Contra atrocities were becoming known despite a news clamp-down. Out of that came the scandal of the decade, Iran-contra.

Iran was an anathema to America since the revolution of 1979, which deposed the CIA's Shah. Islamic zealots seized American hostages, and President Carter's failure to rescue them doomed his presidency. Israel detested Iran for its own reasons, but the CIA was determined to arm the Contras, and cobbled together a coalition involving sworn enemies Israel and Iran, working with the CIA and American arms-hustlers. The arrangement was blatantly illegal, and participants were a who's-who of shady characters from Arab bankers to retired American military officers and a photogenic young Marine Colonel coordinating it with his beautiful assistant.

What made Iran-contra so explosive was the role of George H.W. Bush, Reagan's vice president and Republican nominee for the presidency. Bush had been head of the CIA and had a long history with the agency. He was also was close to many of the Arab bankers and arms dealers involved in Iran-contra. Most damning, he had cooperated in founding BCCI (the Bank of Credit and Commerce International), an amazingly corrupt bank pursued by many governments but vital to the intelligence community, and woven into Iran-contra.

Watergate had been a watershed: the truth came out and heads rolled. Not so with Iran-contra, which continued to fester.

This is the world of **Epstein's Pancake**.

Part I

1

BEGIN on a warm September afternoon in a small old fashioned Manhattan tailor shop circa the '88 elections. Me looking at an attaché case, about to buy it, not sure exactly why. I knew some of the reasons, though. I'd never seen anything like it, and I happened to have the money, and it was a quirky access to power. At a lower price I might have bought it just because it was a really excellent case — black leather, solid and very well made. A little oversized, so you could use it for an overnight bag, and heavy, with the classic hardwood frame. Tan peccary interior, everything included — calculator, battery shaver, Pelikan writing set. Security via large brass combination lock. A tight ship.

It was the end of the Reagan years, a bad time for me. My job was gone, followed by my second wife, and my money was running out. I was investing in something different here. New York is attitude, and this piece of luggage had it. Not twelve hundred dollars worth, but that's what I paid for it when I saw what it was. In the false bottom of this banker-faced artifact was a small green pistol with a remote firing mechanism and suppressor. It was set in diagonally, corner-to-corner, just right if you decided to gut someone in the middle of a disagreement. Not that I'd ever thought of doing anything like that, but in any case I knew half a dozen traders who'd love to own it for a higher price if I wasn't comfortable with it. And owning a gun didn't bother me. In Vietnam I'd seen that people kill each other and get used to it. It's a crowded world, and what with Darwin staring us in the eye and third world hordes threatening to overwhelm us, we find a way to feel all right about it. Bottom line, I was used to guns. In rural New England where I grew up, rifles and shotguns were part of life. A solid, pious little world where the unspoken thought was "Kill not, that you may look down on those who do." I suppose my father thought that way too, until he met a French girl who'd been running around for the Resistance with a Sten gun while he was pushing paper on a troop ship. He was the last of a long line of teachers and preachers from which I escaped somehow. Checked out in his old Pontiac not long after she died. One-car accident on an off-camber curve he'd been driving for years.

The pistol was small and thin, mostly green composite, made by a Swiss company, Michaud-Coubert. There were two loads — a Teflon cop-killer and a mercury load that would turn into a big lead flower more deadly than the poppy. In the false bottom with the gun were ammo, a recorder, and currency compartments. Corner-to-corner metal braces aligned with the barrel to fudge x-rays. Trigger and safety fore and aft in the handle, with a little plate to let you know which end was which.

Where do you get such a thing? I got it from my tailor, Fred, a graying retired Spanish anarchist I'd known for several years who beat me at chess in eleven moves the first time we played. We weren't close and never talked much, but we got along. We met in Central Park, both of us on bikes, and he stayed with me for three laps on an old green Bianchi with steel components. It gave me something to think about, because I'd done some racing and was much younger. Born Federico in northern Spain, Fred had a long, lined, face, eyes like olives, neat graying hair, and a very flat stomach for a man in his late fifties. He was a quiet, civil man who respected good manners, one of these people who seem to take up no space. After years in the same second-floor space, his shop still looked as if he'd just moved in with long pipes running along below the ceiling, and garments hanging from the pipes. Little wood counter with an old cash register at the door, chess table with two chairs in a corner. On a shelf next to the chess set were an old espresso machine and a bottle of brandy. Everything exactly where it belonged, and his work was the same. When Fred fitted a jacket, you looked rich and forgot you were wearing it. Joanna, my second wife, snubbed him, then became wary of him. Once she joked that he could probably make himself invisible and fly. No fool, Joanna.

Fred also worked with leather, and he explained that someone had left this case for repair. After I'd examined it he told me the price and I raised my eyebrows. Then he used a tiny hex wrench to loosen four plastic bolts hidden under the lining and lifted out the false bottom. I saw the gun and looked up at him with an expression I hoped was appropriate. I'd known him for years, but there was a formality about him that maintained a distance.

"It was left a long time ago, several years. I am not eager to sell it, but my wife requires to be in hospital . . . "

I was flattered that he trusted me and sorry about his wife, whom I'd never met. He didn't have time for a chess game but I'd catch him after work another day.

The first thing I did after getting home was take the pistol out of the case, go up to the roof, and test-fire it. It was surprisingly quiet — just a little hissing-squirting *Pop!* When I saw what a mercury load did to a four-by-four I went back downstairs and had a Jameson. Then I cleaned it, reloaded with Teflons, and stowed the case under some loose boards in my closet.

I tried to watch the election news then, but couldn't. I try not to think about politics, but my father taught history at some good schools and some of his knowledge rubbed off. I'd thought of George H.W. Bush as a high level civil servant — Yale, Skull and Bones, quiet man, banking family. Son of a senator my father detested but easy to take, aside from his CIA connection. An okay vice president, maybe make an okay president. Then I'd seen Dan Rather confront him about playing footsie with the Ayatollah on the Iran-Contra arms deal, and saw him get schooled by a pro. No contest — TKO Round 1, CBS bleeding from eyes and mouth. Bush's old friends had prepped him well. The Veep was sanctimonious and slippery, using "out of the loop" to mean not operationally involved, leading viewers to assume he didn't know about it. He kept cutting Rather off, raising a thin, nasty northeast voice, wagging a finger and scolding him, not letting him finish a thought. Then he claimed memory loss and preened. My revised view was, *rich guy no class*. His father's son, and I couldn't stand him. And he was going to win the election.

I turned off the news and went out for a drink. I ended up having several at The Pope's Nose, known to regulars as The Pope, a big old bar owned in part by my friend McVeigh. Mac was a fellow Wall-Streeter and Black Monday victim who was fired the same week I was. It was a slow night, and we talked. As usual Mac suggested doing something about my prematurely gray hair. Grecian Formula this time — always a new brand. I didn't let it bother me, I had a lot of respect for Mac. For one thing, he'd made it through SEAL training and the missions that followed, and after that he'd been a heavy player at a big house. Letting him go had been stupid — he'd made fortunes for them with his instincts and balls. A month later he was an owner in The Pope, with his old friends coming in to talk shop after work. A big, beefy, crafty Celt, McVeigh, good to have as a friend, and you definitely don't want one for an enemy.

Mac had my interests at heart. Six months before he'd offered me five thousand dollars to take what he described as his life savings to an Algerian named Jacques in Paris. Not your average retirement planner, but that was Mac's business. It was a dangerous game, and I'd been ripe for it, though I suspected McVeigh's $140K was IRA funds. Major turning point, though I didn't notice, and the transaction had gone down as if blessed. I found I had no problem helping a friend avoid taxes on what might actually be his life savings for all I knew. Flying home it struck me that I'd lived my life as honestly as I could, and that it wasn't working very well. What was left of my ethics was that I tried not to take advantage of friends, and my word was still good. But I'd come to the point of seeing it's dangerous being too concerned about how you get your money. Takes you out of the flow.

"Y'know, Rob, I'd offer you a job if it weren't for the pith helmet."

Another joke. McVeigh had an aged military uncle who hated colonial Brits and their pith helmets, and the phrase was meant to convey the downside of the white man's burden — if you look right in a suit, you're probably a stiff. Mac thought I was a snob because I speak more than one language and was good at explaining investments to rich old ladies, but he forgave me. We were close enough that we talked about our kids, whom we'd basically lost to ex-wives. Outside the wind was up and a storm was brewing. It was a drinking night.

"And why would I be wanting to work for a smarmy *arriviste* such as yourself then, *Misther* McVeigh?"

"Money, you supercilious dick."

I didn't mind his honesty and he didn't mind my brogue. We traded ethnic jokes as the storm worked itself up, then he went after me.

"Gonna vote for the liberal, I suppose."

I didn't share my thoughts because he'd laugh.

"I'm not voting for either one." I said. "You like the spook, I imagine."

"Don't be imagining, boyo. Mrs. Reagan's got twice the smarts of either one, but will they run her? Of course not."

Then his tone changed.

"I think I might be doing something again with that Jacques fella," he said quietly. "You feel like another little trip, drop in the Louvre, visit the galleries?"

Another tweak. I used to buy art when I could afford it.

"Why not?" I said. He nodded his deal-making nod.

Things were picking up, and just in time. On the tube was our future president, his campaign song in the background — *Don't Worry, Be Happy*, a mindless *a capella* novelty tune written and performed by a black man. I was just about sure we'd have a KGB protégé running Russia and a CIA head running the US.

Outside was wind-driven rain turning to hail. Walking home with my head pulled down into my collar and the Jameson running round my veins I felt change coming. I was thinking that when you're on — when you're really on and know it — people get out of your way. They nod, they smile, they want to be your friend. It had been like that in France, working for Finlay, Kline. Then they'd closed the European branch, and there was the long, losing battle with Doug Finlay. I'd voted for Carter and said so, and he hadn't laughed, or even smiled. Then Kline's heart attack. He'd been my mentor and protector. Soon the sound of one head rolling.

Rock'n'roll was exploding through the floor as I stepped out of my wet shoes. Tom Terrific, downstairs neighbor and keyboard maniac, former college tennis star and leader of the Del Psychos. I left my clothes in a heap, walked into the bathroom and turned on the shower. Then I looked in the mirror at the baby-face under my brillo-mop of gray hair while the water heated up. I've looked pretty much the same since my twenties, but I could see the suet building up. I stood for a long time in a very hot shower sluicing away the drink-sweat, and when the steam cleared I looked better. The funky old green paint and orange shower curtain were sending a message, though — better a white collar criminal than a pith-helmet dinosaur. Tom's keyboards howled and I looked at my mid-life. No job, computer down, dust rhinos under the bed, bills and papers here and there. I'd take my chances and make another run for Mac, but that wasn't the answer. I needed a job.

I turned on the TV and some anchor was going on about the war on drugs. Another government joke — one agency's gunships over Columbia stamping out coca while another one trafficked in it to fund black ops. Cocaine was king, and Wall Street was loving it — hot-pants traders after chilly models, many of them sleeping with cute bisexual photographers carrying The Virus. Not that I hadn't enjoyed a few lines myself when a good-looking woman was involved. I turned off the news and turned on the radio. Led Zep III, loud enough to shuffle the synapses. It had been playing the weekend my daughter was conceived. Layla, child of the much-maligned sixties, my only child. Kidnapped by Wife #1, Felice-of-the-Hamptons, with the assistance of many attorneys and unlimited funds. Thinking about my daughter took me apart. I wrote a modest check for her coming birthday and put it in an envelope, hoping she wasn't using drugs. You never know 'til too late, but it's never too late to tithe.

2

A few days later I thought I might have a game with Fred. It was late afternoon, Indian Summer, a good afternoon for walking. I headed north through Washington Square Park, checked out the chess tables, looked at pretty women, listened to hand-drummers, was accosted by dope dealers. Eventually I got to the seam between Chelsea and the Village, a little rent-controlled pocket where Fred's shop was located. Fred was having a game with a young guy dressed like Buffalo Bill. He smiled and gave a little nod as his opponent studied the board, then asked how things were going, his way of asking if I'd found a job. I smiled and told him things were looking up.

"Keep playing," I added. "I'll be back for a game."

"Closing time on Thursday?" he asked. "We could play then — "

I nodded and stepped out the door into what I called Condition Nam. It comes over me sometimes, a wave of cold irrational rage that just takes over. Sometimes it makes my ears ring, and I don't know what brings it on. Like my father, I had a desk job on an unimportant ship, and we saw action once, if you could call it that, blew up a fishing boat for no good reason. I never got these rages before that war, and since then I've had this Nam-beast living in my head. I felt strong enough to look it in the eye and stare it down this time. But walking back through purplish early dusk I felt like a loner, an odd-duck crazy, getting further out by the day and wanting back in. Then the beast backed off, and I remembered Fred's invitation. It was a first — we didn't schedule our games, they just happened every now and then.

Thursday I found Fred deep in a game with a powerfully built man of about fifty with short, neat, graying hair, herringbone jacket, gray flannel slacks and rep tie. Low-key clothes, but an intense guy with a hard face, very single-minded as he stared at the board. Almost all the pieces were still there, but Fred, playing black, had jammed his opponent's development, and his knights were poised ominously. The game was about to explode. I poured myself a brandy and watched the stranger try to break out with a pawn sacrifice. Fred held him by trading a rook for a bishop. Then Fred lost a pawn and it looked good for white, except that Fred had his Queen on the key diagonal and a horse in the right spot, and that was all she wrote.

"Over twenty moves," said the stranger, with the exasperation of a man who has to accept something he can't deal with and doesn't like.

"Twenty two," said Fred graciously. "You must show more respect for the horse, eh?"

Then, in his courtly way, he suggested that he could show him a mistake from their last game. I knew that Fred kept track of how many moves had been played, but it startled me that he could recall a game from what sounded like a while back. It was unnerving, like absolute pitch or being able to float in mid-air long enough to dunk a basketball, draw the foul and wink at your guys on landing. The man declined, and Fred introduced us, formal as always.

"Rob, this is Morris, whom I have known for many years."

It sounded like a recommendation. I stuck out my hand and we shook old-style. Head on, Morris was tough, with a square face, big neck, thick nose and small glinty blue eyes. He didn't look like anyone who'd be playing chess in Fred's shop. While I was getting used to him, Fred disappeared into the back, which was another odd note. Morris turned on the old tube radio, from which came the news that the President-to-be, despite his CIA tenure, had been in a virtual *tizzy* about the very *notion* of trading arms for hostages, once he found out, after everyone else in Washington. Both of us half-smiled.

"You're looking for a job . . . ?"

It was totally unlike Fred to mention my situation to anyone without telling me. I didn't answer, and Morris looked me over. I looked at him the same way, not very comfortable. I saw the kind of guy who in the old days would join a fraternity and bring it credit by starting for the football team. Kind of guy who respected tradition and kept up his grades. Deferential when appropriate, not to be crossed. Something about him brought Mac to mind, and I guessed that he came with the attaché case.

"You traveled for a Wall Street outfit?"

I was startled, unable to recall mentioning this to Fred.

"Not recently," I said in my office voice.

"You don't mind travel though — "

"No. I like travel. And what do you do?"

"I hire trustworthy people who travel well and get things done discreetly. The work involves extended periods overseas."

I got it then, and didn't like it much.

"Government work?" I asked dryly, thinking about the Dulles brothers, who got us into Nam and kept us there forever making the world safe for democracy.

"Yes, government work," said Morris in a level voice, reading me well.

"I think you might have the wrong impression."

He went for the brandy and poured himself a short one while I re-thought Fred.

"One for you?"

"Thanks."

"I'm always on edge after Federico kicks my butt. Out of my league, annoys hell out of me. Are you interested in a job or what?"

Hard push. I took my time and answered carefully, irritated with both of them.

"I'm not really sure I qualify for that kind of work."

"Well, Fred thinks so, and from what I've learned, I think he's right. I checked you out. Short-hitch Navy Intelligence, honorable discharge. Change jobs too often, get fired for irritating people. Keep your credit line, God knows how. Not going to work downtown any more because you pulled that stuff once too often. Few months ago you did a dope deal in France — "

"*Wrong*, Mister Morris. I don't do that."

The rest was accurate, and I didn't waste his time disputing it.

"Just Morris. What was it? Hot art? You didn't go for your health, and we know you bought art when you had money."

It was getting to me, how much he knew. He chuckled and nodded, a tiny movement of that heavy skull. I felt myself looking at him without expression, the way I'd look at a potentially dangerous drunk. I was not happy with Fred.

"My mother was French, I have family there. Before we go further, how about a job description? And why me?"

"One, you don't look like Clark Kent. Two, you speak the languages, and three you have natural cover."

"Let's talk again sometime," I said, meaning get fucked.

"I'll be gone. We can talk now."

He topped up his drink and turned to me. I put my hand over my glass and listened to the radio chatter.

"Federico likes you, Says your chess keeps improving."

"Would you want to identify yourself?" I said, stepping on his last words. "I like to know who I'm talking to."

He slipped a thin black crocodile case from inside his jacket, opened it, and let me look at an ID card for Morris Pell, employed by some agency I'd never heard of. While I was looking at it, he reached into another pocket and tossed over a greasy blue nylon wallet with a French passport under the name Arnault. In it was a Polaroid of himself in bush hat and khakis, standing with a Kalashnikov on his hip in what looked like a North African village. I was curious as well as bothered. Morris/Arnault was a smart guy who understood people fast and knew how to use them.

Sure, and what else? I wondered, as I always do about certain people. What else beyond the balls and brains, if anything.

He had Fred's approval, that was what else. I sat there and let the silence open up. In the background warbled the infectious-moronic Bush theme, *Don't Worry, Be Happy.*

"I understood you were looking for employment," he said after a while, his voice distant and neutral.

"I've been offered a position."

"Rainbow Rentals? CFO for a black rent-a-car company? Not exactly your style is it?"

I cracked a smile and replied from the heart.

"Better than running around the bush with a bunch of trigger-happy gun freaks."

"Yeah, I can see where you'd stand on that. That's another ball game."

"And what would mine be?"

"Not sticking out, handling sensitive situations. Being businesslike."

"European situations."

"Right. Where you can use your languages. I know you've got good French — what others?"

"Pretty good Spanish, not bad Italian. Some Kinh, no German."

"What we need. You go to Paris, we find you a nice cover job, you go on living as you like, hang with who you want, find reasons to travel."

I was irritated with myself for being so responsive but Morris was persuasive.

"For me to even think about this, I've got to know the downside. Risk factors."

"Not dangerous. You'd be a courier, pick things up and drop them off, routine sensitive stuff that has to be handled by trustworthy people. Not high risk — Joe Courier doesn't carry the Stealth paint formula. If you get bored and want to do more we'll train you."

"I'll think about it. Call you day after tomorrow."

"Good. Call me here," he said, handing me a card.

The card had only a number. My memory isn't great, but I knew this would stick for a while. I looked at it, nodded, and handed the card back. It was a classic move — walk away clean. Morris half-smiled. Then he was gone, and I was alone in the brown silence of Fred's shop, feeling very much alive, which I hadn't been recently. It jumped out at me that seeing and feeling and grasping and remembering sharply are priceless gifts. Standing there I felt them coming back. Morris was a way for me to be in that state and be paid for it. My pith helmet nodded approval. I wrote the number on a card. A Brooklyn number.

Fred reappeared then, and I said nothing at first. Then I suggested doing some laps in the park Sunday morning. He replied slowly, a little apologetic.

"No, Rob, we cannot. It is better for us not to be together for a while."

It took me at least a second.

"So no more chess, either — "

"I am retired, but I worry," he said. "For my wife, you understand. It's better to be single, of course. You'll do well, Rob. We'll ride in the Spring."

I got it slowly, still bothered at having been being set up with the attaché case. Fred looked more like a weary village padre than a spook headhunter.

You clever old bastard! I wanted to say. *Who are you?*

But beating him at his own game appealed to me more, so we did an old-style hand-shaking ceremony, not unlike a pair of Roman senators at the baths, or a couple of Japanese businessmen parting after a visit to Geisha land.

Then he handed me a card: *Jennifer Chen-Garthwaite,* it read: *Martial Arts.*

"Plays Go," added Fred.

And you're completely out of shape.

I saw that Fred had pretty much figured me out over the chess board.

3

Sitting on a bench in sunny Washington Square Park I watched New Yorkers milling slowly in the warm air, looking for something. Under the Arch and overflowing the waterless wading pool were all the kinds it takes to make a world — yuppies, cops, geniuses, jailbirds, artists, college kids, immigrants, fried hippies and endless dealers of crack, flake, smack, herb, hot dogs, soda, falafel and ice cream. Also some skinheads from the boroughs waiting to beat up on gays in the cool of the evening. History lulled me. I remembered pretty girls and twilight music. Bringing my daughter here and teaching her to catch a ball. The crowd churned in the still air as I sat on my bench and allowed young matrons to regard me as a potential pederast while their kids ignored me. It was one o'clock, reality was on hold.

Morris appeared from nowhere in a generic bomber jacket unzipped to reveal a Guns N' Roses T-shirt. In his left hand was a boom-box playing rap, which he stuck between us. He looked ten years younger, as if he was in from New Jersey to do something illegal.

"So? Made up your mind? Wanna work for Uncle?"

"Like to know a little more first."

"Yeah, so would we," he said. His voice planted his words solidly. "Okay, we'll start with a kind of test, give me some sense of where to pick up. Being it's Saturday and we want to blend in, I'm gonna light up for appearances. Join me?"

"Not right now, thanks. More interested in the test."

"You just got an A on part one. Next part is multiple input retention."

He gave me two phone numbers, one U.S., one French, and repeated them. I gave them back, and as I was trying to lock them in, he told me to look at the benches by the toddler swings for a few seconds. I was sweating.

"Okay, that's five seconds, look back toward the Arch.

Wanna give me the phone numbers or the benches first?"

I rattled off the New York number, then half of the French one, then said I'd finish that number after describing the bench-people. I got the benches to his satisfaction but the second number didn't come.

"Well, it's A minus if you remember it while we're here, C plus without it. B is passing. Call it in tomorrow, we find you work in the office."

Off balance and irritated, I smiled, and the second phone number popped up.

"Good. This is how I work. Forty minutes here and I know more than with a half day test battery. Okay, fact one: for now, written communication is by one-time pad. You were in Intelligence, you're familiar with this stuff, right? The pads are edible. I'm gonna give you two pads, pink and green, urgent and later. You'll do two things — encrypt a one-sentence pink-pad message, anything you want. Then you drop it, pick one up for decrypt, and call it in to me. I'm going to get some Crackerjacks, be right back."

I drew a deep breath, looked up at the sky, and found I still remembered the numbers. I was about to write them down, but Morris was back, driving me with that challenging insinuating voice. He had me feeling pretty competitive.

"Next thing we need to know is how you handle yourself. Lotta good desk guys have a problem there, so we have a field exercise. You go to a deli in Brooklyn and order some pastrami from a guy named Boris. Boris the Butcher — make sure it's Boris. You slip him your pink note and he puts one in with the pastrami. Eyes open all the way — anyone picks up on you, be ready to describe them."

"This is the crash course?" I said. It irked him, and I had a new, deliberate Morris. Playing him felt a little edgy but it worked.

"Yeah, okay, fair point. Our outfit is less bureaucratic and we get things done clean that big operations tend to screw up. I know, I've worked for a couple of them. We're small and smart, and we have room for guys like you. And we get things right. Not one fuckup since I've been on board. We're structured like the old communist cells — separation of personnel is rule one. No hanging around the water-cooler learning things you're not supposed to know. No confiding in the girlfriend either."

He paused, smiled, and explained that I'd come in as a C-3 courier, entry-level gofer. He was an Operative, an Op 1, the top grade.

"So, Boris. Boris works at Levine's Fancy Meats, Brooklyn, on Fifth off Sackett. Five-nine, balding, Khrushchev face, nose like a potato, bushy black hair. You ask for a quarter pound of pastrami, then you say, 'Excuse me, make that half a pound, please.' Get him the note without drawing attention, pay and split. Your note's in the package. When you've got the decrypt, phone it in to that New York number. Just 'Mr. B. says' and the message. I might call back if you leave a number. Then you can make a sandwich. It's good pastrami."

"Excuse me, make that half a pound."

It was a good imitation of his voice, my little gift. His little blue eyes twinkled for a second under the dark lids but he wasn't totally pleased. I wondered if he ever wore colored contacts to reduce that distinctive contrast or might be wearing them now.

"Okay, recap our conversation from the top, all the detail you can recall."

I did so, not brilliantly, slowing down and stopping to remember from time to time. Morris smiled.

"Hey, don't get tight — you've been on the beach a while, buddy, you're doing all right. Trick that works, write it down but don't keep it around, burn the notes in a bowl. If you have a problem, train yourself, do it two or three times. In this work paper is bad, good habits are everything."

We both watched as a Rasta-looking dealer was escorted to the wings by two cops, speechifying loudly all the way.

"You can see the Butcher ten to six any day except Saturday. Get it done this week, sooner the better. You should know everything in the manual, make the procedures second nature. Big things for couriers are, do exactly as instructed and know if you're being tailed. Learn how to disappear. And not to sell your ass because you blew your check up your nose, that's important too. Here, take these Crackerjacks — field rations, don't leave home without 'em."

He paused and looked at me pointedly.

"This is an opportunity for a guy like you, Price. No office b.s., which I know you hate. Last point — from now on you're Beachcomber and I'm Eulenspiegel. Spiegel for short."

Good names, I thought. He paused, looking as if he had doubts about me. So did I, but I wasn't going to give him that.

"Okay, Beach," he said. "We're done. Stuff's in here."

He handed me the Crackerjacks and I walked out of the park. I wanted my green card in this world where Morris was a native. Not just because I needed a job. I was thinking I might belong there. I didn't seem to fit in anywhere else, and I was getting to like the game. I shook out some Crackerjacks and the code pads fell into my hand, followed by a small thin booklet. The box had been opened and resealed before Morris got to the park. It was the perfect drop, so smooth I almost missed it.

On my way home I stopped at the Noho Star and thought about it over a Stoli tonic at the little bar where people waited for tables. Morris was about edge. Backing him up a little would get his attention. One of the things about me that irritated Doug Finlay was that I seemed a little laid-back, and maybe he'd been right. I sipped my drink and worked out my message. Sitting in the can a few minutes later I wrote it: *Early Bird Gets Worm.* Then I ate a corner of a page, which was like eating candied newspaper.

Waiting for my train I watched four homeless black men on the far side standing on a cement floor endlessly layered with slime and grime in a patina unique to Manhattan subway stations. In the air was the dead stench of urine and disinfectant. Eventually the F train arrived with a horripilating roar.

New York, I thought. *I'm out of this place. Sauve Qui Peut! Don't Worry, Be Happy!*

Boris was as described, and not surprised to see me. At 1620 hours I was back and had the decrypt. *Mother needs a hat.* Then I couldn't remember the call-in number. What I did remember was Morris's write-destroy procedure, which I'd skipped. I opened a

Dos Equis and skipped through the very unpretentious little manual.

Use phone booths, change booths often. Windows are mirrors. Develop alternate wardrobes and change as appropriate. Protect your ID. Avoid patterns. Avoid credit cards if possible unless establishing a trail.

The World Trade Towers were glinting orange in the afternoon sun, and I went up to the roof to see them against the sky, sitting with my back against a bulkhead. I could call in tomorrow but that would spoil it. The reflection faded as the sun shifted, and I still couldn't remember the number. The sun was setting before I did, and by then I was a much more modest job candidate. I wrote it down four times, burning the paper each time until it was running like a tape loop in my head. At a bodega phone I dialed 958, which gave me the booth number. Then I called Morris and read the message into his machine, giving the time and adding that I could be reached at this number for ten minutes, which was per the manual. I wasn't surprised when he called back in two or three. I was getting a sense of his style. Hard center-line serve, take ball early, go to net often.

"Beachcomber here."

"Nice, Beach, real good, you know how to get a booth number." He was pleased with me. "Maybe I can get you in as a Two. Better pay, more perks. You'll get a call."

"Thanks," I said. "*Ciao.*"

Back in my loft, I read through the manual, which was dry and very clear. Then I took my old Colnago down off its hook, removed the seat post, and worked the rolled-up manual in. Then I took out the bar-plugs and stuffed in the pads. After that I had another Dos Equis and watched Steffi Graf dismantle an ungainly Russian. Like Morris, she took the ball early and got it to move fast on unexpected angles. My perspective was changing. I'd have lost a day and pleased Morris less if I'd dropped in at the Pope. I was sure of that, and I was pretty sure I'd get the job.

A little after nine the next morning I got a call from a young woman with a good accent telling me to expect a call from someone named Crackerjack the next day. This was Morris's boss, the last hurdle. The situation was moving faster than anything ever did at Finlay, Kline. It was exciting and cool, and a little crazy-making. It brought Fred to mind, and I called Jennifer Chen-Garthwaite.

"Dojo." A silvery southern-fried career voice. I didn't mention Fred, just said I was interested in signing up. Then I walked there for the exercise, and to kill some time.

Five flights up a West 26th Street sweatshops-and-studios building I knocked on the door. No one answered, but it was unlocked, and I went into the office. Manual in mind, I memorized it. High metal ceiling. Small black leather couches along two walls, hand-carved ebony coffee table in the middle, matching desk against the far wall. Under broad floor-to-ceiling windows sat two little oak file cabinets with a piece of butcher block across their tops. On it were an electric kettle, cups, and a collection of exotic tea bags. ENJOY, suggested a neat little hand-lettered sign. Not your average karate barn.

I boiled water and stood looking at martial arts photographs on the walls. Gnarled *sensei* flying through the air like human missiles or standing like rocks. One dog, a happy looking Lab on a big lawn — that picture was over the desk. The kettle clicked and I made wheat-tea, which would be a new experience. Through the door to the main room came thumps, grunts and brief comments in that cool smooth voice. I couldn't make out the words, just that it was an expensive voice or a good imitation.

I was sipping my strange tea when the inner door opened and three teenage boys came out, followed by my *sensei*-to-be. A stone fox. Fred's fox? Around thirty, about five-seven. Her smooth oval face glowed with health and had no lines at all. A basically occidental face, but the dark quiet almond-shaped eyes said Asian. Above the smiling rosebud mouth was a long thin Meryl Streep nose. Jennifer Chen Garthwaite was tough.

"Jennie Chen — and you are?"

"Rob Price."

"Right, you called. Welcome to hell week, Mr. Price."

Then we each sat on one of the little couches.

You didn't just sign up — Chen-Garthwaite wanted to know why you were there. I said that I wanted to be able to protect myself in a neighborhood infiltrated by dope fiends. She asked the kind of questions you ask to get rid of loonies, and I told her there had been muggings. Why her dojo? Fellow downtown said it was good.

"I think I might like to study privately if that's not too expensive. I travel, but while I'm in town I'd like to concentrate on this and get somewhere with it."

"I think what you want is some basic disarming techniques, breakaway moves and spins. And some kicks. Practical things."

"Sounds military. I do better if I go slow and get things from the ground up."

"Fine, we're eclectic. Let's start with Aikido and add some harder stuff."

I wrote a check and began filling out a very businesslike form. It was expensive, and would end with one lesson if I didn't get the job. As I was signing away my right to sue for injury, she found me a *gi* and sent me to change.

On my way I passed through the long white chilly main room, which had a row of big windows and two skylights. Three workout areas — one padded, one with a mat, one bare floor. The changing room was pale blue Formica, with a big antique sink and full-length mirror. Behind a pair of louvered half-doors was a steaming indigo-blue hot tub.

I felt awkward putting on the *gi*, and I went on feeling that way through the stretching and warm-up. Then she showed me the *kata* at a speed so slow I could see each element clearly, making it flow even at that speed while talking. I was impressed. Then she had me do it alongside her, and a little behind, so I could see and follow. I stayed awkward and began to sweat in the chilly room. It went on, and I lost any illusions I might have had about being in control of my body. I accepted it; she was a good teacher.

Finally she did the *kata* by herself at normal speed, perfectly balanced, jointless as a snake, her body gliding along, coiling and uncoiling.

"Try to slip through the motions. Start slow and don't push, you're not used to fast. Practice as slow as you like, but once you're in focus, try it faster. Do it a lot."

On my way out she gave me a sheet of paper with the *kata* laid out in pictures.

4

Early the following evening I waited at a reserved table in a small upper east side Italian restaurant sipping San Pellegrino for half an hour and waiting for Crackerjack. It was the kind of place favored by my ex-wives. Thinking about that and them, I experienced my first Jason Olcott Entrance: gray Borsalino and long black coat taken by maitre d', revealing a magnificent custom-tailored dark gray pinstripe with black wingtips at the bottom. Sixty-odd years of tall lanky, shoulders-back, gray-haired American *pukka sahib* strode to the table to deliver a solid one-pump handshake.

"Damn airlines can't keep their schedules any more," he growled in a big stagy old-money voice. "Start late, circle the field forever . . . "

He wouldn't be interested in my ideas about how the airlines got that way, so I nodded and listened. He was a tedious, privileged old boy, but that was fine with me. A waiter appeared and Olcott went with Jack Daniels, soda back. I ordered a Jameson, which brought on a brief discourse on whiskies, Olcott watching my eyes as he spoke. He didn't quite wave the flag, but it was clear to him that good bourbon touched the same spot as Old Glory. He was a classic cold warrior, a Dulles type trying to be more like Mr. Bush. Like all of them, he gave the impression that truth was something validated by him and his friends after due consideration in private council. His scrutiny didn't bother me. Unlike Morris, he had no sense of who I was, and didn't care. Andover or Exeter? Not Choate, they took Kennedys. Most likely Groton. The drinks arrived before I was called on to say anything, and Olcott waved away the wine list, knowing what he wanted. A little blonde pussycat decorating a banquette two tables away thought he was divine.

"Pressed for time I'm afraid, so I ordered ahead for us," boomed Olcott. "Veal piccata, the house specialty, I'm sure you'll enjoy it. Anyway, we're here to talk business, eh?" He paused to get me focused. "Morris is very high on you, and I value his opinion. Very much so — I made time to see you at his request."

His estimate of me was pretty clear. A couple of minutes had gone by, and neither his colorless eyes nor horsey face had changed expression, but then came a large-toothed smile, and a booming, hearty request as he lifted his chin and smiled.

"*So! Tell me about yourself, Rob!* Your background, interests and so forth — "

Morris would have passed it all along, so this would be the smell-test. I had style and accent glued and screwed for the evening — Northeast Responsible. I rattled off my home town, schools, degree, Navy experience, employers, divorce and hobbies, but nothing about my first marriage or my daughter.

"Yes, yes — and you speak French pretty well, I hear."

"For an American. No Frenchman would be fooled."

"Get around on your Italian and Spanish too?"

I nodded. Olcott smiled and fired some fossilized French at me. I replied slowly, with respect.

"How'd you pick up such good French?"

He had to know this, too. I hesitated, then looked him in the eye.

"My mother was French."

"Oh, yes. Often doesn't mean a thing."

There was something about the way he tossed it off that I didn't like. Something between the lines, as if war brides were illiterate sluts, or Frog genes were something to be overcome. He opened his mouth to speak again and I beat him to it.

"Well, it did in my case, Mr. Olcott," I said deliberately. I could have spit in his face, and it must have showed. He nodded with a quick, empty smile and asked about my last job. I told him a little about Finlay, Kline and my work in estate management, leaving out my silly feud with Doug Finlay. As we talked I cooled down and decided he hadn't meant anything at all with his remark; it was just his stupid-rich way.

"In line for department manager, weren't you?"

Touché. Olcott was watching me carefully now, and I answered as if it didn't matter.

"Eventually, I suppose. I'd been working in the French office and I was restless. It got me fired, I was gone in the first wave when the market blew."

"Back up again though, eh?" he said brightly. "Tell me — what draws you to this kind of work, Rob?"

Not well done. Morris had approached me, and he was turning it around. I tried to look thoughtful as plates arrived bearing angel-hair pasta, broccoli and not-great veal. Not a great restaurant, and not someone I wanted to work for. But I needed the job, and my pith helmet was chattering away. A fly on the wall might get promoted if he kept his mouth shut. Might even eventually affect whether some banana-republic reformer was removed or allowed to continue in office.

"This kind of work wouldn't have occurred to me," I replied slowly, as if thinking about it. "But Morris's proposal interested me. My divorce left me free to travel, and I didn't want to go back into an office. It's the challenge as much as anything. It's a job I could . . . take seriously."

"Yes, yes," he said, sounding genuinely pleased. "Any leftist friends down there in Soho?"

For a moment I thought he had a sense of humor.

"Not that I know of. Usual liberals, of course. I'm more or less non-political."

He liked that too. He observed that *the work*, as he called it, was a *group effort by loners like yourself*. I smiled at his little paradox and we began eating. Somehow I knew I was hired, though nothing had been said or explained. I waited a while and agreed with his opinions on white wines, which I rarely drink. Eventually he said that I seemed to fill the bill, so I asked him about salary and benefits. He named a figure that wasn't wonderful. I nodded and gave it two beats.

"I don't want this to be a problem, but I do have other offers," I lied, imagining my alternative future with Rainbow Rent-a-Car. Then he let me in on a benefit of the job: while CIA still required employees to pay back the 'offset money' earned through cover jobs, I'd get to keep mine. Between two jobs, I'd earn upward of eighty thousand, and most of what I spent could be marked up as expenses. And there were *certain tax benefits*. His eyes twinkled and I nodded, thinking how pleased the rich are at stiffing the taxman, be they Felices or Crackerjacks. He paused rhetorically and nailed me with those pale eyes.

"What I'm going to tell you now is classified, not to be divulged to anyone, for reasons of national security. If you should fail in training or leave us for any reason, you must not reveal what I tell you now."

Another pause, then he punched the words out quietly.

"You will work for TelcomCo Systems, also referred to as TCC, of which I'm head. It's nominally a research company, but actually a government operation, though it's also a for-profit corporation. TelcomCo is totally, absolutely, secret. Everyone involved has been cleared at a high level, as you yourself have been. Our mission is to monitor developments in certain technical areas — liaise with people who have certain kinds of information and try to buy it, over or under the table. Occasionally we steal it. Anyway, we get it. Which is to say, the government does."

He smiled a confident, practiced smile with a kind of roguish old-boy threat in it. He might not be super-smart, but he was a tough old bird, and vain about it.

"Courier is not a dangerous job," he continued, "but if ever you find yourself confronted, hide behind the cover job, whatever that turns out to be. That will be substantiated by paycheck records and so forth. Under extreme pressure, you admit to industrial espionage by an unknown employer who pays in cash and contacts you periodically. But you do not mention TelcomCo, and deny knowledge of a government connection. Henceforth, in all except face-to-face situations, you'll refer to me as Crackerjack. In France you'll report to Area Head Alvin Marquardt, work name Slim."

He began talking more easily, relaxing and discussing the wine, which was better than the veal. He was very comfortable with his pith helmet, old Crackerjack. It was just about rotted off. I didn't care. It was how things were, and I'd have a life again. The meal was quick, and he was off in a waiting limo. Walking downtown, I worked it out in military terms. TCC was edge-recon — Swift Boats with muffled engines and big radar. A deniable asset, a cut-out. I didn't care about that either. McVeigh would love it, and I couldn't tell him a thing.

Don't worry, be happy — I was humming the damn thing, buzzing with energy. When I got home the Del Psychos were tuning up and sleep was out of the question. Tom's Hammond organ bellowed and Blinky Bernstein's screaming guitar ripped through the building. Then big thumps announced Sam the drummer, completing the Del Psychos. They played a blues, and then *Country Club Mummies*, Tom's big record, and the building was shaking. They weren't top dogs at CBGB, only the best band.

Packed and ready to go, I picked up a *Post* for laughs and started the day with pancakes and Irish coffee at the Star. *Page Six* featured the disappearance of one Dr. Richardson Smith-Davies, a striking silver-haired scientist of the mind, philanderer, and former Nobel candidate. Big picture, great profile. He was a notorious rake and media magnet. **ALZHEIMER'S OR ANOTHER CO-ED?!** The *Post* wanted to know. The Knicks had lost again, and my horoscope was promising. Over coffee I thought carefully about Morris and my new job. It seemed to fit with something bred into my blood and bone, and in Morris I saw an American my mother would have respected.

5

I met Area Head Al Marquardt at the Aerodrome, a big dreary restaurant so close to De Gaulle it seemed to smell of jet fuel. In front of the place was an old WWI biplane with tattered fabric and a goggled dummy in the cockpit. Overhead was the roar of outbound jets, engines blasting. We sat isolated at a table in the center of a vast empty dining room. Marquardt was around my age, sandy-haired, small mustache, balding, running to fat. He was a fast talker with lots of drive, and quick. He ran TCC France and doubled in sales for an outfit called BioTel for cover. Inside the fat you could see the hungry little hustler. Work-name Slim, another Morris send-up, like Beachcomber. Marquardt explained that he was late because his son was sick with asthma, or maybe pneumonia. I nodded, understanding his concern. The restaurant told me he was more concerned about privacy than food quality, and his French sounded as if it had been jammed into him by computer. He had neither Morris's tightly focused professionalism nor Olcott's born-to-rule arrogance, and he wore no pith helmet. I doubted he'd ever done military service, or real service for any entity other than himself. He could never have recruited me, but he came off likable and unpretentious, and I sensed long experience. He began by discussing a cover job at a French company, Guimard Frères, but he seemed preoccupied, and began dumping information as if I were a human cassette. After a while I asked him to slow down.

"Oh, yeah, sorry, you just got off the plane. I tend to do that. It's all in these notes here. Take 'em to your hotel, learn and burn. No offense buddy, lot on my plate."

His face was suddenly tired and slack, which I attributed to concern about his son. A waiter came and we ordered. Marquardt waited for him to leave, then told me Guimard Frères was looking for an American to work with them on marketing their PC gear in the US. The catch was that I'd have to talk them into a consulting arrangement of a hundred hours a month maximum, and not get locked into an office schedule.

"The Frogs, they'll offer you zilch, but on top of your salary it won't be too shabby for a single guy." Then he talked about the expenses of married life until the food arrived. I told him marriage hadn't agreed with me and he smiled. Watching him tear into his double-thick bloody *biftek*, I saw a man who would manage to enjoy life no matter what. He was reminding me of Finlay, Kline's trading floor until he unexpectedly put down his knife and fork and peered at me, head lifted and cocked slightly to one side.

"So! Tell me about yourself, Rob!" he demanded, in a booming Yankee twang. I smiled. He had Olcott down and didn't hesitate to have fun with it, and that was definitely *not* Finlay, Kline.

"Office joke," he said, mischievous light blue eyes dancing. "You met Olcott's Slant yet?"

I guessed that would have to be my new *sensei* and that I wasn't supposed to know. A cheap remark, but I kept the ball in play.

"Pretty hot," I said, lifting a prawn from my *bouillabaisse* while I thought about Olcott's Slant. Thinking maybe I should have guessed a company connection. Also thinking I might be a little slow, but my new boss seemed pretty indiscreet. Cellular separation had been breached, and my extended interview at Dojo Chen-Garthwaite made perfect sense now. *Why her dojo?* That had been a trick question to see if I'd reveal Fred.

"Trade the wife in a minute," he said. "Bitch put me on my ass couple times. Knew what I wanted, wouldn't give it up. Gotta admit the old boy knows how to live."

Rich is good, Al. I watched a little pile of buttered potatoes disappear and guessed that the ways of hereditary wealth were mysterious to my new boss.

"Anyhow, the gig," said Marquardt. "You'll have this kid, Satellite Sven, works for SPOT, French satellite operation. He'll be around next week and I'll hook you up. No contact, dead drops only. They don't pay him enough to cover his habits, so he's pre-releasing SPOT stuff, which keeps State up to speed with CIA. Drives 'em crazy, cause they're used to bullshitting State. Probably think their own shop's leaking, maybe have a purge one of these days."

A *schadenfreude* smile passed briefly over his features and his eyes changed, the first sign of another Marquardt behind the chatter. He didn't like CIA, and the State Department was our sponsor, which neither Morris nor Olcott had revealed.

Then he went back to eating. He'd learned not to bolt his food, but he was efficient. When the steak was history he started rounding up stray potatoes and continued in a different tone as we finished a good Bordeaux.

"It's rushing things a little, but there's one situation I'd like to get moving on this week if possible. Preliminary meeting in connection with a project called Oracle. Dr. Alain Durry, a.k.a. Fox or Reynard. He wants to check you out. Turned down one of our people already, wouldn't work with 'em. Major Frog attitude. No skin off your ass if he doesn't buy you, we know he's a cunt. But you'll look good if he does, Rob, and your French sounds for-real, which he'll like."

It was definitely rushing things a little. I sensed a problem and was fairly sure this was why I'd been hired and put on line so quickly. Marquardt wasn't casual now; he wanted *yes* and he got it. His eyes relaxed and he passed me an envelope.

"Pictures. Can't let 'em out, so look 'em over."

Durry had a perfect French face of the sharp, angular type — straight high beak of a nose, dark eyes, dramatic Edgar Allen Poe brow from which fell long, dark, artistic hair. Below the nose, a long wire-thin mouth. 5-9, skinny and dapper, with rimless tinted specs. We'd meet at an opening, and I'd be Mr. Beach from Santa Fe, an art dabbler looking for "anything good and new." He'd say there wasn't much of either this year, and if he felt like it he'd give me his number.

"Durry's a big brain," said Marquardt. "Up there pretty high in their nuclear setup. Lotta problems with him. Screws up on work-names, changes the rules, shows up late, fuck-you attitude. So good luck, buddy. Hook him and you'll be golden with Crackers. And me of course."

Crackers. Neither of us had any use for Jason Olcott. He looked at his watch and tabbed the check. Then we took off in his yellow Saab, a big metal muscle that didn't sound like any Saab.

"What'd you do under the hood?"

"Dodge hemi in there. Buy American, dress Euro."

I had him drop me off inside the *Francillienne* route so I could walk off my jetlag on the way to my motel.

"Phone over there — wanna call and make sure your bags got there?"

He waited while I called, and my bags had arrived. I flashed him a thumbs up, the singing Saab took off with a steel-belted chirp, and I strolled away thinking double paychecks, expenses, tax breaks, Swiss account to follow. An end to my fourteen months in limbo. It was cold and dry, perfect for a nice long walk, just me and my attaché case.

Next afternoon I was in a tiny rented Talbot Samba somewhere in Saint-Denis looking for an apartment in drizzly rain. It was half-hearted — I was thinking ahead to the evening's meeting and Alain Durry. Worrying about it, because everyone would be unhappy if it didn't work out, and Marquardt had made it clear Dr. Durry was a prick with ears. I was jetlagged, it was a wet day, and I'd got myself lost a couple of times by mid-afternoon. Coffee wasn't doing it, so I stopped at a local home-style restaurant full of working people who'd know a good cheap place to eat. I had two bowls of a fish soup that revealed the Aerodrome product as steam-table slop. The rain stopped, blood-sugar kicked in, and I felt more optimistic. The sun appeared, and I took in the street from my window. Shops that looked as if the owners didn't take their marching orders from the tube. Baker, tailor, wine shop, smoke shop, grocery, with a big motorcycle shop as the centerpiece. I decided to bag it for the afternoon, go to my motel, and shower before my meeting. Then the Samba wouldn't start.

I walked into the motorcycle shop and inhaled the classic blend of gas, oil and tobacco smoke, and suddenly I felt good. The place was low key, with an old wood counter that reminded me of Fred's. Excellent bikes, including a much-modified rose-petal Triumph Trident with a nifty little custom fairing. A beautiful Brit crotch-rocket dinosaur. No price tag, just a note that said to speak to Marcel. Marcel appeared as if summoned, a big round-bellied middle-aged Frenchman, long-jawed, with an impressive black mustache. He indicated that this miraculous machine was a labor of love created by the incomparable genius of one Monsieur Beauvais, he of the noted Isle-of-Man successes, formerly with Ducati. I told him it was a great bike and he named an astronomical price, so I told him I had to find some rooms first. Then I mentioned that my car was stalled.

He smiled and sent his teen-age son to start the Samba. After establishing that I wasn't a Brit, he mentioned some inexpensive rooms at his aunt's house that might be appropriate for a bachelor sportsman with good taste in motorcycles. While we were talking his son came in shaking his head decisively, long black hair waving.

"*Merde!*"

I said it the way my mother used to about twice a year. The son was startled and Marcel roared.

"Where do you have to go?"

"Rue Plechette. I have to be there by six."

"Terrible Metro trip, you will never get there. I'll run you over if Guy can't get your car started. Meanwhile you can see the rooms, there's time."

The house was large and well kept, yellow stucco on a stone base, circa Degas. It was on a corner, and had three entrances — one onto each street, plus a rear entrance to an alley. Perfect for illicit activities and sneaking around. Marcel led me up a handsome banistered staircase, then a tiny stairwell to a rough two-room garret with slanting ceiling, tan plaster walls and big rickety double-hung windows. Furnished, more or less — a hard little monk's bed and an old wooden table with two chairs, one wood, one upholstered. The price was right and I wasn't planning to entertain, so I took it and paid cash.

"Enjoy rue Marchais and avoid my aunt, who is Alsatian," said the helpful Marcel. I was getting to like him. I remembered a line from the manual: *No one knows where you live.*

Galerie Graffiti was impeccable, starting with the antique blue-gray marble lobby and matching elevator with sexy girl operator. The opening was jammed with affluent middle-aged and older citizens, plus some young ones that looked like art-phonies and models. The Stones were booming and bitching through half a dozen sound columns as I waded through, and the bartender sent me off happy with half a tumbler of Tullamore Dew on three tiny continental rocks. A slow crisscross of the space yielded no Durry, but I found smaller, quieter rooms. At the center of one of them was Alain Durry, drink in one hand, Gallic gesture in the other, skinny but Napoleonic in a fine charcoal suit. The tinted rimless glasses were distinctive. A plump older woman wearing a royal blue caftan was hanging on his every word as he trashed an enormous canvas covered with new and used birth control devices, leather masks, vibrators, dildos, ticklers, etc. Stenciled here and there were pissy remarks in various languages. Durry's wiry body bent this way and that as he excoriated this monstrosity and quoted Foucault. In his hand was what looked like a triple martini, and in his voice was dry total confidence. Crossing the room with the blue caftan to include someone else, his walk fell somewhere between that of a Siamese cat and Groucho Marx. He looked about forty-five, with no fat on him.

I stood looking at multiple silk-screens of dogs fucking, managed a short conversation with a drunken artist and his horny girlfriend, then sat alone at the end of a white leather couch to gaze at a giant green painting full of cascading M&M's that made me feel good. Fifteen thousand dollars and I could have it in my loft where it belonged. The crowd was thinning, and I waited Durry out, sipping my drink and keeping track of him, which I hoped he might be doing with me. I caught a lot that didn't show up in the photos — rubber face, dry smile, and an edgy sense of humor. Eventually I caught his attention with a little hand-gesture as he turned. Then I looked back at the M&M's. In a minute the caftan was gone and I walked over.

"Ah, Beach — American?" he asked quietly. I nodded and he clicked in. There was nothing much to see, he said, it was a poor opening, too many people, not much art. I said I was looking for anything new and good, and he assured me there was nothing of either. Then we exchanged some art babble which he ended by observing that the show was bad enough to please even the Ministry of Culture.

"Can you imagine the dreadful lives of the people who would perpetrate this?" he asked, gesturing to the walls. As I laughed his attention seemed to drift, and I thought I'd lost him. He picked this up, quick as a ferret.

"Yes, I must go, but let's have a drink some time, eh? I am lacking a pen — perhaps you can remember my number?"

He gave it to me clearly and quietly, I gave it back to him, and he was gone. It was all very clean and by the manual, not much more than a minute. I went to the elevator and wrote the number down, out of sight. Then I found a phone and called in.

"Yeah, hi," said Marquardt in a neutral voice: How'd it go?"

"*Alles ist in ordnung, jah?*"

"Good, glad to hear it. Very. See you tomorrow at my office, ten thirty."

6

BioTel's offices were at the top of a tall new building in a busy block on rue Lafitte, flanked by an airline agency and a bank. Inside was a big slick lobby with two sharp young security men, one of whom asked for ID and called ahead. The express elevator opened into a full-floor maximum upscale space that housed his corner office, and his tall, British, self-possessed assistant matched the space. Ms. Brock had such excellent legs that a bruised shin only enhanced the effect. She favored me with an estate-quality smile that I returned to no effect.

"Mr. Marquardt's expecting you," she said, turning apparatchik now that she'd been appreciated. I wondered if I was going misogynist or was one already, but mainly I was blown away by Marquardt's cover job. His office was huge. We didn't sit down but descended through a wood-paneled internal staircase to the floor below. This was another world, a vast, windowless institutional-gray shipping room lit by ugly overhead fluorescents. All around were stacks of cardboard boxes and wooden crates, and a drab, wizened little Frenchwoman was checking boxes against invoices.

"I'll be busy, Françoise," said Marquardt in his unique French. "Nothing until one — no interruptions."

She nodded, and we went back to the shipping office, an unimpressive cubicle with a big old metal desk full of papers. He closed the door behind him and locked it.

"TCC got this floor before BioTel took the floor above, then leased it to 'em under a phony name," he said with a smile. "No one knows we're here. Watch this."

He locked the door and took some files out of a bookcase, then twisted an unused lamp fitting behind them. The bookcase slid out of the way to reveal a steel door with an electronic lock. Inside was TelcomCo France, a long narrow chilly gray space no one would expect to exist. The shipping room seemed to take up the entire floor, and only someone with a floor plan and measurements would suspect anything was there. At one end was a large paper-strewn desk, the one human touch among faxes, answering machines, monitor-phones, and computer terminals. At the far end was a walk-in safe that took up a lot of space.

"Secure-for-sure," said Marquardt. "Wired up the ying-yang, steel sheets in the walls. Took your picture on the way in, tripped this thing on the desk that's flashing when we entered the outer office. Buried phone lines from four buildings away — red one's scrambled. We run Europe out of here, Robbie. Only person on this floor is Françoise, been vetted like a Los Alamos janitor. Dumb as a cow-pie, loves her job."

Then we sat down, him at his amazingly messy desk, me on the chair next to it. A Tizio lamp sat on one paper-pile and a gold brick stabilized another one. He offered me a Marlboro, which I declined, then lit one himself. On his corkboard was a political cartoon: a penis with little legs pursuing a vagina. *De Cockis an' De Bush.*

I let myself laugh, which pleased my new boss considerably.

"Some choice, right? His indifference to the election surprised me. A spook who wasn't for Bush.

"So tell me about Foxy."

"Went okay, I think. Didn't seem to have a problem. Brief, maybe ninety seconds. We talked art and he gave me his number."

He smiled at this news and gave a little nod, his eyes approving. In this room they looked gray, like everything else.

"I forget this is your first go-round. What you do is tell me how you got there and when, venue in detail, anything that caught your attention, whether anyone picked up on you, time of departure, whether you thought you were followed."

I covered this to his satisfaction leaving out Marcel, and said the manual didn't have anything on the procedure he'd outlined.

"Yeah, live contact is unusual for a Courier, but you're right for this. Good French. He didn't like mine at all, or me. The doctor's one difficult SOB. Give him lots of room, Rob, humor him. Oracle's big stuff, could be a real break for you. Let's start by setting you up."

He didn't say any more about Oracle, and I didn't ask, just

watched him go to the safe and start the entry procedure while explicating Alain Durry, whom he hated. Marquardt didn't have a lot of what people call class, but there was nothing wrong with his brain. He could do several things at once without dropping the ball, it was natural to him. A monitor phone rang and he listened.

Banger to Slim, said a male voice. *I'll be on tonight if —*

Marquardt hit one of several buttons on a wall box, cutting him off and letting a machine take the call. I remembered Morris's "cellular separation" and saw that while Al had been casual about Jennie and the State Department connection, he was discreet about other things. The safe made a little chiming sound as the door swung out, and I saw a shiny IBM mainframe at the end. Then Marquardt went in, and emerged with a brown cardboard box which he dumped on the deck after pushing aside some papers.

"Your starter kit."

A few minutes later my case contained tiny binoculars, a device that would alert me to phone bugs, a scrambler, a Minox copy setup, and a make-up kit with hair dye and two real-hair mustaches, one dark, one light. I had to smile at the last items.

"Yeah," said Marquardt. "Y'never know. Couple years before the Glasnost this blonde I knew got tailed in Tempelhof, went to the ladies and cut her hair. Made herself into a brunette and put on jeans. Bag in the trash, walked past two guys going around showing people her picture. You gotta do your hair, Rob — way it is, y'stand out."

He offered me a peppermint ball from a bowl on his desk and took one himself.

"She was an Op — as a courier you won't get into those kinda situations."

I nodded and said I'd take care of my hair, and Marquardt continued, getting serious despite the peppermint ball in his cheek.

"One thing you train yourself to do, keep an eye out for certain faces — people we know about from other organizations. While I'm checking faxes and calls you can look through some photos, especially the ones initialed PAFR and NYUS."

"Are those organizations?"

I'd made his day, his little laugh was real.

"Paris, France and New York, US of fuckin' A."

He left me with a stack of photos, two or three of each person, all shuffled together. While he pushed paper I matched them up and studied them feature by feature, starting with the eyes, per the manual. From time to time phone monitors babbled into space while Marquardt did paperwork. After a while he stood and stretched.

"Got 'em?" he asked, walking over.

"Pretty much."

"One of those faces pops up, call me. Probably won't, but keep 'em in mind. Have a look through every few weeks, check for new ones, refresh your memory."

Then he gave me access codes to some areas in the computer.

"You any good at this?" he asked.

"Not especially. I can run basic programs."

"Yeah, you're a touch player, that's why they gave you Fox. This is the future though, buddy. I love computers, I can forget everything when I'm in here. I was learning to write code, but no time, just too busy. They're workin' on units so small you can carry 'em around — plug in a phone line and *bingo*. I got money in some of those companies."

It was the end of the session. We both stood, and on the way out I noticed a tennis racquet and a driver in a corner near the door, both black composite and new-looking. I picked up the racket, and it felt good. Then something strange. Marquardt seemed to go blank before he settled on embarrassed. It was out of character for a fast-thinking guy.

"Come spring," he said, as if Paris didn't offer indoor tennis. Then patted his gut. "Can't find time. Gotta do something, I guess. Free equipment, but I'm lousy at both."

I knew from the Saab that he liked you to notice his toys, but not these.

"I run my people loose," he said then in another voice. "Not big on paper and meetings. Been doin' it forever, Rob, and that's what works for me. Just keep me up to speed and let me know if something looks wrong, even little things."

I nodded, he threw me a thumb-hook handshake, and that was the end of my first and last training session with Alvin Marquardt.

I met Durry next at the Olympia, a small ugly neighborhood bar in Clichy, with a bearded, half-comatose proprietor. In the background was the rush hour traffic roar of the *Périphérique*. The place was empty except for three old women in a corner, and I heard the roar of a soccer crowd on the tube. As far from the Graffiti Gallery as you could get, but there was Durry. He was standing in the near-dark, sipping vodka and watching the game very intently, piss-elegant and totally out of place in a mauve silk jacket and black slacks. He flicked an eye at me and nodded curtly. I said *bonsoir* and he said hello in snarly English. I smiled as if I enjoyed his company and ordered myself a vodka that came out of a Stoli bottle and tasted like kerosene. When he saw that I knew something about soccer, he loosened up. Then we went to a table to eat terrible sandwiches made of a single slice of nameless cheese on stale bread. He kept an eye on the TV as we talked.

"I have a sister in Belgium whom I rarely see," he began, speaking good English in a flat, meaningful voice. "A long drive, but I plan to visit her in a while. In Ghent."

To make conversation I said that the only place I knew in Ghent was the Velodrome. His long thin mouth formed a bent-wire smile.

"*Extraordinary!* There is the big six-day event, final day, *le cyclisme* at its best. I plan to be there, to make some bets. My weakness."

"A lot of them are fixed, you know."

"So I am told. There are many things to bet on beside the final winners, of course. If you learn anything significant, you must tell me. I share winnings."

He stopped, and when he spoke again his delivery was slow and precise.

"I will be there for the last night, the 15th. Between ten-thirty and eleven I will be near the Stella Artois concession inside the track. Between the concession and the band, eh? The racing will be hot, people will be distracted. A newspaper under my left arm. If it is on the right, something has made me nervous. As in pass left, not right.

"'Left side right side, right side suicide?'"

He laughed hard, showing small tobacco-stained teeth.

"Exactly. Except in England, where everything is backward, eh? The people most of all. You come up behind me during a jam, and you poke my back twice in the same place with your thumb, quite hard. I drop the newspaper and place my foot on it. You replace it with one containing the payment. I walk away and you step on my newspaper. Then you stand there three complete minutes."

I nodded and he looked back toward the TV. There was no reason to meet at all. The manual was very clear on that — dead drops were the m.o. for a courier. But I'd been warned not to cross him, and if Oracle was French secrets, a Belgium drop made sense. On the tube, the blue goalie blew it, the crowd roared, and Durry cursed.

"*Damn!* In the name of God! I have such a pile of francs on these Italians, and they throw the match away!"

We went back to the bar and watched until the Italians finally pulled it out, Durry chain-smoking Gauloises, eyes glued to the screen.

Afterward I called in, trying the scrambler in an outdoor booth. Marquardt sounded like Lear in the storm, and I could barely hear him over the hissing and howling.

"Good . . . just go along with him, don't push . . . little fucker has to run the show, so let him . . . "

Next afternoon at rue Marchais I dropped my bags in the middle of the room and then stood looking out my big front window at a quiet pale-blue day. Up around ten thousand feet, the wind was driving thin pink cirrus clouds in the last of the sun and a breeze was coming through the window frame. On the street below were small European cars and a tranquility I enjoyed. A safe place for normal people and myself, address unknown to anyone but me and Marcel.

I looked at the mail I'd picked up at my motel. A forwarded letter requesting my blood type for insurance purposes and a cheap mail-merge document from a rental-car company catering to English-speakers. Halfway down the car rental ad the word-processor had blown up and the inane prose was replaced by meaningless clumps of letters. I smiled and re-read the beginning: *The English Speaker has special needs to which we cater most expertly.* Only the French would make car rental sound like a sex service.

I let Marcel sell me on the Trident point by point, putting him on with questions about Jap bikes, the pair of us standing in his shop alone and having a good time at the end of the day. It was right there with the top bikes, courtesy turbo, big pistons, hot cam and fuel-injection. Gas suspension for handling that would get you away from anything "normal," as Marcel put it. It worked in steps — you could cruise street-legal on soft suspension and standard headlight or you could go turbo, open the pipes, tighten suspension, and have a screaming beast with a blinding and illegal halogen beam. There was also an illegal switch to cut the rear lights.

"A man's machine, not a quick toy," summarized Marcel with a Gallic flourish.

The price was ridiculous until I started talking cash in US dollars, at which point he knocked off a huge chunk and we were cutting a deal. He threw in a year's maintenance and sent his mechanic home, then took me to his office. On the way he pulled a set of used leathers off the end of a rack.

"You're going to need these. My old ones, and we're the same size. No charge — I can't use them any more. My wife. One little spill . . . "

Great leathers, and they'd fit. I hung them over a chair and Marcel poured calvados from a bottle in his desk, watching with interest as I opened my shirt to get at my cash belt. After the transaction we lit Cuban cigars and drank to good luck in my new rooms. I took a drive then, and found some clear road. The Trident was everything Marcel said, and it cornered on rails. I was confident about getting out of almost any situation that became an emergency.

No one knows where you live, I thought. *And no one knows what you drive.*

7

The little old Ghent Velodrome was a monument to old-school track racing. It had dried-up boards and tight, steep banking that threw riders into the straights like crazed hornets. They were jamming hard as I stood watching at the rail, glistening with dope-sweat, jerseys advertising everything from ice cream and videotape to banks and condoms. It was the final-night feeding frenzy, crowd screaming, stretched-out pack eating its tail, the stands jammed like a Grateful Dead concert, smoky blue air like nuclear fallout. It was a good choice for a live drop. I stood there feeling history — I'd substituted as an amateur here, went down twice the first day learning the hand-sling.

I waded up through the screaming crowd with my leathers in a nylon bag under one arm, case in the other hand, pouring sweat in my thermals. The only seats were up in the stratosphere, but the glasses from my kit brought the beer concession clearly into view. I looked it over and settled back to kill some time while figuring out the race, which featured ancient Alf de Vos. De Vos went back to my time — we'd raced together, and the man had to be pushing forty. Still pedaling the same way, toes down, body halfway over the bars. He was leading, but he was definitely *in distress* as the Brits say, and his allies were busy bumping people around to slow things down. Then a little German and a pop-eyed Frenchman full of God knows what broke loose. They stole a lap right there in Alf's house, and the crowd went mad.

Boche! Nazi! bellowed two old men next to me, full of beer and patriotism, *Baby killers! Rapists of virgin nuns! Filthy swine!*

I started working my way down to the infield tunnel, the newspaper with the pay envelope inside my jacket. The infield was packed, but I was exactly on time at the drop. No Durry. A great roar announced the De Vos counterattack, led by a teammate and a Dutch ally, with Alf tucked in behind. No sign of Durry. The Germans tried to chase and were harassed by the Belgian combine. The fix was in, but not completely. A hard day's night for old Alf, lots of jamming and slamming. And there was Durry in front of me, *très chic* in a tan suede sports jacket, with a beautiful blond half his age on his arm. His newspaper was under his left arm where it belonged, so I poked his back twice with a thumb, medium-hard.

"*De Vos to win, Germans take sprints,*" I said, breaking the rule against speech. Durry's paper slid to the floor and he put a foot on it. I slipped mine in its place as he made a note in his race booklet. Then he looked up, seemed to spot a friend, and pushed off through the crowd with his blond. I looked at my watch. Three minutes, he'd said. Until I picked up that paper I was a virgin. Waiting for the minutes to pass, I watched Alf eke out his escape with his allies. The crowd was on its feet screaming as he stuck his tough old beak into the foul air, entering agonies of oxygen debt. The Dutchie took a long pull and dropped away, then his Belgian ally ran out of gas. Alf was out there alone, swimming in lactic acid as the band struck up some Sonny and Cher idiot music. In howling patriotic tumult he caught the pack and I left with Durry's paper. I hadn't pumped so much adrenalin in years.

Outside I saw that it had rained, leaving a murky humid night with the unique fecal aroma of slow moving canal sewage. It sent me down a time warp to my year in Ghent, racing with blue-collar kids who were going to be the next Eddy Merckx and win the Tour. Me riding away from myself and my contribution to a war that stank like the West Bank, getting my ass kicked by Alf and his friends.

Et voila! Felice-of-the-Dainty-Feet, a sexy little rich girl looking at art, soon to conceive my only child during a protracted sexual frenzy that kept us warm the next winter in Vermont. I lost track of myself, walked past Muynck Street, then circled back, considering the greasy-wet bread-loaf cobbles. I knew from experience how dangerous they were. Was I being followed? Didn't seem to be. Near the bike, I stopped in an alley to slip Durry's newspaper under my sweater and put on the leathers. I was almost into them when a dark-haired girl stopped on the street twelve or fifteen feet away.

"So what are you doing in there, anyway?"

Casual, as if she knew me. It was provocative.

"Exposing myself of course."

"I think I'll stay out here."

"Most girls would."

The light behind her cast a yellow halo in the damp heavy air, and I glimpsed a sharp profile, head held high. She wasn't leaving yet. Was she trying to pick me up? That's what it looked like, but she didn't seem to be a whore. She moved a little, and I saw a thin, sharp face. I looked down for the case, and when I looked up she was gone. I was even more wide awake then, but I stood without moving for a couple of minutes to be sure she was gone.

My eyes were everywhere when I got to the bike and strapped the case to the rack with multiple stretch cords. The engine gave a big wet bark and I bounced away over the cobbles, very aware that I couldn't hit the throttle. The more I thought, the more suspicious I was, weaving around Ghent to elude pursuit, then stopping at a big service station where I filled the tank and had a double espresso. In a reeking men's room stall, I got rid of the newspaper and glanced at Durry's envelope before slipping it under my sweater. It was large and thin, with a slick plasticky texture. Doing business as dictated by Dr. Durry was bothering me.

Back on the A1, headphones plugged into the radar pickup, I started feeling good. *Round peg escapes square hole! Don't Worry, Be Happy!* I was buzzing as I watched the mirrors for a tail, but there was too much traffic to know. The girl bothered me. A cut above ordinary, good French without the Belgian burr. Maybe five-five, slim, dark, jeans, red jacket. Not cheap, not special. Attractive, and a little cocky. I remembered Belgian girls traveling in pairs after dark, and she'd been alone. The minx of Muynck Street.

The manual was big on common-sense, and I tried to see it that way. A woman, because women are less threatening. Maybe to have a look at my face, which hadn't been visible in the dark. I'd turned many corners before going to the bike, but if she did have a look at the plate, that was fine — it was a dead one from

Marcel's yard. My little exercise told me I had nothing, just that she was slim with sharp features and smooth French.

Traffic thinned out and I got off the A1 to see if anyone would follow. I found myself in patchy ground-fog on a small empty secondary road. Two cars exited with me. I sped up, and the radar started beeping. I slowed down and one of the cars passed me, a small Mercedes with a couple in it. Then it didn't pull away. I was in a sandwich, one car ahead, one behind, alone on a back road. There was a stone wall on the right and a grassy bank on the left. Down the road a traffic light turned red and I had nowhere to go. In the mirror I saw the second car start moving out to pass, all wrong with a light coming up. Without thinking about it, I dropped my gear, hit the gas and put my faith in the bike, cutting away from him and flinging the bike up the bank in a berserko dirt-bike move. Dangerous game on a road machine with smooth tires, and it left me slithering on the grass, almost going down. I came sliding back down behind the two cars and saw a ditch coming at me, so I leaned back and yanked on the bars. It bottomed the suspension and dragged the crankcase, but I got a leg down and wallowed up onto the pavement. Then I almost lost it again in a fishtail when I hit the throttle too hard, but I was gone, flying down the dry strip at the center of the road in fourth. No rear lights, courtesy Marcel's rear light switch cut-off. In a minute I was past the A1 with nothing in my mirrors.

Four wheels good, two wheels better — no car could turn around fast enough to catch me. I stayed on back roads, calmed down, and critiqued myself: forgot to re-set suspension, nearly lost it on the grass, twisted my ankle, didn't get plate numbers. No proof I'd been followed, but two cars turning off like that and getting me between them was too coincidental. And Durry was way too much of a gambler for me.

I was sleeping it off and out of focus when the phone rang. It was a woman, British and cool.

"Hullo, Yank."

"Yeah, hi."

Who was this? I was still half asleep.

"Al asked me to give you a call. I thought we might have a drink and exchange notes. Free at one by chance?"

Millie Brock, Al's assistant.

"Your place or mine?"

"Neither for now. Do you know the Tic Toc?"

It was fun for a minute, then it wasn't. Now there would be live contact at both ends of my run. And she had my phone number, which didn't feel right, and she worked for BioTel. But she was Al's minion and so was I, so I agreed to the Tic-Toc, a big trendy bar off the Champs Élysée.

I made coffee, shaved, and dressed as warmly as I could without my leathers. On the way I bought *l'Equipe* and the *Tribune*, then folded Durry's envelope into the Trib and put both under my sweater to protect my chest.

The Tic-Toc was vast and loud, a cream-colored international zoo full of journalists, embassy people, politicos and hustlers — Americans, Brits, Germans, Arabs, Swiss, all kinds of Asians. Not a good place to be passing an envelope from a man in the nuclear commission. I had a brioche and coffee at my little table, the only quiet person in the place. I couldn't read the *Tribune,* but *l'Equipe* was interesting: the Knicks were said to covet a Croatian giant, and a defected Polish weight-lifter was looking for replacement kidneys in return for an exposé on Polish sports medicine. And Greg LeMond was still recovering from a hunting accident.

Millie was late. I picked up a *Figaro* that was lying on an empty chair, and on the front page was Richardson Smith-Davies, who'd been in the *Post* the day I left New York. He taught at the Sorbonne, and the French knew all about him — he was an intelligence theorist and academic hero. **STILL MISSING**, it said under the photo. The article gave him a lot more respect than the *Post*, but the weakness for girl students was noted. I guessed it would be mutual — Doctor Dick had a marvelous profile and a poet's mane of silver hair above his youthful face.

"Oh, hullo, you'll be Jimmy!"

I smiled politely and rose. On her feet, Millie Brock was even more impressive. Close to six feet, casual and balanced, with long straight shoulders and clean classic English features under a neat cap of brown hair. Her eyes were a kind of violet, her bosom nonexistent under a chaste white blouse. She chattered confidently, an upper class English female to the core, and an attention-getter.

"I'm just so glad you could come! Mother's begged off and I really don't know what to do."

You could stop talking. It went on and on, with a strident insistence that made me think she was Marquardt's side action and wanted me to know. I wondered if she was a little thick, or thought I was.

"Drinking?"

"Vodka gimlet. After that, could we go somewhere else? I dread these places, but I just don't know my way around. And mother's taken up with this terrible Frenchman and she's off to the States. They want to go to the clubs. God — *parents!*"

Strange. She'd chosen the place and now she wanted to leave. It was stagy and manic, and she was too old for it. A waiter appeared and was distracted by her legs but managed to take our order. Then I told Millie that her mum might feel a bit lost in the New York clubs.

"Yes, really! Dying to visit them myself, actually. Could you put me in touch?"

"Sure. Parents have lives too, y'know."

Her look said that was none of my bloody business, and it was established that neither of us wanted to know the other. I got my drink down in three swallows and said I had a lunch date.

"Can I drop you off?" she asked in that invincible rich-Brit warble. Abruptness didn't ruffle her a bit, she was born to it.

"Just around the corner, thanks anyway."

I had to get away from her. She picked up her drink and I noticed her hands. They were too large and rough-hewn for the rest of her. Strong, reddish, big-knuckled farm-girl hands that didn't fit the rest of her elegant self. Sad. She'd kept them tucked away. I did a fake smile and put down some francs, but she wouldn't let go.

"I hear you're quite the success."

I laughed it off as if I didn't know what she was talking about, but my smile was turning to wax. Before she could do or say anything else I caught her eye, glanced hard at the *Tribune*, and walked out with a quick good-bye, putting on my jacket as I left.

I calmed down driving home and considered the politics. Millie was a little nuts, and I doubted fat Al could really handle her. I was glad to be rid of the envelope, but having his red-flag girlfriend in my face scared me. I was seeing him as a wild and crazy guy and wondering how he got his job. Olcott wasn't my kind of guy either, but Al was part of my daily life.

Guimard Frères was in a large dignified old corner building twenty minutes from the office, and you could smell the difference between BioTel's flashy new Texas money and the old European money of Guimard just walking in. Totally respectable, a great cover job. They had two upper floors of tall old-fashioned offices with windows that looked over slate rooftops to Montparnasse. Felix Guimard was an urbane, solid Frenchman in his early fifties with the three-day beard of a new-age mover and shaker. A ladies' man with a business head, he'd moved from office equipment to computers before the crowd arrived. The techs were all on the lower floor, and there was no hardware in his office, just a fine antique walnut-burl desk, two comfortable chairs, pale green wallpaper and a very nice old rug. Over excellent coffee served by a pretty young redhead who thought he was God, Guimard told me about his dream. Their PC peripherals were the best, he said, widely accepted in Europe. He wanted into the American market before it was too late, and he seemed to think I could help. Sitting behind his wonderful desk in his sunny corner office, he spoke about the perils of long-distance business — mistaken assumptions, mutual arrogance, cultural dissonance, dangerous misunderstandings. He knew he needed a reliable liaison and a solid American-style business plan. I told him I'd worked on Wall Street and that I could provide one, which I could. Looking out over the sea of slate, I forgot TCC. We'd spoke for a while, and he low-balled me with respect. Then we worked it out the French way, direct but polite.

Before he died, Joe Kline told me the way to get ahead was to make your job your hobby, and I took his advice, many years late. I followed the manual, picked up a range of clothing, and found a good barber who tamed my hair and dyed most of the gray out. Sometimes I put a little pad of paper in one shoe to change my walk. I kept myself too busy to think about anything except work. Between my useless role in a stupid war and two failed marriages and a daughter who never wrote, I was a real piece of work and I knew it. But I'd found a job where repressed hostility was normal. The job gave me a routine, and I was fine with it. Wake with the birds and work on Felix's business plan for a couple of hours. Coffee and a croissant at one of three cafés I could make calls from, a light workout at a little dojo run by a young Taiwanese named Hu Shi, then a solid meal, often at the restaurant across from Marcel's shop.

Aside from Durry, the work was simple. Keeping my eyes open and not being noticed were the major requirements. Afternoons and evenings I visited my postings, never approaching them the same way. There were little signals that usually fell on certain days — a piece of tape under the sink in a men's room might appear on Tuesday afternoon, or a dark thumbtack in a wood post on Fridays. Wednesdays I'd look for a touch of spray paint on a wall at knee level. Usually there was nothing, but if a posting was go, I'd visit the drop and pick up an envelope in a towel dispenser, or maybe taped to the underside of a table in a dark corner of some restaurant. Or under a rock — cemeteries were popular, especially the one where The Doors' Jim Morrison was buried, not far from Balzac and Flaubert. It was ghostly work without human contact until there was an envelope. Then Marquardt would meet me. Not recommended, but he probably knew I needed to talk to someone in English occasionally. He was easy to get along with, and I didn't let him know what I thought of Millie and his procedures.

My new hobby was challenging, and I developed a private agenda. I wanted to become one of those people who can beat a polygraph, and I wanted more money. And I was determined to deliver Oracle. I'd flunked out of America, but I was doing all right as an expat following Dylan's advice: Don't Look Back.

8

I was reviewing some Guimard numbers one night when the phone rang. Hoping for Durry, I got a self-important young voice with a sing-song accent asking if I were the Beechcraft rep for the Paris area. I said no, try the phone book, and hung up. But Al had prepped me, and I knew from the accent that it was Satellite Sven. He was no Alain Durry, so I followed the manual and did nothing, but I was irritated with Al for giving my number to him. Sven sounded like an immature kid with flap-tongue virus. The next day I got the drop, a large envelope barely concealed under a cemetery stone. It was unsealed, and I stopped in a café to have a look. Two photographs and a crude hand-written note:

Krasnoyarsk — something new happens, compare photos.

The monster Krasnoyarsk radar installation was to Washington as our SDI boondoggle was to Moscow, and in 1983 the Russians had shot down a Korean airliner for violating that air space. I had a look at the pictures, but couldn't make out anything, and called Marquardt.

"This Scandahoovian friend of ours called last night, sounded like he'd been drinking. He left me something this afternoon. Can we talk?"

"Yeah, this phone's secure. Sorry about that, shouldn't have given him your number. Kid's a real little weasel, thinks a high I.Q. makes you smart. I'll talk to him, don't worry about it."

Good, I thought, *talk to Millie while you're at it.*

But when I thought more about the call I remembered that he'd been on a pay phone, and mine was too new to be tapped. I relaxed and watched the news, which was mainly local events and ads, and then the smiling American President-elect. He was in a jet, happy and unworried, as advised by his little song. I was a little worried but reasonably happy. The job was interesting and my boss seemed to be okay, if casual about procedures. I didn't look that gift-horse in the mouth until later.

I started the Friday before Christmas with Hu Shi knocking

me around his dojo, and ended with a surprise phone call while I was doing Guimard work.

"*Ici Reynard!*"

Reynard was French for Fox, which was Durry, who wasn't supposed to bother with work-names. I told him I was with a friend but would call back in half an hour. Then I walked about a kilometer through a frigid glittering night to a fresh pay phone. Durry was waiting and organized, proposing dinner at an inn out near the Le Mans race course. Worth the trip, he said, for the exceptional cuisine and wines. It would be a long cold drive, but I told him I'd meet him there, and he gave me directions.

On the way home I stopped in a big stone church I'd been seeing since I moved in. Roman Catholic, my mother's rejected heritage. It was very cold and nearly empty, and I felt free to look around. I sensed the age of everything around me. It had been there centuries before Madame Pompadour, Marat and Napoleon. Up front was a *retable* like one by the Van Eycks in Ghent, the faces dementedly innocent. It seemed better to kneel in a pew toward the front rather than walking up to look at it. I settled down after a while and considered prayer — what it was about, how it was done. What a gift it must be. I smelled damp old stone and incense, very aware that this was a real church, an authentic working model complete with ambience and participants and belief. It struck me that my kind of thoughts and feelings were sacrilegious and out of place. Trivial. I didn't have the nerve to pray was what it came down to, so I just kneeled respectfully and soaked in what was there. Leaving, I passed a young couple, faces radiant, eyes sparkling at each other, unaware of the cold. I didn't seem to have the nerve for that either any more. But come hell or high water I was going to deliver Oracle, whatever it was.

I drove a long time under a cloudless pink sky before arriving at Mme. Gauthier's, half-frozen despite leathers and layers. Her inn was a rambling old stone country house with wings sticking out in all directions, presided over by the gracious and imperturbable white-haired lady it was named after. Only person I ever met who remembered the battle of the

Marne, which put her around eighty, and totally in charge. She showed me into the bar, a long room with windows along one wall and silvery-tan wallpaper on the others. At the far end was a big wood fire, and the room was full of heavy old provincial furniture. In the corner near the fire was an antique chess table with squares cut from stone. I ordered a vodka and sat thawing out, admiring an old secretary desk in a corner. Halfway through my drink I heard a roar and scattering gravel — my man Durry in a shiny black turbo-Peugeot. His mood was obvious as he stalked though the doorway. He spotted me, threw his trench coat over one chair and himself into another while ordering a double Stoli, all at once. Mme. Gauthier ignored it all, and I became unnaturally calm. Durry looked into the fire dramatically after I greeted him.

"You are quiet. You do not enjoy the holidays?" he asked in biting French after he had his drink in hand.

"Not very much," I said after a couple of beats. "You don't seem to, either. I'd like to know what's bothering, though."

"I'm sure. And it will bother you as well, *ami*."

He delivered this with total arrogance, flippant and irritating, as if I was probably a waste of time like all Americans. It was a big change from our phone call, and it was getting to me. He was the cornerstone of my new career, and he didn't feel very solid. I gave it some time and replied in a neutral voice.

"If we have problems, I'd like to know."

"Not between ourselves, but a problem, yes! Financial. We must renegotiate."

"I'm not authorized to do that, but I'll pass on your request."

"I'm afraid it is a demand. Somewhat negotiable, but not very much. All that I won at the velodrome with your advice, I lost a few day's later. Government pay is ridiculous, I'm drowning in debts. I will take another loan until I am paid."

He paused and shifted in his chair, hesitant for once. Then he struck a pose and made a little speech.

"There is something else I wish you to understand. While circumstances force me to appear greedy, I think it important for you to know that I am not selling government secrets, but

54

products of my own creation. I say that because I would like us to continue to respect each other. It may appear otherwise, but I am a good Algerian Frenchman."

"I suppose we could begin — "

"With another drink!"

Now it was my problem, and he was going to enjoy his evening. Mme. Gauthier was gone but a bartender had appeared, and I ordered two more vodkas. Durry seemed indestructibly confident, sure that he could think or bluff his way through anything. Alcohol made him more dramatic, but the computer didn't slow down.

"My attitude about money disturbs you, I can see this. Since I wish us to be friends, I will explain myself. My thoughts on money. Not to insult your powers of observation, but surely you have noticed how the rich do as they please? It is one of the few reliable rules of life, we see it everywhere. How the police hate to invade an expensive home! Their case must be perfect and still they may pay dearly — their superiors will distance themselves, lawyers will make fools of them, and inevitably they will lose favor. Because the rich accumulate influential friends, creating an *entente* which multiplies and consolidates influence, and this creates an entity which prevails as a law of its own until there is an upheaval, and the process begins again."

He saw my detachment and went up a gear.

"The point is, in this world of yours, these same rules apply. Who was that British spy a while back? Connected with Philby. *Blunt* — Sir Something Blunt. Not just a spy, clearly a traitor, but extremely well connected. Curator of the Queen's art, I believe. He was dealt with very gently, as he no doubt knew he would be. And what did they ever get from him? *Nothing!* Partly because he was clever, but mostly because he was allied with the rich, an intimate of the Queen. Others ran, including Philby, who was not rich, only a kind of genius. Blunt remained, and survived with just some embarrassment. *Formidable!* The point — only money can bring safety, privacy, tranquility. Time to think, to work, to play. *Time!* Yes, money is the one thing the Jews are right about."

He looked at me as if he'd made a brilliant point. I nodded, as if his view was shared by all us good Christians, but I was thinking about the impoverished Blinky Bernstein, who had the misfortune to play guitar for my neighbor, Tom Terrific.

"I would like you to indulge me in something," said Durry. "I know this menu, which is excellent in its specialties. May I order for both of us? You must tell me if something disagrees with you, of course."

I said that was fine, glad to move on.

"I have in mind a light local white wine that you Americans have never heard of, thank God, there is not much of it to be found. The asparagus soup. A great platter of mussels. A more robust white, and whatever seafood and vegetable Madame recommends. Then *Boom!* — the mousse. And a fine brandy they have here."

"If you will let me pay."

"Let me, Rob. Your advice in Ghent saved me from a bad mistake, and this will not cost very much. Drive two hours, pay a fraction of the price. My family was ruined when France abandoned Algeria, but not before I became accustomed to the good life. But if I come to places like this two or three times a week I am able to carry on . . . "

To slow down the drinking I suggested a game of chess. The board was already set up.

"Excellent. I am rather good, of course."

"I have a friend who is teaching me to make more interesting mistakes."

He smiled, drew white, and launched a queens-pawn blitz. I buttoned up and he made a mistake Fred would never have. It was pretty even, and I thought we might draw, but then he sacrificed a horse and stole a rook. I was finished. Durry leaned back, in a good mood.

"You are not really so bad, but you must attack, Rob. Countering only works with mediocre players. You cannot fight round-by-round, you must have a plan of scope. Like Ali in Zaire, if you recall. The famous rope-a-dope . . . "

"The game went too fast; all I could do was look for a mistake."

"Yes, and I made a bad one. Actually, that is how some good

players play me. And I make the mistakes, because it's only a game and I don't care. It is the pleasure of risk without punishment."

A thin teenage boy in a dark suit with very precise manners came over then, and led us into an immaculate pale salmon-colored room with an enormous glass chandelier and widely spaced tables. The boy seated us at a good one, and a serious old-fashioned professional took over. We ate vastly, two bottles of wine disappeared, and at the end came a dry mousse of "unaltered" chocolate, as Durry put it — the stuff Montezuma ingested before servicing his wives.

"The mousse," said Durry. "The mousse, eh!? It bounces straight up to the brain."

"Uncompromising," I said, belly pleased and my head full of wine.

"*Exactemente!*" he said, sounding fairly drunk. "Uncompromising. That is how one senses the closeness to perfection. Which is all we are given to know, don't you think?"

"'Euclid alone has looked on beauty bare.' Millay."

"Indeed. Which Millay is that?"

"Edna St. Vincent. American poet who burned her candle from both ends."

He smiled his bent-wire smile and announced that he was off to a week in the Caribbean. Then he gave me a bright-eyed birdlike probing look that caught my attention. The vacation meant something.

"For the sun," he added, eyes twinkling maliciously. "The islands — St. Croix, St. Barts. St. Marcus — that one is best. Immaculate, entirely rich, enormous yachts. Now, tonight's transaction — it is on the original terms, as I do not wish to make a problem for you, and this may help establish you with your superiors. But not again, and your superiors must understand that this is no bluff."

"You have another client?"

I was killing time, waiting for him to throw out an impossible number, wondering about his references to those Caribbean islands. He seemed to think I should know what he was talking about, as if it had something to do with our business.

"Yes, I could have another client, although I would prefer not to do business with them. But I could, yes. It is important for Marquardt to grasp this."

I was rocked by his knowing my boss's name, trying not to show it.

"You must give me at least some idea of your demands," I said.

"I *must*? Indeed! No, Beach, you are not in the position to tell Alain Durry what he must or must not do!"

Drunk after all. I slowed way down.

"In that case — well, I'm only trying to do business."

"I'm sure. But Alain Durry does not do business on command."

"Of course not," I said cheerfully. "No offense intended."

He smiled and said it was nothing, just a misunderstanding, and that we would do business, of course, but when he was ready and the number was right.

"I've only recently joined the situation. Perhaps you could review your understanding of the deal as it stood?"

"It no longer stands, of course. I originally agreed to deliver packets of information as I developed it, at a hundred and fifty thousand Swiss francs per delivery, beginning in July. One every three or four weeks, with double payment for the last. Two of six have been delivered. This will make three. But I know now that the value of the product was concealed, and the sum agreed on is not sufficient for my needs."

He didn't say any more, and I didn't push him. Both of us drank a lot of strong coffee in a friendly mood, and as we were leaving he casually drew an envelope from under his shirt. I didn't expect it, and was shaken by his casual way of doing it.

I drove back carefully on deserted roads, lining up facts. Durry knew my boss by his real name. My boss had used his idiot cover-job assistant to pick up Oracle material, and she knew my phone number. Satellite Sven was another idiot with my phone number. Those were facts. And Alain Durry was a wild and crazy guy who liked to play you and let you know it — I took that as another fact. I'd been thinking I could handle him, but now I was wondering for how long.

And what did his Caribbean vacation signify? St. Marcus had felt like bait, a clue tossed out to see what I knew, and I'd let him think I might know more than I did. One very big fact was clear. TCC France was not a tight ship. I spotted a phone in a small town and left Al a message: Durry had delivered, but we had a problem.

I was too wired to sleep when I got to rue Marchais, but I got in bed and tried. The phone rang around five, and I answered in cheap slurred French. It would be Marquardt, and I was curious to see if I could fool him with my voice. Instead I got a young sing-song late partying voice. I squawked some more gutter French about stupid shits dialing wrong numbers in the middle of the night and hung up. A minute later the phone rang again and Sven got the generic answer-box message. He stuttered something and rang off. I enjoyed it for a minute, but it bothered me. Al hadn't spoken to Sven. I was beginning to think of my boss as the anti-Morris, and wondered how he got away with it. A jerk like Sven shouldn't have my number — that was another fact.

Marcel made me a friend for life by inviting me to a fine Christmas Eve dinner with his wife and son, but in the morning I came down to earth when I picked up my mail at the motel. A Christmas card from my daughter, with a note:

Thanks for the check, it was totally timely. Great about your new job! Hope all is going well for you in la belle France, I know you like it there. School is fine, I have a little car, and I really love being up here.
Best, Layla

Best what? Layla was sounding like Felice-of-the-deep-pockets, whose attorneys had blocked visitation long enough to finalize a break that never needed to happen. The note reminded me that I didn't know my daughter any more. I didn't even know how to read the note, which was as much as I'd heard from her in close to a year. At sixteen, she'd declared her independence of me, and I'd never figured out what to do about it. Walking through the parking lot I saw myself clearly. Another failed parent hoping to make things right. I drove home and spent Christmas at my desk.

The next afternoon Marquardt asked endless careful questions about my Durry meeting. We were in the vast, always-empty Aerodrome with its interchangeable waiters, Al was sleek as a seal, elusive and confident, pleased that Durry and I were getting along. He seemed satisfied, not disturbed by the undefined financial demands, and leisurely, as if he'd had a couple before I got there. At one point he paused, and I waited for Sven to come up, but we stayed with Durry.

"Didn't let on who the competition might be?"

Not smooth, he'd already asked that.

"No, just that he preferred not to do business with them. He doesn't talk about business, Al. He drops it on you and goes on to other things — the state of the world, how smart he is, food and wines. He's going for a vacation, by the way."

"Great timing. Don't ya love this guy? Well, gotta see the good side, right? Delivered again. Guy gets along with you, so that glass is half full. Yeah, we'll pay for his holiday, that's what it's probably about."

It would be more than that, but I let it go. After the second drink I knew he wasn't going to address Sven, so I did. He didn't want to hear it, but he let me finish. Then he let a silence develop before replying.

"He's a dick, but he delivers, Rob. Krasnoyarsk is very big. Sometimes you have to bend a little. No such thing as perfect security at this level — you'll see that when you've been around a while."

Perfect security. Funny, but the Nam-beast didn't think so. I slowed myself down.

"He's trouble, Al. He probably tells girls he's a spy to impress them. He's a *kid*."

When he didn't respond, the beast encouraged me to observe that Sven was a complete fucking idiot who shouldn't have my number. Al showed no reaction to my change in tone, as if I was entitled to my opinion and manner of expressing it.

"Gotta suck it up, Rob, no choice."

I nodded, but I was still feeling exposed and contentious, so I told him about the girl in Ghent. He relaxed and shook his head, blue eyes all-knowing.

"Not to worry. If they were on to you, you'd've never made it home with the material. European girls are different, she was probably looking for some action."

Al Marquardt, authority on the Continental female. I was irritated enough that I held back my little escapade off the A1, glad that he didn't know about the bike. Telling him Durry knew his name wouldn't help my case either, and I didn't even consider bringing up Millie. I'd learned that much from Joe Kline. Then out of the blue he asked would I help him with his French — just speak with him in French once in a while.

"I had this woman I'd spend a little time with each week, just hang out and talk French, but then I fucked her and screwed it up."

It broke the tension, and I asked him in French how that had happened. He couldn't handle conversation speed, so I slowed down, separating words.

"It was her idea. She said she liked large men."

Did he mean to be funny? I was finally relaxed, cracking up at his French. He sounded like a machine assembling parts at high speed, all out of alignment. We kept it going for five or ten minutes and I agreed to do it again from time to time. Then he surprised me again.

"You could take a few days stateside while Durry's away if you want to. I know you came on zero notice."

"That'd be great. I left some things hanging I can't handle from here."

"No problemo. With our guy on vacation there's nothing I can't switch off. If it's okay with Guimard, it's okay with me. Take a week, have some fun."

His reaction puzzled me. I'd been out of line pushing Sven at him with such a hard edge, but it hadn't seemed to bother him. Did he value my services enough to take that from a very junior guy? It felt like yes. Oracle was that important. He'd stayed cool, defused me, and made sure we ended on good terms.

In the airport taxi I watched sleet form on the windshield and decided to put my boss on a need-to-know basis about some things. Then I pondered TCC. How did you put a Morris in charge and then stick him with a wild card like Al? How did Al get to be a senior exec at an operation like BioTel? Whatever they were, they were very big.

At the airport I slipped the Air France man three fifties and put myself on standby, then considered my issues over a Stoli. I understood Al sending Millie to the Tic-TocBad idea, but it was the kind of thing guys do to impress other guys. I understood indulging Durry, too, he had no choice. But Sven was just a jerk kid who could be scared into behaving himself. His calls were stupid, and there wasn't anything in the manual about dealing with nonsense. But aside from Sven, I liked the job, and the freedom, and having two incomes, and tabbing everything to expenses.

Thinking about those things was safe but I couldn't keep it up, and soon I was thinking about Layla. My daughter was the real problem. Should I call her when I got back? It had been a year since I tried talking to her, but now I had a job, and she was away at school, and things might be different. Then it came through the vodka with a quiet *thump*. Getting in touch with my daughter needed some thinking about. TCC had rushed me through, and they'd missed my French marriage to Felice, along with Layla. I was pretty sure of that, and I didn't want my employers to know she existed. Morris could talk about cellular separation but I'd heard Al spill the beans about Jennie and our State Department connection. I continued with the vodka and kept dropping by Air France. Before I was buzzed I had a flight.

9

I got to The Pope bag in one hand, case in the other. It was holiday time and the place was jammed with traders, lawyers and rich kids and locals, all going after the models. Very loud, everyone half drunk and shouting over bad rock music. I got the end seat at the bar, and the wind hit my back each time the door opened. The world was holiday bright but I was still in my TCC head, studying fistic history on the wall: Joe Louis taking a pop from skinny Billy Conn, Jack Dempsey tearing someone's head off with a hook from hell, Ali standing over Liston looking crazy.

As I waited for a drink, the smiling president-elect appeared *en famille* on the tube in a festive setting. I looked away and spotted McVeigh working the far end, and he gestured to show he'd seen me. A minute later a barmaid came over with half a tumbler of Jameson and ice water, of which I had a swallow, followed by a hit of the Irish.

"Been a while, Rob," said Mac, appearing a minute later with one for himself. We both tossed off a slug.

"Been out of town — "

"So that's it. You're a real mystery-man lately."

"Eat your heart out, Mick. Got a for-real job in France, left on short notice."

He didn't ask about the job, just nodded like a cop. His big red face had an expression that didn't make sense. Had TCC been to see him? They'd checked out several friends, though the friends didn't know it. Mac probably would, though.

"Cheers!" he said. It lacked the holiday spirit, but we lifted our drinks and took identical slugs again. I was waiting for him to ask about my new life, but he was somewhere else.

"What's on your mind, Mac? I'm not here to borrow money, just pay my tab and get schnockered among friends."

It wasn't my usual voice, but he wasn't his usual self. He looked at my chin and tried to look casual.

"Trouble at home," he said unwillingly.

"Sorry to hear it." I wasn't very surprised. There was his

fiancée Carol, and there were all these hotties that wanted a piece of him, and Carol was nobody's fool.

He still had the wooden expression, and he didn't say any more. I had a swallow of ice-water and gave up on it, but when he saw I was ready to leave he spoke.

"German girl," he said. "How come you just disappeared?"

"I didn't tell people when I left. Not even you, dear heart. It was a gamble. If it didn't work out I didn't want to be talking about it."

A believable lie, given my circumstances, and it settled him down.

"Good luck with the new girl — "

"She's not the 'new girl,'" he said.

"Well, just good luck, then. How about that?"

"Sure, why not."

I looked in his eyes again and decided he might have had more than a few before I walked in. His voice had a crooning softness, and I got the message through the drunken holiday roar. A kind of warning. This German had him by the short-hairs while Carol still had a grip on his black-Irish mop. I guessed he wanted both and they wouldn't go for it. Solution, pick a fight. I reached for my wallet.

"On us," he said. "Forget it, Rob, I've got my head up my ass. And of course I'm feeling like a shit about Carol. Christ, she's wearing my *ring*. I just can't seem to tell her, Rob. Never had a problem with these things, but Leni's different. Leni Hartt."

His voice was serious in a different way now, calm and thoughtful. Carol was long-term, they owned each other and he knew it.

"Do me a favor, just forget it. Another Irishman acting the fool, let's talk about you — what are you up to over there, Robbo?"

Lighten things up, tell a good lie.

"Same old thing, investment advisory. Foreign outfit, BCCI, good people."

Mac exploded. The Bank of Credit and Commerce International was a notorious bunch of crooks under investigation in a half dozen countries for every crime known to the industry. When he was through laughing, Mac looked at me in a normal way before knocking back the last of his drink and glancing down the bar.

"I've gotta help out, we're getting backed up. I'm sure whatever you're up to is making you rich, but I wonder if you might do that delivery I mentioned when you go back. Frère Jacques — "

"Maybe so, let me sleep on it. If it blew up I wouldn't know who to call."

"Got that worked out. By the way, that's a fucking awful tie. Is it French?"

I shrugged and then saw another job perk. A low six figure currency violation would probably be no problem for a TelcomCo employee. From what I knew of Al, he'd probably like me better for it.

"Let you know in a day or two?"

"Fine. Maybe no one in the middle this time, simple bank deposit."

And then some words came out of my mouth that I would come to regret.

"Someone tipped me to an outfit that might do something. You still in touch with people who can check that out?"

"Yeah, the guys all come in and talk. Maybe I can find the people who shopped it. Get 'em loose, introduce 'em to some lively bush. How'd you get tipped, if I may?"

"We do business with an outfit that works with them. The company is called BioTel, and I don't know anything about it. It was just some tech talking, but there might be something there. Strictly private inquiry, no waves. Just you and me."

"Why not, market's still dead. Are you thinkin' you're gonna do that other thing for me then?"

"Your retirement, right. Or was it those Sisters of Celtic Sanctity? Yeah, I think so. I'm going upstate to see family, I'll be in touch when I get back."

"And I'll see what I can find out about this BioTel."

"Strictly between the two of us."

"Understood. *Jesus*, but I hate insider trading! That Boesky

— *terrible* person. Commencement speaker at Stanford then gets caught in a scam? But what the hell — can't beat 'em, join 'em."

I climbed my stairs hoping for the Del Psychos, but the building was silent. Just a few of months, but everything was different. I felt my civilian life floating off into history, leaving me in spook limbo with Al Marquardt. Then I opened my door and there was a series of shattering *clangs*. I turned off the alarm and when I turned on the lights, I saw my old life, stale and dead. I threw open the windows and turned on the jazz station. *Bird with Strings*. Excellent. I turned it up and sat in my coat on my old horse-hair sofa with a December wind sweeping through. Then Bird was gone and a femme-fatale DJ told me who was at the clubs in a breathy brainless voice. I was ready to settle for a game with Fred, but he was off limits.

A group effort by loners like yourself.

Crackerjack wisdom, and not bad except that I was sure Jason Olcott maintained a conventional wife and family. I turned off the radio and watched the news. In Queens, a gang of white kids led by a dwarfish South African teenager was on trial for what amounted to a lynching. One dead black man. Then the mayor, blaming his troubles on predecessors going back to the sixties, then holiday murders, date-rapes, jail-rapes, and the President-elect with a garbled *Be-Happy-Don't-Worry* holiday sound bite. He didn't speak well. On another channel cops with taped badges were beating on homeless people camped in Tompkins Square. I was home. Then I was asleep, fully dressed.

In the morning I couldn't wake up. I had coffee, showered, got most of the dye out of my hair, and tried the *kata*. I did it badly and missed Hu Shi. After some more coffee I remembered my original *sensei*, with whom I still had time on the clock. Her cool smooth voice was the same, but I heard it differently since Al let me know who she worked for.

"Thought we'd lost you, Rob."

Neat little deception there, light touch, well done. And could I come in at four?

I could, and my day had a point now. At the Star I had steak and eggs while catching up on the smoldering Iran-Contra scandal in the *Times*. Congress was still foaming at the arms-for-hostages trade, the whole thing being blatantly illegal under the Boland Amendment. The executive branch and its spooks had bypassed the legislative branch, and Cabinet members who hated each other agreed on this with fiery quotes. They'd been bypassed as well. Barred from making such a deal, Carter had tried to snatch the hostages, failed, and lost the election. But it was pretty clear to sharp journalists that CIA had cut that deal behind Carter's back, with desired results. Carter disgraced, hostages freed, arms to the Contras. All facilitated by those same dirty Iranians, working with their sworn enemies, the Israelis. Politics makes strange bedfellows.

The Israelis had been represented by one Amiram Nir, a mystery man, now gone. Dan Rather had mentioned him in the Bush interview, but he'd been lost in the hullabaloo. I was curious about Nir, an intelligence liaison who doubled in gun-running and died in Mexico just before the election before he could present his views on the matter. Trying to corner the avocado market, they said, which was controlled by a fellow Israeli. The stench from this giant can of worms couldn't be contained, but the investigations were dying.

The hero of the moment was a photogenic and patriotic Colonel North, who was drawing attention away from the real players and might yet end up on trial. Those players had really excellent lawyers though, and North was media-ready, a dashing young officer with a very hot secretary. Hot secretary's mother just *happened* to work for the National Security Advisor, and her delicious daughter had just happened to lose track of several million embarrassing dollars somewhere in Switzerland. The President-elect was naturally disturbed. Extremely. *If only he'd known!* Career CIA and former agency head, but somehow out of that endless international loop.

The Nam-beast didn't like it, and I had a few hours to kill, so I got on the subway and went to the mid-town library, where I applied the skills my father had taught me. Soon I was finding all manner of interesting things. Secretary of State Schultz was still furious. He'd been bypassed and ignored, and lost his temper at length in a secret no-notes meeting that Bush could not recall. Others remembered it and said so, but there was no media follow up. The CBS debacle had scared everyone off.

Then I discovered that the president-elect had actually admitted his knowledge of Iran-Contra earlier in an FBI deposition. Why would he do that? Skull and Bones meant keeping your mouth shut. Looking closer I saw that no *involvement* was admitted, which by Bush's definition kept him out of the loop. I learned that he was very active in oil and banking, with associates including many prominent Arabs, all of them knowledgeable about money and/or weapons, as well as oil. These included one Adnan Khashoggi, rumored to be the richest man in the world, recently profiled in *Time*. Reading up on him, I came across another old Bush associate, Khalid bin Mahfouz of funky-stinky BCCI. Another Bush associate was BCCI's founder, Agha Hasan Abedi. Another was Kamal Adham, former head of Saudi intelligence. Kamal Adam owned a whopping big chunk of BCCI. Woven through the whole thing was an Iranian middleman named Ghorbanifar that no one seemed to trust. There were too many names to remember and my eyes were getting tired, so I took a break.

After that I focused on BCCI, a financial legend in its own time, always under investigation by several governments. It was difficult to corner, because it had no real home, having been designed to avoid regulation. Audited in some sense by Price Waterhouse, it had endless enemies, but no real problem.

How did BCCI achieve this invulnerable position? That I understood — it was designed to avoid prosecution, registered in lenient Luxembourg. Journalist Joseph Trento noted that " . . . *with the official blessing of George H.W. Bush as head of the CIA, Kamal Adham transformed a small Pakistani merchant bank into a world-wide money-laundering machine, buying banks around the world to create the biggest clandestine money network in history."* BCCI was insured against almost anything by its special relationship with CIA, and a French probe had revealed that the President-elect had a personal account with them. Not very discreet, but maybe he didn't have to be. I was rocked, and the beast was pacing. Trento was legitimate, a two-time Pulitzer nominee.

But the Senate had not been completely fooled. A couple of years before, the Kerry Committee had outed North's guns and funds network. Accurate information, but with unnamed sources, and somehow overlooked. I respected Kerry, a swift boat captain who got his boat out of a shore-fire trap by running his boat up on the shore and winning the firefight. Not PT-109, but not bad.

Finally I looked into the mysterious Mr. Nir, who turned out to be a boy wonder Israeli journalist who had married power and weaseled his way into intelligence and did gun running on the side. Not Mossad, but he'd been Israel's man in the big Iran-Contra meetings and Col. North wanted to make him a scapegoat. He didn't like that, so he talked to Woodward and Bernstein about writing an Iran-Contra memoir from his POV. Then came the avocados and a timely Mexican plane crash before the election.

I'd had enough serious for one day, and walked out with a wild hair up my ass, thinking about my father. He'd detested Bush's dad for many reasons, one being an attempted coup after Roosevelt's election known as The Business Plot. It was outed by a Marine general they wanted to front for it, but Bush senior had good lawyers and got out of it. Undaunted, he'd continued doing business with Nazis into WWII until FDR stopped it. Good lawyers got him out of that, too, and ten years later he was a senator.

I tried to walk off the mood, but it was still with me when I got to the dojo. I was early, but the door was unlocked, and I stood in the office listening through the inner door as Jennie gave a lesson. The wooden file cabinets under the butcher-block caught my eye when I went to make tea. Al had revealed Jennie's TCC role, and I wanted to know more. The old locks looked easy, and I scanned the room. No camera. I threw the front door bolt and got lucky. The top left file opened without much encouragement, and the first thing I saw was her diary. Blue leather, unlined pages, a graceful hand. The voices continued in the other room and I flipped to the day I'd signed up.

New student via Fred. Not a great prospect, past forty and pretty blobbed-out. Gray hair, quiet, not stupid, a little burnt.

Seeing Keith for drinks tonight, why, we don't know. I'm bored. My gig is too easy and I'm not getting any younger. This is a sick business that cuts you off from people.

Cut off, yes, but I wasn't blobbed-out anymore. Lesson-sounds kept coming through the door and I kept looking. The drawer below wouldn't open, but I got a hand through the split bottom of the top drawer and unlocked it from inside. I was beginning to sweat, but the lesson-sounds continued while I flipped through her files. And there I was, as Beach, on blank stationary — a three line note to someone named Bill saying I'd be okay. Offhand, like a social note, vague and minimal but clear. Not just Olcott's mistress, but vetting TCC candidates.

Then silence in the main room. I slid the drawer closed, unbolted the hall door, and stood looking at the martial arts photos and listening for her voice to start up again, which it did. Less than two minutes, but my pulse was still racing. The kettle squealed and I poured water over an exotic teabag, thinking about the new game. Part of it was knowing things other people didn't think you knew. Now I knew that Jennie was part of TCC, reporting to a Silver Spring, MD address. I also knew that she was casual about security, and that she had no problem with me. New equation — she'd known more about me than I did about her, and I'd turned that around.

I was drinking some kind of herb tea when she walked in, and she really caught me up. The glow of health, the understated walk, the serious little mouth with its reserved little smile. Over the smile, that long thin nose. Topping all this, those serious Asian eyes and perfectly black hair in a punky new cut. Above all I saw her composure, the God-given natural grace that can't be faked or forced. Having seen her diary, I let myself see her. Delicious. I was detached about it, though. I was developing a detachment in this job that surprised me. We smiled at each other.

"Are you in town for a while, Rob?"

Cool and businesslike, standing at her desk looking at a big calendar.

"Maybe a week. Do I have any time left?"

"Three lessons. You look better — have you been working out?"

"Four or five times a week. I found a dojo in Paris and got into some sparring."

"Well, let's see if they ruined you. This group will be gone in a few minutes."

No smile, dead serious. Three middle aged women walked through several minutes later, looking rejuvenated. *Showtime*, I was thinking. As I dressed, I knew I was going to surprise her. I was lighter and faster, and sparring had sharpened me. When we did the *kata*, I saw that Hu Shi was a mechanic. With Jennie it was a war dance in slow-motion. I felt a mask-like detachment come over me. When we finished, she nodded.

"Good, much better. Now I'm going to teach you an application. It's a counter to a blow or knife thrust — any attack with the arm coming from below."

We worked on this for a long while. Her moves seemed to change angle and pace in mid-air, and a lot of them got through. My strength was useless but something was opening up in me. When it was my turn to attack, I knew that in some intuitive way I had her number. Almost. Something about my timing seemed to distract her, and I got through. Then I almost did it a second time, and the door closed. I was sparring with a ghost, a disembodied series of subtle shifts that kept me continually off balance. I couldn't get near her. Without transition she began touching me, again and again, different places, one tap after another, getting harder, jarring me. Then she put me on the mat without striking, just getting me off balance and giving me a little push. She did it again. I was pouring sweat but she wouldn't call time, just came down a gear and made me keep going. When we stopped, she scolded me.

"This is supposed to be full contact on your side, and you're holding back. You're not really trying to strike, and you're not good enough to just touch, it makes you slower. I can handle it, that's what you're paying for."

We went at it again, but jetlag was catching up with me. One time I surprised her, but she flew out of reach like smoke.

Finally she called time and ended the session, after which we bowed, faces fixed. After that she spoke in a lighter voice.

"Post-party syndrome?"

"Little jetlag, too."

"Alcohol in your sweat. But you're improving, Rob, keep working out with your Hu Shi. One more thing . . . "

She walked away and picked a small brown object off a shelf.

"Beanbag. Good for balance."

She tossed the little bag in the air and kept it there with little taps of hands, feet, elbows and knees, moving it around in front of her, then circling it, striking it in cycles, then changing the cycles and mixing the moves until it became a kind of fugue-dance with flashes of cool white thigh as the *gi* flew around. Then she tossed me the bag to take with me.

"Anyway, that's the idea — we'll go into it next time. You might like to get in the tub for a while if you have time."

She walked off to the office and I went to the hot tub. I'd never been in one, and it was hotter than I could believe, sperm-killing brain-boiling hot. Just getting in took my mind off everything, and then it hit like a narcotic. Time was melting and sweat was pouring out of my face. When my metabolism leveled off I was smiling and empty-headed. How long to stay in? My body hadn't felt so good all winter. Then I hauled myself out, weak and dazed, staring at blue tile, muscles so loose I felt helpless. I pulled my mind together and dressed at half speed, waiting for my body to come around. I didn't want teacher seeing me like that.

Jennie was writing checks at her desk when I came through, not quite smiling, but she knew where the tub had left me. It was light-touch humor, nothing said. I enjoyed how polite we were with each other, which let me think well of myself. And I really enjoyed knowing what she was up to with TCC and without her knowing that I knew.

10

I slept like a rock and woke at noon to a cold dark day, rain drumming on the roof, phone ringing away. I let the machine take the call and a big rich sound filled the room — the voice of Morris Pell in a good mood.

"This is Junior from Spiegel's deli. We have your pastrami and celery sodas if you wouldn't mind picking them up."

Working with Al had enhanced my appreciation of him and I didn't mind at all. I climbed into my clothes, went out in the rain, and called from Fanelli's, a quiet old bar full of artists and film people. When I called, a machine told me I'd reached an entirely different number, but it was his voice.

"Beechcraft here and holding until one-thirty," I said, and read off the number.

Then I ordered a rare hamburger. Halfway through it came the callback. He wanted to meet for dinner at Wohlfurt's, a steak house in Brooklyn. There was no spin on the ball, and he sounded friendly in his sardonic way, as if he'd had a good report on me.

"Just over the Williamsburg. Eight sharp. Dress."

"See you there."

Finishing my burger, I wondered what the surprise would be. I remembered the way he'd set me up that day in Washington Square. Face deadpan as he observed my delay-time, little blue eyes glinting, mouth cherubically relaxed. The Crackerjacks. There would be a surprise and dressing for dinner was the clue, but I missed it.

Wohlfurt's was an unpretentious place full of white tablecloths, and a solid feeling of the world circa 1960. I'd just joined Morris at a corner table when the surprise arrived: Jason Olcott in black coat, gray fedora, big black umbrella. Wohlfurt's was informal, but someone appeared to take his belongings. He walked over with long shiny yellow teeth bared in a benevolent-despot smile and pumped my arm. Then we sat down and had

73

whiskies neat all around. I remembered Olcott's taste for bourbon and ordered Jim Beam. Flattery will get you everywhere, Felice used to say.

Very quickly the topic was me. How I was getting along on the job. Chapter and verse, if I didn't mind. I sensed that Marquardt was being undercut by this little out-of-channels meeting and I didn't like it. I had my issues about Millie and Sven, but I still didn't like it. Maybe it was his sick kid, or just his easy-going way. Olcott presided, filling gaps in his Washington Insider manner, confidential and cheery, and false. He wanted to know everything I'd been doing, what I thought about this and that, who I saw socially. I lied about my address without thinking about it. He seemed pleased that I was too busy to meet people other than a martial arts trainer, and I let him think I spent time at Guimard. My work had become my hobby for sure, and the mask was becoming the face. I was relieved when the steaks arrived, but there was no break. They took turns leading me in a review of events from day one in France. I piled on details, surprised at how much I remembered.

"Any significant personal contacts in your work?" asked Olcott.

Even Morris couldn't smooth that away. Contact was outside the job description and shouldn't be occurring. I waited a couple of beats and organized myself.

"One. Dr. Alain Durry, work-name Fox. Several phone calls and three meetings."

"Yes," said Olcott. "How did that go?"

He had to know already. He'd done the same thing in the interview when I was hired. It was clumsy, and I was starting to think of him that way. I answered carefully.

"Not badly, but he won't do drops, he wants contact. Someone I know as Sven has called a few times wanting contact, too. When I declined, he dropped some photos of Krasnoyarsk -"

"Al's reaction?" asked Morris. I remembered Al's sick kid and covered for him.

"He was interested in Krasnoyarsk and asked me to bear with Sven's calls."

"And Durry?" asked Olcott, bypassing Krasnoyarsk as if

cabinet level careers didn't hang on what happened there. His crudeness startled me. Why was Al interested in Krasnoyarsk when his boss wasn't? And why wasn't he?

"He's made two deliveries and we seem to get along. By coincidence, I knew something about a race he was betting on. He won and he was pleased about it, but he wants to renegotiate."

"Heavy bettor, is he?" asked Olcott, showing no interest in Durry's new demands.

"I'd guess into the thousands, pretty often. Tennis, horses, soccer, basketball — it doesn't matter." I realized I was volunteering information, and stopped.

"Any problems?" asked Olcott, elaborately casual. I'd already told him, so I spelled it out.

"Insists on live drops, so there's repeated exposure."

"Keep going," said Morris. It was clear that Durry's high risk m.o. was incidental. Whatever Oracle was, it ranked Russia's super-radar for TCC. It was none of my Courier Two business, but I couldn't help wondering what could be that important.

"Durry won't set a price on his new demands. He got angry when I pressed him."

"And . . . ?"

"Dislikes Americans. Opinionated but not political. He seems to think the world is a chaotic mess run by people who will probably blow it up sooner or later."

Too strong for Olcott, so I finished by saying that Durry was typically French, fond of himself and his ideas. Morris's eyes twinkled, but I saw Olcott shift uncomfortably before speaking again.

"This is an unusual situation we have here, Rob, you and Dr. Durry. What we have is a brand new Courier running a very high level source."

It was obvious, and he sounded foolish saying it. I was sure this was exactly what Morris had hired me for, and got the sense that he was handling Olcott like the trusted employee of a rich old retiree who was losing his marbles and didn't need to know much. While I was digesting that, he spoke.

"Sounds like a real cunt to me," he rumbled cheerfully. "You're going to have to winkle that material out of him and try to keep the price down. Our read has always been that he'll go any direction, not controllable. Think he'd sell to others as well?"

"I don't think so. That's just a personal impression, but he's no fool."

Olcott gave a perfunctory nod. "We'd very much like to know who we might be in competition with," he said stiffly. Morris came in right on his heels.

"Of course, broaching the subject even indirectly could set him off. Might come out in negotiation, though, if you get close to him. Al's had problems with him, but he thinks you're handling it, and so do I."

Olcott gave an emphatic equine nod at this, reversing himself without effort. It was Morris's show, and I was starting to relax, but I was uneasy about my slapdash good-natured boss and his sick kid. Of course Durry preferred me to Al and his mangled robo-French, it meant nothing. I looked down at my steak, cautious and thoughtful. It was all right being golden, but I was concerned about what might come with it.

"The Durry material is a series of installments, and given the insistence on personal contact, we're not very comfortable with the situation," said Olcott gravely. "This is a special case, and national security could be involved. Morris feels, and I agree, that you should consider being armed when you have the material in your possession."

"As a courier, Jason . . . ?"

I said it in a casual, matter of fact way, to get him off me. Over the drinks he'd suggested I address him on a first-name basis, but the challenge flustered him.

"Oh, of course — work that out, yes," he said quickly, head tilting slightly.

"Not a problem," said Morris soberly. His expression took me to the edge of a smile. We understood each other perfectly, starting with the attaché case. I had power at this table, and it didn't bother him. We both knew it was my cock on the block, that I could go from valuable to expendable in a heartbeat. Olcott had handled me wrong, and we both knew that, too. Morris used his heavy, solid voice to ease us along.

"Another precaution, Rob. We think it would be wise for you to re-enter France under fresh cover. There are two sets of Canadian I.D. in this envelope."

He drew it from his inside pocket and I put it in mine. There was nothing routine about this meeting, and my antennae were full up. I took time to think before speaking.

"Onto me already?"

I let myself look first into Olcott's face, then Morris's, and saw nothing.

"In that case I'd rather fly to London and take local transport into France."

"We've had no indication that any other party is aware of you" said Olcott. "But additional security's a plus. Your work is very critical."

Then he excused himself and went to the men's room.

"You're not comfortable with this," said Morris.

"Not yet."

"Price you pay, Rob, comes with the responsibility. It levels off after a while. I know this is op work and we'll work that out."

We were talking about the best way to re-enter Europe when Olcott returned, followed by the waiter with a bottle of brandy. I was their boy. It felt good, but a calm, lucid paranoia came with it. The fact was, we were all professional liars, and they had seniority. Another fact was, I fit right in.

After that I was wide awake, pacing my loft and trying to settle down. Something was missing. My pith helmet, it felt like — my boy-scout requirement for some credible entity beyond myself, and my obligation to it. Instead I was feeling a simple selfish need to know more and cover my back. And get paid more, because running sources wasn't in my job description, and Olcott didn't want me armed for no reason. Around dawn, rebellious and feeling used, I was understanding how people were doubled. It didn't have to be money or ideology or blackmail. You might just meet some person from the other side who was more convincing than a Jason Olcott. Not hard to find. I lay there thinking about it until it was getting light out. Without Morris, Olcott was nothing.

And what was TCC, exactly? Sealed off in my cell with Al, it wasn't something I could research, but maybe Al would say more, or Mac would come across something while checking out BioTel.

Layla, I thought unexpectedly, and put TCC aside. No paper trail. Renting a car without using my plastic would be the main problem, but one of the going-broke film guys at Fanelli's had a car he'd probably let me use for a price. Pay for everything with cash, because money has no smell. It felt safe. I decided I could see Layla, but very carefully.

Day's End Inn was a classic place-to-meet-Daddy. It sat in the snow in front of a stand of birches, big, white and colonial. I felt my roots, and I felt like a drink. Just a single Jameson, which I sipped slowly, sitting alone in the long clean bar, eating cheese-fish and tiny pretzels while being observed by an old skin-and-bones Yankee bartender with a hard little mouth. But my daughter walked in with a big uncomplicated smile, not shy of me. She ran over to hug me, and after those bad years, things were fine again just like that, I didn't care how or why. Her face was full of color. A long, serious face, a young woman's face now. She was a tall girl with superior legs, my daughter. Looked good on a bar stool.

"You're really not mad about my not writing, are you," she said after we settled down. It wasn't a question, she could tell. The bartender stayed at the other end and I began to like him more.

"You're right, I'm just glad it's over, I'm glad we're here. I'm super-happy about it, Layla. Would you like a drink?"

"Yes, I really would. Vodka tonic. Daddy, you're being great about this. I feel so good. It's such a fu . . . great relief. Whenever I'd start to write — "

"Yeah, big fuckin' relief," I said gravely, and she laughed. I waved at the bartender and ordered her drink. She was a very adult eighteen, with my mother's cool pale eyes and her premature-gray gene. In Layla it showed as a single streak that came off her forehead like a warning flare. She was smart enough to act like a pleased kid, and she was easier to talk to than I'd ever been. Naturally social, like Felice, and she had Felice's fine chest. We took our drinks into a big cold dining room and were led to a window table. Then she got down to it.

"I've come to see that I'm mother's whole life, she said. "It's not the healthiest."

A waiter came over, we ordered the scampi, and I added an overpriced wine.

"Now that I'm at school it's actually harder to deal with. Lots of phone calls, and she talks about money all the time."

I could feel from the careful way she was speaking how uncomfortable she was about Felice now that she was old enough to understand her.

"Most rich people think about money all the time. That's why they tip the way they do. She'd have lost some last year, but she can hardly be hurting."

"I didn't think so either, and she — well, she says that I have to keep down expenses. I have this *miniscule* scholarship, and of course I can't get a better one because of her money! I mean — I can't cost much more than her shrink, can I? I wouldn't have come here if I couldn't have a car. It's this *archaic* Honda Civic, so there's this maintenance, plus insurance, of course ... "

For a moment she was about to lose it, but then she was in control again.

"The point is — my insight for the semester — I was just imitating Mom when I sent you that awful letter. She's still pissed at you, it's like her career now."

I smiled a rueful smile and my daughter smiled back. We understood each other.

"Your mom's thing with money," I said, "I have a saying — 'The rich are poor, ask them and they'll tell you.' Those trusts are well and wisely locked up, I know all about them. She doesn't have access to the capital and she's taking it out on you. My view. But I'm doing well now and I can help, and when you're twenty-one you'll have a little income of your own from the estate. Also — well, you're competition now, and your mom never liked that."

The look on her face said I wasn't shocking her yet. She

asked about my work and I dodged, saying it was a great job but involved classified information, so I couldn't talk about it. The wine arrived and I smelled the cork thoughtfully, like Durry. When the waiter was gone I suggested it would probably be better not to mention me to Felice.

"No kidding! That's what I saw after I finally got away up here. You and I can be friends, it's like completely separate."

I smiled proudly. Outside, large wet snowflakes were falling from a colorless Vermont winter sky. We talked art history and felt snug, and the shrimp appeared. I saw that my daughter had Felice's elegant manner with knife and fork — no clumsy left-right shifting. No clumsy anything. We talked about things that had happened a long time ago, and what she might do with her summer. Just before we left I pulled out an envelope with ten near-fresh hundred dollar bills as my perceptive daughter looked at me.

"Now, you may be curious about this envelope, which contains cash instead of the usual check, but your dad is not paying any Star Wars taxes he can avoid. I suggest you put it in a deposit box and dispense as needed. There's also a card in there from a man who owns a motorcycle shop that you could call in an emergency."

"But it's like this man's shop and we shouldn't take advantage?" she said. "You're just the same, Daddy — you're funny. Secretive. I don't think Mom ever realized how funny you are. You're so serious, but you're a stitch with all your — methodology."

"Nobody's perfect — "

"Or you could tell me the truth Daddy, whatever it is you're really doing with no phone. I don't care — I can see now you never belonged in an office."

Her voice was quiet and clear. My mother's voice, low key and logical. Seeing that in her, I could feel my face change.

"Or you could trust me, daughter," I said gently.

"Oh, I will, I do. And I won't say a word. Do you know what I always wanted to tell you? How much I like my name. It's such a killer name, everyone envies me. I know you and Mom must have been really in love when you named me."

"We sure were," I said, wondering.

After the old blue Civic drove off I sat marveling at what God had wrought with our love, or whatever it had been. Lusty for sure. Pretty sexy spoiled little rich-girl Felice and me of all people. History now, except for Layla. Very American history. I sat with the window open to the country air and let myself see how much I'd lost in Nam. Home, for openers. It was there when I shipped out and gone when I got back, not a thing left. I had a great daughter though, and I was clear about who I owed what. TCC made Layla vulnerable, and I would protect her any way I could. Lying through my teeth, no problem, I was getting good at that. Just a little money would buy her some independence and get Felice out of her face. Envelope money, which she'd understood, along with the phone. She was my mother all over, minus the sharp edges. If anyone came near her, well, God help that sonofabitch, be it Jason Olcott himself.

11

The next afternoon the sun came out and I took a long walk that ended at the Pope. Then I wished I hadn't. Mac poured me a Jameson and started talking at me across the bar in a mechanical way, not meeting my eye.

"Guy was in here looking for you name of Mardigan, said he knew you from a few years ago."

"Madigan? Bill Madigan?"

"Not Bill. I've met Bill."

McVeigh's voice was dull and metallic, and his eye had a speculative look. I didn't like the way he was talking but I trusted his instincts.

"So this guy, what did he look like?"

"Five-nine or ten, black hair. Older guy, some kind of accent and a fat dumb mustache. Had a Remy and left. I told him I hadn't seen you lately."

"Oh Christ, I think I know who this is. You didn't give him my number I hope?"

It worked. While I searched my mind for who it might be, McVeigh gave a slow, twisty smile and shook his head slowly.

"And why would I be givin' such personal information to complete strangers who might be from a collection agency, not to mention the IRS?"

"This guy — I tried to help him write an offering once," I lied. "Big waste of time. The name's actually Mertegun. Persian, he said. Never finished paying me. Anyway, I came in because I'm leaving soon and I wanted to get straight on our deal."

"Oh, I could see you were having problems with that. Something went wrong you might get off but lose your job. I've got someone else, so it doesn't matter."

I kissed the money goodbye and agreed it was probably for the best.

"So what are you really doing over there, anyway?"

"Using my cockamamie multicultural magic for a computer outfit, Guimard Frères. Trolling the bars for a rich good-looking

French woman of a certain age."

"Sounds like a plan."

"See you in church," I said. "If that Persian phony comes back, I'm in California."

He was smiling when I left, but I wasn't. I had no clue about this mustache man, and it struck me that Paris felt safer and more predictable than home. Crazy contacts, crazy boss, but no Olcott surprise meetings or Mardigans. Or money smuggling deals falling through. Now that I was making money, I wanted more.

It was windy, and the sun was coming and going between fat gray clouds rolling in from Long Island. I walked to the East River to calm down and watched high school kids in gray sweats running laps on the track in the little park. Who was Mardigan? No idea. At the Wohlfurt's meeting, I'd asked Olcott and Morris if anyone was on to me when they talked about being armed, and got nothing. On the way home a light buffeting rain began, and I walked fast, staying to the lee side of buildings. By the time I got home I was wet, still thinking about the mysterious Mr. Mardigan. I changed, heated a can of soup, and watched Hawaii Five-O to distract myself. Heartwarming period piece complete with period ethics, cops clearly distinct from crooks. Mardigan had bothered Mac enough that it showed. Given his instincts and experience, that was disturbing.

So be careful, I thought, follow the manual. I checked my phone for a bug and found none; then I checked it for a line tap. Nothing. On my way out, I pulled a horsehair from a sofa cushion and placed it in the crack at the bottom of the door so it would jump out if the door opened. On the same impulse I took the case. I was counting on the workout to change my state of mind, and I couldn't wait to get back to rue Marchais. My vacation was getting too complicated.

I found Jennie sitting on one of the office couches smoking a cigarette, which I hadn't seen her do before, sitting next to an open window. Something told me not to sit down.

"I have a problem, Rob. I tried to call but I missed you. How about tomorrow?"

"Fine," I said, certain she hadn't called me. "Same time?"

Before she could answer the door opened too fast and a tall, well dressed black man in his thirties came in too quickly. He was wearing aviator shades and a trench coat, and he was holding his right hand to his shoulder. The other held a tan leather case. He kicked the door shut and threw the bolt, not seeing me because I'd been on his far side. My case was at my feet. I saw red on the fingers of the hand held to his shoulder. He started to say something to Jennie, then saw me and froze. Then his eyes went to hers.

"It's okay, he's family," she said.

He nodded and walked through to the main room as if familiar with the place. Jennie followed him without a word. I hesitated, then decided to stay, very curious and thinking I might be of some use. The black guy, actually light brown, had been lucky, hit where a bullet would do no serious injury. He'd been blessed in other ways, too. He was very handsome, like an actor or model, but with sharp eyes. When Jennie came back, I spoke before she had to lie.

"Don't bother explaining — we both work for the same people."

She gave me a half-guarded, half-distracted look. "You're not supposed to know."

"Right. People talk, cellular separation and all. How's he doing?"

"Not serious. I dressed it and called the doctor. But I could be compromised. His car's out front."

Her eyes asked would I take it away.

"So give me the keys already, the man doesn't need his car towed on top of getting shot."

She handed me the keys with an odd look, as if I must be crazy to be making jokes at a time like this.

"Red Monte Carlo parked near a hydrant, Maryland plates."

I went down the steps two at a time, case in hand, brave as only a woman can make me. The Monte Carlo was on the far side, still without a ticket. A pre-emissions SS, spotless and beautiful. I stepped into a doorway and peeked back. It was a dark afternoon, and the street was full of rain, cars, umbrellas and honking horns. I couldn't tell a thing, so I walked over, hopped in, and was hit by an amazing tobacco stink. I drove with the window open, and when I got to the remains of the West Side Highway I floored it. Then I watched the mirrors as I weaved through traffic. The car was a tiger.

A late model blue Chevy responded, and I kept going, cutting in and out of lanes. The Chevy wasn't losing ground until I made it past a clot of traffic and saw a light that would trap the bunch. It turned red and I ran it, and the Monte Carlo was flying when I cut across two lanes toward the next exit. I clipped an old Honda, touching bumpers with a clang. Then I got stuck at the next light behind another car, with the Honda-man two cars behind beeping his little horn like a kid. I could see the Chevy trapped at the back.

Then came my first smile of the day — a siren, followed by a cop pulling alongside the Chevy. The light changed and I was gone. When I had the car in a garage I called.

"Hi, this is Bobby. I left my Daytimer home — am I on your schedule this afternoon?"

"Yes, Bobby, why don't you come up and have some tea?"

I felt unbelievably excellent.

Jennie was holding a little blue teacup full of vodka. She didn't say anything, just threw the bolt and poured me some. It was over for me, but not for her, and it showed. She seemed to think I'd get it, and didn't say a word when I gave her the parking slip.

"How's he doing?"

"Fine, missed everything important. The doctor just got here. Rob, how long have you known about me?"

"Almost from the beginning. I learned by accident."

"Morris does find interesting people."

"I was easy, I was broke."

"Tell me about it," she said. "By the time I got started here I was living week to week. I really didn't know what I was doing, bank loan I couldn't afford. One day Morris came in and signed up. He's a gym rat — he's done time in half the dojos of the

85

Western world. He'd come in, we'd work out, and I'd give him problems because I could read him. He sent me clients but I wouldn't date him. One day he hurt me, and it was intentional, he just walked through me, bang, knocked me down hard. He's strong enough to do that. I told him he was getting too good for me and sent him to a friend who broke his nose."

She stopped for a slug of vodka and I had to smile. Coming in that smooth civilized voice it was a funny story.

"Then he called and apologized. Came over with his nose in a splint and said it had been too much for his ego, a woman, and so forth de blah-blah. He was, as they say, a gentleman about it. Then he recruited me, which took me out of debt. I don't like it any more, but I can't quit, I'm dependent. I'm used to not worrying about money . . . "

And never had to, I thought. Not with that accent. I didn't know what to make of it, just saw she was vulnerable for the moment. She shook her head, slightly drunk. Instead of volunteering how I'd been recruited myself, I just nodded. Then we heard footsteps. When they came through, the black guy was wearing the doctor's coat and hat, and carrying his bag. I sat behind a magazine, and they were gone before I could get into the latest exhumation of the Rolling Stones. Jennie threw the bolt and sat down, then was silent for a while, not looking at me. Then she looked at me.

"This happened once before. I'm a safe house, too — I get an extra couple of hundred a week for that. Come on, I'll show you my trick wall."

She picked up the bottle with an expression that told me she really wanted to put this behind her. I followed her through the big room and the changing room, into the tub room, where she took one of the big brass towel rings and turned it. Then she pushed, and the tile wall slowly pivoted. Inside was a silent, softly lit *trompe-l'oiel* fairyland, a blue-sky cloud-puff ceiling blending its way down to sand-dune walls. On the floor was a rich rose-colored carpet and a futon with a blue sheet and quilt. The privacy was intense and exotic.

"Keith and his fucking Marlboros," she said, and hit the switch for an inaudible exhaust fan. Then she looked at me shyly.

"This isn't exactly the way it appears, Rob. I'd've joined you in the tub the other day, but there were too many secrets. I'm glad you found me out."

She said this in a quiet private voice, then put the bottle on a table, took a step forward, and looked up at me with the hot innocence of a teenager. Then she softly pressed herself against me. It was a nice fit, and I was almost shaking, instantly painfully hard. She gave me an endless, shattering, wide-open kiss, lips slowly moving, and I felt something yielding, fatalistic and totally un-American in her.

We ended the kiss and she spoke in a soft voice.

"You just gave me such a feeling then," she said. "You can't tell, can you — ?"

"Us Yankees can be dense."

"And shy," she said. "Your eyes were so hungry, but you weren't going to ask."

Then we were kissing again, and taking our clothes off. Her *gi* and silk underwear were off in seconds, revealing a slender, solid, dancer's body that didn't look especially strong or tough, just perfect. She smiled and started helping me take my clothes off in a smooth efficient way, as if I were a child. She noticed an old scar from a crash and looked up at me curiously.

"You're quite a piece of work, Mr. Price. You make me feel purely like a piece of ass, in case you're interested."

"I guess you can see it's mutual, I replied, cock quivering like a mad thing. "You're so damn . . . delicious."

"I'm really hot is what I am. You really do it to me."

On one knee, she finished removing my clothes with the gentlest hands I'd felt in years, then took me in her mouth. I came in about three seconds and was ready again right away just looking at her. Her eyes were wide open and unwavering. She was right, I was starving, and she was the first woman I'd really wanted in a long time. We lay side by side kissing and touching. She was so ready that my breath caught in my chest as I listened to her breathing, feeling for the spot, watching her face.

"Now, Rob — I want you in me now," she said, in a hot tight whisper.

She rolled over to let me in, then looked up at me, eyes wide open with the calm composure that was in her every move. I was dizzy with the knowledge that this beautiful woman really wanted me, that it was her pleasure. Her small subtle movements told me so, and then the way she let herself come, and keep coming, until I was ripping with lust. And on and on, until her eyes were melting. Then she blinked slowly and I saw they were wet. I came again, hard enough to get dizzy.

"*Hsieh-hsieh*, she whispered after a while. "Means 'thank you' in Chinese. I cry. It doesn't mean anything, runs in the family."

She'd gone right past every defense, totally got to me. When someone brings you back to life, you like anything they do. She sat up and folded her legs, and I did the same, so we were facing each other, looking in each others' eyes. She was so fine it almost hurt to look. Her face had the perfect poise of innocence, and I couldn't look away.

"You're nicer than you know," she said, taking me in her hand.

When I was hard again she climbed onto my lap in a neat little move, still looking me straight in the eye and began those subtle little movements again. It was very natural and easy. She really loved to fuck, and I was under her spell, hypnotized by the pleasure in her face. This one lasted forever.

Then I was asleep. An hour or two later Jennie woke me up with a gentle shake.

"I'd like you to stay, but I have a class at eight and I have to sleep. I'd open another bottle if you were here, and we'd just go on and on."

"It's fine," I said, very relaxed. "You're right."

"*Huh!*" she said. An abrupt, funky, distinctly un-American sound, bawdy and humorous. We were ready to start over, just that little sound and our eyes brushing. I looked away and began to dress. She'd said it was time, and I knew that one of the rules was not to be greedy. As I dressed, she sat on the bed in a blue silk robe, perfectly composed, little smile, reading me like a book. She played a CD, and a romantic singer floated in on a diaphanous film of music. We'd put the afternoon behind us.

I thought about it all the way downtown, listening to

kamikaze raindrops splattering the cab. How did that Jennie coexist with the *sensei* who was Jason Olcott's mistress? I didn't think about it, I was feeling too good. What exactly had gone down, aside from the best sex since Felice? A favor-fuck for moving the car? Break-the-mood fuck? Definitely that. Mercy-fuck, brought on by my hungry eyes. Probably. Maybe a little more, given what I'd seen in her diary. No mirrors, just a little tasteful lavender smoke. For reasons I couldn't fathom, none of it bothered me. Whatever else, she knew the difference between fucking and fighting, and that was just fine.

By and by I understood that it would be wise not to make further demands. Let the game come to you, they say. It hadn't felt like a game, but it had to be played that way until I knew more.

12

Going up the stairs I was walking on eggshells. I had the light from my key chain in hand and wasn't very surprised when the horsehair was gone from the crack in my door. It could have sprung free but I didn't think so. I just stood there listening, knowing I'd set the alarm. If someone was inside, it had to be Morris. Whoever it was, I wasn't worth shooting. Not yet, anyway. I walked in whistling *Sugar Pie Honeybunch*, trying for lighthearted, safety off, very pumped.

Nothing. Using my left hand, I turned on a table lamp. More nothing.

Then a big dull jolt. In the shadows at the far end of the room a man was sitting at the table. Not Morris. Smaller, with a mustache. He was facing me, about thirty feet away, slumped in the chair, perfectly still. Like dead. Case armed, I walked slowly and carefully toward McVeigh's Mr. Mardigan. Halfway there I saw it was Fred, his hair trimmed and dyed, relaxed enough to doze. He blinked, straightened up, and cleared his throat.

"Please excuse the intrusion," he said in a rusty half-speed voice.

"I didn't recognize you. I might have shot you, Fred."

My voice sounded normal to me, but I was shaky and furious.

"Not you, Rob, that is one of your virtues," he said quietly. "Please accept my apologies. We can't be seen together, but this way is all right. When we spoke last, I was abrupt. I don't have so many friends that I can afford to lose one. A game of chess, I thought."

"It's good to see you, Fred," I said. "Certainly, a game. I miss it."

I might have added that Mac was no dummy and blowing smoke up his ass had done me no favor, but I was glad to be rid of the mysterious Mardigan, and Fred had found me a job when I couldn't do it on my own. While I made coffee he discussed Spain's Tour possibilities with Delgado and expressed sympathy for LeMond's hunting accident. While we talked I poured brandies. When the coffee was ready I added some cookies from the fridge, and served it all on a tray like a good host. Then I sat down, and he startled me again with the news that ex-wife number two, Joanna, had been in. To have some clothes altered and ask after me, he said. Fred did only men's clothes.

"Joanna always liked you, Fred."

Not quite true — what she'd liked was his work. But she'd want a new man to be well turned out. Probably brought him in and expected Fred to pass on the news.

"A lady," he said diplomatically.

I smiled and got ready to kiss my ass good-bye as I set up the board. Playing white and not caring, I went with Durry's queen's-pawn opening, which seemed to upset Fred. Then I had a lucky stroke around move fifteen, but six moves later I gave the game away. I conceded and poured brandies, waiting to hear what was on his mind. I was wishing he'd say his piece and leave so I could unwind and dream about Jennie.

"Not bad at all, Rob. A single mistake. The queen's pawn game has always been my weakness — it puts very much at stake quickly, yet it seems natural to you."

I chewed on that and waited. This visit was not about chess or ex-wives or Spain's chances in the Tour. When he said no more, I remarked that I still wasn't sure how Morris felt about me. I didn't really think that, but I wanted to get Fred talking.

"It's safe to say that you are doing all right in his eyes."

"I'm finding myself uneasy for no particular reason."

I was fishing, but he nodded firmly.

"It is from sensing the limits of one's knowledge. No doubt Morris is concerned about something, but it is not you. He would let me know, since you came through me. In the end, it is all about information, Rob, and you are good with information. Discreet. That was one reason I brought you together."

He paused and spoke with special care.

"But also, Rob, when you are doing well you may find yourself up where the air is thin."

He was dead serious. I looked for the right words.

"My inexperience seems to make people nervous."

"Yes, they are afraid someone will turn you, that you could be doubled. This will pass when they know you better. I have said as much."

"Another espresso?"

"No, thank you. I must go."

He hesitated, not looking at me.

"My wife died last month."

"I'm very sorry."

"It was for the best, she had been sick so long. Too long. It was as if she was already gone. I was more sad before, when she was suffering. I was already alone."

He nodded to himself, his eyes unavailable, then continued.

"I am not a believer, but I went to church because she wanted it."

It was as personal as he'd ever been with me, and my head was spinning for a long time after he left. Why had he come? Not to play chess or drop Joanna's name or mention his wife's death. To take my temperature and pass on a report? Maybe just to make that observation about being doubled. Fred perplexed me more and more. I'd been so blind about him that I didn't trust my judgment, but when he left I was sure he'd tell Morris I was fine. Somehow I didn't think much about Jennie. That had been a kind of miracle, and I wished she wasn't TCC. I was seeing that these company people were real-world smart. And Alain Durry was smart enough to change their rules and get away with it. With his help I'd finally disrupted Fred's chess game.

A college station was playing music for the discriminating insomniac, Bartók quartets, each wilder than the last. Lying on my back, unable to sleep, I knew the old pith helmet was still there after all. I'd felt it when Fred mentioned being doubled. Whatever I thought about all those people living in our streets and how our leaders failed us and lied to us and sent us to die for no good reason, no matter that great nations are predators, us included, my sense of self was tied to being an American. It ran in the family. I envied Fred's unencumbered thinking, though. It didn't strike me as dishonorable but it made me thoughtful. My job was bringing out a wariness I'd always lacked, and some humility. I wasn't as clever as I liked to think — I was a predictable creature to Morris and Fred. I didn't like admitting that, I wanted to go on thinking of Fred as an equal.

I was dreaming when the phone woke me. Jennie and I fucking magnificently under the sun in the tropics, her bent over, hands on a fallen log, lovely as a doe. Me the old buck in rut, my teeth in the perfect curve between shoulder and neck. I lost the dream and got myself out of bed. Except for the erection I was asleep, but halfway across the room I remembered to let the machine pick up. Wrong number. There was no getting back to sleep so I started a pot of coffee and ran up the blinds to a soggy gray morning, a little slow after my long day and short sleep. I really wanted out of New York now that I was okay with Layla. In the shower I saw that I could take a bus to Hartford, then fly Hartford-London using the fresh Canadian I.D. But first wake Tom if he was home, and take him for a feed and some company at the Star.

No answer, so I headed to the Pope for an Irish coffee and some food. A woman was sitting in my usual place, facing away, and I sat next to her without intent, preoccupied.

"This is an approach, yes?"

European voice, aggressive, intelligent. Challenging. I looked at her and saw a tough earthy blonde. My mouth ran itself.

"Oh, yes. Why wouldn't it be?"

"Vell — big man other side of bar maybe? Far end."

"Oh him," I said. "He won't mind, we're old friends."

It was stupid; she brought it out. After Jennie she came off as trash.

"Not a problem for me," she replied. "You're sure you know who I talk about?"

"Big Mac?"

She laughed. "Good name, quality beef."

"And you're Leni."

"I'm Leni."

Mac appeared from the other end of the bar and walked toward us. I could see he was getting a laugh out of the situation, which I wasn't. I didn't like Leni Hartt. Mac was rough, but she was coarse. Coarse and clever, but I played along.

"Two of what the lady's having, my good man."

"Do I laugh or just rip off your head, you Protestant weasel?"

Leni was having a good time, but he was jealous, which was unusual. Mac went through women like jelly beans.

"Elie Weasel at your service, endangered species member. I came to talk business but this beautiful woman distracted me."

"I can't stand the other kind," he said. "Let's not waste our time on business, I want to see Leni drink you under the table on the house."

"Some other time, I've got a meeting coming at me."

"Guy talk," she said in a gravelly German voice. "Also endangered. Women taking over any time now. Soon ve take away your footballs, yes?"

"She's crazy," said Mac affably. He was besotted. Leaving was the thing to do, because it could all turn around on a wrong word. Leni Hartt had a big motor and no brakes, and I wasn't blowing up a friendship to amuse her. I wished Mac hadn't seen her flirting me up, but I smiled my way out and left without eating. It was bizarre. Replacing lovely Carol with a Euroslut was not the McVeigh I knew. I was still thinking about it in my loft when I got a call that changed my plans.

"Yo! It's Junior from the deli, give us a call about your bill, mister." There was no mistaking the voice.

"I thought I was okay."

"No more credit, mister."

"So I'll call you already."

Morris had talked to Fred, and Fred had vouched for me. Or he knew I'd been to bed with Olcott's girl-friend. Or he had another surprise — I had no idea and I wasn't ready.

"I'm booked to leave town. I'm expected at the office."

He asked if I'd like to hop a ride to Atlanta with him in the company jet and pick up a flight there, which he could arrange. It wasn't an order, and he didn't press me. I agreed, forgetting that I'd have to pack and get to the airport real fast.

"Teterboro, runway seven, south end. Big dark blue jet off by itself, no ID. We'll hold till four."

I called Jennie then. The machine answered and I didn't say much, just that I hoped everything was fine and that I'd be in touch.

Running through the drizzle with my raincoat flapping and a bag in each hand, I felt like a kid trying to make the school bus. The plane was easy to spot, a corporate jet, metallic midnight blue, three times as big as a Lear, no name or logo, just its number, which I tried to memorize. The closer I got, the bigger it looked. The engine-howl was high and I wasn't sure I'd made it, but the door opened and stairs came down. Then I climbed up into a plush teak-and-blue world featuring big Recaro seats in soft navy leather. Morris was half-reclining in one of them, looking brown around the edges. He smiled a weary smile, and before we'd said anything the black guy who showed up at Jennie's with a bullet in his shoulder came out of the cabin. Keith. He stowed my bags with no sign of recognition, but it was the same man, and he was favoring his left arm. After throwing the safety latch he went forward to get us half a tumbler each of Scotch, with a little jug of ice and a bottle of water. It all fit into a tray on a little pop-out table between us. I was curious about Keith, but they were doing cellular separation, and Morris never addressed him by name.

"Buckle up, Buttercup," grunted Morris. "Welcome to Big Blue."

I hooked my belt and straightened my seat. Morris continued in his half-reclined position, belt loose, as warned not to do by a blinking sign. His eyes were half-closed, and he looked cherubic as the engines screamed and Keith went back to the cabin.

"Don't ever let me see you doing this on takeoff," said Morris. Then he smiled a carnivorous Op smile as we moved down the runway. "Glad you made it, Rob. Fred was right, you're gonna be okay."

The reference to Fred settled me down. Whatever he'd said, Morris didn't have a problem with me. We were accelerating hard and took off at a steep angle, with Morris's seat still reclined and his belt loose. At a fairly low altitude we changed direction but stayed in the climb. When we leveled off, Morris spoke.

"I know you had things on your mind you couldn't talk about at Wohlfurt's," he said in a tough, tired voice.

It wasn't corporate, and he was no draft-dodging Doug Finlay, getting rich and fucking with me. He wanted to know what was bothering me.

"It's just that I'm getting a lot of unnecessary exposure. Durry's one thing, I have to play his game. But meeting in public for drops — "

I stopped myself. Morris's half-supine body didn't move.

"Well, that's Al."

"Millie. He sent his cover job assistant."

He wasn't excited or shocked, just looked at the ceiling for a while, considering his reply.

"How do you know she's not TCC, Rob?"

"Does it make a difference? She does it all wrong, like 'Hey guys, look at my great legs.' The manual says be invisible."

Morris grunted and looked thoughtful.

"Fuckin' Al. The guy who put this outfit together and hooked us up with Uncle Sam died a while back, and we're — less flawless without him. People get bad habits, happens with any agency. Big part of my job is to know it's happening and clean it up."

He stopped and looked up at me more seriously.

"Two underlying problems. One, different pay basis. CIA employees aren't supposed to keep what they earn through cover jobs. In theory, anyway. We do, and that sets a tone. Two, an Area Head has a lot of latitude. Because we're so decentralized, he has a little fiefdom. And by the way, you saved his bacon — he was having big problems with Durry. There it is. All off-record. Now, double off-record: do you trust the guy? I know you were covering for him at Wohlfurt's."

I couldn't believe what he'd said.

"No reason not to," I said carefully. "It's just the exposure. I do things by the book, then Millie calls open-line and says to meet her at a bar full of high end hustlers, journalists and . . . observant people."

"I see. Yeah, well, live with it 'til spring. We get the Durry material, you get promoted. You're right, of course — there should be cut-outs and we should follow our procedures, but Al is Al, and he's good. He gets closure. Of course, the company itself is a cut-out for the government by being a business as well. Plausible deniability. The fallback is that we're just a bunch of civilians who got out of line. As contrasted to those Frogs who blew up that Greenpeace boat or Ollie Fucking North."

He paused and I spoke.

"Okay. Mind telling me what I'm sticking my neck out for with Dr. Durry?"

"Right, Oracle. I'm the ranking Op and I don't know. It's big though. Major-major. CIA isn't onto it — that we know. They hate us, of course. Anything else I can't tell you?"

"What about Millie?"

"That's Al. He's one of these bridge-and-tunnel hicks rather bang a rich Brit than someone who wants to and knows how. Clever guy otherwise. Met his wife, Jackie?"

"No."

"To understand Al you've gotta meet Jackie. Jackie Jugs. Beautiful woman."

In his voice was a fatalistic acceptance of what he had to work with, and respect for the fact that Al got things done.

"Any other problems, excuse me, *issues* . . . ?"

"Yeah, this Sven kid. He keeps calling. I ignored his calls and he did the drop."

"Right move. Okay, we'll get him off your plate. Use your answer-box and don't return his calls. That's a general procedure — screen calls and return them on pay phones. Left that out of the manual. And memo Al on a 104 Form. The 104's like a little red flag — copies go up the line to me, and to Jason. It'll get his attention, trust me — 104 opens the loop, keeps an area head on the leash."

He flashed a dark smile and seemed to be weighing what he could say. Did I want to know more? Yes, but what I really wanted was the job I signed on for.

"Sven's not as dumb as he acts, that's just the kid in him. He's a hacker. Little Sven and his little friends have a little club, and they know how to break into really big systems. They've figured out how to go backwards through the networks into restricted government areas. The old guys in charge of security can't keep up with the kids attacking it. But Sven can't keep his mouth shut, so every whore in Hamburg knows about it. Anyway, he's Al's boy, special relationship. He'll handle him after the 104, don't worry about it. I'm gonna close my eyes for a few minutes now."

He seemed to doze, leaving me to think. If Marquardt crashed and burned with Sven, I didn't guess it would bother Morris a lot. While I was working that out, the black co-pilot came back. Handsome Keith, another mystery. One way or another I was getting through cellular separation, but I had no real idea of what TCC was. I wasn't supposed to, but I was getting more curious.

Keith went to a little galley and put two meals in a microwave. When he brought them over, Morris came back from his nap.

"Thin-kew!" he said brightly, like a perfect Royal. The accuracy jarred me more than his sarcasm. I was beginning to sense the mosaic of words, accents, inflections and attitudes that were the voice of Morris. It was urban and sarcastic, but sometimes it had a clipped northeast WASP effect that didn't fit at all. Maybe a smart tough voice from the boroughs, or the product of a very mixed marriage. There was a hard glottal-stop at times, and bent vowels that sounded like Mekong. It must have been quite an odyssey, Morris's life, and I could see why my problems would amuse him. I finished my drink and began eating. Morris put his seat in the upright position, stretched his arms, arched his back, and breathed out very completely, rolling his neck without inhibition, a bear rousing itself. He chugged some coffee in silence, and asked for more. He didn't say another word, but started eating like a very hungry man. As we were finishing, Keith's voice came over the intercom giving us ten minutes to Atlanta.

"I got you on a Brussels flight," said Morris. "Those things we were talking about — not to worry. Finish Durry, you're out of there. With your languages you can go places. Jason doesn't understand you, but he doesn't interfere."

A little later, as I was about to leave, Morris gripped my hand firmly in a thumb-lock handshake and looked into my face.

"Don't hesitate to call if things get hairy. It says not to in the manual, but so's a lot of stuff we have to do. Use a booth and don't say anything, just leave a number and wait. If I don't get back to you, try again in a few hours."

Lying across a row of seats in the half-empty 747, I analyzed TCC's civil war. Morris had the authority and Olcott's ear, but Marquardt had his European empire. That was Finlay Kline all over, except that Doug Finlay would have allowed Marquardt to fail, and been rid of him. If I had it right, Morris had chosen to save Oracle by giving me to Al. It was something to respect, and it let me forget about Jason Olcott. Forgetting Jennie Garthwaite would be a problem only solved with another woman, and I couldn't imagine that woman.

13

Al and Jackie Marquardt had a large stone house in Versailles where they lived extremely well, assisted by a serious fiftyish French woman who cooked and ran the show. The fifteen foot ceilings, antique rugs, and mauve silk walls had nothing to do with a government pay scale, and had to be paid for by his cover job. Their problems were obvious, though. Having been through a couple of marriages, I sensed the failure of this one as soon as I walked in. Jackie was a fine looking woman in her thirties, tall, with long honey-blonde hair, splendid breasts and crazy green eyes. It was an old formula — most-likely-to-succeed marries prom queen. It wasn't real, and there was a big hole in the middle where the heart goes. Al had impregnated a woman clearly meant by God for an all-pro linebacker. They were dissatisfied and bored with each other, and the air was heavy with it. I guessed they were staying together because of their twelve year old son, Billy, and that didn't seem to be working either. Al was as bad in the daddy department as I was. The boy lay on a rug in a far corner of the vast living room, reading. At the other end, I sat drinking with the Marquardts and watching Saturday Night Live on tape. When her husband went to mix the third round of gimlets, Mrs. Marquardt leaned forward, laid the crazy green eyes on mine, and gave me a good look at her breasts. Then she smiled, and there was no mistaking her look — the Marquardts were cohabiting but going their separate ways. I wondered if getting to fuck each others' women was part of TCC culture.

"Are you meeting people here?" she asked in a tone of unconcealed desperation. She had no fake in her at all, it was hot naked need, very appealing in the chilly spook world after a couple of drinks. Jennie had turned me on, and it hadn't stopped.

"Not really," I said, as if I didn't understand. "Still getting it together."

When she told me she felt like firing the help and doing her own housework, I knew she was telling the truth, and that she was fairly drunk. She had everything, and it didn't mean anything to her, and she was going crazy. At dinner she looked at me very frankly from time to time, nipples gliding on silk as she moved to pass the duck or broccoli di rabe. Marquardt didn't mind; he needed me. I guessed that whatever he was making between TCC and BioTel, he was spending it all, and that Oracle might be critical to his cash flow. Only young Billy, a precocious skin-and-bones kid, had anything to say, and he was holding it in. He was bilingual, and I made conversation in French, telling him about Hu Shi, who'd studied martial arts as a boy and worked his way to Europe on a ship. Billy was intrigued, and I felt his parents watching as we talked. After dinner he went upstairs and there was a brief silence.

"He never talks to anyone," said Jackie soberly. "We've moved so many times, and the asthma just keeps coming back."

I nodded, and Al suggested cards. The French woman brought coffee and a brandy that would have run six figures stateside. Then we played rummy, five hundred, Marquardt winning all the way. I tried harder, but he went on winning, and it dawned on me that he was a card-counter, remembering everything the way Fred would remember the moves of a chess game. Finally I begged off, and Jackie went upstairs. Happy in victory, my boss smiled.

"Jet-lag," he said comfortably. "They say don't eat and drink, but what else is there t'do? You read about that couple got arrested for oral sex? Everyone was asleep but the stew turned 'em in! Other passengers told her to fuck off, but they busted 'em."

I laughed, then went to the bathroom. Someone was using it, and Marquardt waved me upstairs. After a long walk I relieved myself in a large pallid space with ornate gold fixtures. On the way out, something cracked under my shoe. Slightly drunk, I bent over to see a piece of glass that might have come from a goblet or a test tube. I had no idea what it was, but I looked in the waste basket. More shards. It bothered me, and I wrapped the largest one in tissue and put it in a pocket without thinking. When I went back downstairs Al was smiling, ready to play, but I said I really had to go.

"Yeah, you look beat, I'll run you home."

"Metro's fine. Might pick up a girl."

"Good hunting buddy, I'll drive you to your stop."

In the car I had the feeling he knew something significant had happened in New York. As he barreled the Saab through the quiet streets, I was hoping Sven would come up. If we solved that, I'd skip the 104 report Morris had recommended, but he was focused on Durry.

"Keep me up to speed on the Doctor, Rob. Every call."

It was a little too firm, and my reply must have been lacking. He repeated himself, which he didn't often do. I pledged allegiance to Oracle and forgot about cutting him any slack on Sven. But then he parked the car at the Metro and waited with me for my train, and surprised me, speaking his uncomfortable French.

"Come often, Rob, call at any time. Billy likes you, and also the history of the Chinese martial teacher. I like the dojo. My son is intelligent but must be more active. Jackie and I have difficulty with him."

It was painful, but I maintained my end of the conversation. I could tell he'd rehearsed the opening and guessed it might be easier for him to talk about personal things this way. There was definitely a human side to him. Alone in an empty Metro car afterward I thought about the three of them struggling along, and my own hard times with Layla. Would Billy forgive his dad the way she had with me?

When I got home, my answering machine was empty except for a boozed-up indiscreet Sven call. I saved the tape, filled in the 104, and went straight out to mail it before I had second thoughts.

The next day I was out of it, thinking sporadically, pacing, looking out the windows and drinking tea to hydrate myself. I was meeting Durry for dinner, and that was the point of my day. In mid-afternoon I went to my dojo to wake myself up.

"You still slow boat," said Hu Shi after the bowing at the

end. "But you get better. Remember — *okay hurt teacher!* Good for teacher too. Wake up teacher is special favor. You try see me on floor, okay?"

Jennie's advice, and there she was. I went at it with Hu Shi, but she was back when I left. Jackie Marquardt would be a potent distraction but complicated and crazy-making, and I decided to do without. Serial monogamy ran in the family, probably killed my father when my mother died. Walking through the early dusk I remembered Jennie's upturned face before we kissed. Then I thought about it and decided I had to scrutinize her the same way I was doing with everyone and everything in TCC. It made sense and I hated it.

Durry's restaurant was a big lumpy building set too close to the street, nothing like Mme. Gauthier's. I stepped into a bright loud bar, tipped the bartender to stash my leathers, and waited for Durry. He arrived on time, very buttoned-up. One drink, no jokes, no reference to our last meeting. Before the mood turned to cement we had a table in a much better room than I expected, small and quiet, with smooth, shimmering conversation. A waiter took us to a table where I agreed to Durry's suggestion about the crab soufflé; things always lightened up when I agreed with him. We talked soccer, and I felt him edging toward reality. The price was going to be bad news, but Rob Franglais was going to field it with Gallic aplomb. I asked him about his vacation and he was coy. I told him I'd been home, and when he asked about it, I lied and told him about my mother and her golden memories of The Liberation.

"Statistics indicate blacks carried the day."

Rude. The Nam-beast noticed. Then he added something about black babies in case I'd missed it. Extremely rude, worth a full-contact Jennie lesson. The beast was for it, but I managed to look bored and superior.

"For those in the streets, I suppose," I replied, as if descended from ancient nobility. Then I shrugged and looked at this *pied noir* polymath as if forgiving someone at the mercy of a brilliant but incorrigible wit. Of course Al hated the man, I was getting there myself. But his nasty remark left him vulnerable. I gave him a two beat silence.

"These negotiations we're not talking about," I said, neutral and distant. "They won't happen overnight."

"I am sure it can work out," he said in a conciliatory voice, knowing he'd crossed the wrong line. "But now that there is rumor of possible success, others will pay more."

Rumor of possible success. I waited, but he stopped — he'd said more than he meant to. His beak-nosed face looked at me in unconcealed scrutiny, a shrewd, ballsy guy under the foppish exterior, tanned and confident since his Caribbean visit.

"These others are already working along similar lines?"

He ignored this with a smile and announced that he was doubling his price for the remainder of the material. His face gave him away. *What can I get away with? How hard can I push?* I shrugged as if he was killing the deal and gave him back some attitude while he was off balance.

"I've been told to negotiate, Alain, but what can I do with this? It appears that you committed to the deal, and that we've kept up our end — "

He quietly cut me off.

"I know your employers perhaps better than you. They take this line to make you deal harder, but such arrangements are inherently . . . 'flexible' shall we say? Subject always to renegotiation, like any extra-legal agreement. That little affair with Iran and those arms — what did General Secord and his friends take for themselves on those illegal arms transactions? Or that Monsieur Bagdosian of BCCI, the good friend of Mr. Agha Hasan Abedi, who created it with your kinder-gentler President? People here know more than Americans about that affair and found Bush's account with that bank. They know about the Israeli, Nir, who was in the meetings with Mr. Bush, and conveniently disappeared before your elections when he was fool enough to talk about his 'memoirs.'"

I thought he'd lost his point, but then he modulated his voice.

"Do you think the prices remained stable in that situation?"

I was startled at how much he knew, and gave him my mother's Norman shrug. We were both on the same side of this one. He continued in the same quiet voice.

"Everyone knows that this 'Enterprise' of theirs doubled and tripled prices on equipment for your sainted 'Contras' and made fortunes on the cocaine as always, but no American seems to care. And your new CIA President — is it really possible for an adult to believe he was not involved? So please — no critique of how I do business. I am a scientist selling an experimental technique that belongs solely to me. I have signed no agreement, I may sell to anyone."

I couldn't fault him, but I smelled compromise. He'd screwed himself with that black babies remark and he was working uphill, trying not to look like a complete shit. He cared about that, apparently. I went back to business as if nothing had happened.

"I don't care about the numbers as long as it works out. It might facilitate the process, though, if you could let me have this installment as originally agreed."

"Well — as you recall, I said no. But why not? For the 'good faith.' It is useless without the rest, anyway. I have it with me. And your proposal?"

"Not up to me. This will go to the top, and will require some time. They're going to feel very jerked-around."

His eyes twinkled at the prospect of jerking around powerful Americans.

"They could end on their knees, your employers. They have the money, and the work is unique. They must have it to continue this project — "

"What are we talking about? What is this 'Oracle,' Alain? It may become important that I know something about it."

"I hesitate to say. I really feel I must not."

"For me to have background would help me negotiate on your behalf. It suggests mutual confidence and strengthens my hand. And the way things are looking, it might also spare me a dangerous problem."

It was instinctive, based on Olcott wanting me to be armed and Fred's remark about finding myself up where the air is thin. Durry looked at me sharply, black eyes intent, serious and concerned. He'd said something contemptible, but he didn't want anything bad to happen to me. I kept the beast in its cage.

"They did not feed you that line," he said. "You believe you are in danger?"

"More and more as we delay, Alain." I was laying the words like bricks, Morris-style. "Your work is no longer secret, but no one kills the goose that lays the golden egg. For delivery boys there are different rules, and these live drops are dangerous. Those 'others' you mentioned have spotted me already if they're any good."

Durry sat and thought in silence for half minute or so.

"Yes," he said abruptly. "They are very good, and how they learned of my work, this I don't know. And of course you must have something to yield if taken by them. I cannot tell you everything, nor would you understand it, but this much may be helpful: first, I wish to stress again that while I am currently employed by our national nuclear system, that is irrelevant. The material you are negotiating for has to do with a recent development in the field of artificial intelligence. A radical new approach."

He paused and I shook my head. It wasn't much and we both knew it.

"Two years ago I worked in the U.S. for a year, in your intellectual Mecca of Cambridge, Massachusetts. I had a visiting professorship, poorly paid as usual. I was invited to join a 'think-tank' led by a bright and annoying man who had very 'far-out' ideas. He was too secretive for real collaboration however, which created problems. An infuriating man, and, I suppose I should add, a Jew. He would pose us 'problems out of context' — that is how I thought of them."

He was wound-up, eyes sharp.

"Dr. Jakob Epstein. He saw us as assistants, clerks, privileged to be involved. Also to the point, he was sloppy. I am precise, I caught mistakes, he was unable to admit error. Then I pointed to such a mistake in front of the group, and he grasped, I think, my boredom and antipathy, this man who wished to create a computer without chips and knew so little of my field . . . "

He broke off with a shrug and a flick of his black eyes. I

waited, and he self-started, anger still pumping.

"You and I have never touched on these matters. What do you know of computers?"

"Not very much. I can run the usual programs."

He smiled.

"Are you familiar with term 'fuzzy-logic?'"

"It's a term used by a computer theorist who is supposed to be either a genius or a fraud — "

"Neither. Dr. Zadeh is clever and practical. He uses what is available. Fuzzy-logic offers a system of approximations closer to human thought, which he is able to simulate crudely, and this simulation works with certain problems. But its limits are obvious. Zadeh also says he can compute with words rather than numbers, but we challenged this with a totally original approach. Rockwell likes Zadeh. BioTel likes — "

BioTel. Marquardt's employer of record.

"Durry and Epstein."

"Working in isolation, as I was forced to do because of Epstein's secretive nature, I saw no point in continuing. I later resigned, but not before copying everything, reviewing the project exhaustively with other members, and committing to paper significant points that had surfaced and died. My memory for this kind of thing is excellent. Then I created doubt, and others followed me — Henke, Kagan, Kemmer, Donegan, and Davis also, who came before me. Epstein was lost without us. Ethically speaking, how could I do this? It was my view that he had been drinking blood from our veins. I retaliated by tapping an artery."

Henke Kagan Kemmer Donegan Davis. I broke the silence with my one thought.

"It's my impression that software is the big creative area, and that the Cray does more or less everything a silicon-based machine can be expected to do. I mean — improvements won't give any basic change, just more speed. Was Epstein proposing a carbon-based intelligence or . . . what?"

"Amazing. With no training or preparation, from the backyard of a layman's mind, you seize upon the only element of interest — the least probable! Yes, something happens in one's head that does not occur in any computer. That was the starting point. 'Organic cybernetics,' we called it."

Durry's voice was getting quiet again, and sharpening.

"This Epstein was not a problem-solver, and he could not work with those who were. He could not be honest and open in pursuit of truth, and hid away things that we needed to share. As a scientist and as a person he put himself into a dead-end — a low, cunning, man with a single obsessive idea. A poor creature in human or intellectual terms. An Israelite of the worst kind."

Without transition he slipped into a classic diatribe on The Jew that reminded me of my uncle Elbert who died railing about Kabbalists in Washington. I eased him off the subject with another guess from the backyard outhouse of my clearly ordinary mind.

"Yes, they're everywhere," I agreed. "And now we must outbid them, I suppose."

"And you must! Your people certainly have the money."

He'd identified the competition, exactly as Morris had foreseen. Israel. Mossad or some cousin, and Mossad was notorious for doing what they had to and a little more. Getting some courier out of the way, no problem. Durry was still talking.

" . . . and while I have this deep suspicion and distaste for the Jew, having lived peaceably and enjoyably among Muslims in my childhood, I have also a taste for the good life that is even stronger. Not to mention my concern to avoid repercussions from those from whom I have unwisely borrowed."

And who would lend money to Alain Durry? Who else, though he wouldn't know it. This ivory-tower anti-Semite was up to his neck in Jews. It would have been funny except for the look his face. He was in deep, and our misunderstandings were history.

"Alain," I said in my most American voice, "I'm your advocate. The better my sense of what you're providing, the stronger my hand with my employers. I think we can probably get you most of what you want, but my employers must be allowed to save face."

"You are a very odd American."

"I suppose. My mother was in the Resistance — "

"Of course! There is always an explanation. We drink to her, then — "

Later we stood between two cars in the freezing pitch-black parking lot and exchanged envelopes again, a procedure so crude and stupid we deserved to be caught. All the while I was thinking about Mossad. If they were onto Durry, they'd be onto Marquardt. After I was in the leathers I remembered. *Henke, Kagan, Kemmer, Donegan, Davis.* I found an envelope and wrote them down. Then I took a very indirect return route, weaving around, rear lights off, eyes on the mirrors as I went over our meeting. His nasty little joke had infuriated me, but I took his revelations as quid pro quo. A sign of class, in a way. I was about to turn in when the phone rang. I let the machine take it.

"Hey buddy, it's Slim. Give me a jingle when you're in town, we'll have a drink."

His voice reminded me of the piece of glass I'd picked up in his bathroom. I took it out of my suit pocket and held it under my desk light. There was residue on the concave side. I touched it with my tongue and there was a very faint chemical taste. I was looking at the remains of a freebase pipe. It chilled me. Smoking cocaine put you on a planet where other people were beside the point. My boss was strung out, I was sure of it, with no idea what to do about it. It left me disturbed and sleepless, needing to think about something else. I walked off my mood and called Mac.

"*Christ!*" he said, "Don't you ever sleep?"

"Sorry, I forget. Now that you're awake, have you turned up anything on our research project?"

"Not really, but I know who to talk to now."

"Might end up being something, Mac."

"Do tell."

"Just bar talk, but the man was not stupid."

"Learn anything more?"

"Only that people are aware of something going on at that company."

"I'll step it up. My guy will be in again this week."

"Nothing rash. No third parties, strictly a MacRob enterprise."

"When was I ever rash?"

"True. There's an old guy standing here shifting from foot to foot, probably wants to pee in the booth. I'll get back to you."

I hung up before he could ask for my number. He was as good a friend as I had, but TCC had changed me. If Mac was popped for one of these mysterious money transfers, I didn't want my number in his book.

14

The tiny lobby of the Marquis was a masterpiece of low-rent Gallic ennui, lightless and lifeless. Beckett came to mind. There were cooking odors, two undersized armchairs, and an old wooden bench that had seen better days. At the desk a pretty blonde was staring into space like a model. I'd chosen the place at random and was dressed down in sneakers, jeans, windbreaker and a cap. My boss was sitting alone in his usual suit, half out of sight in a little alcove, his butt jammed into a small chair while he read a paper. He looked terrible, jowls slack and body sagging, as if he'd done an all-nighter. I walked past him into a long empty bar with a single line of little wood tables without tablecloths. I sat at one that let me see the bar mirror, ordered a Stoli, and put my *Figaro* on the table. Al waited a few minutes to see if I'd been followed, then came in and sat down heavily.

"Everything okay?"

The bartender came over with my drink and took Al's order. I waited til he left.

"I don't know. The upside is, Fox delivered. Downside, he's talking double or nothing for the rest of the material, and he thinks the competition might be onto me."

It was me thinking that, but I wanted Al's full attention.

"Yeah? He say who it is?"

Al wasn't concerned. I felt anger so intense that it automatically concealed itself.

"No. You have any ideas?"

There was a pause while he thought about it. The Nam-beast was waking up, and I was trying to put it back to sleep with long slow breaths.

"There's another access to the office, avoids the lobby," said Marquardt, as if indulging me. I'd covered for him with Olcott, and now I wondered why. The beast said I should knock him backward out of his chair and step on his face after his head bounced. The waiter arrived with Stolis and Al continued, oblivious.

"Yeah, you go into the bank on the corner and walk left past the officers. Locked glass door, opens into Rhys and De Loache. Through the next door you come to an elevator. Get off on the 6th floor and walk around to the main elevators. I'll take the key off my ring when I go to the can, I never use it."

"So what do we do with Fox?" I said.

"Negotiate. He's not serious."

"He's serious, Al. This is how he does business. He's got debts, and he came back from his vacation real confident. We're not in control, it's a bidding game."

This time it got through.

"*Shit . . . sonofabitch . . . gonna be rough . . . do what y'can . . . don't bend over, y'know . . . love to hit that cocky bastard, take a knee out, do the world a fuckin' favor . . . *"

The words had no force and the flesh hung like putty on his face. Except for dark patches under his eyes he was colorless. After a few quiet seconds he finished his drink.

"I'm gonna take a whiz and get that key off my chain. Order us another round."

I didn't care if he lived or died. He'd put me at risk out of lazy indifference — I saw no other explanation. I slow-breathed the beast into its cage, and when Al came back I told him I'd enrolled Billy for Aikido. He brightened, and I handed him Hu Shi's card.

"He can call any time and set up a schedule," I said. "Give him something to do after school, work up an appetite."

"Yeah, he reads too much. I should've thought of it myself, good idea," he said. "Jackie'll be real pleased. Tough bringing up kids over here."

Tough anywhere, I thought. Then I threw him another curve.

"Foxy is going away again for a couple of days and I need to go to Switzerland."

Durry wasn't going anywhere, but I wanted to slow things down and have a cool-off period. Marquardt smiled, assuming my trip was about hiding money.

"No problem, buddy, actually it's perfect — you can do a drop there, 'cause that's where it's going. Just keep it and take it with you." He was back in gear. "So okay, Zurich. Phone booth on Thalerstrasse, southwest corner of Girondon. Plastic piece above the phone comes out, got an empty space under it. Pry it up with a knife, put the envelope in. Okay?"

I was caught off guard but gave back the directions and he nodded.

"Eleven a.m. Tuesday. If you can't get at the phone, try again at one and three. Then call me if it's not done."

"Okay." Then I hit him again. "You get that 104 yet?"

"104?" he said sharply. "What're you talking about?"

"Sven. He's fucked, Al — he's calling me up drunk, another totally wasted message while I was away. Slipped my mind the other night so I dropped it in the mail."

His face showed an uneasy mixture of respect, hostility and acceptance. I had him halfway out of his wrapper, and it felt good. As if we were even now, more or less.

"Yeah . . . well, you were right. He got himself popped on a computer thing while you were in the States. But the 104 — you wouldn't know, the manual says use it, but it makes me look bad, Rob. Copies upstairs, Spiegel and Crackerjack."

He was fully on line, using work-names, little blue eyes letting me know he understood my move but not making an issue of it.

"Ah, shoot," I said. "Sorry, won't happen again. Y'know, Al, I got like no training before they sent me. Nothing, zip. Copy of the manual."

As if I still didn't quite get it. But I was done covering for him and he knew it.

"Yeah, courier's supposed to be light stuff, you're a special case." He paused.

"I'll take Sven off your hands," he announced, as if it wasn't automatic.

It was sprinkling lightly and I was edgy on my way to the Metro, bothered by Marquardt and thinking I was up where the air is thin. I folded the Durry envelope into an inside pocket and tossed the newspaper. Two blocks from the Marquis I looked at my watch and turned back as if I'd forgotten something. I memorized the four pedestrians, then turned onto a side-street and waited half a minute before looking back. A compact medium-sized man in a raincoat on the other side of the street was looking in my direction. Then he walked straight toward me as if we were both out in the open now, and there was going to be contact, like it or not.

I had thirty yards on him and was wearing the right shoes. I've always had good wheels and was confident. I scooted up a tree-lined residential street at an easy run, looking for a place to disappear among the big old houses but seeing only blind alleys. Then I saw one leading to a yard and ran into it. It was an empty space about thirty feet square with dead grass, toys, and a red tricycle shiny with rain. Past the house I saw that the picket fence extended all the way around, as tall as myself. No exit, no foothold. I hadn't had to get over anything like that fence in twenty years, and I had to make it the first time. The raincoat man would be there soon, and his face had been all business.

I measured my strides, trying to remember how to do it, but I got too close, timed it wrong, and barely got an ankle over. I yanked myself up and onto the pickets and made it over the top, an ugly process that seemed to take forever and ended up ripping my hands and pants and bruising my groin. I fell across sideways, landed on one foot, jumped up and flew through another yard. No witnesses. Running down the parallel street working my way toward the Metro I was angry with Al all over again. I'd been careful to get to the meeting clean, and Al hadn't bothered. But I'd dodged the problem and I was cool. Brilliant bulletproof Rob. Rounding a corner, I slowed down to get my bearings and heard quick, choppy foot-strikes. The raincoat man, much too close.

How the fuck?! Had to be Israeli. I stepped into a doorway remembering the tough little guys who built that tough little country. Blew things up when they had to, didn't worry much about civilians. I was ready, and I was afraid. I knew a lot about the raincoat man from how he'd looked at me, and found a way to stay with me. As the flying footsteps came near, I tensed. As

114

he passed, he flicked his eye, we saw each other, and I made my move. One jump-step and a rib kick. I got it right, and he went down hard.

Not hard enough. He rolled away and was getting to his feet all in one move. Fear turned me into an animal. Before he was up, I launched another kick. It wasn't as solid as the first, but it knocked him down again. Before I could do any more, he'd rolled over again and was on one knee, reaching under his raincoat. I kicked again and got his head with a glancing blow. He went over backwards. Then I was jumping on his chest, stiff-legged, four or five times, like a crazed animal. It knocked the wind out of him, but my sneakers took the edge off. He was out of it, but when I saw a pistol half-hidden by his shoulder I head-kicked him hard. The soft shoe saved him, but his head flew and I heard him grunt. The grunt told me I was safe — there was nothing in it, just a shapeless sound coming up through his body. He was out, arms thrown loose as if he'd been hit by a car. I kicked the gun away, heard shouting and took off. Two men on the other side of the street were staring at me and folding their umbrellas — two big, young, law-abiding citizens in their twenties. They missed the gun and started after me, and I really began to run. Four blocks to the Metro, with two corners, and I had to lose them. A woman with a grocery bag turned to look. I was full gas, flying on fear, and then I was starting to cramp from running on bicycle legs. Running as hard as I knew how, and really hurting.

I glanced back as I turned the last corner, saw I was alone, and shot down the stairs, both calves cramping. I couldn't run any more. Three old crones stood at the track edge gossiping away, not noticing my heavy breathing and general craziness. I stood with my back to a wall, chilling in my sweat, envelope still in my pocket. No idea what I'd do if the umbrella guys showed up. Put my hands on top of my head, I decided. Get myself arrested and let Al pull strings. If it was the raincoat man, he'd be armed and I'd be fucked. I pulled out the envelope and dropped it in a trash can.

My wind came back, but my legs were locked up and painful. Finally a train muttered its way into the station. A ghost-train, almost empty. I had no idea where it was going, but I retrieved the envelope and followed the three chatty old ladies. Sat down and felt my bowels vibrating as the train grumbled its way out of the station. I remembered jokes about guys losing their shit in combat, and really got it for the first time.

Back in my garret I put on a heavy sweater and sat at the table with a mug of very Irish coffee debriefing myself. The manual had a procedure for any situation including this one, and it gave me something to do. On a legal pad I started with a list of things I didn't understand or know what to do with: the girl in Ghent, Millie, the Israelis and Durry's mystery trip to the Caribbean. Al's drug use. The raincoat man.

Fact one was the raincoat man. Fact two was his engaging openly without hesitation. He knew who I was and what I looked like. Fact three, everyone had seen it coming. It was why Jason had popped up with Morris, and why he wanted me armed. Why I'd been given new I.D., and why Marquardt had no reaction when I told him I felt something coming. Brilliant bulletproof clueless Rob.

Forget courier, they'd be thinking — *walks like an Op, talks like an Op . . .*

And this afternoon I'd fought like one, so I smelled like one, too. That would be fact four.

What I knew, or thought I knew, was dwarfed by what I didn't know. I couldn't be sure the raincoat man was Mossad. Why not the Russians or the Chinese, or some company working along the same lines as Durry and Epstein? Morris had left the door open for me to call, but I held back, and I didn't even think about telling Al. I poured half a tumbler of Jameson with a dash of water and sipped it slowly, thinking it would be really excellent to fall asleep. Before I did, I added one last fact: Alvin Marquardt didn't give a shit, or a hoot or a damn. He had good instincts though, and didn't call.

15

The manual said that disappearing yourself was the thing to do when in danger without backup. I spent the next two days in my chilly garret waiting to hear from Durry, doing Guimard work, reading Beckett and thinking about Switzerland. How to be invisible. Unused Canadian passport for openers, and a car without a paper trail. Sitting in my restaurant looking out the window over a bowl of stew I saw the answer to that.

Marcel smiled when I walked in. I hadn't spoken with anyone for two days and it felt good being in his shop. So far he'd sold me an expensive motorcycle and rented me an apartment, and he could probably foresee another business opportunity. I told him I was really happy with the bike and we retired to his office for a Calvados, where I explained why I was there. He lit a Gauloise and exhaled thoughtfully.

"Just 'a car,'" he said. It was rhetorical; he understood. I stayed businesslike, as if it was all completely normal for an American.

"I need it the day after tomorrow for two or possibly three days. Something reliable, and I'd want to pick it up in early morning. Early as possible."

"I could rent you my wife's Renault for a few days. Seventy five dollars a day, fully insured. I can have it in my lot the night before, and you can leave the Trident — it's due for service."

What would I do without Marcel?

Durry's call came the next morning and revealed nothing, but I heard in his voice that making him wait had been a good idea. I said I'd call back, dressed and went to a nice big warm café where they'd bring the phone to your table.

"I do not hear from you — there are problems, eh?"

"Just normal delay," I said, letting it sound doubtful. "But you'll have to give some ground, Alain," I added in a diplomatic voice, as if this was just another business deal, and could go wrong like any deal.

"Perhaps so. I have made your role difficult, but I must have the money. I can expect to hear a number from you — when?"

"Another couple of days. Maybe as soon as Thursday," I said. "It's gone to the top, which slows things down. But I don't think it's negative, and Slim thinks as I do — "

"Ah, yes," said Durry. "The thoughtful Slim. So I will wait for your call?"

"By the weekend almost definitely."

I dropped the heavy old receiver onto the phone and left a big tip. Outside was what looked like an all-day drizzle, but I was dry under my plastic hat and leather jacket. Somehow the incident with the raincoat man wasn't distracting me, just making me very careful and focused. I was learning a lot in a hurry, and whatever I was turning into, I hoped it was less of a fool. If someone offered me a trick attaché case now, I'd know it wasn't a friendly favor and a sign of trust.

How to play Durry and Marquardt? They were like a pair of big racing yachts approaching collision at a course-marker buoy with me sitting on top of it. On the way home I called Al and wished I hadn't — he wanted me to come in before I left.

I entered the building via Rhys and De Loache, took the freight elevator, and had Françoise call him on the stockroom intercom, which was how it should have been from the top. Then I waited at the paper-piled stockroom desk. Al had a field man's contempt for office routine. He walked in a few minutes later and asked for a Durry update before the door was closed behind him.

"We talked on the phone, and he'll come down some. We'll talk again soon."

Marquardt grunted and locked the door, moving swiftly to get us into TCC. He was an edgy quick-thinking butterball today, a different man. It was uncanny.

"Good thing you're still on terms," he said when we were inside. "The doctor's m.o. is to break off when things don't go his way. I talked to Olcott. We're going to bag all other contact situations for you until his stuff is in."

It was meaningless, Sven was gone with the 104. We sat down, and Marquardt faced me across his desk. He still had that edge, and I was wondering where we stood. I wasn't mentioning the raincoat man, but I was over being angry and wanted to ease things between us.

"So Al — how many years before they find me a cover job like yours?"

He smiled a genuine smile.

"Take a while, buddy. That gig goes back to before we had agency status and we were their security. Good friends to have."

There was a lot packed into that. I filed it for thinking about as Al kept talking.

"You're here now because there's something we have to talk about, Rob. These live drops — you should be armed when you're in possession of those documents. You need to be."

Walks like an Op, talks like an Op, armed like an Op. I looked at Marquardt.

"I'm a courier, Al."

"Sure. But you start running people like you're doing now and who knows."

Running people was not in my job description either, but I didn't bother to say it.

"I guess. Well, a guy followed me the other day after we met. I got rid of him, but it was close. I ducked into the Metro as a train pulled in. Pure luck."

"See what I mean? I'm like you, avoid trouble if I can, but shit happens. Tell you this much, Rob — I'm out of shape stuck in an office, but I carry a weapon around the clock and I'm good with it. Once a week at the range, and then out at our country place."

I waited.

"This request that you be armed comes from upstairs," said Al. "Humor them. Gets me off the hook, maybe save your ass one day. Think about it."

I already had. I knew I had no choice, but I was going to play him a little.

"My deal was no guns. It was a condition of my employment, and Morris accepted it. It's also in the manual —

couriers aren't armed."

"Optional for a C-1, which is in process. Another twelve thou and some perks."

He walked to the other end of the room and came back with a single-malt from his collection, which gave me time to think. Morris hadn't mentioned the attaché case, which worked for me. While Marquardt was thinking pistol-on-my-person, the reality was the case, which I kept with me since the raincoat man. He poured Scotch and glacier-water chasers, and we drank. Then he reached into a drawer and pulled out a walnut box. In it were a Perssons .40 mm with suppressor, shoulder rig and wire stock. He removed the stock, leaving an empty space.

"Handy for personal items," he said. Then he paused and started again. "Rob, I know this goes against the grain. Whatever he said back then, this is Morris's idea, not mine. It was like, 'talk you into it, but not pressure you'. He's telling me your profile says non-violent, and not to piss you off. But make sure you do it."

I chuckled politely and didn't reply. It threw him off.

"Look, Rob — if everyone upstairs wants somethin' t'happen, it's gotta happen."

He didn't like pushing me, and it hit me that Morris's insistence was a warning.

"Don't like chrome, Al. Black disappears, chrome catches the light. Jacket falls open, guy across the street can see it."

"Black it is, couple of days. And thanks, Rob — last thing I'd ask on my own. You got your unarmed skills together at all?"

It sounded innocent but it didn't make much sense if I was going to be armed.

"I work at it. Three times a week, it's in my expenses. Your pal Jennie thinks I'm coming along."

"That's good, she's important. She vets people. Jennie gets the wrong vibe, people don't get hired."

I'd found that out on my own but wondered why he was telling me.

"Good to know," I said. "What's the deal with her and Olcott, anyway?"

"He's the über-dude, buddy," said Marquardt. "Plus he's

loaded and has more clothes than God. No use on the job, but his wife's cousin is Jim Wilcox, Assistant Secretary of State Far East, and between 'em they've got relatives all through State and congress. BioTel Director, too."

BioTel Director. I dipped my face so he couldn't see it and sipped my drink.

"Hard for the girl to say no."

"You got it," said Al. "Whereas it's men like us could do that woman justice."

Took care of that, boss.

I took the Perssons out of the box as if it mattered. The Michaud had the basic, raw look of something created without cosmetic concern. This was shiny-sexy, a techy consumer product. While checking it out, I was adjusting to the idea of Jason Olcott as a BioTel Director hooked up at the State Department. I'd thought he was clueless, but now I understood how he got his job. I put the Perssons back in its box.

"I'm gonna have to work on this. My experience is with long guns."

"No problem," he said. "Why don't you kill forty minutes and do a status report on our favorite Frog. I've gotta meet Jackie at the bank, then we'll go to the range."

Being left there on my own was beyond irregular, and I was cautious as well as thoughtful. He'd mentioned a camera, which I could see overhead, but there might be a videocam. I pulled the Durry file and sat down at Al's littered desk to look it over. The file had never come up, but it didn't seem to matter. There wasn't much there, just the kind of facts that could be pulled from civil and academic records and a couple of clips. He'd graduated Polytechnique, which meant smart with attitude, a certified mandarin. The clips were from science journals, but at the bottom was an amazing one from a newspaper. In June of 1977, Alain de Montes Durry had become engaged to marry one Claudia Rothschild, a fact of no apparent interest to anyone but me. Three column picture, hot couple. Mlle. Rothschild was gorgeous, with unforgettable eyes, a cousin of jazz legend Nica de Koenigswarter. She had the invulnerable look of a very social woman for whom brilliance without a Nobel might be just another positive attribute, like good skin or nice teeth. *No marriage*, said a handwritten 1980 note.

How had Durry felt about money before getting jilted by a Rothschild? Or Jews? I put the file aside and moved some papers to make space, then wrote a report on my recent activities, leaving out everything important. A headache was coming on, and I closed my eyes, resting my head on my hands. I lost track of time, and when I half-opened my eyes I found myself looking at the papers strewn on Marquardt's messy desk — letters, documents, scribbled notes, phone numbers without names. The sloppy minutia of a disintegrating man. But still a clever one, I was sure of that.

A monitor-phone squawked: A woman's voice.

This is Bunny, where the hell are you? C'mon, pick up!

Who was Bunny? It didn't matter. A while later someone named Banger asked for contact. I didn't care about him, either, but I was curious about those desk papers, looking at what I could see without moving anything. A letter caught my eye because the letterhead included a tennis racquet and golf club, which reminded me of Marquardt's strange reaction when I picked up the racquet near the door as we were leaving that first day. I got a slow, cautious buzz. I didn't move anything and didn't have to. Most of the text was uncovered. It was addressed to BioTel, and didn't belong in this office. Pictured with racquet and club was something that looked like an old Tinker-toy construction with balls attached here and there. And a pair of panels. Solar panels — it was a satellite. Without moving, eyes still half closed in case there was a camera on me, I read what I could. A California composites company called Uniceptco wanted BioTel to know they'd be pleased to help the People's Republic of China build a plant, and would train employees. The next paragraph stated that, as Mr. Marquardt surmised, the technology for tennis racquet and golf club were applicable to all sorts of items requiring a high weight/strength ratio and unaffected by temperature, exposure to sunlight, etc. Such as bicycles. The rest was covered by a sheet of paper, but I'd read enough. It was a silly letter by some overpromoted tech, and the bicycle part was moronic. Composite bikes were cutting-edge costly, irrelevant to the Chinese market. Uniceptco would do anything for money — that was the message.

Yawning for the camera, I blinked a few times and stood up and stretched like a man who started drinking too early in the day.

At the coffee machine I thought about Al's reaction when I asked about the racquet. Not that of a flip, quick-witted guy who made jokes about his boss. His wife coming on to me hadn't bothered him, but my interest in that racquet definitely had. I guessed Uniceptco would be a way for Al to score, and in my eyes that was worse than the Rosenbergs, Kim Philby and Sir-Something-Blunt all together. Those were people who believed in something, and I doubted this little porker believed in anything but his belly. And he was flirting up China on a technology with all kinds of military uses to pay for his extravagant life. Not proven, but it felt that way. I felt BioTel lurking down there like Grendel's mother. Maybe CIA didn't know about Oracle because it was really just a BioTel deal. But if Al had the balls for it, which I guessed he did, Oracle might be a huge score. Get the Israelis bidding and the sky would be the limit.

Again not proven, and I started backing away from my speculations. There was a lot that smelled bad about Al Marquardt, but there were reasonable explanations. A letter from Uniceptco was not a drop-the-soap reply from Al, and the whole thing might just be part of his day-gig or something he planned to pass on to State. *He trusts me*, I thought — his son goes to my dojo and we're friendly. He trusts me enough to leave me alone here. He doesn't feel like a traitor to me, just a hustler. What do I really know?

Somehow, some way, Al Marquardt had got close enough to me that I didn't want to burn him, much as that might please Morris. A monitor-phone squawked — Al telling me he'd meet me at the range, and how to lock up. Another unauthorized procedure.

The range was small, with a high end clientele that looked like businessmen in their forties and fifties. There was a small crowded lounge with comfortable chairs and a heavy tang of gunpowder and tobacco. The manager recognized Al and let us in to shoot after giving us earplugs and binoculars. Inside was worse air with more cordite and the sporadic *crack* of handguns. Someone left, and Al took the slot while I stood back with binoculars. Surprise — my boss was the best shot in the house. Firing his Glock quick-draw from a belly rig, he was as accurate one-handed as any of the others taking their time with both hands. And fast. When he was through I shot for a while, not very well. Then we went for a drink and spoke French for a while. It was never going to be real French, but he didn't forget much.

In the Metro, I considered Uniceptco. Was Al selling secrets to the Chinese or was BioTel weaseling them out of the country through chinks in the law? Or was it legitimate, with government blessing? Not impossible, not at all. I looked around the clean subway car at its unarmed civilians with their reserved French faces, riding a good train, looking forward to a month off in the summer. Why couldn't we have that? Why were we hung up on guns, drugs and our unique wonderfulness? Fucking Vietnam. Before Nam we were ourselves and the country worked. After Nam the deluge, and no end of BioTels. Which reminded me.

I got lucky from a booth outside the Metro and caught Mac in a good mood.

"Nice timing, good to hear your snotty Puritan voice. How's that Frog bush?"

"Clammy. I was kind of hoping for a business conversation."

"Sure, I'm on it, Rob. I did some more looking around and found out a few things about this BioTel. The name is new, came after a merger four years ago, but the operation dates back to the fifties. Electronic weaponry mainly now. Trained mercenaries through a subsidiary, case I'm ever looking for a job. General military consulting, government work, ours and others. Big solid outfit, no takeover rumors. Sounds like the officers have a free hand and do real well for themselves. Long-term Pentagon contracts."

"That's it?"

"So far. Unless there's a nice big war or some new toy that would jump the stock. I'm not done looking, Rob, I've got a couple more names."

Some new toy. Something mysterious called Oracle? It was just a hunch, but it didn't feel wrong.

16

Solothurn, Switzerland was very cold with a steady wind. The two-story brick Michaud-Coubert building sat behind a tall metal fence in the middle of smooth snow with a neat path to the door. No special security, very good manners. In his neat little café-au-lait office, a plump and expert Swiss sold me a second pistol like the one in the case. Then he arranged auto-fire conversion for both, along with a lecture: auto-fire was limited to short bursts and wasn't recommended with an enclosed weapon. Unreliable, could be done. A couple of hours later I drove off through the Alps with two identical mini machine guns, one in the case, one in the shoe bag under my shirts — one for each side of the Atlantic. Airport security was an issue in Europe, but if I got through, I was home free. If not, Morris would bail me out and have a laugh at my expense.

I drove until I was gritty-eyed and took a room outside Zurich. It was expensive, like everything else in Switzerland, with a big TV and a mini-fridge full of booze and soft drinks. I lay down on the bed and poured a tiny bottle of Scotch down my throat, chasing it with Perrier. On the tube, a Belgian scientist was comparing SDI to the Emperor's New Clothes. I dozed through a commercial and woke up to Euro-comedy at the expense of Colonel North's document-shredding party with his assistant, a younger Jackie Marquardt look-alike. Then came North himself, telling the world that he did not buy lingerie for the lady, whatever some dirty-minded political persons might think. After that came a second tiny bottle of Scotch and extended footage of the assistant. Well coached, winning smile, still unclear about those darned misplaced millions. Annie Fanny guides the ship of state. Of course they were laughing at us, why not? We'd asked for it.

Zurich at drop-time was a picture postcard. Clear, dry, icy-bright. I walked along Thalerstrasse among scattered pedestrians with an oversized nail clipper open in my pocket, file extended, ready to pry the panel open. No luck — I could see that a hundred feet away. A large gray-haired woman filled the booth, and when I got closer I could hear her squabbling in German-Swiss. She was still at it ten minutes later when I made a reverse pass on the other side of the street, so I had two hours to kill. I saw Lindenhof Park and started walking toward it. It was about as big as two or three Washington Squares, but less urban, with bushes and benches here and there. A good place to sit down, look at my map and freeze while cleaning my fake glasses and checking for raincoat men. No raincoat men, and I headed for the old town, where I climbed narrow cobbled streets looking for a place to kill time and eat. I found a quiet little bar on the side of a hill and went in to warm up. Looking out over the town, I drank San Pellegrino and sipped a brandy against the chill, not yet hungry. I was halfway through my drink when a tall, yellow-haired, respectable-looking kid in his early twenties came in and sat next to me. He wore an old tweed jacket with a navy turtleneck, and offered a pleasant smile while striking up conversation. His inquiries were very Swiss, quiet and polite, delivered in good English. He could see I was new in town — did I perhaps want some nice hash? Or maybe some really nice heroin, yes?

So much for my impersonation of a European. It puzzled me, since I could often get away with it in France. I told him no thanks and had another sip of brandy. I couldn't enjoy it until he left, but it was a handy prop. He thanked me for my patience, ordered a beer, and asked might I by chance be in need of a woman? I declined in a civil way and he explained that while he must sound like some kind of criminal, please not to be misled, he was working his way though law school. I said I was on my way to meet a ski instructor but he didn't leave, and we pretended to converse briefly on everything from punk rock to French universities and the good life in Canada, my home. He was comfortable but I wasn't, so I begged off, finished my brandy and put down some francs for the check. The phone booth delay, the Durry envelope and this too-friendly kid were having a cumulative effect.

Outside, I turned at the first corner and lost myself in small winding old streets full of people who didn't mind the cold. A few corners later I found an inset doorway and checked my watch. Leaning out to look up and down the street I saw nothing suspicious, but I was jumpy, and also lost. My jacket was reversible, and I turned it blue side out, put my red scarf in the case with my hat, which I replaced with a cap from the pocket. Squeezed flat in the doorway, I studied my map until I knew where I was. I was freezing and hungry, and just about as nervous as I get. The blond kid seemed young for the game, but he was too much of a coincidence.

A few minutes later, standing at a corner and looking for a place to eat, I froze. Driving slowly through the intersection ten or fifteen feet away was the kid. He was with a very angry lady friend, a real stunner. I saw them for a long moment, and they were too busy arguing to notice me. She was really giving him hell. It was a moment I'd never forget — citizens, tourists, little old buildings reeking of time, yellow-haired kid at the wheel of an ancient green Fiat Strada, cowering before his raging woman. She seemed older than he was, long and lanky in the little car, with wild black curls and bone-white skin, eyes set off with makeup. I had a strong déjà vu flash. Had I seen this exotic beauty before? In a movie maybe. I turned away puzzled, then walked into the nearest restaurant, impressed by her rage. It locked her in my mind, and I gave her a name: *Lorelei*.

The phone booth was empty and there was no one close. The panel popped out and I squeezed the envelope in. Then I walked away, eyes scanning everywhere, wanting to be out of Zurich. I was cool until I got near the car and saw a pair of cops, and another pair at the far end. They meant nothing, but traffic was barely moving and it felt like I'd never get out of Switzerland. I tossed the cap into the back seat and squirmed out of the jacket, replacing it with a tweed sport coat I'd left under some newspapers on the floor. Then I put on a pair of tinted driving glasses. Traffic inched along, and at the corner my route was dictated by cops who were sending everyone down Thalerstrasse. Nothing I could do about it — all traffic was being routed past the drop at about five miles an hour. I kept my face aimed ahead as my eyes swiveled, glad I'd changed my appearance.

My composure collapsed in stages. First I saw Morris, the model Swiss citizen, sturdy and solid in green loden. He had a neat salt-and-pepper beard and steel-rimmed glasses, and looked completely at ease walking away from the drop. My watch said the Durry envelope had been there slightly over twenty minutes. I'd been a little early, so he was right on schedule, but something told me he didn't belong there.

Then I passed the yellow-haired law-student pimp-hustler walking in the other direction, his face pinched and inward. A wave of perspiration came over me that seemed to freeze on my skin except for the droplets running down my rib-cage. I was sure I hadn't been spotted by either of them, but I guessed that TCC's civil war was getting close to Gettysburg and something like a neutron bomb was about to descend, perhaps on me. I'd been playing a few games myself since New York. This was no little tweak-prank like embarrassing Al with that 104 report. Huge escalation. I was sure Morris wasn't the intended receiver, and I'd just witnessed him short circuit a delivery on TCC's major project. Even Olcott would see that.

Calling Morris had been my hole card if things went wrong. Now it wasn't even an option.

17

Françoise was vacuuming the shipping room at eight a.m. when I returned. I went into the little office bone-weary after driving straight through and called Al, who said he was running behind schedule. In front of me was another messy Marquardt desk, this one covered with shipping orders. Al might not show for an hour and Françoise couldn't see me, so I had a peek at the orders. Since the Uniceptco letter, I was very interested in Al's other life with BioTel.

There were three loose paper-piles — shipping printouts in and out plus a small group of hand-typed shipping orders. I could see the door Al would be coming through, so I risked looking at a few of those hand-typed orders. A few seconds later I stopped and took a deep breath. Stapled to the orders in this pile were notes in Marquardt's neat clear writing. It was clear from them that BioTel sold its wares to pretty much anyone, but not directly. Limited-distribution superchips went to France, thence to Germany, Australia, and finally Japan. Radar components and upgrades for F-15 guidance systems went to a Belgian outfit hooked up with a German company that had got rich trading with Libya through Ed Wilson, a CIA crook-legend, now serving twenty years. Identical field radars wound up in both Syria and Israel after the same kind of shuffling, and orders for an all-aspect Sidewinder followed a Byzantine routing through NATO countries that got them to South Africa via Israel. TCC might be battling Mossad for Oracle, but BioTel needed those Israeli way-stations that kept popping up. After Iran-contra I wasn't surprised. Al Marquardt was making a ton of money for BioTel. He was in touch with operations all over the globe that were cleared to accept restricted hardware and would ship it anywhere. Super-special items got moved via loss-points, where theft could be claimed. There was a hand-written list of loss-points that had been burned, and what had been "lost." It was obvious that oil producers could buy anything BioTel sold, especially Iraq, our proxy-war ally against our pal Iran, which had expedited arms to the Contras.

There were also several envelopes, and I found the nerve to open one. It contained a hand-typed order for six *krytrons*, whatever a krytron was. Al had had these stolen stateside, then reported, and he'd indicated subsequent routing with names rather than locations or companies. *Teak* to *Juice* to *Alben*. With these were orders for depleted-uranium artillery shells, whatever they were.

Françoise turned off the vacuum. I put the slips back in the envelope and went back to my expenses. Marquardt walked past her as if she didn't exist and appeared in the doorway with his face set in a hard smile. He locked the door behind him and we went into TCC without a word. At the coffee machine, face turned away, he popped the question.

"Go okay in Zurich?"

Then he turned to look right at me, his expression flat and hard. I wasn't taken off guard, but this wasn't any Al Marquardt I knew. He was unreadable, and he meant to get the truth out of me. I answered as if I didn't notice.

"Yes and no," I replied. "Phone was busy at eleven, so I had breakfast and went back. It was in the box at one and no one was paying attention that I could see. Only thing that felt wrong, I thought maybe someone made a pass at me in a bar before I got it in the box. Maybe I should have another look at those surveillance shots."

He said nothing, just pulled the box from his desk.

"First Durry," he said then, sounding like himself again. "Deal now is, we finalize before he gets any more bright ideas. He could still be trouble."

"He could. He's seriously in debt — "

I was referring to Durry's gambling, but the ricochet got Marquardt.

"So's most of the world, Rob," he said. "Problem is, he won't play by the rules. I told Crackers he's not bluffing, so we don't look real great to the front office this week. Washington wants the stuff yesterday. They'll go to seven hundred thou Swiss. Two thirds hike. That's authorized. Try him at six and bargain with him. On my own, I'd go eight and just take the flak.

Even eight-fifty. . . but this is key — "

He was looking down at the desk as he spoke.

"We need a complete copy — the whole entire document, asshole to eyeballs. All the installments, everything from word one."

Right. Because Morris had disappeared the Zurich installment. It struck me that people in this line of work who carried guns and smoked cocaine might kill someone at some point. Accidentally, sort of. Not me though, not while I was still mission-critical.

"Isn't he still working on the material?"

"I don't think so, Rob. This has been going on a long time. The original schedule called for the final installment by the first of the year, and he never asked for more time — I think he's parceling it out so he can keep jacking us up. But if he's under pressure like you say, he'll go for it."

From his tone I was sure that he didn't suspect me of anything worse than being a boy scout and maybe not too clever. The phone rang and emitted one word: *Snyder*.

A senior voice, professional, European, and impersonal. The authority in it changed the mood, and the name stuck in my mind. Before Marquardt got to the red button Snyder was gone and I was thinking. Bunny and Banger had had the voices of young adult Americans. Snyder was anything but that. I saw cellular separation working when it mattered. With all Marquardt's loose talk, I still knew next to nothing about TCC.

"Another thing," said Marquardt. "Civilians can get cute. Remind Durry that if he sells it twice, we're gonna have t'do somethin' to him, which we will. Not violent, just make him uncomfortable, fuck up his life. Easy to do. Scare him a little, Rob. Washington is on my ass like a hot-tub full of piranhas. We need this behind us."

He took a call then, and I walked away. I was having an Al Marquardt type idea and doing numbers in my head. Big trouble was on the way as Al and Morris fought it out. Whoever won there would be a shake-up, and I could be out of a job again. I was expensing everything and saving my salary, but it didn't amount to much. I had to look out for number one, because no one else would, and the job was about money, like any job. Al was about money, Durry was about money, Olcott would not exist without money. I had to think about it too, and I could fiddle the situation like everyone else. And I needed to, because I had no seniority or job security. If things went wrong I'd be gone with minimal severance and no references, and close to broke. There was no way I could let that happen, if only because I couldn't let Layla see that daddy.

Al got off the phone.

"So what's this about someone making a move in Zurich?"

"I was killing time and having a brandy after my first pass at the booth. This kid sits down and starts trying to sell me everything from Afghani chocolate to his girl friend. I got away from him, but then I saw the pair of them having a fight in his car and she was really giving him hell. He was no pimp, Al. I think he knew who I was, and what I was doing there. Staked out the booth was my guess."

He looked at me for a moment, then went to the end of the room and came back with another walnut box and another Perssons, this one in black. With it was a belly rig like his.

"I'm better off without it till I can hit something Al, and they're doing spot-checks at borders. I should look over those surveillance shots, that girl friend rang a bell."

He nodded.

"Don't cross any borders for now. I can hook it up for you to carry anywhere, but it'll take a week or two. We'll go to the range later, and next weekend you can come up to the country with me and we'll shoot outside. I'll work with you — doesn't take that long once you get the draw. So what did this pair look like?"

"Both tall, barely fit into this old Fiat. The kid was early twenties, about six-three, skinny, good-looking, long straight blond hair, blue eyes, good English. Beat-up green Strada, Swiss plates, couldn't get the number. The woman I saw for just a couple of seconds. Lanky, on the flat side, but she had the look. Hot. Very white skin, wild black hair all over the place. Intense. She was all over him, furious."

A monitor phone started up and he hit the red button.

"Make-up, hair, skin — all that can change," he said. "Tall hot and lean is what we've got. Anyhow, look at the shots. I'm under the gun today, Millie's out with the flu."

I sat drinking coffee and flipping through photographs, the complete stack, slow and careful, putting them face down on a work station as I went. I had no luck with Lorelei or the blond kid, then *bingo* — the minx of Muynck Street. I remembered that sharp profile. Older than she'd looked in Ghent, caught from an unflattering angle while talking to a heavy middle-aged man. I went on through the pile and she came up again, getting in a car. On the back was her origin code: TAIS. I walked over to Marquardt.

"No luck on those two in Zurich, but there's a face here I can almost place."

I carried the photo over and watched his face as he looked at it. The reaction was there, a kind of stillness in a face that wasn't made for it.

"Dead file, Robbie, shoulda been tossed. Sorry, guy — suspected Stasi a few years ago. No confirmation, probably married to the mob, y'know — seen with her old man or whatever. Happens all the time."

Too many words, and I didn't see how TAIS would indicate East Germany, or why it was there now and hadn't been before. Marquardt put the stack back in his desk, and then I got it. If NYUS was New York, US, TAIS would be Tel Aviv, Israel. I didn't say so, and Marquardt shrugged, smooth as snake-oil.

"Don't go away mad," he said lightly. "We've all had that feeling, Rob — Slants at the market, KGB in the Metro . . . "

After the range we went to a piano bar, a big expensive room with an old black society-bop player doing the American songbook for people so rich they could wear last year's clothes. The floor was tan marble but the piano player had a fine touch and didn't bounce the sound. Marquardt ordered Stolis and talked handguns through a Rogers and Hart set while I thought about that night on Muynck Street and the raincoat man. Al was explaining the Zen of the draw.

"Big thing is getting your first move smooth, the sweep.

That's off, everything's off. If the sweep's good you have time. Clean draw, time to aim. I used to practice at home, drive Jackie crazy. I'd set my watch-timer to go off every fifteen or twenty minutes, keep changing the timing. Keep doing what I was doing and draw from whatever position I was in when it went off. It works, there's fucking few people out there that can beat me. Including your friend Morris."

My friend Morris. Probably still true if I kept my mouth shut about Zurich. Al ordered another round I didn't want. I hadn't slept or eaten much in a long time but I had to drink with him, so I kept eating gravlox and caviar hors d'oeuvres to stabilize the booze. An expressionless old waiter kept replacing the tray as soon as I ate a couple. I was thinking about the Minx of Muynck Street. The Israelis had been onto me from the start. My boss had known, hadn't said a word. Why?

Then he was telling war stories. Something about the Chili Run and someone called The Major. His voice burned like a hot coal in the cool rich room.

"The Major — ?"

"Morris, der Eulenspiegel. He made Major in about six weeks from second Lieutenant. Inchon, Korea — big deal, kid war hero. Came out of the reserves into Nam, walked away when he saw it was crap."

"So what's the Chili Run?"

"Latino snuff."

He closed one nostril with an index finger, sucked in audibly, then popped his eyes. In that room.

"Chili Run's a normal first assignment, see what you can handle. CIA, same deal. Check out Jupiter Island some day, but don't get caught doing it. Coolers of blow from Nicaragua for those *contra* guns that never happened. When they skipped you over the Run I knew they had plans for you."

"They knew I couldn't shoot straight, Al. I'm a courier, next thing to a tourist. Not that anyone seems to give a fuck."

Al laughed so hard his roly-poly body shook. Why was he courting me?

When he was through laughing he leaned forward and spoke seriously.

"You're a smart guy, Rob, good school, Wall Street. This business is about cash and contacts. The Run has both — the cash is untraceable and the guys with the product control the governments. There's your Latin deal, basically — the people you do business with own the politicians, staff the military, computer access — all works together."

Al thought that was really excellent. With no real sleep or food for many hours, I was about drunk enough to explain that his neat Latin deal didn't work any better than the nifty Nam deal had, or the cool Shah-of-Iran coup, or the cockamamie Contras. I wanted to show him shots of what they'd done to whole villages, slaughtering everyone, kids included. The Nam-beast was pacing and I was getting crazy. *Change subject.*

"Strategic Defense Initiative," I said. "Whaddya think? Better than Mutually Assured Destruction?"

Al looked at me with a new expression, as if seriously considering me for the first time, and what to say. It was very unusual, and it brought me right back down.

"I don't have to think about that, Rob, I know. Reagan took the bait, and then he made a speech with no idea what he was setting off. Lotta people know Star Wars is just a movie but he didn't, and the money was huge. *Is* huge. Basic problem, too many ways around it even if they get it to work. At low cost."

He hesitated and continued quietly.

"What that speech did to the Russkies — well, he's saying we'd never start a war, but it's obvious if SDI works we win and they're fucked. They're afraid it might happen, and they're on a hair trigger watching those tests. Scary things have been happening that don't get out. Remember Flight 007, Korean airliner they took out?"

I nodded. Another pause while he thought.

"1983, that was the big year. We did a giant naval exercise in the Pacific to test their radar and so forth. Huge. Forty-something ships, lotta planes. Violated their air space, freaked 'em out, notes exchanged. They had enough, that's how come 007. Everything was going wrong. In July their systems registered a launch — nukes in the air. Their back-up cameras couldn't verify or deny because of the weather."

He stopped and looked at me.

"Their silos were open, right? But someone on their side had more sense than Reagan. Guy on duty gave it a couple of minutes, got more pictures. No nukes. Fucking computer glitch. *Way* closer than the Cuban missile thing. Know what I'm sayin' Rob? The Russians were *scared*. Still are, and this shit kept happening. Lotta close calls before that Korean flight, which they had every right to hit in their air space, KIA bein' a branch of CIA and us playin' spy-plane all the time up there. Big planes, easy mistake."

He glanced at my eyes and saw I was getting it.

"And Right after 007 the Able Archer war games. Total clusterfuck, never got out. You can't do war games without the possibility of it's being for-real, and the Russians were paranoid already. They just didn't know. Kept escalating up to DEFCON 1. They had a guy inside NATO, but until he called in, it was real close, Rob. Open silos again. They're still shitting marbles and we won't back off SDI. All about the money."

It was another Al Marquardt. I was back on my heels, totally rethinking him.

"They had their silos open twice that year?"

"Little known fact. Ronnie's a Hollywood jock, no idea what he was setting off with SDI, and they sure weren't gonna tell him. Reason I know, this all happened while I was with another outfit before TCC."

I didn't doubt any of it. I was rocked, and it felt like time to leave.

"I've gotta hook up with my new best friend and start talking numbers."

I walked off the booze and looked for a place to eat, all the while puzzling over that conversation. I'd seen a completely different Al Marquardt, a knowledgeable thinking man, clear and sharp. Why had he opened up like that? It wasn't about SDI or the Russian reaction. It was about this other Al Marquardt wanting us to be closer. Did he think I knew something and I might share? I did — I knew the minx of Muynck Street was

Israeli, and probably the raincoat man, and what happened in Zurich. Not to be shared.

And I knew there were Swiss francs to be skimmed on Oracle. TCC was asking a lot and no one was talking combat pay, but I didn't like it much. I found a restaurant and had a bowl of soup. When I was leveled off, I made my first call.

"Beach! So you have heard something?"

Durry was ripe.

"Yes, we should talk soon. When can we get together?"

"Today if you like. That idiot's bar where we watched soccer? Four o'clock?"

Time to shower and get the bike, but no time for a sit down meal. My next call struggled forever through the French lines until finally I got a familiar Hell's Kitchen bark and a lot of background noise.

"McVeigh. Who'm I talking to?"

"Is it a fact you operate a pub of the old sort in lower Manhattan, Misther McVeigh?"

He laughed.

"I *knew* it. I fucking knew it was gonna be you, I've got you timed. Well, I've got a free minute here, so let me bring you up to speed on this BioTel. I think we're onto something boy-o. It's the old tangled web, but it turns out that when they changed hands about four years ago, it was an odd deal. BioTel started out experimental, owned by some egg-head named Epstein who ran out of money. The new owners were super-connected extra-wide Texas assholes. I got this from a kid at Bohr and Surtees, and I made sure some very fine trim met and welcomed this young genius. He'll be dropping in to see her and keeping me up to speed.

"It was a pretty strange deal. Basically they re-named themselves, but it's the same old arms business. Hooked up every which way — Pentagon, congress, other governments. CEO is a guy named Arvin Telemann, a top thief. Corporate structure like Chinese boxes — no figuring out who really owns what. Delaware, Switzerland, Bahamas, Channel Islands, you name it. Ever hear of an outfit called Chinko?"

As in Pinko, I thought. *Good one, Mac.*

"Sure, it's a loss leader. What I'd *like* to know is who BioTel's really in bed with. When it's government contracts, that's everything — "

"Is that a fact? How extremely perceptive, yes, governments do buy arms, mustn't forget that. But as a practicing liberal, aren't you a bit bothered by this kind of thing?"

"Definitely. As a law abiding Christian Pinko I'm very uncomfortable. Very. But as a man trying to make his way in the world after a difficult year, I'm rather pleased with myself. So what will they be selling in a couple of years, I wonder?"

"Right? Well, I get the picture of an operation that does business real well, but they're not gonna invent the wheel. This Epstein may have had that in mind, but after the company changed hands they retired him."

"So why would these Beltway cowboys bother with a tiny company that had nothing going? For a name that doesn't mean anything?"

"Yeah," he said. "I had that thought, too. Not to worry, I'm gonna keep digging."

"Could be a bear down there, Mac."

"I know what you're saying. Discreet's my middle name. One more thing."

His voice had a ball-busting leprechaun innocence he saved for special moments.

"Arvin Telemann's brother-in-law is Menat Bagdosian."

When I said nothing, Mac asked me if I read the papers.

"Yeah, I know who he is."

Menat Bagdosian was the fat smiley-face Persian BCCI banker I'd learned about during my library visit while looking Iran-Contra. Tight with Sheikh Mahfouz, lived in his Boeing 737 when he wasn't on his yacht scoffing up starlets and buying senators. BioTel was connected up the ying-yang.

I walked down a dreary side street to the Olympia listening to the traffic roar on the *Périphérique*. I was exhausted, and only Durry would have kept me from crashing. When I got there, it was a perfect replay. Same small damp little room, same bleary proprietor, Durry at the bar watching TV as if he'd never left.

Tennis this time, Steffi Graf blowing away some irritated Italian on clay.

"Can we move to a table after this set?"

"I've seen this match before but I love to watch her," said Durry. "What a perfect Aryan, eh? And yet so human."

After we moved, the proprietor came over and I ordered one of their godawful cheese sandwiches and Durry smiled, waiting.

"It's like this, Alain. I've made the case for you being a difficult business partner, now receiving other offers — "

"They already know how difficult," said Durry. "Slim must love this."

"Not much. It went over his head and he wasn't at the meeting. I'm permitted to raise our offer to six-thirty Swiss for the remaining material, but you deliver it all at once, complete. Half payment on delivery, balance when it's decrypted and reviewed."

He nodded, thoughtful and calm now that we were finally down to it. He said nothing until we'd both had a pull of vodka. The proprietor brought my sandwich and I ordered another round.

"An excellent choice, as I recall," said Durry, smirking at the sandwich. "You must try their soup."

I almost laughed.

"But we must be serious. The number is wrong, Rob, and what would they know after this 'review'? It is a laboratory procedure — until it is accomplished, it is just a lot of words, numbers and symbols. And I must tell you that this offer is already matched, with full payment on delivery. More than matched."

Not great, but I guessed there were strings attached to the other bid.

"That's what I'm authorized to offer," I said carefully. "It's a very big jump, and you know we're reliable. Sole possession — that's obviously a condition. Is it ready?"

"It could be, yes. And I would not be such a fool as to sell it twice. But the price is not right, nor the terms."

I studied the tablecloth.

"Alain, this can happen as quickly as you want, but we should come to terms. What is your absolute best price? I have to know."

"Well . . . seven seven five, Swiss. I deliver all of the material, you become sole possessors — I retain no paper or electronic copy to be stolen. Cash on delivery, the entire amount, used bills of fifty to five hundred francs. Which is all agreeable to the competing group. More, if I play a little, but this could have dangers."

"Yes — I might be unemployed. If you could accept seven fifty, I think we'd have a deal. I could force it. Just to be clear, I'm expected to deliver the complete document, including earlier sections — everything as bargained for, complete."

His eyes relaxed and he smiled.

"*Okay!* Done. At Mme. Gauthier's, and celebrate with a good dinner."

"I'll call in the morning."

He nodded and I let a few beats go by.

"Alain, I'm concerned about your Israelis. You know the term 'hardball'?"

"Yes, they kill rather freely. They did it in France several times, we expressed our irritation, and they now favor Belgium. But in any case, they would not do that — I have value to any government."

"I'm thinking of myself. I've developed a high profile."

For a moment he looked impatient, as if he wanted to say something revealing.

"They know who you are then — definitely?"

"Yes. I was followed the other day."

I told him about the raincoat man in some detail, and as I waited for the reaction, something happened that I wasn't ready for. Alain Durry gazing into my eyes too long, with sad, naked, uncalculating desire. It didn't shock me, but a mistake could send everything down the tubes. I pretended not to notice.

"It was violent, Alain. Brutal. He had a gun, but I surprised him before he could use it, if he intended to. Kicked him to the ground, ran, was pursued — "

He bypassed this diversion.

"You are my first American," he said gently. "I like you a great deal. You are someone to be trusted. I feel comfortable with you, which is very rare for me. It allows a general mingling of the mind and senses, a strong affection quite difficult to express — "

He said something quiet in French I didn't get.

"I like you too, Alain," I said carefully. "I like you better than most of the people in my life, actually. But it's not me. I'm — set. Like glue, or a crystallized solution. Don't be offended. Basically, I'm just another bourgeois."

He handled it without rancor, his voice still friendly. He had an intellectual's way of making personal questions sound like rational inquiry.

"Be serious now — you are clearly of a liberal persuasion. What is your real reason? Fear?"

Because it was ridiculous? But Alain Durry could not have a ridiculous idea.

"Perhaps afraid I'd get to like it. Disturb my fiancée."

He laughed a hard, rattling Algerian laugh. Durry had decided I was okay, whatever I was.

"The notorious Hemingway 'grace under pressure.' I drink to the American style. And you should not be offended either, eh? For you there is always the wife of your employer, or his big English one who found me so charming."

"Millie Brock is a Tory — she detested me immediately on instinct."

"Yes, she would have to. I also enjoy women, but not that one."

Then we went up a couple of gears.

"Rob, this raincoat-man incident. I think it is time for you to know about a man named Snyder who worked with me last summer."

I tried to show nothing, and Durry continued.

"He fell abruptly out of contact, which was peculiar, since we were compatible. It went like this: first was Marquardt. When we did not get along, Snyder appeared. It went well, but after three meetings he disappeared, to be replaced by the Brock girl, also unacceptable. Awkward for Marquardt, but then you arrived."

Snyder. I remembered that one-word call. The impersonal distance in the voice. Who was Snyder? And how could Al put Millie in the field like that? What had Morris said? How did I know she wasn't TCC? I didn't, but I didn't believe it. Olcott was a fool, but the people TCC hired were not.

"Tell me about this Snyder, Alain. Did Marquardt feel threatened by him?"

"Perhaps. Marquardt could as easily been working for him. He was older than us by ten or fifteen years, with good French and English and probably other languages. Polite, well spoken, average European height, not heavy, graying hair. I could not say where he came from — he had the deracinated quality of many professionals in your business, but definitely European. We met last July, and at the second meeting we were close to agreement. When the girl replaced him I broke off."

He paused and went back to the Israelis.

"They puzzle me. They want possession of the material, but seem ambivalent about the value of the work, which is — understandable."

It didn't compute. He was as vain as they come, but there was doubt in his tone. For half a moment he seemed depressed and inward, then it was gone.

"They have only a few pieces of the puzzle, but they very much want the material. I'm not sure why, because they don't really know what they are bidding on, and I tell them nothing. Strange! My genetic manipulations solve only a few of the problems. But it works out in your favor, because they wish to engage me for other projects, and they will not injure a friend of mine under these circumstances. I can make this point with effect."

I was fascinated that this virulent anti-Semite might work for Israel.

"How would you feel about just openly working for us?" I asked, not thinking.

"You are truly a hero, Beach," he said with a devilish smile. "In that case I could do nothing on your behalf with them, could I — ?"

I was annoyed with myself and he saw it.

"A mere lapse, brought on by stress and hunger — you were able to eat even that dreadful sandwich very quickly. You are tired, and I embarrassed you. You need rest and I need to play."

"Eight o'clock, day after tomorrow. I'll confirm by asking if you are free and you will say no. Be careful you're not followed, Alain. Be very careful."

"Yes, definitely," he said. "The Jews are clever, but so is Durry. I will leave Paris tomorrow and stay with a friend, then leave the estate by another exit in one of her cars."

Then I asked if he happened to know what a krytron was. He stopped dead and gave me a look. Then he told me in a quiet voice that a krytron is a nuclear fuse.

Driving home, I couldn't think. I was bonking, nothing going on from the neck up. The legs keep moving for a while but it's soft-pedaling. One idea kept recycling itself: if Iraq's nuke facility had recovered from the Israeli strike they'd need krytrons. BioTel was there for them — they were fighting Iran for us, and that was leverage. Cooperative dictator, lots of oil. I steered through narrow back streets watching my mirrors and trying not to think about it too much. When I got home I ate half a loaf of black bread dunked in olive oil and a big piece of the local cheese. It calmed me down and I remembered Durry's puzzling modesty about his work. And doubt, a self-critical moment. It stuck in my mind because it was completely unlike him.

I put it aside and thought about my situation, finishing off the bread and cheese with a couple of apples. I was an open secret, but with delivery thirty hours away I thought I could pull it off before the other side was ready. And someone in Washington needed to know about those krytrons. Someone not from Texas.

Hold that thought. I could hear Joe Kline, still advising me from beyond the grave. Bargaining with Durry had brought back my recurring money issue. Olcott was in it for power and perks and Morris was a mystery, but the über-game was basically about money. Al was into it big-time, and BioTel's *raison d'être* was profit. CIA didn't care what they did to get it, and their retirees went into the arms business for big money. And it was Jennie's native habitat. I didn't want to know that, but I did.

And I needed some of my own. The skim would come to almost a hundred thousand US. Not really a whole lot given the circumstances, but it bothered me.

18

I met early the next day with friendly, normal Felix Guimard, with the sun just beginning to show itself. We usually met briefly, but this time it was over coffee served by the beautiful red-head, and he seemed unconcerned about time. When she'd left the room, he asked me to take readings on employees he was considering for the U.S.

"I want your opinion as someone familiar with Americans. Your sense of each person — could they cross the water as you did, and be accepted? That is my concern."

"I could do it today. I have only one meeting, which can also be lunch."

He was pleased. "I'm aware, Rob, that along with the language problem, 'too French' can be a disqualification. An American girl was honest enough to say it once, and I saw that she was right."

On my way to breakfast I was thinking that this quiet little dawn meeting was a vote of confidence. He liked my business plan. Cranked on caffeine, I found a phone and called Al on the scrambled line — I didn't want him to hear what might be in my voice.

"*We're on — it's set,*" I barked above the roar.

"Our terms?"

"He took it to the max. Your final number, payment in full on delivery. Eight-sixty Swiss, used bills. He could call any time."

"*I hate this bastard!* How soon?"

"Any time. Tomorrow. He says we're being stupid about the payment delay, that it's impossible to evaluate the procedure until it's applied, so I gave in."

"Yeah. That was Crackerjack. I'll get it. We're go, tomorrow, confirm with him."

"I pickup one p.m. tomorrow and confirm — "

"No — today, we'll do a brush. One p.m. *École Militaire* Station, north side, middle of the platform toward the back.

Folded newspaper in your left hand, keep your right ready. I'll be coming from your left. And keep me up to speed on Foxy."

He was gone. I'd never done a brush before but I knew what it was. His newspaper became mine, and vice versa. But it was like any trick play — getting it and doing it were not the same, and it had to be perfect. Marquardt's confidence was infectious though, and I accepted it. By and by I knew for sure that I would be skimming the difference between our best offer and what Durry would accept. A hundred and ten thousand Swiss, a little less in dollars. My bad feelings about doing it didn't matter. It was what you did, working for an outfit like TCC. Especially if you knew what it was to be on the balls of your ass for a year.

I confirmed with Durry and returned to Guimard, where Felix's redhead began plucking candidates from their desks without notice. Getting them off-balance was the beginning of the process, then letting them see their personnel folders on my desk. I turned into the Morris of Washington Square, messing with them *a l'Americaine*, talking fast, using slang, switching topics, changing rules. Nasty game, I didn't enjoy doing it, but in a short time I had a pretty good idea who'd go Frog under stress. I put my notes in an envelope and looked out over the peaceful old rooftops, not very happy. I wanted to stay with this and be in on the ground floor of Felix's American move, and I knew he wanted that too. It would be honest work that didn't involve screwing anyone, but I'd got the job through TelcomCo, which gaveth and could taketh away. The possibilities taunted me.

Al was perfect, and the hot drop was invisible. Arms laden with packages, in Olcott clothes and fedora, he passed in front of me like a total stranger as a train was coming in, slipping me a newspaper and taking mine without slowing down. Perfect sweep. Then he got on the train. It was beyond professional.

Back at rue Marchais, I counted out a hundred and ten thousand Swiss francs from the payment at the table, then put them in a second money-belt separate from my travelers checks, ID collection and other cash. When I got back to the office, Felix and I quickly agreed on two of his employees who could probably deal with New York. Then he took it up a gear.

"I was thinking that you might join us on a different basis, and in future divide your time between here and the US, Rob. Would that appeal to you? We need people who are less technical and more focused on relationships. In an executive position, of course."

It suited me down to the ground and I said it was a great idea. It was a future. But out in the street I was back to the exchange at Mme. Gauthier's. The huge plate-glass window of the Tic-Toc caught my eye and I stepped inside for a drink. The cream-colored room where I'd met Millie was packed with well-dressed hustlers jamming away in a dozen languages, but the upstairs bar was almost empty. I sat with a Jameson and looked at myself in the long amber-pink bar mirror trying to see my future. In a while I'd be forgetting how to talk with anyone but spooks. Could I replace cheap thrills and have a life doing something sane with Felix? That depended on Morris. If I came through with Oracle, I'd have served my basic purpose, and he might be open to my going full-time with Felix, part-time for TCC. Maybe. Or maybe not.

Other people sat at the bar and I studied them in the mirror out of habit. Three seats away was a quiet woman who drew my attention. Italian, I guessed, in her mid-thirties. There was an empty stool beside her and I was deciding to buy her a drink when a man in a suit sat between us and started talking.

"American?"

"Sorry, Canadian," I said distantly, still focused on the woman in the mirror.

"Naturalized?" he said sarcastically. "Gotta be a Massachusetts accent."

I forgot about the woman. My two words hadn't given me away. Still looking in the mirror, I tried memorizing his features. It wasn't easy — he was any big young lawyer/MBA type around thirty with dark brown hair. Regular features, grotty manners, homogenized voice. I shook my head and said *sorry*, meaning I was sorry he was there. He gave up.

"Harry Dreher. We're in the same line of work."

"Oh? What's that, then?"

I was doing a voice, and whatever I was sounding, it wasn't very American. I hadn't looked at him except in the mirror and the hostility was building.

"Your name is Beach and you work for a fat little guy — "

"Sorry. 'fraid you're mistaken," I said, cool and dry, and a little snotty.

"Look buddy, you're the one's gonna be sorry if you don't cut the b.s. You want to see my I.D.? Fine, then we talk. We're gonna talk one way or another."

He placed a black leather case in front of me and I spread his I.D. out on the bar, tilting it to the light, scrutinizing it, looking back and forth at him and his picture and drawing attention until he reached a slow boil. Then I shook my head slowly in amazement, simulating outrage and projecting my voice.

"You're from the *CIA*? This is ridiculous. I'm Canadian and we're in France."

"Okay, you've had your fun," he said quietly, putting his ID back in the case. "We can't talk here now, we'll go to that empty table — "

"I don't think so, Yank. Whatever you're about, I'm not who you think I am. I'm a Canadian citizen employed by a French firm, and I don't feel obliged to cooperate in any way. Let me be very clear — I will have the bartender call the police if you try to intimidate me. We've got his attention and I should think he's about ready. This isn't your jurisdiction and you know it."

He backed off but didn't move. Then he started up again.

"You people operate with our consent," he said quietly. "You know that, Beach."

"My name's not Beach, and I've no idea what you're talking about. You've shown me some documents that might or might not be genuine, and you seem to suspect me of something. D'you think I'm a *spy*? Is that it? We're not really, ah, big on spies in Canada, y'know."

He smiled. It was a brotherly, competitive kind of smile, as if we were rival journalists playing each other over a drink. Then he moved to pick up our glasses and I got to mine first. It began as a gesture of independence and ended with me slamming it down and smearing my prints while raising my voice. I had an irritating un-American accent going, and manic anger to mask my fear. Another thought came.

Think Crackerjack. Loud and lordly, looking down nose as if born rich and thick.

"We'll talk right here, with people about us, very briefly. This is not the US, Mr. Dreher. Pushing people around over here could lose you your job, if that *is* your job, and you're not just some industrial snoop. I know we're of interest to others, Microsoft's trying to buy us. Say your piece, I'm on my way to dinner."

Dreher took it like a good soldier.

"December second, Graffiti Gallery. You spoke to a scientist connected with the French nuclear commission. He gave you some information and you left."

I stared at him silently. That meeting had been clean and quiet, and very brief — art chat, no exchange of cards. No one near us, so he would have observed from a distance and couldn't have seen anything except a minute of social contact. Then Durry himself showed me the way out, and I drawled my reply in an affected, irritating way.

"Really! *Information.* Well, what do you know about my friend Alain except that he is a scientist? What *could* you, actually? There's an obvious answer to your confusion, you know."

He really didn't like my tone or the smile, but he didn't get it.

"Which is?"

"A shared taste for the arts and — other experiences beyond your limited ken, let's say. Will that do?" I smiled some more, cute as a bug.

It unsettled him, and things got more formal.

"You're telling me you're gay — is that it? And that's the connection?"

"You do seem awfully upset over nothing."

Now he really hated me.

"Nice try. How about your being seen on your way in and out of 261 Rue Lafitte three times in the last month?"

I shook my head slowly as if amused, letting some time pass while I thought it out. Then I continued in the same queenly patronizing tone.

"If you'd done your homework you'd know that my employers do business with a company in that building. And I'm not going to tell you any more than that, because *that* is privileged business information, and *you* smell like an industrial spy. They gather here. If you are what you say you are, Mr. Dreher, you will let me be. If you don't, I will send a registered letter to the American Embassy and copy the CIA home office, Sureté, Interpol, and the French Foreign Ministry. Do we understand each other? I don't know a damned thing about nuclear energy except that it's a poisonous mess, as Dr. Durry would tell you himself."

He was going to let it ride.

"Good evening, Mr. Dreher. If you interfere in my life in any way, those letters will go out. Bad for your career."

We stared at each other. When he still didn't leave, the beast got involved, and I was offering my views on spooks who wanted to make foreign policy and start wars. I stayed with the affected, superior tone, staring into his face, pushing him. The beast was dancing and we just about wanted to kill each other. The bar had gone silent. Suddenly Dreher was gone, leaving me to pay for my drink. We'd both lost it, but he'd blinked. He went downstairs and I left by a side door the bartender showed me.

All I could think was that if Al had set me up to enter through Rhys & De Loache at that first meeting, Dreher wouldn't have had anything to put together. I was hemorrhaging adrenalin, hanging on to one thought. If I could make it through the next day, I'd be golden. I was locked-in, pedal-to-metal.

Walking away and calming down, I guessed that Dreher would have a partner, and I wanted a look at him for future reference. Ten minutes later I stopped to look in a shop-window. Lingerie. The girl inside gave me a not-amused look, but I just smiled and glanced down the block. Everyday people moving through the dark on their way home after work. *Disappear*, said the manual, but Dreher had changed my mood. I strolled on, not trying to evade pursuit, not feeling threatened. It was somewhere between risky and crazy, but I knew what was going on, or thought I did.

It was the hour when sidewalks clear for dinner, making it easier to spot a tail. I drifted west through sprinkling rain, looking for empty stretches that would expose a tail. Toward the river the neighborhood went downhill, and I saw an Olympia-type bar where I could be observed through the window. I went in, stood at the end of the bar, and started drinking vodka, dumping most of it in a dark corner. Two fat locals at the other end were immobile, and the bartender never looked away from the TV. I left walking looser, then leaned against a building and made sick noises as if to heave the drinks. A figure dropped into a doorway quickly, not like someone getting home from work. I kept walking, and in the next block was a high wooden fence with an open gate. Inside was a lot full of big old trucks sitting in the dark like a herd of sleeping buffalo, and I could see another gate through them. I stopped to urinate against the fence and saw only two men down there arguing in blue-collar Parisian.

When I got to the corner I turned and ran along the fence, then entered the lot through the other gate and worked my way to a place in the shadows not far from the first gate, crouched between two trucks. There was a streetlight, and I thought I could see well enough to recognize whoever it was if he showed up again. I was dead-still, totally wired and sure of myself. I knew a figure would appear, and it did. Not big, but intimidating. The raincoat man, and I wasn't sure of myself anymore. For the first time since buying the case from Fred, I thought I might have to use it. He looked completely unafraid, and my guts said Israeli. I didn't move a muscle, just waited while he thought a moment before continuing down the block.

Now there was the possibility he'd enter where I had, and I found a new spot covering both entrances. I didn't hit the safety, but he'd been armed last time, and the Michaud was part of my thinking when he appeared at the other entrance. He looked in again for fifteen or twenty seconds. Enough time had gone by that I could have left by the other gate, and he seemed to give up on it, walking away in the same direction, away from the lot. I waited a few minutes and left where I'd come in, crossed the street fast, and went into an alley. Then I waited another five minutes, ears cocked, remembering how I'd been unable to lose him last time. Right. He was a pro, and I was making it up as I went along. Finally I came back out onto the empty street, turned at the next corner, and saw a metro station. I went down the steps slowly and quietly, safety off. No raincoat man, so I stood with a half-dozen other people and boarded the next train. It was like having a gun taken away from my temple. I stayed on for one stop and didn't even smile when I found myself back at the Tic-Toc.

Coming down from it in a cab, I thought about my daughter, and the father she'd meet next time. He couldn't be a twisted guy who went around with a concealed weapon. She was too smart, she'd feel it. At rue Marchais I made a deal with myself: deliver Oracle, then forget Zurich and call Morris.

I woke up late and stood drinking coffee at the window looking at a sky like a dirty sheet with leafless trees shivering in the wind. I had some more coffee and sat down to digest the past few days. I was an open book, fact one for sure. The raincoat man, whoever he worked for, had probably picked me up at Guimard, and I assumed he was Mossad. CIA also knew who I worked for. Who else? Until Zurich I'd thought I had some idea of what was going on, but I knew now that I didn't have a clue. Oracle made me the locus of forces I couldn't identify. The phone rang and I let the machine take it.

"Good morning, Mr. Beach," said the bright cold voice of Millie Brock. "We were wondering if you could possibly come in a bit earlier for your meeting. One, say?"

I picked up. "That will be fine."

What meeting? There was no meeting. I guessed the shit was in the fan, but it didn't seem to matter. Whatever it was about, everything important rested on Morris, and I might be able to use Dreher to get my way. Morris could fire me as a loose cannon and use me off-record for special situations like rifling drops and bedeviling area heads. I smiled as I put the receiver down, and it was my last smile for a long time.

19

Behind Marquardt's cleared and spotless desk was Jason Olcott, wearing his government face. It was Star Chamber time, and it was his pleasure. I had no idea why he was there.

"Unfortunately," he began, "Al could not be present."

I nodded as if I believed it. Then he said it was good to see me again. Another pointless business lie, which I reciprocated. After that he rumbled on about the nature of our work, and I saw this wasn't about the raincoat man. My CIA contact was so recent that I couldn't be faulted for not reporting it, and no one knew what I'd learned about BioTel's krytrons or what I'd seen in Zurich. I couldn't figure it out, so I just sat with a respectful face. Price faculty members had been dealing with stuffed-shirt headmasters forever. I knew the drill and assumed Olcott had his head up his ass as usual.

Without transition, he reached below eye level and placed an archaic Norelco cassette on the desk, then started it with a *clack*. It was so crudely intimidating that it would have been funny, except for the slightly crazy look in his eye. As if he'd seen a video of my night with a woman he thought was his.

"Something's come up, you see," he said after a silence that he seemed to think I might be fool enough to break. "Security issue. Your employment's supposed to be absolutely secret. We talked about that . . . "

When he was finished he tilted his head back and looked down his nose like Woodrow Wilson about to blow it at Versailles. As if I should know what he was talking about. The sound-sealed room was abnormally quiet without the monitors and ringers.

"I've mentioned TelcomCo to no one. It's never come up, and I'd give Guimard Frères as my employer if it did — "

"Yes," he said, cutting me off. "Well then. Someone called several days ago asking for you, giving the definite impression you have a connection with BioTel. Had your name."

I was stunned. My heart gave a single thump. We were

silent for a few seconds.

Why BioTel?

"Is the assumption that I've been indiscreet or that my cover was penetrated some other way?"

Blunt tone. I had to back him up.

"No, ah, way to know that," he said, flustered by the second possibility, and I saw again how unqualified he really was. He hadn't bothered to think that far. But I had no idea who'd connected me with BioTel.

"I've told no one," I said. "I cover my movements carefully, and all calls are through public phones."

It was true, and the tape would withstand voice stress analysis to the end of time. He nodded, but it meant nothing. After some seconds of dead air I spoke.

"Am I permitted to know who's connected me with BioTel? I've stopped using the express elevator."

Very respectful. He seemed to appreciate that, but didn't answer the question.

"Called twice. First by phone, then in person, showing some — annoyance, I'd call it. An element of bluff perhaps, but I've listened to the phone recording and think not. Could you have slipped somehow? After a few drinks perhaps, back home on holiday?"

The clue was there, but I wasn't seeing it yet.

"No, Jason," I said, drawing it out. Using his name might slow him down if it didn't get me fired. "I drink no more than most people in this work, and it doesn't affect me that way. If it did, I'd stop."

Right. I'll just lose a little judgment here, little memory there, one day I'll be an old fool like you.

Then I settled down. He wasn't going to tell me anything, and I was going to have to lay out every contact in my life, business and social. It would take a long time, and I had to keep Layla out of it. I was glad I'd slept, and that he didn't have anyone to help him. After some more questions leading nowhere it felt like time to drop my bomb.

"Actually, it's good you're here. CIA approached me last night."

It hit him like a torpedo in the boilers. He opened his mouth to speak, then closed it. Then he stared for a moment, and made a little speech on security and procedures, quoting the manual.

Ask me what happened! Don't you want to know?

"You didn't tell them anything — "

"I did not. I claimed Canadian citizenship and mentioned my cover job. I was approached in a bar. After we talked a few minutes he seemed to give up and left."

Olcott looked relieved, started rambling, reversed himself, and ended telling me what quick wits I had and what good work I'd been doing.

"Thank you, sir. But where does this leave us regarding the security breach?"

"We carry on!" he brayed. "I'll set Morris on it. We carry on. If you're quite sure you've told no one . . . "

Then someone backtracked from Guimard. I waited for questions, but he was lost without Morris. Looking in his eyes I saw that we were done and reminded myself that as soon as Oracle came through I'd be talking to Morris about this, and everything else. Everything but Zurich.

"Yes, I'm told you're doing excellent work," said Olcott. "Had to let you know about this though, see if you had any insight. You're not under suspicion in Alvin's eyes, or mine, now that we've spoken. Clearly a leak from elsewhere or some kind of misunderstanding. Quite often is."

Exiting through Rhys and De Loache I tried to make sense of this strange non-event. There was no love lost between Olcott and me, and he was a guy who would fire someone for personal reasons. This had been a good opportunity, and he hadn't. Someone had to be pulling his strings or I'd be gone, and that could only be Morris. But someone had inquired about me at BioTel, and actually gone there. I didn't doubt that, and my antennae were full-up, because it couldn't be over just like that. I was looking for a tail, and knew the Metro stop. Halfway down the stairs I sprinted to the photo booth, then pulled the curtain and squatted on the seat, leaving a gap in the curtain. Eight or ten seconds later Pox Britannia appeared, leggy and tweedy, and cautious for once. A different Millie. She glanced around and saw nothing, then went to the track and looked both ways. I left the booth and walked up behind her as she surveyed the opposite side, my footsteps covered by the sound of an approaching train.

"You're in over your head," I said quietly from inches away.

She froze. Professionally speaking, she was stark naked, and furious, ready to kill. Her color was high and she wouldn't look at me. It felt very good seeing her lose her composure.

"Just say I'm taking the day off to think it over," I said, as if talking to a child. The color was draining from her face. She'd dropped the ball and been scored on, and didn't know what to do but walk away. I got on the train wondering what she was up to, and for whom. It wouldn't be Olcott, had to be Al. But that didn't really make sense.

A bell rang, and I saw what had probably set me up with Olcott. I got off the train at the next stop and started calling Mac's numbers from a pay phone, getting his machines and not leaving messages, walking from booth to booth through a light rain. Finally his fiancée, Carol, answered and put him on the line. By then I'd thought it through so many times my voice was as bland and cheery as a detergent commercial.

"Pinko here — how's my timing?"

"Not great, I was sleeping. Get back to you in fifteen?"

"Fine," I said, and read off the booth number. He wasn't especially happy to hear from me but he sounded like he wanted to talk.

I stayed in the booth and watched rain trying to become snow. I'd got off my train when I had my idea and had no idea where I was. From the booth I saw a long straight avenue of solid peaceful middle-aged buildings, different but similar, like those citizens in the Metro. Waiting for the callback, I thought about the Durry meeting and the long cold drive to Mme. Gauthier's. Even after the raincoat man and Olcott's surprise meeting, I had no second thoughts. Part of that was professional vanity, but basically I wanted this win so I could approach Morris more easily about bailing TCC. And I wanted those Swiss francs, because I'd be needing them if things went wrong.

The phone rang and I said hello. Mac had gone to a booth.

"So Robin, what's going on?"

"I'm wondering if your friend Leni might be over here. I got a message from an assistant that doesn't make any sense."

"Yeah, she — I gave her that thing you were going to handle for me."

He was disturbed but under control, and the rest of the call was me telling a bunch of lies to distract him. It was depressingly clear — I'd met Leni at the Pope and she'd come on to me, fucking with Mac's head. Now she was fucking with mine. He'd mentioned BioTel, and she'd guessed the connection. Got pissed when they denied my existence, walked in, and blew Millie's limited mind.

I got off the line and stood there watching it rain. The phone rang, and I let it ring. There was no point talking, Mac had it all figured out — Lily von Schtupp was the Virgin Mary and I was Satan, and she'd flown to Paris to kiss my dick. Love had turned off his bullshit detector, and Leni had nearly busted my nasty little career. *Girls Just Wanna Have Fun* — that would be her song, and trouble was her idea of fun.

When the phone stopped ringing I took the scrambler out of my case and dialed. A schoolgirl walking past saw the black box and glanced at it with nervous eyes.

"Slim here," said Marquardt.

"Beach," I said, "Let's go private." I turned on the scrambler and the electronic hailstorm began.

"What's up? Everything okay?"

"Don't know. I had a talk with the great white father, and he's got a big prickly hair up his ass."

"Yeah, he does this stuff sometimes. He doesn't know crap from apple butter but we're fine. He's on his way home, doesn't know anything about tonight."

"Is this how he gets when he feels he's being overcharged?"

Al thought that was quite funny, and he didn't seem very bothered.

Back at rue Marchais I got a case of the flutters and went to my restaurant when it passed. There I drank red wine and ate among sane, common-sense men and women who held normal jobs and lived life as if it mattered personally. Then I ate some more, to keep me warm on the bike. My stomach was at peace but my life wasn't. I was feeling unclean. Any questions about the trajectory of my life had been set straight when I lost it with the CIA guy, and I knew that I had to get out right away. It was self preservation. I was determined to salvage that nest-egg, though, and work for Felix Guimard if I could.

Sitting there with my second glass of wine as the restaurant emptied, I looked through the steamy window at Marcel's shop. The only people I knew I could trust were Marcel and Durry. And maybe Jennie, but that was asking a lot.

20

Durry drove up forty minutes late in an old maroon *Deux Cheveaux*, a tiny joke of a car designed in the thirties. I watched from the bar as he strode across the parking area. Durry the Victorious, eyes shining, coat thrown off with a manic grin as he entered. He could see I had his money and he was on top of the world, planning to make a night of it. We went to the chess table corner and Durry began talking about chance while tossing down vodkas. Did God shoot craps with the universe? Very Jewish question, Durry thought. I tried to listen, time passed, Durry drank, and I found ways to dump my drinks. In the dining room he talked non-stop over the soup. I was wound so tight I could have jammed his napkin down his throat. When he paused for breath, I asked how he thought about our chances of getting home unmolested when we left.

"Yes, I considered this," he said. "I left Paris by a different route yesterday, very fast, and switched cars at a garage. As you saw, I switched again at my friend's estate. I have done nothing to alert my other suitor. To assure stability I continue those negotiations, although I would not be fool enough to sell to others now."

Totally professional. He paused and gave me a tolerant look.

"I put the odds very much against either of us being assassinated, but you might be robbed. I would be careful about returning to home or office. If you should be taken with the material, you will be out of work, but perhaps we could work together for your competition if it came to that. They lack finesse and could use your talents."

I found his concern with my welfare considerate, but I really needed a time out from Alain de Montes Durry.

"I couldn't do this kind of work for another country."

He nodded, enigmatic and superior.

"Yes?" I said. He looked at me soberly.

"Two things, Rob. First, I think you may be deceived.

Perhaps you are only technically employed by your government — wait, let me finish. It is in the nature of this ah, shadow-world, that one's real employer may be concealed."

I thought about it briefly, and dropped it. Whatever I thought about Jason Olcott, he didn't need money, and he was too patriotic to be working for anyone else. Durry changed tack.

"You spoke last time of being concerned for your safety after that raincoat-man appeared. This man Snyder who preceded you — I have a feeling about his disappearance. It made no sense. Possibly someone wanted to disrupt our business and arranged it."

I thanked him for the information and didn't mention Snyder's phone call.

"It will turn out to be nothing of course."

I agreed and remembered something.

"You mentioned genetics last time we spoke — "

"I thought you had overlooked that," he said, looking pleased.

"Information might save my life. The Israelis may think I know more than I do. I must have something of value to give them if things go wrong when I no longer have your document."

"Yes, I remember our talk. And I feel you would do the same for me, so how can I hold back? Especially now that you have worked things out so well for me.

"So. . . the concept Epstein and I arrived at independently has to do with the nature of the 'mistake' — the flaw in thinking. The apparent flaw. Understand first that the type of mistake a silicon-based artificial intelligence makes is different from the mistake a human being makes. The computer mistake is more rare, and is technical, caused by a defect in hardware or coding.

He paused to focus me on his next point.

"Most important, the machine's mistake is not productive — it does not lead to new lines of thought. It is mechanical, it provides no clue, it is not related to inhibition or false association, or inspired association. Thus a certain kind of feedback does not exist that can lead to unlikely solutions. The human mistake often contains part of the real solution. It is the truth of what is called the 'Freudian slip.' Epstein and I, among others, had remarked on this characteristic of human thought coincidentally in different articles. That is how I came to be in Cambridge."

Duck a l'orange appeared and Durry smiled wolfishly. What he was saying was interesting but vague. Then I saw it.

"To explore the possibility of living tissue as a basis of artificial intelligence?"

"Exactly. We made jokes about it. We called it the Hydroponic Brain, or Epstein's Pancake, because useful development could not be accomplished normally and it would have to have such a form. *Difficile!* Scale was a problem — start with an Olympic pool or perhaps a hundred bathtubs. But here is the key: we wanted interactive areas of thought, as human beings have. It would have to interface with conventional computers, and linkage was a great problem — how to access living matter? With other living matter, and there again they came to Durry. But the original problem was to take a bit of tissue and keep it alive, developing in a useful way. From a proper donor, of course. It can be done. Already one can create human skin. Brain tissue likewise — but not without Durry."

He looked at me.

"You are familiar with stem cells?"

"No."

"Stem cells are a current research topic, largely in the UK — two men and a woman with whom I correspond. These cells exist in the human body and can adapt to become other types of cells, which may allow the body to repair itself. But they may also do other things of interest to me. They are attempting neural stem cells in vitro. These are things you can mention if you find yourself in such a situation."

He paused and smiled a faraway smile I hadn't seen before. A dreamer's smile.

"Imagine, Rob, imagine — a totally focused human intelligence, untrammeled by neurosis, greed, prejudice, fear, desire — all the things we live with every moment. But there is the possible cost, of course."

I knew he wasn't talking about money.

"To the donor?"

"There is always danger. Forget what you may think you know — one does not yield a scraping of the brain with impunity, and the area from which this scraping derives is critical. Certainly this sacrifice comes not from the brain of Alain Durry."

"How far did Epstein get?"

"Through his arrogance Epstein managed to lose key members of his group, and without them this — *crêpe* — could not come into existence. First myself, followed by others, as I have mentioned. Then he lost his company. I suppose the new owners saw he was at a dead-end and got rid of him. I speculate he may have gone mad. He was a man of ideas, not execution — he had difficulty even to follow what some of us were doing, and he was already paranoid when I left. I helped him to be."

Tight as I was, I had to smile.

"You are familiar with Descartes' ideas about the pineal gland?" asked Durry.

"I believe it turned out not to exist."

"No, not exactly, there is a gland there, but . . . "

For once he hesitated, considering his words. "It was not what Descartes thought, it did not connect body to soul nor distinguish man from other mammals. But it was a very convenient concept which provided employment for many philosophers and was most acceptable to the Church."

"And this project would employ many scientists — "

We were at the root of his ambivalence about his work and he couldn't conceal it. Doubt, complicated by jealousy of Epstein. After a moment he answered.

"Yes, it would employ many, and take a very long time, and require a great deal of money. Tens of billions. Hundreds."

Then he changed the subject. "But more immediately, you have that long cold ride," he said, and called the waiter.

"You must find a container to hold perhaps a pint," he instructed him. "I wish it to be filled with espresso and brandy."

In a few minutes the waiter returned with an antique aluminum *bidon*. It looked like a Tour relic from the days of Fausto Coppi.

"Bacteria circa De Gaulle," observed Durry, then addressed

the waiter. "Fill it half-way. Two parts espresso, one part Hennessy three, six teaspoons sugar. First clean it very carefully, then rinse thoroughly with a lesser brandy."

I thanked Durry and watched him go at the duck. My mouth was dry and I was wetting it with wine I couldn't taste.

"Did they have some application in mind?"

"Do you Americans ever do anything for another reason? Consider that there are certain problems which seem intractable at any given time. Really big problems of the type most often solved by gestalt thinking — by sensing a new underlying pattern and making a leap, rather than through being methodical. In modern warfare exist such problems, eh?"

He had my full attention. He smiled the bent-wire smile while his index finger made a deliberate skyward arc followed by his eyes. I nodded. SDI, the ultimate cash-cow, Reagan's great gift to the National Defense Industrial Association.

"Dr. Teller is wrong this time, eh?" said Durry. "I see this in your face, and you are correct — this 'Star Wars' does not ever fly, nor does it solve the real problem, which we are just learning about. Russia is finished, they have no money. War is changing. Now we have small groups of fanatics that blow up aircraft and abduct political figures. Businessmen arrange elaborate protection. You recall that Italian Premier — Aldo Moro? A significant case. The Baader Meinhoff Group, the Red Brigade — it is guerilla warfare, and big bombs will not work. But Generals still love them."

He shrugged. "I digress."

"Why 'Oracle'?" I asked without thinking. He smiled.

"Because it embodied the idea, and I knew it would be appreciated."

We finished eating quickly. My *bidon* of coffee-brandy arrived, I picked up my leathers from the bar, and we walked out across the gravel. Then I put on the leathers and started the Trident, and left it running while we sat in the old Renault and I took the envelope of francs from under my shirt. Durry riffled through them and unbuttoned his own shirt to pull out one of his waxy yellow envelopes. Inside it was a small one.

"The key to the cipher," he said. "It has already been

delivered, but Slim specified 'everything,' eh? And now something tells us to go. I have, I must admit, some anxiety for you, *ami*. I borrowed a pistol for the occasion. You will exit to the right to return, so I will pull out and stop in the road for a while with my hood up to block the road behind you. *Bon voyage*, Rob."

I stuffed the envelope into the leathers and we shook hands. Then I climbed out of the little car and strapped the case on the carrier. Finally I put on a ski mask and liner. The beautiful afternoon had turned into frozen moonlight, with a nearly full moon that was bright enough to drive by. Durry drove out and straddled the road with the *Deux Cheveaux* then, and pretended to stall it. When he lifted the hood I left quietly, with no lights. After two bends in the road I turned on the halogen beam, reset the suspension and opened the pipes. The road was fairly straight, no traffic, and I was flying behind what looked like the landing beam of a jumbo jet. Nothing in my mirrors. After a few minutes I passed an Alfa sedan stuffed full. Soon its lights were far behind, and on the curves they disappeared. I slowed down to a normal speed, and after a minute or two a set of lights appeared in the mirrors.

I dropped them, but when I backed off again there were two sets of lights behind me. I remembered getting sandwiched on the back road after Ghent and took off, which left one set behind. What was in Durry's envelope was worth killing for, but I still had the option of doing it myself with the bike. Or maybe luring that car into a curve it couldn't handle. I had super brakes, and Marcel's tires let me lay the bike down at a serious angle. I opened up some more to test that pair of headlights and they were gone before the curves began again. Then I roared flat-out through an intersection and backed off, hoping the guy behind wouldn't know which way I went. Waiting to see what would happen, I slipped the *bidon* out of my pocket and had a slug of coffee-brandy. As I zipped it back into the pocket, the lights reappeared, and I began to push, braking hard and working the gears, jumping out of corners, engine screaming. It was getting dangerous, but I lost the lights, and only an occasional faraway flicker told me my man wasn't giving up. I decided to turn at the next cross-road, and every one after that, and figure out how to get home later. After a few kilometers my beam picked up a white fence I remembered. There was a side road ahead, and I downshifted. The lights reappeared in my mirror, far behind. I downshifted again and killed my headlight.

I nearly killed myself as well. My eyes couldn't adjust, and I was flying blind for many seconds listening to the Trident's snarl, hoping to hold a straight line. My vision came back in time to pick up the end of the fence as I was about to drive into it, and I went into the side road out of control. Then I lost the bike in loose gravel and went into a slow-motion slide that forced me to lay her down and pray, skidding over the shoulder and down a bank, with the bike landing on my leg. I was on my feet in seconds, ripping the case loose of the cords, then flat on the ground, peering into the dark. Then I moved away from the bike into some brush, the case in my hands, safety off. I was scared and out of options, ready to use it. There was no time to get the Michaud out of the case, and as I waited there a pair of lights appeared through the trees.

Then another surprise — the familiar howl of a hemi-powered Saab with tuned pipes. A moment later my boss flew by. Half a minute later he hit the next curve, tires squealing. As I was getting to my feet, another car flew by. A little later there was more tire-squeal. I felt relief, ignored it, opened the case, and removed the Michaud. I was so wired that I managed to do it by feel in about a minute flat, and get the bolts and wrench safe in a pocket. Then I set it on auto-fire, made sure the safety was on, and lay there waiting, concealed by brush. If they came back they might spot the bike, but I'd surprise them from a covered position lying flat, with an automatic weapon. I wasn't sure how the suppressor might affect auto-fire, and removed it. I had a twenty round clip, three or four bursts, and I'd never tested the auto-fire.

After the second car passed, there was dead silence. A few minutes more and I decided they were gone, and that I should be, too. The Trident was flooded and the starter was out, and my twisted knee didn't like kicking her over, but the engine caught and I got back up on the road. I followed Marquardt's path, lights off, pipes muffled, idling along in second gear. I was ready to U-turn at the first sign of trouble. Had Al made it through that curve? Or the other guy? I remembered his shooting at the range, and there was no telling what he'd be packing in a game like this.

The yellow Saab was sitting at an angle, half off the road. I saw it from the top of a little hill and rolled to a stop. The moon was ahead of me, and I'd be almost invisible in the leathers. There was no sign of life. Al didn't bother with seatbelts, and I wondered if he was inside, unconscious. It didn't look like the kind of crash people get killed in, and something was pulling at me. Not company loyalty, something personal. He'd changed things when he opened up in the piano bar. I had good reason to turn around and leave him there, but I kept watching the moonlit scene, thinking about it. Had Al been riding shotgun unannounced? That was no crime, and after Zurich, it figured. I unzipped the leathers far enough that I could get the Michaud out easily, and was about to approach. Then I stopped. How had he followed me? It would have been tough — our phone calls were clean, and I'd left the autoroute for back roads on my way to Mme. Gauthier's.

I dismounted and began a slow, careful, hand-search of the bike, all surfaces not too hot to touch. It was on the underside of the rear fender, in an area scraped clean. A small round box. He'd been following the beeps, but couldn't stop in time. I put the box in my pocket, angry and afraid. Then I drove slowly down to the Saab and found Al lying on his back in the road next to it, his face a shiny clot of blood. A sick wave of shock rolled through me. He looked as if he'd been shot in the face with a mercury load. His jacket was open and the Glock was still in its belly-rig.

There was no chance he was alive, and my instinct was to get out of there, but as I backed away I saw a chunk of blood-covered bone and gristle shining up at me in the moonlight. I forced myself to look at it, and saw what was left of the center of his face. Al hadn't been shot. He'd been killed barehanded with a Tae Kwan Do technique I'd heard about years ago in a Saigon bar — index and middle finger through the eyes and into the brain. For good measure, hooked fingers rip out a chunk of face. It didn't feel Israeli, it felt stark raving mad.

For a few seconds I felt paralyzing fear and couldn't think beyond escape — escape and disappear. Then I remembered the beeper in my pocket but I was so rattled I almost threw it into the brush. I wiped it down and put it on the Saab to create some confusion, and got out of there as fast as I could go. Running scared with a head full of questions, I was sure of one thing — Al had known his killer. He'd climbed out to talk and been caught unawares, making no move to draw. My time was up, I had get out of France. To do that, I needed my bank books, spare I.D. and some clothes, all packed in my carry-on, which should have been with me.

Did the killer know where I lived? I'd been careful that Al didn't learn about the bike, but someone had put a beeper on it. I tucked myself into the fairing with a little prayer and shot down the empty road. My chances of getting to rue Marchais first were good — the second car had had a problem staying with Marquardt, whom I'd been able to drop. The rest of my mind was a scramble of questions. The second car had never got close to me. Did the driver know I was on a bike, or was he just following Al? Who put the beeper on the bike? Had Al been playing some game with his killer and paid with his life, or had he been covering my ass? How would I handle a killer who could out-slick Al Marquardt and kill him barehanded?

There was a shortcut to the autoroute, and I hoped I'd beat the killer to rue Marchais if he was headed there. The A11 was straight as an arrow, and I stretched out, feet on the high pegs, and wound up sixth gear until the needle was floating up around 170K and I could barely hear the howl trailing behind me. I trusted the bike, but if I hadn't beat the killer to the A11, he could veer at me when I passed. I could cut my lights when I saw tail lights ahead, be invisible and pass very wide, but it wouldn't take much. Flying down the empty road flat on the tank, face and hands freezing, I tried to compute the killer's head-start in terms of arrival time. No choice about returning — I absolutely needed that bag.

There was a thick hedge on the street parallel to Marchais. I hid the bike behind it and approached my building via the alley, pumped and crazed. Fear was overriding any calm thought. I went in the back door, Michaud on auto-fire, safety off, and very quietly climbed the endless stairs. All I needed was a couple of minutes. I got to my door, listened, then unlocked it, gun in hand. Stepped in like a cop, terrified, ready to spray it with mercury loads. The room was silent, two shafts of moonlight slanting down through the windows. I grabbed the carry-on and flew down the stairs unconcerned about silence, thinking that once the bike was moving I'd be okay, and that I really wanted to live.

Outside was complete silence until a dog started barking. I sprinted to the bike and strapped the bag on, quick and sloppy. Another dog joined in as I drove off, lights off, staying on back streets. When I came to a parking lot, I slipped into the shadows and re-strapped my bags. A few minutes down the road I saw a pay phone and had a very coldblooded idea that might buy me some time. I dialed Marquardt's number at home. His machine picked up and I spoke through the scrambler.

"It's me," I said quickly. "We've got problems, buddy. I'll call when I can."

TCC could give that all the voice analysis they wanted. Between the scrambler and genuine fear, they'd have a hard time. But I still needed to get out of France, and that wouldn't be easy. As I headed south through the night I sipped cold coffee-brandy and passed through the chalk-white houses of sleeping villages. I relaxed enough to think: Durry had said Snyder was his original contact — who the hell was Snyder? Who killed Al, and why? How did the beeper get on my bike? Where to go?

Italy. By morning I was through Beaune, and another beautiful winter day was starting. I wasn't hungry, but stopped to eat in Lyon and get warm, loading up on eggs, sausage and soup, and coffee for my *bidon*. Next door I bought a cheap leather jacket, jeans, and cans of spray-paint. When I found a dirt road leading into some woods, I drove in. Half an hour later I was back on paved road in my new clothes, driving a blue bike. Stopping only for gas and coffee, I made Briançon by late afternoon and found a garage that would take the bike for storage. Then I ate again, and walked to the bus station, where I locked myself and my bags into a smelly pay-stall in the men's room. In there, I dyed the rest of the gray out of my hair and remembered Al's story of the woman in Tempelhof dying her hair and walking past guys with her picture. *Never happens to couriers.* Unless it does.

The bus was heated, but I stayed cold and began to get shaky. Fear and confusion were corroding my guts. I couldn't think straight and I had no plan, not even a next step. The mood locked in, and it felt as if I was holding onto my life by my fingernails. I hadn't quit soon enough — just had to skim those francs packed around my belly.

In Milan I ran out of gas like never before in my life. I lay on a bed in a cheap, smelly, mold-green room in the kind of hotel where no one gives a fuck and you sleep with your valuables. The radiator was hot and I was freezing. It was worse than viral flu or vomiting on paraquat-grass. It was worse than the hangover produced by the three-day drunk after Felice's lawyers blocked my visitation rights or the brain-dead month after Joe Kline died and Finlay fired me. In my TCC kit were sleeping pills and tranquillizers, but they didn't change anything. I wasn't awake and I wasn't asleep, and I had no appetite. The same thoughts circled my mind like patient buzzards. Who killed Al, and why? What set the raincoat man onto me down by the Seine? *Who was Snyder?*

And what exactly had gone down in Switzerland? Not just an escalation of the Morris-Marquardt feud. The blonde kid and his bitch-beauty girlfriend — who did they report to? *Lorelei.* She'd reminded me of someone or something.

I needed help. Morris probably, but maybe Fred first. We'd known each other a long time, and his showing up at my place after the Wohlfurt's meeting told me he was more in touch than he admitted. I tried to think, watched Italian TV, dozed, drank vodka by the glass and looked at myself in the bathroom mirror. A wild, hard, bony face with straight dark-brown hair stared back. I couldn't carry a thought from one room to another, and

I'd stick out in an airport like a red flag. If detained and searched, I'd have to explain a big pile of currency and multiple IDs, which would eventually lead to the Michaud in the case even if I left the other one behind, which I'd have to do. I needed the money and the gun in the case, but if found they'd be advertising me on Interpol, making my presence known to TCC, the Israelis, and whoever killed Al.

I stayed in the room, fear shorting out my thoughts, my scanning machinery locked wide open, with stress twisting my muscles and joints until I hurt all over. I nodded off and jumped up wide awake going for the Michaud. Did it again. Fear paralyzed and constipated me, and then my guts ran like water. For a while my pulse went way down, and then it was racing. Finally I fell asleep sitting on the can and fell on the floor. When I got to the bed I slept about fifteen hours.

It was afternoon the next day when I woke up. I drank a bottle of mineral water and realized I was starving, so I dressed, put on my money belts, and went out with the case for coffee and pastries. Then I walked a while on shaky legs and went to another place for some pasta, which cleared my head. It was time to get home and call in — only Morris could bail me out. After a bath and shave, I put on my suit and took a cab to the well-named Malpensa airport to take my chances. The airport was new, spotless, and nearly empty. And peaceful. The Red Brigade had moved to France, and few Italians are cops by nature.

Part II

21

Mac stood in the doorway of Carol's brownstone looking like a holdover from the seventies, blue-bearded and squinty in a plaid robe with a small cup of coffee in his big hand. It was morning and neither of us was at his best.

"You look like shit, Rob."

I told him it was mutual, and he gave me a sour morning smile.

"Damn restaurant business. What's your excuse?"

"Jet lag," I said. "Overwork."

I followed him down the hall into a sunny kitchen where we drank warmed-over coffee and tried to find a common frequency. We were in Carol's excellent condo on West 75th and I was thinking that she was wasted on someone who'd get involved with a Leni Hart. But I had an idea that involved him and I was putting off TCC contact until we spoke. He wanted to talk BioTel, about which he expected to know more in a few days, which was fine, but I was thinking more directly. Go to Cambridge and talk to some of Epstein's associates. When it mattered, Mac could get people up and talking.

"Waste of time, Robbie, he's history."

"My information is, it's gonna be a back-burner development that jumps the stock. One of his ideas."

Mac didn't say no but his face said we were playing in different keys. He went into the bathroom while I sat drinking coffee in Carol's big warm kitchen and looking at the pumpkin-pine hutch and table she'd found in New Hampshire for next to nothing. He returned with a white patch in his left nostril that suggested a major wake-up toot. He leaned on the table with both elbows and we both started to talk at once, so I yielded.

"Since that last call, I've had the feeling you might be holding out on me."

Pretty blunt. He was looking very large on a wooden colonial chair intended for skinny New England behinds. I tried to look puzzled.

"In regard to what?"

"What d'you think Rob — chicken futures?"

"BioTel or Leni Hartt — "

"Yeah. She's missing, never came back. She left a number, but there's no answer. And it's not about the money, she delivered."

His eyes met mine squarely and I saw naked pain. He was begging me to level with him. I told him part of the truth, that I hadn't seen her, and the words burst from his tortured guts.

"She's gone, Rob, she's gone. It slips my mind for a minute and then it's back — I go to sleep with it, I wake up to it . . . "

He revealed his fear in terse halting phrases, and I listened. I felt sorry for him, but more so for Carol, a subtle, quiet woman with a gift for old fashioned devotion. When the market went belly-up, she'd helped Mac buy into The Pope while other guys were twisting in the wind along with their families. And I was preoccupied. With Al dead and the Oracle material missing, I'd be suspect until I called in. That was my reality, and I couldn't work up much interest in Mac's love life.

"All I can do is wait," he said, standing up, buzzing on the blow and embarrassed at revealing his emotions. "Maybe it's good you're here. Okay, we go to Cambridge as soon as I meet with my BioTel boy. Trip will do me good, I'll call you."

He wouldn't be able to, but I didn't go into that. I'd call him.

Walking downtown with no place to go, I envied Mac his snug harbor. TCC would be keeping an eye on my loft, so I'd be staying in a hotel until I was straight with Morris. Beyond that I had no moves except the Cambridge trip. I needed to know what was happening in France, though, and morning was a good time to call. I found a lobby phone off Central Park and caught Marcel at his shop. I felt him out by asking about mail.

"Nothing, *ami,* but you did have a visitor several days ago," he said in a careful voice. "A tall English girl with wonderful skin. An old friend, she said. She said also that she saw you driving out on a pink machine. I said you brought it in for a tune-up and were not satisfied."

Between the lines I heard that he'd seen through Millie Brock, and probably me, and that he wasn't very bothered.

"She had a bruise on her cheek," he added delicately.

I remembered the bruise on her shin the day we met and said she had a reputation for being difficult. Then I thanked him for his discretion and changed the subject by asking if he could have the Trident picked up. When I told him what I'd done to it there was another pause.

"If this can wait until next weekend, my boy will get it. Should I keep it at my house perhaps, in the paint shed?"

"Good idea. This girl — you haven't seen or heard from me since that tune-up."

"Of course not. You were not satisfied with my work."

I loved the man.

A minute later I was still sitting in the old-fashioned wooden booth. How had Millie tracked me down so quickly? Who was she working for now that Al was gone?

I tried Durry and was lucky again.

"Alain, is there any reason we should not talk?"

It was my rotten-Parisian-waiter accent, aggressive, cheap and offhand, not easily identifiable. He got it.

"Of course not. I was asleep, but where are you, handsome?"

I almost laughed, then realized how clever it was.

"Far away with a friend, but back soon. 212-620-5944. Call me quickly, eh?"

I didn't like giving away that I was in New York, but we couldn't talk on his line. I sat in the booth trying to figure my next move until the phone rang.

"Hello?"

"I am glad you were not taken, Rob, and that you have called. I had a visit from Snyder. You remember that story, eh? So you are all right?"

"Yes, now. That was a bad night after I left. Tell me about Snyder."

"He is very concerned about you and will call me again soon."

"You haven't heard from me. Tell me about him —

what did he want?"

"You. I said you had disappeared. His appearance has changed, he has a goatee and longer hair. He caught me in my hallway, from which he had removed the light bulb, so there was just the street light. A bit like being in the confessional."

"To what did you confess?"

"Nothing. I never do, just little things. You are very sought-after, Rob. Because you are so adaptable to our country, it is thought you are still here, but I would not count on this for long. You have the only copy of the material, and they want it badly. I said you were chased down the road after we met. Was that Slim who was found out there? They have shut that story down like a nuclear incident, but a car like his was mentioned."

"Yes."

"This number is good for you if I learn more?"

"No, we'll have to keep doing it this way for a while."

"One thing I did notice. Snyder's French is rural, like that of a friend from the Pyrenees. A self-made man, I suspect, but a very quick intelligence."

I took a time-out in the hotel coffee shop and decided it was time to call Morris.

"You've reached Walkowitz Furriers of Brooklyn, home of the silver fox," said a lugubrious Eulenspiegel voice. "Normally we would love to serve you, but there's been an unfortunate death in the family. New Year's greetings just the same, however."

It gave me a smile and cleared my mind. I wanted a read on him and Fred, and there was only one person who could give me that. I continued walking and weighed the risk. Finally I walked into Jennie's unannounced. She walked into my arms without a word and we kissed for a long dizzy half minute. I'd guessed right, and it was a huge lift.

"I'll cancel my one o'clock," she said. "Keep smiling like that while I call."

But when she tried, one of her students was unreachable.

"I've got an hour and a half, but don't let's start something we can't finish," she said. Then she blushed and looked at me seriously. "And you're in trouble of course."

She paused and spoke again. "Mr. Price — why didn't you *call?*"

I shook my head. Jennie nodded and said I looked like I needed food. Then she took me to a tiny sushi bar where the fish was flown in from sacred waters, and I spent a hundred and sixty dollars in less than an hour. The *sake* was served in little wooden boxes, but Jennie couldn't drink before teaching, so I drank for her. As I did, I saw that I had to open up. Everyone else in TCC would have the same agenda, but I got something different from her. It was personal between us, and I was easing up for the first time since customs.

"So what happened, Rob?"

I hesitated. What to tell her? An expurgated version, but no lies.

"Will you stop me if I start getting into things you shouldn't know and couldn't lie about?"

"Like your being here? But yes, okay."

"I was the contact on a project called Oracle. It was a very big deal, and the source was French. Algerian French with attitude, but we got along and I scored. It was installments, ongoing. Then one final big one."

"And you delivered?"

"No, it was going to Al, and he died that night."

"Oh. So you still have it?"

There was no point lying. I nodded.

Her face didn't move. I summarized what had happened since I saw her, leaving out Morris in Zurich and the nuke fuses.

"The way Al died — he was killed by hand. That Korean thing where you put two fingers through the eye sockets and jerk back."

"Oh boy," said Jennie. "Not a whole lot of people can do that." She hesitated. "It would be — well, a lot would have to go wrong. Al was nobody's fool."

"A lot easier if he thought you were a friendly and unarmed. Whoever killed him, they knew each other, I'm sure of it. He was the best shot I've ever seen, and really quick. He never went for his gun — it was holstered when I found him."

She nodded. There was a silence and Al echoed in my head

for a few seconds. His knowledge of the Able Archer games and the Russian silos had come from the real Al Marquardt, a guy with sources beyond TCC. His take on SDI as a high stakes con was the same as Durry's.

"I don't know what he was doing there. Riding shotgun, I think. The exchange was hours outside Paris and I was supposed to be doing it on my own."

"What are you saying?"

"He was never supposed to be there, Jennie. There were two cars chasing me, Al and the killer. One of them had a beeper on my motorcycle."

She digested it and I waited.

"What do you plan to do, Rob?"

As if she knew it was only the tip of the iceberg, but not pushing me.

"Talk to Morris. I tried, but I got a machine."

"He'll be over there cleaning up the mess."

"Can't be Olcott," I said.

"Why not?"

"I skipped the part where he called me on the carpet and accused me of breaching security, which I never did."

Except with Mac.

"Well, Fred then. He got you on board, and he's trusted by everyone, been around forever. You need to touch base mister, or people will think you killed Al. Weren't you supposed to be a courier, by the way?"

"Yeah, then they gave me a gun and said You The Man."

That disturbed her, but she just looked at her watch and said she was out of time and had to prep for a class.

"We've got to go. Get a room and pay cash," she said firmly. "Under a new name. Don't even think about going home. Call me from a booth as Jack, and we'll meet somewhere. Please. Okay?"

"Jack Winter. I'll be downtown somewhere on the west side where I'm not known. I'll name a corner for us to meet at and hang up. I don't want my voice on your phone, but I do voices and I think I can sound different enough that they wouldn't guess. I'll be two blocks north of where I say — come at seven and I'll be there."

"Deal. Take a shower, Mr. Winter. Do you have money?"

I nodded. I'd be safe at the Chelsea with the freaks.

I took a tiny room, showered, and fell into my first untroubled sleep since Al's death. I woke up in the dark, slow and disoriented, unable to find my toilet kit, but I did find the second Michaud, still in the shoe bag. I'd taken it through customs without knowing it. It took my breath away, and I sat down for a minute looking at it and thinking about Milan. I was awake by the time I called Jennie from a booth, using a black voice modeled on Miles Davis's grit-gargle. Then I went back to the room and sat thinking that I just couldn't make any more mistakes. Forgetting the second Michaud really shook me.

When I got to the corner, Jennie was double-parked in a Rabbit GTI that lived in Manhattan and had the scars to prove it. Instead of starting the engine, she sat and looked ahead for a few seconds, her profile flickering in the passing headlights. Then she looked across at me.

"I've got such a damn crush on you," she said. "I might as well have been sleepwalking through those classes. D'you mind?"

"Do I mind? I haven't looked at another woman since I left. I started to once, but this CIA guy showed up — "

"Not funny," she said. "Over-thirty Asian woman one jealous cunt, mister."

"So that's how it is."

"It is if you want it to be. Or we can just fuck. Is that what you want? Just tell me what you want me to do."

"Jesus H. Christ!" I said. "You are too *much*, lady."

She laughed a throaty little trill and told me round-eyes were sitting ducks.

I surprised Fred and locked the door behind me. Nothing had changed. Same soft light, warm air, Gauloise smoke. Chess table by coffee machine, clothes hanging from pipe racks, all unchanged. He was unreadable, but his handshake was lacking. His eyes reproached me, but he didn't seem completely sure of himself.

"I know," I said, "I shouldn't be here, it's an emergency."

Nothing changed in his face, which had the shape of a doubtful smile.

"Fred, I'm in trouble. You got me into this, and I don't know how to get out on my own. Talk me through it. I know you want to stay out of the loop, but you have to help me out here — "

"I cannot, Rob. If I do, I get information which is incorrect for me to have. I'm a consultant. You took the job, you know who to report to."

It wasn't exactly a rejection, but it wasn't encouraging. I ignored it as smoothly as I could and continued.

"I can't reach Morris, and Jennie thought we should speak. You came to see me when I was in town — "

"Very different." There was the barest flicker in his eyes. "But I seem to have no choice. We can talk in back. As you might guess, I've been asked to call if you come here, but I will wait. Do you have documents belonging to someone else?"

"No, of course not."

He seemed to buy it and didn't ask about the money, just led me back through the clothing racks to a small sitting room furnished circa late Franco. The furniture was dark wood and the lighting was southern European, bulbs well-shaded. The fine old rug caught my eye. Fred went to a doorless cupboard that was his bar, reached for a bottle, and poured two brandies. I sat down on a small blue plush couch, Fred on a matching chair, and we faced each other. It was hard to read him, and his voice was the same as always when he lifted his glass.

"To your luck, Rob, which you may need. I wish to know no more than absolutely necessary. No names, no specific information. As little as possible."

I was in deep shit and Fred didn't want spatter. It was clear that those years of a friendly relationship counted for nothing; he was tight as a clam. It wasn't a complete surprise, but I'd been hoping he'd cut me a little slack. A clue, a hint, something. I tried a flanking movement, asked how he'd ended up in the U.S.

"It suits me," he said simply. "I am not obliged to be here, it is my choice."

We lifted our glasses and drank, perhaps to the U.S. I was impatient with him and put a pawn over the line.

"You respect it then, what we have here," I said. He caught it.

"Yes. Of course."

He didn't know this side of me and he was wary. Smart as he was, Fred was no intellectual. He knew I was going somewhere, though.

"No Hitler, no Franco, no Shah — "

His black-olive eyes said he was getting it, and not liking it. I'd never pushed Fred before, but I needed him to open up a little and give me some kind of hint.

"My father taught history," I said. "He taught me not to be sentimental. It's impossible, but it helps to try. My point is, while I know that this country is not all we say it is, I think we still have something worth saving."

He reminded me of an adult politely listening to a young fool who might reveal something significant.

"Listen to me, Fred." I spoke in a slow, deliberate voice. "This operation I work for, or one of its employees, is selling secrets. To a foreign power."

Full attention. The phone rang as he started to speak. He glanced from it to me, unguarded for a moment, a very bothered man. I was calm. I knew what was coming.

"Might as well answer it," I said. "You haven't done anything, Fred. I just barged in on you with my problem."

A Rob he hadn't met before. He shook his head, as if I'd been really promising for a while there. He picked up the phone, and then he looked tired.

"Fine, of course, yes . . . yes, the back way."

He dropped the receiver.

"All right," he said. "Jennie will be here. She'll come from another building. It will take a few minutes. I think it is time for another drink, my friend."

Then he shook my hand, which felt a little crazy. Was he was congratulating me on my game or was it goodbye and good luck? He sat down again.

"So, how did you get in all this trouble?" he asked in a

resigned voice. "Only what you need to say — the minimum, no names."

"What happened was unavoidable. This fellow employee I referred to was casual about security and told me things I didn't need to know. Things were going wrong, and it turned out he was on drugs."

"Go on."

"He talked a lot — about drug-running, about Jennie, about Morris's background. He failed to warn me when he knew I was in danger. Then I was approached by CIA, and it wasn't friendly."

"You said someone was selling secrets?"

"Same man. I saw a letter. He seemed to be in process of negotiating the sale of classified technology to a foreign government."

"If this is true he must be mad!"

The words ripped out of him with Latin fury. It was what I'd been waiting to hear. I kept it up, watching his eyes, queen's-pawn all the way.

"He was killed. Fred. I'm seeing TelcomCo as a wildcat operation. Using their government connection for profit."

His face stopped me. It didn't matter that Fred was from a Loyalist family and married a Basque, he wasn't that guy any more. I kept on anyway.

"The tail is wagging the dog, Fred. The dog is the United States, and these companies are the tail. The attorney general is right there under the tail, saying it smells okay. I think I've been doing industrial espionage."

Fred's look was dry as dust. It said that talk is long and life is short, especially for people who talk too much. Then he eased up.

"Yes, I understand," he said. "The key for you is that you suspect your employers abuse their mandate. But how can you know this?"

"The CIA man had no idea what was going on. He knew who I was dealing with, but had no idea what kind of information was involved."

"Still not proven," said Fred calmly, "and do not tell me

what kind of information. If indeed the man was CIA, it does not follow that he knew very much. Your employers can be working within rules he is unaware of."

A knock interrupted him and he went to a back door and let Jennie in. She kissed him on the cheek. An apology kiss, it looked like. However Fred had felt about his wife, I doubted his relationship with Jennie had been casual. Then I noticed that the rug on his floor was a sibling to the one in her safe-room. A bad night for Fred, but he was calm, almost courtly.

"Ah, Jennie — I gather you have heard about Rob's problem."

"He told me he was burned and had to run."

Her tone made her position clear. Rob not to be screwed. Fred maintained.

"Then you will excuse us to finish speaking privately for a little while longer?"

"No," I said. "I need a witness to this conversation, Fred."

A little nod as if I'd snapped up a loose pawn.

"Very well. First, Rob, if you have done nothing wrong, I do not understand your reason for leaving France."

I started to review the night Marquardt was killed without naming him.

"I shouldn't know this," said Jennie. "I'm leaving. Good luck, Rob."

As if passing me off to Fred and ending her involvement. A big smooth lie without words that kept her clean. She left and I continued.

"Our man was killed by someone he knew. He'd never drawn his gun, and he was very good with it. I had to get out — "

"Leaving the impression you'd been killed or taken."

"I tried to. I was completely exposed."

"Yes, this man was mad. It happens. The stress, and in this case drugs. But that is not to say the situation is what you think. These disturbing activities may have been cleared. They may have been part of an entrapment. There are many possibilities."

"Recently I made a drop. When I returned to my car, I found myself re-routed by traffic police back past the drop, no way to avoid it. I saw someone pick up the delivery — unauthorized, apparently, because my boss had me get another copy."

He stopped me with a gesture and asked where he could reach me. I said I'd call.

"I have some latitude, Rob, but I must report that you were here. I will say that you are convinced you were betrayed from within the organization and are distrustful."

That was it. I nodded and he wrote a number on a blank card.

"You should do nothing at all for a few days. Go home, get some rest, and eat, you are too thin. Call me at this number if something happens. I will think about all this, and see what I can do. The important thing is to speak with Morris, of course."

22

I stepped out hatless into a light powder snow and headed up Eighth Avenue waiting for Jennie to pick me up as agreed. I was in shock at what I'd revealed about Zurich. Maybe recorded. A few minutes later she pulled up and I got in. While I mopped my frozen skull with her handkerchief she came down on me hard. How could I take such a tone with Fred, who was a long-time family friend, close and trusted?

There was a silence while I tried to recall exactly what I'd revealed to her close and trusted family friend. I hadn't named Morris, but it didn't matter, that cat was out of the bag. What happened at the Zurich drop exposed the depth of antipathy between Morris and a dead area head. And telling Fred that I'd found Al dead was stupid. I couldn't deliver to a dead man — ergo, I still had the Oracle material. He was very good. He'd opened me up, not vice-versa.

"Let's get out of this damn city," said Jennie in a different voice. "Morris is the only one to fix this, and he could be gone for a while. I want to leave it behind for tonight. I'm gonna fuck you half to death, round-eye."

"You've got that backwards," I said, as she was sliding her hand up my inner thigh and sending shivers through my groin. Then she removed her hand and swung the wheel abruptly. We did a neat little skid and were turned around, headed downtown against traffic, and then into a cross-street. It was so smooth it didn't even feel illegal.

"What was that about?"

"Nothing, really, just in case there was a tail, but there wasn't. I thought someone might be watching Fred's."

"You're a fucking Op, aren't you — ?"

"Yup. Jennie the inoperative Op. It was too much, so I quit. These days I just run my gym and vet people. Teach civilians like you how to stay alive."

We entered the yellowing tiles of the midtown tunnel with

the GTI's pipes yammering all around us. I couldn't stop thinking about Fred. How he'd turned himself into Mr. Mardigan and showed up at my place. That he was a mercenary, which I'd managed not to notice. I'd counted on something that wasn't there and dug myself into a very deep hole. His suggestion about going home had been extremely bad advice; it made me afraid of Fred, and I didn't want to see him or talk to him. We came out of the tunnel and I watched snow hurling itself at the windshield, wondering if I should I try to explain myself. I didn't have it completely together, but we needed to talk.

"This stuff that's bothering me, Jennie — it's all the same to Fred. He's not an American, he's a citizen of the world. In his terms I'm a bad unit that reflects on his little employment agency. In my terms he's — "

"Parasite? Would that be the word?" she asked in a dangerously reasonable voice.

Bingo. But I couldn't agree.

"Monarchist, probably. I don't think Fred concerns himself about where things lead long-term other than professionally."

I caught a little tilt of the head in the corner of my eye. I was fine in my place, said this haughty little movement, maybe not a bad hungry fuck. But the lady was Beltway-born, a citizen of the world herself, and she wished I'd just shut up. It was my night to talk too much, and I spelled out my take on TCC and BioTel.

"Al's cover job was his real job, Jennie. He was sloppy, I saw the orders. BioTel's just a bunch of high-tech gun-runners. The CEO's brother-in-law is Menat Bagdosian, Persian financier who was involved with Iran-Contra CIA and that stinky bank, BCCI —"

I was working up to the krytrons but she cut me off.

"Look, it was his cover job, so he did it, all right? And you may not know what you think you know. I've never heard anything like that about Jason or Fred or Morris and I don't see how you can get so caught up in all this speculating when you're out of a job with your ass in a sling, darling."

Jason Olcott is a BioTel director.

But I'd said enough for a while. Her voice was going

snippy, the warning sound of a turned-off receiver. I shut up and watched snow attack the windshield thinking that she'd be wanting me to come in and cut a deal. She wouldn't say so yet, and I didn't see how it could happen. Olcott and I disliked each other too much. We fell into a silence.

"You're in deep doo-doo, Rob," she said after a while. "Right or wrong, it doesn't matter. Why push it? Why don't you just resign and write a book about it?"

"Because they won't let that happen. Don't you read the papers? That Israeli with Iran/Contra who talked too much and disappeared before the election? Nir, Amiram Nir, he started as a journalist, he was planning to write about it."

I heard myself and stopped.

"Well, fuck you then! I'm just trying to help." Then she wilted, southern style.

"I don't read a lot, I'm dyslexic, Rob, okay? It was sports and dance for little Jennie. But I do *get* it. And even if it's true, which I doubt, I just don't see what you can do. My father had a saying — 'In the end we all crawl.' My father was a proud man, but he accepted that about life."

"Okay," I said quietly. "There's other stuff going on here, Jennie. Personally. I was down the tubes when I signed on. On the beach, nothing to lose. Sleep till noon, start the day with an Irish coffee. TCC brought me back. Multiple identities, private jets, steady income, patriotic redemption. Stimulating, makes you feel important. I'm completely tangled up in this now, it's like a drug. I know too much to just walk away, and now Fred knows I know. I spilled my guts."

She got that. What she didn't get was my take on Fred, which was a toxic mix of fear, respect and distaste. I guessed that his wife's long sickness and death hadn't just left him broke, but probably killed everything in him that I'd liked.

In the midst of hurtling traffic Jennie set the blinkers and pulled off onto the tiny concrete shoulder. Then she brought her forehead down to her fists like a little girl.

"I'm tired and really hungry, that's the problem, I haven't eaten," she said after a while. "There's a way, I just can't think now. Wake me up when you find a place to eat."

Then she slipped between the seats into the back and curled up under her coat. I climbed over into the driver's seat and drove north until I spotted a clean-looking place called the Shore Lodge, where I booked a room. Jennie slept until I drove into the parking lot of a restaurant. I reached around and touched her shoulder and she woke up as if we'd never had that little fight. I'd lucked into a nice quiet roadhouse for people who like solid food and soft music, and it was nearly deserted. We took a booth and started with vodka martinis. Our skirmish was history, and we ate big steaks slowly with Frank Sinatra's encouragement. Then an old bossa nova with dessert. After eating her own tiramisu and half of mine, Jennie looked at me over her espresso in a businesslike way.

"I think I may know something about Oracle, Rob. I think it's what the Pentagon calls 'Project 38.' Jason reported on it to a secret committee last year and brought me to take notes and suss things out. Computer issues were making SDI look bad and Jason was shopping Project 38 as the solution. New type artificial intelligence."

She was over her irritation, moving toward me. I remembered Durry's gesture at that last white-knuckle dinner, his finger sweeping skyward with sardonic amusement.

"The great cash-cow in the sky."

"The simulation tests were a disaster. There were program breakdowns all over and nobody seemed to have any faith in them, you could see them praying it would all work. The whiz kids playing SDI kept losing to the ones playing Enemy Missiles. Jason was telling them that by the mid-nineties he'd have something they wouldn't believe. They were calling it Double-I then, for intuitive intelligence."

And Olcott wouldn't have been there for TCC, he'd be speaking on behalf of BioTel. The more she said about it, the less likely it seemed that any real scientists had been present. More like lobbyists and techs trying to talk the Pentagon out of a jam. But Olcott had been taken seriously, she said, SDI being a Reagan priority, and Durry was right again. There would be endless funding. Gorgeous bottomless money, with the missing link in my case. Of course Al had been obsessed with Oracle.

Living large was his weakness.

"There was a lot of talk about this procedure where you put electrodes on the subject's scalp and pick up brain waves to operate controls. They showed videos of a guy operating boats and light aircraft without touching the controls. The generals loved it."

"And Keith was along," she added. "Who came in that day needing a doctor? He drove us there and picked us up afterward, but he wasn't in the meeting."

It struck me that if she was inside and he wasn't, Jennie ranked Keith. Or Olcott liked showing his girlfriend off, like Al with Millie.

"Busy man, Keith," I said. "He was co-pilot on Big Blue when I hitched a ride. I don't think Morris likes him a whole lot."

"Well, Jason loves him. Keith was FBI out of law school, top forty with a bullet, but he gave evidence in those discrimination hearings, and then he had to quit. People call him Olcott's token Black, but Jason really believes in him. I think he plans to get him out of ops to the next level, which would really get under Morris's skin. You didn't happen to pass a nice warm motel, Rob?"

She was looking at me with her other face now, the sexy, innocent one.

"I booked a room while you were sleeping."

She went to powder her nose and I sneaked in a quick call to McVeigh. He was off and running at the sound of my voice.

"Yeah," he said. "Tomorrow," he said. "Nine sharp, Acropolis coffee shop, west side of First Avenue up around 55th. Keep an eye out for my car."

Instead of ripping each others' clothes off at the Shore Lodge we talked and watched a *Cheers* rerun. At the end she turned it off and looked at me, neat and prim on the edge of the couch.

"So what *do* you plan to do, Rob? You look like a man with a plan."

"Little exploratory tomorrow with some researchers who

worked with an Oracle guy in Boston. They won't know who I am."

"Don't be so sure," she said. "There's a logic to what you're doing. If I see it, others can."

"Well, I'm going up tomorrow morning — drop in unannounced and disappear. False name, and I'll be gone in a couple of hours."

She looked unconvinced.

"I can't just sit, I have to do something."

"Actually, you can and you should, but you won't."

She opened a mother-of-pearl case and lit a rare cigarette, a Sobranie.

"One secret to surviving in this world is doing this, what we're doing now. Take the moments when they come."

"Love the one you're with?"

"You'd better, darling." Then her eyes stopped twinkling.

"Ops get debriefed. It's how you stay sane. Al played you, Rob. That's part of what's happening in your head. He was a pretty twisted guy, and very experienced. Nobody wanted to talk about Al, something in his background."

"He played everyone, Jen, I could feel it. The guy was strung out."

But there was also the Al Marquardt that laughed at Reagan, and accepted the Russians taking out a passenger jet in their airspace.

"So he did coke," said Jennie. "Half of the government is on drugs, they're just legal. Al could have been doubled. That happens." She paused. "You're caught up in something big, Rob. And different. TCC is known for staying out of trouble and people not getting hurt."

"I left out someone named Snyder. He was the original Durry contact. He dropped out, but then showed up out of nowhere at Durry's a few days ago."

"What do you know about him?"

"Just Durry's description — maybe sixty, a pro, fluent French and English and probably other languages. European, southern French accent. He had Durry's respect, and they cut the original deal quickly. But then he was gone, and Marquardt involved Millie, who was his BioTel assistant. She found out where I lived, by the way, which I told no one. She came looking for me where I bought my bike."

"You spoke to him?"

Very calm.

"Yes. Marcel and I were pretty tight in a French kind of way, we understood each other. He didn't know anything about my work, but he knew she was up to no good and lied to her."

"And you trust Durry."

"Except about money. He's a gambler."

She nodded. Then she opened up.

"I know Al let it slip that we report to State, but it's more than that. We're *priceless* to them. CIA competes with State, and they don't share information. CIA loves deposing governments and creating policy. That fight has been going on since the Dulles bothers left. Keeping State in the dark gives CIA power, so of course Casey wanted us gone."

"Yeah. The CIA guy made that clear."

She said nothing, just looked thoughtful.

"So this is debriefing?"

"Sort of. Without background I can't really direct it. But you have to share with someone, it's basic. You have to have some trust somewhere. Morris was your guy."

"Or you get like Al?"

"You got it, round-eye. Zero trust. He was just *layered* with secrets, but he was valuable, and they let it go."

And super-valuable to BioTel. Al had been connected above Morris, and it must have been driving him up the wall. I came back and focused on Jennie. She wanted a little interregnum while we waited for Morris, and I wanted to find out more while I could. But she was what I had, all I had, and I knew it. I didn't know what I might say next, and needed a break.

"Enough," I said. She turned on the TV, and there was the new president, making noises about his disappointment in Señor Noriega of Panama, an old cohort. Lately Señor Noriega was turning out to be responsible for all sorts of bad things — lynchpin of the drug trade, playing kissy-face with Castro, thumbing his nose at CIA — very egregious. And he knew way too much about the Prez from early days.

Bush's whining northeast voice rose in irritation as he threatened his former ally.

"Contentious, isn't he?" I said. "For a kinder-gentler new age type of guy. Do you think he got that speech impediment from lying so much? It can't be hereditary, his dad didn't have a problem."

Jennie gave me a look that almost turned into a laugh, and I risked asking about her thoughts on Fred.

"It bothers him, you and me," she said soberly. "We've known each other for years. Half my life, and I'm older than I look. His wife was ill forever, and one night we ended up in bed. He was — I don't know, it was just friends drinking too much. Lonely. That's another downside to this work."

I guessed it was more than that, but I appreciated her delicacy. *Treat history with respect*, my dad would have said.

"You think it would be safe to check my answering machine?"

"Do it from a pay phone," she said. "They'll know from Fred that you're back. You know your problem, Rob? It fits you, this work. But you can't seem to back off."

"How do you know all this?"

"From in bed. You're really hungry."

She looked at me, and it started to happen. But after she turned off the tube, she spoke in the voice that made me listen. She was sitting back in the corner of the couch like a thoughtful poker-faced cat.

"This isn't a problem Morris can just fix, it's too big. Think about survival, Rob. Please. Think about you and me. Alive and well."

"Give peace a chance?"

"Give this piece a chance, okay?" she said. "What do you think about you and me?"

"Not much thinking involved. I'd kill for you, Jennie."

"Guys will say anything to get laid. Can we stop talking yet?"

We lay side by side kissing for a long time, wind whistling at the windows, tongues touching. She slipped around on top of

194

me and began kissing my neck, then tiny bites along the shoulder as I held her sweet little breasts and gently squeezed their big sensitive nipples. Then she was going through the gears, nakedly carnal, a tight little cat sound in her throat. We found a lot of gears, locked together, sometimes barely moving, and then she was gone.

"Don't stop, darling," she muttered. "*Oh! Oh!*"

I took her lovely little ass in my hands and squeezed, and she was there, with a strangled little sound as she went over the top. I kept her there, both of us trembling. Then a big boom from down around my knees when she bit the inside of my arm.

Wasn't over. Without a word she rolled back, pulled me over, and I was on top, fucking her hard. As hard as she wanted, as long as she wanted, and we were both starving. Another earth shaker, and it shook me into a deep silence. The ghost of Felice was burned to a crisp, and we were lying side by side again, both a little dazed by what could happen between us when we let it. I closed my eyes and Jennie kissed them. When I opened them a while later she was looking into my face in the dark. Then we talked. Her mother was Chapel Hill via D.C., and her father, Jean-Pierre Chen, was a businessman who got out of Nam before the deluge. A natural Beltway man, he married perfectly and advised his daughter to travel under Garthwaite, since she was three-quarters round-eye anyway. J.P. had died some years before, and she'd resumed using his name. I sensed sadness and darkness, how much she'd loved him, and a mystery about his death. And a scandal, it seemed; I didn't probe. Whatever happened, it was still with her and she needed to talk about it. And she trusted me. It was mutual. One way or another we'd hooked up, and it was solid. I'd forgotten what that was.

" . . . mother is Southern, as in men are bastards and you put up with it. When I was in high school there was a rumor about J.P. and my teen-age cousin. Later that year daddy was found in the garage, where he was supposed to have sat in his Rolls listening to the radio and forgot to turn the engine off. Loudest thing is the clock, they say. There was enough alcohol in his blood that it was taken as an accident and people whispered about mother letting it happen . . . "

I nodded. She had a sweet little way of delivering these radioactive nuggets. Along with the candor I felt quiet rage. And something secretive and self-protective, as with all beautiful women. The thing with her father was powerful and unresolved — I knew about that from Felice. J.P. Chen's death had set up a tape loop that was still playing. It was quite a life, and Clan Price came off pretty dull. She didn't seem to mind.

"Rob," she asked shyly, "am I the best?"

"God, yes! You are, you really are." I wondered how could she ask. Then I buried my face in her and prayed hard.

Jennie was sipping tea before I was out of the shower, and there were containers of coffee on the desk with donuts. I dressed and drove to Manhattan through fast, tight, rush-hour traffic, sucking up coffee. Mac had caught me without a real plan for Cambridge, and I was working it out on the fly. Jennie was silent, listening to the radio. It was the same music I'd noticed our first time together, romantic singer with smooth arrangements.

"Who is this again?"

"Sting. Used to be with The Police. Are you going up there alone?"

"With my friend Mac. He doesn't know the deal," I explained. "He thinks it's business research."

"I hope so."

"I need to know more, Jennie. That's the problem working alone. That's why I'm going there."

"As Fred could tell you, recruiting friends can have complications," she said. "And you're not exactly alone."

"You signing on then?"

"Don't do that Rob, it hurts."

I apologized and she accepted.

"If anyone asks, I'm going to say I dropped you at Kennedy," she said. "It's a normal move, and it takes me off the hook."

"I'll pick you up for dinner when I get back. I guess Fred's reported by now."

"He has to. It's how he presents it, and if he leaves some

things out. You said too much, you made it difficult for him."

"I know. It's because I knew him so long and still thought of him as a friend."

"Oh, I almost forgot," said Jennie. "Can I have a baby, Rob?"

"That's what you want to do?"

I could barely get it out. It caught me flatfooted and I sounded as if I shared the President's speech impediment.

"I just thought I'd ask."

"Have a baby with an unemployed guy on the lam?"

She started giggling.

"I didn't mean to frighten you, Rob. It was a joke. I'm not sure I can, anyway."

Walking up First Avenue, I was cold, damp and happy. There was a phone booth in front of the Acropolis so I called my machine. Through the roaring traffic came old messages — a neighbor, Mac, a party invitation, Tom Terrific waiting on a recording deal and needing a loan. Then I called Morris and got his Walkowitz Furriers message and left one of my own that said nothing. I had a pocket full of quarters Jennie had given me, so I tried Durry.

"You have reached the telephone of Dr. Alain Durry," said a precise metallic voice. "You may leave a message, but I am on holiday, and my reply will be delayed."

Strange, since he'd just come back from a vacation; I guessed he might be in Monte Carlo with his Oracle money. I went into the Acropolis and had the ham-and-egg special. I was down to two allies, and I couldn't forget totally losing it with Fred. I'd just have to level with Morris when the time came. I had more in common with Fred and we'd known each other a long time, but I felt closer to Morris.

23

Flat wet gray sky, Mac the Seal fighting his big mustard-color Mercedes into traffic before I had the door closed. I said good morning and he grunted, bulling his way across lanes toward FDR Drive. *Toot-toot! Outta the way!* We were zipping up the drive before he spoke.

"Something you oughtta know, Rob. This trip isn't business for me. Only reason I'm doing it, it might lead to Leni."

"How?"

"I saw you two that day at the Pope. It was her, I knew that, no fault of yours. She likes to fuck around and you were a challenge. Mystery man walks away before she can hand him his ass." He paused.

"So anyway I gave her that delivery for Jacques, and before she gets on the plane, she hears the word BioTel, God forgive me. I was gonna give her a little piece of that if it worked out. She goes over there for me, chance to make a few bucks she can use. She doesn't know what BioTel is and she's got no fear in her anyway. Pokes around looking for you, looks like she knows something, and gets their attention. Those outfits have their own security, thugs and all. Things go wrong, she runs her mouth, sayonara. Or maybe hooks up with someone there and decides to stay. She could take care of herself, that lady." His voice was deadly. "BioTel isn't a game for me anymore. She was the one."

"She never found me."

"I know," he said, then did a one-eighty as we flew up the Drive.

"Iran-Contra," he said.

"I didn't know you cared." I was glad to leave Leni Hartt behind.

"There were a lot more crooks in that mess than anyone will ever know," said Mac. "One of the names on the BioTel board came up at one of those congressional hearings. Pierson, Wolcott, Prescott, Pisspot — something Wasp like that, it'll come to me. My guy at Bohr, Surtees got shitfaced and mentioned that. Mean anything to you?"

"Half the people in Massachusetts have names like that," I said, and went into brain-lock for a couple of seconds, glad he couldn't see my face.

"Yeah," said Mac. "Made their bucks and didn't get caught, my guy said. No follow-up, they had big juice. So will you fuckin' come to Jesus now and tell me what's really going on?"

He was driving Autobahn-style in the tight traffic. I kept talking as if we were business buddies on some kind of plausible errand.

"That's what we're trying to find out, Mac. Along with a way to leverage our position and make some money if it turns into something."

My voice was level and bright, and I hoped it was boring.

"Money's not an issue, I can always get money," said Mac. "This kid tells me his shop has a whole goddamn phony department that liaises with CIA. It's pretty cozy — Bohr fronts for them, invests dirty money, shuffles it around in the wash, expedites transactions that need to stay quiet. Not uncommon, he says. Keeps the SEC away. I think BioTel's gonna be kinda like that, Rob."

"And?"

Mac swung onto the throughway at about twice the legal limit, then spoke again.

"This is new to me, Rob. I'm telling you, mister big liberal, that this fine old company devotes a department to spook games and you're saying so what? Sounds like you're used to it."

"I don't give a fuck any more, frankly."

The car was flying through the icy gray morning and I was sweating.

"What're you into, Rob? Who do you work for?"

Sound of one punch landing.

"Outfit called Guimard Frères, PC peripherals. I'm their US expert, they want to come over here and they don't know how. Year from now we'll probably be shopping them, which mustn't get around or I could be out of a nice job."

A pretty good lie. The car slowed down and dropped into the right lane, and Mac turned to give me a big toothy smile.

"*Gotcha!* Guimard Frères is in bed with BioTel. Betcha didn't know that."

A surprised grunt came out of me, then I was relieved. McVeigh could have this laugh at my expense. I kept it going, innocent as Girl Scout cookies.

"What? In bed how?"

"Business partners, maybe more."

"Well, it figures. This guy talking up BioTel met me through Guimard. But being out of a job for a year — changes your perspective. Guimard can play footsie with who they want, I like my job."

"You? Mister Pith Helmet? You used to be quite the boy scout."

"Hey, come on."

"Vote Mondale?"

"Didn't vote that year, trouble at home. Joanna's miscarriage. Bad time, beginning of the end for us. Plus that fucking empty smile he kept stuck on his face."

Lies and truth woven without time to think, but good enough to divert McVeigh.

"But you're still a liberal, right?"

Something in me conveniently snapped.

"Am I still a liberal. What is this, talk-radio? Sure, but I'm also convinced we're dead meat if we don't make English the one and only language here pretty quick, so I'm kind of a skinhead too. Anything else you'd like to know?"

"Not really. You were always a superior bastard, and lately you're a tricky one as well. How do you feel about the Pledge of Allegiance, Rob? It's coming back, y'know."

"How do you feel about arms for hostages?"

He replied slowly in a different tone, as if discussing sacred matters.

"They were just out there having fun, Rob. Doing what comes naturally. I used to know some guys from our outfit were into that after Nam. It's like — well, there's just something about an operation. Nothing like it, it's the big high."

"Lotta fun for an old B-movie actor and a Wall Street thief."

"Best we had," said McVeigh, pleased to see me irritated.

"Two good Irishmen."

"Sure, and this CIA President owned a bank with some of those Saudis that were in on it. Leave out Carter and we've had twenty years of these patriots, and y'know what? Waving the flag is a license to steal, people are selling everything — codes, weapons, presidential memos. We've got no secrets, it's all for sale, whole fucking government."

"Sure, aren't they all? You're sounding a bit wild this morning, Robin, if you don't mind my saying so. In case y'never noticed, things got different real quick when they got rid of Jack and Bobby. There are a lot of Directives that show Jack was backing away from Nam. That would be very bad for business. Outfits like BioTel need wars."

"Okay, Mac, what do *you* think happened in Dallas?"

"A crazy twerp with a piece-of-shit mail-order rifle made a remarkable shot with a magic bullet. Only known instance of a frontal entrance wound inflicted by a shooter from behind. Look — the Kennedys had the stones, Rob, they couldn't be bought. Like the Roosevelts, so they had to go. Of *course* it was a conspiracy! Everyone wanted them gone except the voters. Cubans, CIA, arms gang, oil gang, mafia, Pentagon, all those Texas assholes."

I sat there waiting for more.

"Jug in the glove box. Must be noon, wouldn't you say?"

It was nine-forty and we were shooting up the throughway, the big Benz dodging trucks and hopping lanes like a Porsche. I had a taste of Stoli and passed the flask as Mac kept throwing the big car back and forth. One patch of ice and we'd be airborne. He was in bad pain about Leni Hartt and wanted to kill someone.

"You've had your fun for today, big guy. Let's talk Cambridge. You're a headhunter for Research Frontiers out of DC. They need high-level consultants for artificial intelligence. Theoretical stuff. Say ten grand and expenses for six weeks out of their summer. Cut the deal, shake the hand, paper to follow. Somewhere you mention that the name Epstein came up. First name Jakob, with a K. We'd like to reach him, too, and can they help. I've got a voice-activated cassette — "

"You've really worked this out."

"You bet. That's where I fail as a liberal, too hands-on, short on ideas. I've also got some nice cards for Michael Patrick Donleavy, corporate consulting. Useful when I drop in on our competitors looking for work and peeping their cards. Shopping bodies, that's all you know — money to burn, and here you are. If they get interested, tell 'em you'll mail the details. Also — key item — names of colleagues who might be appropriate. Net-net, delivering Epstein should look like a guarantee of employment."

After a while he spoke in a thoughtful voice.

"Until you did that run for us, I never thought of you as a very adventurous guy, but I always had respect for your intuition, Robbie."

"Right, like before Bloody Monday."

We both laughed big sudden laughs, two guys who fell off the same boat and took a bath together.

"You're getting pretty devious here, fella."

"For a liberal."

The radar detector went crazy then. Mac braked hard enough to loosen me in the seat, and a few hundred yards further we drove by a State trooper but Mac and he ignored each other. Down the road we had another pop, I dozed, and then we stopped for coffee at a dying Howard Johnson's outside Hartford. I went to the head, then placed calls to Epstein's former associates at Harvard and MIT. I was after the five men of Durry's list, of whom I reached three, and one sharp assistant. There were a number of Davises that didn't seem to fit, and I had no first name. Two of them would speak with Mr. Donleavy , and one demurred. When I said Mr. Donleavy was flying out that evening, he came around. I was surprised at pulling it off so easily. There was a whole new self inside there, lying like a real pro.

In Cambridge we circled until Mac somehow found parking space. Then he pulled a Vidalia onion from the cooler, bit off a piece, and chewed it slowly. Then he gargled some mouthwash and opened the door to spit it out, drawing the insulted glances of several young citizens with book-bags. Then he was off to see

Dr. Henke while I sat in the car listening to B.B. King, watching the kids stream by in floppy clothes and innocent privileged faces.

What's Layla doing today? Will she marry one of these kids and eat him alive? I closed my eyes and the next thing I knew Mac was climbing into the car.

"Nothing," he said. "He'd like the money but wouldn't turn me on to other people. Silly bastard. Remembers Epstein, but no help. Disliked him and wouldn't admit it. Never heard of Davis."

"Might be your breath. Interesting mixture, mouthwash with the onion."

I wasn't goading him for fun, I wanted to get his A-game going — Big Guy leaning ever so gently on these unworldly men, soft-voiced and hypnotic and bearing good tidings. He could do it with intimidating charm. Another gargle and he was off again. I listened to the Henke tape twice, and heard a tight-sphincter academic who revealed nothing except a desire for the money, followed by a quick shutdown when Epstein came up. Had Epstein exercised the old *droit du seigneur* with Mrs. Henke?

Mac was back quickly after trying Kagan.

"*Nada*," he said. It was understatement — on the tape Kagen barely admitted his name, as if he might have sensed something. We went to MIT then, where Mac did the perfect interview with young Dr. Kemmer. Mac was easy, modest, tough and persuasive, smelling of big easy money. It was subtle but clear — delivering Epstein was entrée to a fruitful summer. Kemmer wasn't available, but wanted to help. He had no idea where Epstein might be. So far, no one did. For an in-your-face guy he had disappeared himself pretty well, and it didn't feel accidental.

Donegan was our last hope. Waiting for Mac to return, I speculated about Morris. What to say about Zurich? Mac returned and didn't say anything, just sat down, pulled out the recorder and spun the tape back and forth a few times until he had the right section.

"*Epstein is the kind of person who — well, he's pure scientist, all he wants is resources to work. He came by when I was pressed for time,* and then he dropped in again. It wasn't like him, and he wasn't comfortable about asking twice. He's a fairly open person except about his work — a lot of original thinkers are."

"Just not making progress?"

"No, the opposite, he was excited. He thought he had a way out of the binary process. Carbon-based, he said, operating on patterns like the human neural system. Very bold thinking."

"I never heard of anything like that before."

"Right, it doesn't exist. But he wouldn't say any more. Very secretive, wouldn't tell me what I needed to commit. Not until I signed on, which in the end I decided against. But Jake Epstein's your man for big ideas in artificial intelligence."

"You didn't want to get involved until you knew more?"

Mac's probing was perfect — normal, innocent, irresistible. I knew that earnest face and the way he'd barely nod, no smile, all respect.

"Partly that. Partly I was — I didn't want to disrupt my life. I sensed he might be onto something big, but I have to be frank — he's a driven man. Womanizer too. It wasn't going to be just a summer think-tank, it was going to be demanding and unpaid, and he'd take all the credit. Maybe go after my wife. He's notorious."

How did Mac get people to open up like this?

"He's in California, in a town on the coast called Rodman, no, Rodney, living under his wife's name, Graves. I happen to have his address because he was, well, he was having an affair with one of his students, and she wanted me to write him. Awkward. Very bright guy, but inconsiderate. You're not the only ones after him — couple of weeks ago a man from a drug company wanted to talk to him."

"Thanks very much for the information, this is very helpful. We're going to need others in this field — any you might want to recommend?"

"Well, if you could find Smith-Davies from UCLA, he's as bright as they come. Richardson Smith-Davies, he was here for a while. And of course anyone who was working with Jake at the time. But the group was at loggerheads . . . "

Durry's "Davis" was Smith-Davies. I was wide awake now, and Mac caught it.

"Gonna let me know why we're so happy all of a sudden,

Robby?"

"Read the papers, Mac. Richardson Smith-Davies is a notorious space-case genius and pussy hound — *Page Six* of the *Post*. Knew Tim Leary, they were both up here."

"Find out anything else about Epstein?" I added

"Yeah, he was in a group picture, he looks like a skinny toad with glasses. Bad dresser — Hawaiian shirt with wing-tips."

He started the car without a word and headed toward the Turnpike, pushing through the traffic like the tormented beast he was since Leni Hartt came into his life.

Not until then did I wonder what a drug company would want with an artificial intelligence theorist. Help develop the new gingko biloba, maybe. Nothing came to me and I fell asleep.

24

The dojo door was locked, which was odd, but I had a key and went in. I knew something was wrong when the office lights were off, and in the half-light I saw that the inner door was closed. That was wrong too.

H-A-I-E-E-E-E!

It came right through the door, a martial cry like nothing I'd ever heard, a crazed feral howl. Then a thump, and I was through the door. The big room was dark too, but in the moonlight from the skylight I saw a figure in black flying through the shadows at someone on the floor. Jennie. She rolled away, but as she came up the tall figure caught her with a glancing kick that put her down again. By then I was into the room with a scream of my own. I had the case in hand, and all I needed was to get the guy's attention and have him coming at me.

No problem — the figure whirled, ran a few steps, and flew at me feet first, high in the air. I caught a penumbra of woolly hair in the half-light as I tried to release the safety. It wasn't there, the case was backward. Before I could duck, I was slammed off my feet with a kick that would have caved in my chest if I hadn't turned and got my shoulder up. My skull bounced off the floor and everything went into slow motion. Detached from the case, I performed a dream-like escape roll and came up in a groggy imitation of combat stance. The black figure had turned back to Jennie, who was on her feet, behind a pillar. Dazed witless, I stumbled through the shadows to where I thought the case should be.

H-A-I-E-E-E!

Jennie was dodging, trying to get her opponent to strike the column. I had no chance without a weapon, and was scrambling for the case like a demented rat. I found it against the wall, and heard another scream. Not much of a scream, Jennie was out of it, but it was a distraction. She'd gotten away somehow, and as the figure came at her again, she flipped through a handstand to bring her feet over the top upside-down. It was crazy but it was a headfuck, tangling up her attacker and buying time. I had the case and was on one knee releasing the safety. Jennie took another bang and got slammed off a column.

"Hey, asshole!" I screamed. *"You're gonna fuckin' die!"*

Full attention. He whirled and came at me again with another flying kick. I fired deliberately, still on one knee, firing up to avoid hitting Jennie, not trying to dodge. The Michaud was on auto-fire, but barely got off two rounds before I took another stiff-legged kick that spun me around. Not as bad as the first, but it knocked the wind out of me, and my head hit the floor again. I was in the twilight zone, unable to move, about to be kicked to death, because Jennie could do nothing. The case was gone, and I couldn't make myself move, couldn't breathe.

Nothing happened. I fought air back into my lungs, smelled the fired gun, and got to my knees. Everything was incredibly slow. But I hadn't missed. The black figure was sprawled on its side like a spear. I crawled to the case and got my hands on it, ready to empty the clip. When the figure still didn't move I got to my feet and approached, very cautious.

It was Lorelei of Zurich, the woman I'd seen screaming at the blonde kid in the old Fiat. She wasn't moving, but I didn't trust that. I was stunned that a woman could be that strong. Slowly and carefully I backed toward Jennie. She was breathing, but she was out of it. Without looking away from the woman in black, I knelt beside her. I glanced down and touched her cheek, afraid to move her head.

"Jennie — it's me, it's okay."

Her eyes opened but she was very dazed and said nothing.

"It's okay — I think she's dead. Not moving."

"Good. You're good, Rob."

Her voice was slow and small, unfocused.

"You gonna be all right?"

"I think so. She landed a lot, really hard. The worst."

"Everything working?"

"Spine's okay."

She showed me her that hands and feet were operating.

"Ribs maybe," she added.

"What happened?"

Her hand fumbled for me like a small blind animal. I took it and squeezed gently, one eye on Lorelei, one watching Jennie as she pulled herself together. I took off my coat and folded it under her head.

"She called and wanted to see the place before signing up," said Jennie, her voice barely audible. "I was turning on the lights and she came at me. She got a nerve center and my left arm went dead, and then she chased me around. She was too good, I couldn't do anything, all I could do was duck and dodge."

Long pause.

"She knocked me down a couple of times and I got away, but when my arm came back, it was too late. If you hadn't showed up I'd be dead, Rob. That's where it was going." Then she spoke again, with a little more life in her voice.

"Did you ever see her before?"

"In Zurich, just for a second. Any idea what to do with her? I was thinking the roof. Like a suicide."

There was a long pause.

"She's dead — ?"

"Think so. She hasn't moved."

"Well, I guess the roof then. The downtown side. Let me rest a minute, Rob, I can't talk now."

Sometimes God smiles. My mother the atheist would say that sometimes.

I walked back to the dead woman. Her face was in shadow but her profile gave me a chilly déjà-vu, same as the first time. Case armed and aimed, I backed toward the lights and turned the dimmers up slightly.

When I went over for another look I saw that the black hair was a wig. Under it was the neat brown English hair of Millie Brock. Then I saw those big-knuckled hands that she kept out of sight. Hands that missed killing Jennie only because McVeigh drove like Dale Earnhardt. I remembered making fun of her in the Metro after Olcott grilled me. I was lucky to be alive.

She was wearing a kind of black crypto-*gi* with two deep pockets. In one was an international mix of coins and small bills and the other was empty. No ID, one generic key. No sign of life.

I locked the front door, then made Jennie a mug of strong black tea, all the while keeping an eye on Millie. While the tea steeped, I went through her money. French, British, Israeli and U.S. After that I rolled her over and looked for blood. There was a patch on the polyurethaned floor, but it came clean with detergent and paper towels, which I balled up and put in my pocket. By then the tea was steeped, and I loaded it with honey.

Jennie was coming around when I brought it over, sitting with her back against a column. She sipped it in silence and I didn't say anything. She was thinking very hard about something, but I didn't ask. When she looked up I spoke.

"That's Millie Brock, Al's girl-friend assistant. She was after what I've got in my case. I've got to leave town, Jennie. I'm too hot."

"I know."

"Do you want to come?"

"Yes, I think I'd better."

It sounded like she had a reason I didn't know about, but I didn't ask.

"How fast can you be ready?"

"Twelve or fifteen minutes. Pack a second bag and get files into the safe room."

"I'm going to drop her off the roof and meet you on the landing. We need to be out of here once she's off the roof."

"Yes. There's just a dead-bolt up there. Be careful. The building's empty after six, it's non-residential but sometimes people work late."

Getting Millie to the roof seemed to take a very long time. First I went up to open the bulkhead door, and it flew out of my hand as the wind sucked it open. Then the nightmare of getting big Millie up the narrow stairwell with warm building air rushing through it like a wind tunnel, followed by a long, slow, clumsy trip across the roofs to get her away from Jennie's building, dress shoes slipping on snow and ice, feeling nothing but urgency. After slipping and falling twice, I dragged her there by an arm.

At the edge I leaned the body over the parapet, caught my

breath. The cold air snapped me out of it, and I looked down. There was just a couple near the corner, walking away. My watch said it was only nine minutes since I'd left Jennie, and I wanted a smooth exit, so I waited another two in the icy wind, sweat chilling, hands going numb, mind sharp and empty. I looked down again and saw an empty street.

When I started to lift the big inert weight I heard a groan. Then another. Millicent Brock wasn't quite dead. I froze, then exploded in a crazed burst when she groaned again, a violent motion that sent her flying like a sack of laundry. I thought I heard a scream. Going back across the roof I felt trapped inside myself, guilty as hell and not guilty at all. Then I was on the landing with Jennie and no memory of getting there. I desperately wanted to be gone before anyone found the body, and picked up two of the bags with my free hand without a word. We went down the six flights without speaking.

"Wait inside against the wall, she said then. "I'll get the car."

That took forever. I waited in the dark with the bags trying to guess what came next. When Jennie pulled up, she climbed out and said "you drive." I didn't feel like talking, and she let it be. I could see she was much better, but after a while I had to ask.

"I'm okay. I'm tough, Rob, I really am. Lot of bruises, nothing broken."

Her voice told me she was coming around faster than I was. Then my breath caught as she reached toward the cassette.

"Please — no music."

"No music, Rob. Phone tape."

She rewound it and I heard a tough grainy familiar voice that made my gut lurch.

"I'm gonna make this quick. If you want to see your loony-toon boyfriend again, get to Brooklyn as fast as you can."

" What? What are you talking about, Spiggie?"

"Get out here! Beach won't say anything, and he's going to have a very bad experience if you can't talk some sense into him. He's taken something very important and he's in big trouble — got it?"

"I don't know what you're <u>talking</u> about! Look, I'm finishing up

here with a class, I'll call you back in ten — "

"SEND THEM HOME! TELL THEM YOUR MOTHER HAD A STROKE! GET OUT HERE! I WANT YOU HERE IN FORTY MINUTES, MAX! GET GOING! NOW!"

"For Christ's sake — "

"I mean it! Get them out and come here. Do It! Now!"

"All right! I'll be out as soon as I can."

Took my breath away, but Jennie was back in focus.

"Then your friend Millie showed up, so I decided to give her ten minutes. I knew Morris was lying because you were in Cambridge, and I wanted time to think."

She paused. "Setting that crazy bitch on me — that wasn't like him."

"No, it wasn't. I think he was expecting me to be there, and then he realized what he'd done. He had to know she was crazy."

"I told you he doesn't understand women," she said. "He really doesn't."

I grunted something, lost in thoughts about my mentor, now my enemy. An enemy with secret weapons like Millie Brock. My life felt like an endless row of giant dominoes about to fall. The first domino was leaning against the second one, and the second one was teetering.

"I don't guess you ever had to do that," I said. "Millie, I mean."

"No," she said. "Almost. I had problems with it, so I kind of retired."

"She wasn't dead, Jennie. Up there on the roof I heard her groan a couple of times. I just threw her over — I killed her twice."

"You saved my life, Rob. She came to kill, and she was enjoying it. She could have taken me from behind, one twist of the head, she was strong enough, but she gave me half a chance and then took her time. I guess it was supposed to look like a student had flipped, and they'd think it was a man."

"You were probably right about coming in. Not so easy now, that tape totally incriminates him."

She sighed. We'd picked up my bags at the Chelsea and

were circling Central Park. I was looking for a next move, feeling hollowed out, still not myself.

"Rob, we can't just run. I need to talk to Keith about what happened. You won't come into it, I just want him to know. He's never trusted Morris, and next to him he knows the most. He spends time with Jason and hears a lot. We go way back, and he owes me. I want to hear what he says, he won't hear about you — "

"Fine. We didn't really hit it off."

"Think of it as a business relationship."

A dark little laugh jumped out of me.

"What I'm trying to get to, if you'll let me, is that you may not be on the same wave-length, but it's — well, you have things in common. Keith's a classy guy, victim of a TCC fuckup, critical of certain activities. Ethical stuff like you care about."

"And?"

"And you're not going to make it on your own, buddy."

A pregnant silence. I didn't touch it.

"I know you don't like this much."

"I don't know anything about Keith except that you say he's close to Olcott and he used to be a cop. He could be critical of things within the company and still, y'know — follow orders. What's his story?"

"Just a fellow ethnic."

"Didn't like the Chili Run?"

I said it on a hunch. Keith had looked clean to a fault.

"You got it. Keith totally hates dope. He wouldn't go to CIA because they shop dope. Right here in the US, he says. 'Unacknowledged genocide,' quote-unquote. The Chili Run got to him, he almost quit. Anyhow, top credentials, automatic Op Two, made One right away. Three languages, MIT, Boalt Hall. Doesn't drink, didn't come on to me. He was rising at FBI but he wouldn't beg off on that discrimination thing."

"I thought that was Hispanics."

"Exactly. Not mad about Hispanics, but he gave evidence. Thinks black leadership is b.s. and says so to black people. He doesn't win the popularity contest, Keith."

"Except with Crackerjack?"

"You can't afford to think like that, Rob. You have things in common. That afternoon he came in — he thinks he was hit because of a TCC screw-up, maybe a setup. That's not so different from your own problem, is it?"

I got calm and thanked her. The instinct to trust wasn't there with Keith, but I could see that Morris might be a problem for a virtuous FBI Negro. And Keith had seen through him, when I hadn't. I was starting to recover from Millie.

"Your call. I'll talk to him if you think it's a good idea."

I drove out of the park and waited for her in the car while she called, thinking hard, trying to catch up. I'd thought Morris was my hole-card but what I really had was a woman I didn't deserve, and maybe an ally she'd found for me. Plus my pile of cash and the Oracle envelope.

When Jennie returned I spoke first.

"Know what? I think Millie Monster killed Al. She worked with him, handled his schedule and slept with him. She was his blind spot."

"She was up to it," said Jennie. "Rob, I had to tell Keith about you."

"That's okay."

I started the car and toured Central Park again. By and by I saw the obvious — Millie had been Morris's asset, and she'd nearly killed one of Jason Olcott's most favorite people. With Keith so close to Olcott and Jennie priming him, that would come out, and Morris would have problems of his own. Then another piece dropped into place.

"Morris told Millie where to find me in France," I said. "He was the only one who knew, I told him at a meeting when Olcott went for a whiz. She put that beeper on my bike. And on that tape I hear three things — he wanted you for a hostage, he knew Millie was coming, and he knew she didn't mind killing."

"And he didn't want me killed," said Jennie. "I told you, Morris just doesn't *get* women, and things were moving fast. He knows what happened between us last time, and figured you'd be there."

She stopped to think. "Millie was working for him, but I think she was after you for herself, Rob. You and what Durry gave you. With me out of the way, she could wait for you, kill you, and have sole possession of that Oracle document." She stopped again.

"It fits, her killing Al. She must have hated sleeping with him. Morris misses things like that."

"Me too. I thought of Millie as a beautiful rich girl who was too tall for most guys and had someone else's hands."

"She wasn't born with those hands," said Jennie. "She built them. Millie Brock was the real thing, she was a killing machine. Look, Rob, I should call Keith again and tell him you'll meet him. You okay with that?"

"Yes."

"Good, it's the only thing to do. Anyway, I picked up some fresh I.D. for us. Someone outside TCC," she said. "I had a feeling."

25

Son Sung was the man who'd broken Morris's nose for Jennie, and his Dojo was in Red Hook, Brooklyn. He was built like a large fireplug, about five-nine, a hundred and ninety fat-free pounds. A class was in session, and he stopped it to lead me to his room without a word, walking like a tank. It was a soldier's room, spotless, minimal and strictly organized, futon folded against one wall, metal desk against another, straw mat on the floor, wooden chair. One picture — the head and torso of an old *sensei.* There was no door, so he could see in when Keith got there. On Jennie's suggestion I put five twenties under a lamp on the bureau, then sat on the futon.

I expected to think things out while I waited, but nothing came, and I watched Son work his multi-ethnic group. An advanced class, six warriors. It was reassuring to have all that beef around, and I felt safe. The front door was in clear view, but Keith slipped through my guard, just appeared, the way Morris had in Washington Square. I stood as he entered Son's room, and he nodded.

"Call me Keith," he said, a busy man with a new problem. No handshake.

"Beachcomber. Beach."

He unbuttoned his trench coat, revealing a good gray suit, blue button-down shirt and a red tie. He sat down and started right in, voice quiet, pushing me like a cop.

"What's this about Jennie? She didn't say much."

To avoid looking at him, I watched Son working with a big Hispanic kid. It was Korean, hard and direct, and they weren't faking the contact.

"She told me she was blind-sided," I said. "Took a hammering. She said she was lucky the gun was in the drawer."

"What gun?"

"I didn't ask."

"What else did she say?"

Had Jennie mentioned the Morris call tape? I took my time

replying and watched Son knock the Hispanic kid on his butt and add a light follow-kick.

"Jennie thinks it's time for us to talk," I said bluntly.

"We're talking," said Keith, drawing a pack of Marlboros from his coat pocket. From that point he smoked a cigarette every ten or fifteen minutes. I accepted one, lit it, and let it burn in the ashtray. He got it, and after half a minute he asked what I wanted to talk about. I picked up the cigarette and looked at it, then at him.

"Saving my ass, basically."

No movement, just a tiny flare of caution in his eyes.

"I'm persona non grata with our employers. I guess it's not out yet."

"The implication being that I haven't been told? Perhaps I have. What are you up to, Beach? I'm only here because of Jennie."

His drill-down was crude and irritating in a genteel way.

I just killed someone for the first time, I thought, *and you're one very ordinary dude.* I looked at him as if noticing his skin color for the first time.

"I told you. Saving my ass, and possibly Jennie's. That incident at the dojo may be connected to my problem. She's not involved, but that might not be understood."

"I need to know what happened there — "

"She'll have to tell you, she didn't want to talk about it."

"Are you willing to tell me your story without any guarantees on my side?" he asked in a lawyerly manner. Not promising, but he seemed to be coming in a bit.

"Okay. I'm a brand new Courier Two, first posting France. I'm assigned to something that's already out of hand. I'm supposed to patch things up with a difficult guy and turn the situation around. It's working out, but it's loose and sloppy. One night after meeting him I'm on a motorcycle being chased up the road by a pair of cars, and manage to get away. When I come out of hiding and head home, the Area Head is lying dead in the middle of the road. I decide to get out."

"Understandable," he said, not sounding very interested. "What do you want me to do? You know the procedure."

I yawned, a real yawn after my long day. Then I gave it two beats.

"Why are you acting like I'm in your office by mistake? This was Jennie's idea, and you agreed to it. To flesh things out, let's say that I was beginning to have reservations about certain TCC activities, and I think this was picked up. I was recruited for a government job, but I'm beginning to wonder."

"You're new," said Keith in his superior way. "Knowing who you work for in this business can be unclear," said Keith. "Colonel North thought he had the President behind him. What about this operation you were on?"

I looked at him squarely and said that North *did* have the President behind him, and the Vice President, until it got embarrassing. Then I looked away and watched chunky old Son topple a man a head taller than himself with an amazing roundhouse kick. I put out my cigarette with deliberate *gravitas*.

"I'm a courier. I wasn't told the nature of the material and wouldn't say if I knew. It had major priority."

Keith nodded, a small movement in the silence. First sign of respect.

"Jennie thinks you're a victim. It may true but I don't know if I can help. These things happen, Beach. Sometimes they're misunderstandings that can be worked out."

Olcott had talked about "misunderstandings" the same way, using the word to exit an awkward situation. I looked Keith in the eye and decided he was too comfortable.

"I don't think so," I said in a mellow, sarcastic tone. "Selling drugs is not a misunderstanding. Selling classified technology to a foreign power is not a misunderstanding. My boss getting killed was no misunderstanding. I'm not a happy camper, Keith, I know too much and I'm scared. Now you do, too."

"Not really," said Keith. "So far I know what you believe on the basis of isolated incidents and limited experience."

"Do you want to hear what I have to say?"

"Of course, but I can't offer confidentiality."

A lawyer cop. It felt like being Mirandized, but I started him off with the Uniceptco-China deal. The air in the room seemed to change.

"I see. We've been here long enough, we can continue this in my car."

Without thinking I did a little voice impersonation.

"You checkin' me for brains, man? This a *neutral* zone here, safe place. Know what Ah'm sayin'?"

His eyes said he didn't like that vernacular at all, but he didn't react.

"Has it occurred to you that I could be at risk here, too, Beach?"

I didn't see how, but I decided to trust Jennie's judgment.

I waited Keith out in the cigarette-stink of his Monte Carlo. He was the whitest black man I'd ever met, a lawyer covering his own ass, and I had no idea where he stood. I was bothered by his closeness to Olcott and was having second thoughts about this meeting. He started the engine when I didn't volunteer anything, and began cruising.

"You were saying?"

His tone was reasonable and settled me down.

"Morris." I threw it out on a hunch. "What's your read on Morris?"

"Very qualified. Maybe overqualified."

"Bother you?"

"Anything illogical bothers me. I'd like to go into your internal affairs issue first."

Cop talk for the Unicepto business? I told him what was in the letter without naming the company.

"Is that it?"

"No."

I told him about the orders I'd seen on the BioTel shipping room desk, leaving out the krytrons but including what was going to Arab states through Europe. Then I threw in South Africa. No response.

"Okay," I said. "You don't seem too concerned, and I've said all I'm going to until you say something that let's me think this meeting was a good idea."

He gave himself time to light another Marlboro, exhaled,

paused, and began talking in the flat, even monotone of an office report.

"About a year ago it came to my attention that quantities of untraceable cash are generated for operations through use of company facilities to transport drugs. The Chili Run. In November I was with Morris when we saw two known Sforza family members driving away from an airfield we use in Texas. A government airfield. Afterward he made a joke about them and I didn't respond. He's intuitive, and I think he read me correctly. A month later I was shot, the day I came to Jennie's, and I suspected I'd been set up. I was FBI before joining TelcomCo, and still have access to Bureau data. I began checking out anyone who might be involved and got positive I.D. on the man who shot me. He's associated with the men I recognized with Morris. I think your friend Morris may be Walker Schultz, assumed Mossad for years, never confirmed."

My friend Morris. I ignored it and told him about the girl in Ghent, and how my boss denied her Tel Aviv origin code. We stopped at a light and Keith rolled down his window to toss his Marlboro. I opened mine further and the smoke began to clear.

"I'd guess the Israelis bought in with Marquardt for insurance," he continued, "but their primary line would be Morris. For the record, Beach: I took time to check you out in the computer and found that you're listed C-2, but with a J-rating, which indicates firearms, and that you were recruited by Morris, seen as a protégé. That impression was reinforced on the flight to Atlanta."

He pulled the car over. We were in a desolate area almost under a bridge, a dead zone of lofts and empty lots. I didn't like it, and had no feel for the situation. I turned to face him.

"If this is a prelude to taking me in, forget it. I'm backed up, everything I know."

"After what I just told you? Only way I'd bring you in is dead. But Jennie vouches for you and your story checks out. Did you know you were being talked up to take over France?"

Sometimes I laugh at odd times, and this was one of them. A sudden little bark of a laugh.

"Take over France? With my experience? That's ridiculous."

"Fact. It would be Morris running things through you."

Then he observed that prosecution for drug running would never happen, and I finally heard that drive in his voice that I'd been waiting for. I went for it.

"That's the nub, isn't it — not being accountable. Doing jobs no one wants, and learning secrets. It gets to be blackmail. Like that Israeli, Nir. He was in the big meetings with the Prez and had a story to tell. Gone before the election, very quiet."

"Some people you do not blackmail," said Keith. "Even the Israelis. I'm going to get the tape I've been making and you do the same. I'm going to destroy them."

"How'd you know?"

"Little blue light here indicates active microphone. I started recording when it went on."

He took a cassette like mine from the back of the sun visor and I gave him my tape. Then he took an eraser from the glove box, plugged it into the lighter socket and raced the engine while degaussing them. While the magnet hummed, I asked him what he knew about Dr. Jakob Epstein. He wiped down the cassettes and tossed them into the gutter before replying.

"Only that he had some research project. It was before I joined the company."

"Caribbean connection?"

"Possibility. We go down there from time to time, but his name doesn't come up."

"He's involved, and scientists who worked with him seem to be disappearing."

"Uh-huh. This is getting interesting, Beach."

Talking was doing him good. His pith helmet must have weighed a ton. While he was feeling cooperative I moved on.

"It may influence your thinking to know that it was someone in TCC who almost had Jennie killed. Someone working for him."

"*What*?" he said sharply. "You can back that up?"

"I'm going to play you something."

I played Jennie's message tape with Morris's unmistakable voice, and he didn't say a word for a while. I didn't either, and when he spoke he was on autopilot.

"Given Jason Olcott's character and his affection for Jennie, that's enough to get rid of Morris right now."

"Sure," I said. "Termination with prejudice. But when word gets out that someone is ratting, all the information on those krytron shipments will just evaporate."

"What are you talking about?!"

"One of many fine BioTel products Marquardt was selling under the table. His cover job."

Another silence. He had a cop's way of thinking at his own pace.

"What other surprises do you have, Beach?"

"None for now, but we should stay in touch," I said.

"We can't use my phones."

It put the ball in my court, and I had to think about it.

"I don't have one now. I'm good at accents — how about I call you asking for someone with a peculiar name and voice, and you say it's a wrong number. Then I call you at a pay phone fifteen minutes later."

"Could work. What will you do now, when I let you off?"

"Get out of town. Write up what I know in detail and get it in a deposit box."

"I'll need that. Chronological narrative, names, dates, commentary — all of it."

"Everything. There's a draft version in the hands of my lawyers. If I up and disappear I'll go out with a bang. They move twenty four hours after I miss a call-in."

I hadn't had time to even start that, but Keith accepted it. He reached into a pocket, took out a pen and pad, and wrote for a few seconds in the dark, using his left hand. Then he asked for the Morris-Jennie tape, and I said not before I made a copy.

"One more thing — I spoke with Fred when I got back."

"He's just a consultant, talent spotter. What'd you tell him?"

"That my boss was killed, and I ran. That I was suspicious about things going on around me. Enough that he was pretty unhappy."

"I'm sure," said Keith. "He'll have to say you were in touch if he hasn't already. There's nothing he can do for you — stay away, better for both of you."

He handed me what he'd been writing, two sets of numbers.

"Numbers that will reach me on the left. Numbers to the right are pay phones I can usually get to. Try me half an hour after the dummy call. Try them in order, then again in ten minutes. Cumbersome, but this is a very problematic situation for me."

Keith started the big V-8, then drove onto a bridge ramp and dropped me in Chinatown.

Standing in the wind waiting for a cab, I reviewed our talk. It had ended better than it began, and I should have been pleased, but I could feel time and space bunching up on me. I'd been thinking I could lie low and Morris would self-destruct, but I was doubting it. The tape notwithstanding, Keith wouldn't do anything yet, and Morris was resourceful. Resourceful and quick, which Keith was not.

Out of nowhere I heard Durry's voice, plain as day.

You must have a plan, you must attack. Countering works only with mediocre players.

My plan started with avoiding the tri-state airports. Whatever I came up with, I knew Keith would want to move slowly. He was used to bureaucracy.

26

Laura Graves Epstein was a knockout who'd been knocked out by life. She was in her forties, tall and sexy, and it was obvious she'd been a beauty since she could remember. She wasn't past it by any means, a hot woman with gray-streaked auburn hair that fell in long curves, and large empty green eyes like Jackie Marquardt's. Her breasts flowed forth deep and primal, and her mouth had a shocked voluptuous fatigue. She'd deserted an old Boston family (hers), and a fortune (her first husband's), to join forces sixteen years ago with a would-be genius who looked like a bright-eyed toad and drove everyone crazy. A guy who understood she was meant basically for fucking, I guessed. Now she was stuck in a falling-apart beach house in Rodney, California, with a rocky waterfront and undertowed waters that sometimes featured sharks, according to a large sign near the beach.

I stood in the Epstein doorway with Jennie, California sun baking me in my suit, and tried to explain who we were without obviously lying or telling too much of the truth. She wasn't going for it. To her I was one of *them*, convicted by suit, shoes and voice. She was poised for hysteria, eyes glazed, a lovely persecuted slow-brain beauty. Jennie cut in, just in time.

"This is a long story and it's missing some pieces," she said in a quiet, matter-of-fact voice, as if I worked for her and had trouble expressing myself. "I'm afraid it has to be. There are things we can't say because we're afraid of the men who stole your husband's company. You don't have to talk to us, but . . . "

But she was going to stand there and make this mindless queen understand that they were sisters under the skin, born hot and rich, natural allies. She'd keep it up, and eventually Laura Epstein would talk, because Jennie spoke her language and was about four times as smart, and because the need to unburden was as strong as the paranoia.

"Come in," she said finally in a quiet cigarette voice, and we entered a house that would only exist in California, a flimsy bungalow that resembled an oversized summer-camp cabin. She offered not so much as a glass of water. I wondered if she was on lithium and wished I could take off my jacket when we sat down in the family room. Epstein, she said, was "out of town," and Jennie didn't press her. A few minutes later, just as Jennie finished an entertaining fiction to account for us, the door opened and a tall unattractive blond boy of about sixteen walked in with a major attitude. He knew what we were.

"Sit down, Zack," said his mother. "These people are here about Dad. This is Noreen and this is Jim."

You two are definitely full of shit, said his glance. *And I — I am Wunderkind, son of Übermensch.*

"Noreen," he said thoughtfully, holding the name up for examination.

"Norrie, if you prefer," she said, quelling him with a look. He was his father's son, responsive to the ladies. I spoke carefully, looking right at him.

"We think your dad was kidnapped because the people who took over his company couldn't continue his work without him."

"So do we," he replied, smart as hell, completely at ease.

"All we know is that he boarded a plane for New York to attend a seminar and disappeared," said Laura without emotion.

Page Six material, like Smith-Davies. *Who's Stealing America's Scientists?*

"Yes," said Jennie. "We have him surrendering his ticket, but apparently not boarding." She was making it up as she went along, but Laura thought she was nifty, and didn't hold back. Epstein had left them high and dry, she said without rancor, and what little estate there was, was tied up. Likewise insurance. They'd been stuck in Rodney running up bills since he disappeared.

"It's a hard thing to say, but finding out definitely one way or the other would help you. Legally as well as personally," said Jennie.

"You want to know if he's been in touch," said Zack. "You figure he would have set something up — "

"Do we look like the IRS?" I said. "If you've got something

to say, don't make a game out of it, it's your dad's life we're talking about."

It came out harder than intended, and I saw fear ripple through both of them. The mother was ready to freak.

"Okay-okay," conceded Zack. "But we don't know anything. It's just — you reminded me of a guy that came by last week."

"That's something. Can you describe him?"

"Shorter than you, and real solid. Short dark hair with gray in it. About my dad's age, around fifty. Kind of blunt nose and hands. The way he talked, he made you listen."

Morris. He was traveling as Kammler now, and I had a feeling he was also the drug company headhunter who passed through Cambridge ahead of us. His mother was following the boy's words in a way that told me she had something to add. Zack paused and I waited, but she never said it. Then he told us that after "Kammler's" visit, a man from the insurance company had showed up, except that the insurance company had been in touch, and the man didn't seem to know. Two days earlier. It was too close, and I was glad I'd parked a few blocks away.

Jennie detached Laura Epstein for a *tête-à-tête* and Zack invited me down to the beach. He brought along his bow and arrow, which turned out to be serious equipment. He was good with them, and I learned some archery. We shot against a high bluff cut out by the ocean, with the desolate beach and breakers behind us, me still baking in my suit. There were strong gusts of wind, and Zack went to the house for his cross-bow. When he returned I saw that it was a kind of compact model that had begun as a commercial product and been rebuilt. At half crank it sent a bolt through a piece of three-quarter plywood and the wind didn't seem to affect it.

"Your dad let you know he was in danger?"

"Yeah. We bought the 'bow last summer and hot-rodded it. Didn't help him."

"Has anything happened recently?"

He hesitated.

"I think maybe, depends on what you mean."

"How so?"

"Coming home from school on my bike sometimes I see cars that don't belong here, and someone kind of like you will be sitting in the car. Off and on, different places, not near the house, but in sight of it. People here don't sit in their cars, and they have their own taste in what they drive. These are like generic, government cars or rentals."

I took off my jacket and drew the spare Michaud from the small of my back.

"Wow. Pro gun," he said, appreciative but quiet about it.

"Okay to fire it here if we're careful?"

"Yeah, we're deserted. Rotten beach and rip tides. Nobody ever comes around except sometimes at night to smoke pot. Dad liked it that way. My dad's kind of strange some ways."

He set up a fresh target and I explained the Michaud to him, then fired twice, hitting close to the small circle. Then he fired, and surprised me by hitting in the same area. We took turns, and then I put the Michaud on auto and fired a burst, spraying a little. Then he did, and controlled it better. He was a natural, like Marquardt.

"I didn't mean to get you ticked-off before," he said.

Not easy for a kid like him to say. I shrugged and there was a pause. I opened up a little while reloading with mercury-tips.

"The same people that have been coming around here are looking for us, Zack. And we know more, which makes us dangerous to them."

He nodded, then looked the Michaud over carefully while the clip was out. He and his father had been in a gun club, he said, and I saw that he knew the drill.

"You keep the bow with you at night in case one of those guys comes around — ?"

"Yeah," he said, looking me in the eye. "I sleep in the study now, so they have to go past me. My mom can't handle weapons or information, or anything stressful. That's the way she's always been, I guess. I'm more like my dad."

"Nothing's happened yet besides this Kammler; and the phony insurance guy?"

"No, but I think they have my father and they need us to make him cooperate. Kammler, he's pretty scary. I feel like I've seen him before, but I don't know where."

When you were very young, your mother gave it away.

I'd disliked him at first, but I remembered being fifteen, living in the country. I was seen as reliable, and no one would have been very put out if I shot a burglar. Zack Epstein was a year older, and had more need of a gun than I'd ever had. I was sure he was equally reliable, not to mention smart as they come. I weighed it while he took down the target. Whatever weapon he had, he'd use it, I was sure of that. Getting off a surprise shot with the crossbow in the dark, he might kill an intruder. More likely he'd miss or wound, and end up dead himself, because the reload took forever. With surprise and an automatic weapon, he would kill or scare off the intruder. I wouldn't blame him, and I doubted a jury would. A kid who killed to protect his mom would get off, and rightly so in my view.

"How much is a gun like that?"

"A lot. It's a custom job, kind of like your bow."

"Yeah. I know we need a better weapon. Dad was talking about a pistol before he left, but he's such a perfectionist he like never found the right one."

"He was right, Zack, and this is the right one. I'll trade you for your crossbow until this is over. You can take someone out with the 'bow, but if you miss, you're dead."

"Yeah," he said. "I thought about that. Well, now I know for sure you're not a cop or a friend of Kammler's. About my dad — I think he knew he might be going away, but not the way it happened. Like he might be gone for a while, but he'd make a lot of money, and we really need it. He was staying in touch, a letter or a card every two or three weeks, mailed from different places. He relayed them through friends and he'd sign with a name that didn't mean anything. He knew people all over the world to forward them, so it was easy. The cards came for a while, then they stopped coming six or seven weeks ago. My mother never knew what was going on. It was better she didn't, he said. So I like know my dad could be dead, but she doesn't."

"All you really know is that the cards stopped coming, Zack. People don't kill the goose that lays the golden egg. Was there any pattern to the cards?"

"No, just 'howdy-guys' stuff and a fake name and handwriting. To look at them, they were totally unrelated, just cards from friends. He had so much correspondence they wouldn't draw attention."

"I'd like to see them."

"The deal was, I had to destroy them, so I did. My dad was pretty nervous. You too, I guess."

I nodded. It felt like time to leave.

"This is on automatic. Here's the switch, here's the safety. And these are shoot-to-kill loads in the clip. They tear up whatever they hit, so aim for the center of the body.

He knew it already.

"And wipe it down completely, so my prints aren't on it. Clip and ammo, too. Everything, Zack. Do that first thing."

"My dad's gun, right?" He was sixteen going on thirty.

"It's a bad idea for us to be here any longer. I'm parked on Buena Vista, and it looks like we could walk along the beach and get there without drawing attention — "

"Yeah, if you go that way a couple of hundred yards you'll come to a public boat pier that leads onto a dirt road. Go right on Delmar and it puts you on B-V."

"Good, thanks."

"Another thing — I think I know where my dad might be."

"Oh?"

"Dad would never come out and say things, he'd drop hints. He had an old globe in his study that he never looked at, but one day he started spinning it, and talking about the Caribbean, what a great place it was for a vacation. It was a joke, he'd never take a vacation. He needs to have his stuff around him all the time, files, computers, books, what he needs to work with. He came back to this Caribbean thing again, and just sort of dropped it that St. Marcus was the place to be down there, with all the millionaires. I think I was supposed to let that out if something happened. He really hates rich people."

I remembered Durry being cute about St. Marcus at our first dinner, as if it should mean something to me.

"One more thing. I think maybe Mom used to know Kammler, or maybe she'd met him before, but didn't want to say.

He didn't take off his jacket either, I guess he had a gun too."

I nodded, sure that we'd barely missed Morris. When we went back inside, Zack disappeared into his room to stash the Michaud. The two women were sipping coffee like faculty wives. Iced tequila-coffee.

"We've got to go, Noreen," I said. "We have a drive ahead of us."

"Yes, we really do," said Jennie to Laura in a warm voice. "I'll call."

Epstein's stunning wife nodded in complacent agreement, never looked at me, and didn't seem to notice that we left by the back door.

"She's crazy," said Jennie as we walked down the beach.

"I think he does that to people."

"She was always crazy. Jake is talking to her in her dreams — everything is going to work out and not to worry, just trust the crystals. She showed me her crystals and explained how they work."

Then she noticed.

"*You're not wearing your jacket!*" she said, looking me up and down in sudden rage. "Oh boy! You let him have the gun, didn't you?! Damn it, he'll get himself *killed!*"

"Traded him for his crossbow. It's in my case."

"How *could* you?"

"With the bow there's no second shot — miss and you're dead. The Michaud's auto-fire."

I'd never seen her angry. Her eyes were smoldering, her face set. Then she exploded again.

"How *could* you, Rob! He's fifteen years old!"

"Sixteen this summer, and he needed it, Jennie. He sleeps in the den so he can see his mother's door, and he keeps the 'bow next to his bed. Zack can handle a gun, believe me, I checked him out. He's trained, he's in a gun club, and he's a minor. If he shoots some SOB who breaks in, it's over and he's a hero. He is one smart kid, Jennie."

"They're *wack*, Rob, they're all crazy! It's so *dangerous*. And now you have no weapon."

She was so angry that I didn't say any more. I was stung. I

still had the other Michaud and Zack's risk was greatly reduced, but just like that we were on a new footing, negative and uncertain. I hadn't seen the righteous rich girl before, but I understood, and I did something I never could with Felice. I shut down and stayed on course as if it was a minor disagreement When we were in the car I spoke.

"You ran tape?"

The recording was perfect, but there wasn't anything there until toward the end.

"Do you know a Doctor Donegan?"

"Yes. I doubt he's connected. He was on Jake's enemy list — he didn't want to join the group. I think he wanted to be paid. Jake put everything he had into research, and everyone was supposed to cooperate. Not to expect money, just meals."

"There was a Doctor Derry, too, or Dearie — "

"Durry. He was French, another enemy. Jake has a lot of enemies. He said it was like Teller making the H-Bomb. Durry was supposed to be very good. They really got along, but then something happened. Something went wrong."

Her voice had no affect, as if it had been created electronically to answer phones.

The little car rolled south along the coast road and we were silent while Jennie made a list of calls and I tried to figure out what to do with this dangerous truce. No matter if I made sense, she wasn't buying it. I had a next move, but it wasn't time.

27

The silence extended until Jennie said we should look for a phone. I spotted a booth next to a deserted Exxon station, where I dialed Keith and looked out over a dusty golden field behind the station. Keith finally answered and I asked for 'Astrid' in a Nordic drawl. He chuckled.

"You've got the wrong number, fella."

Keith was not a laughing guy, and I knew things were okay. While he was on his way to the pay phone, Jennie called Olcott. She identified herself as Charmaine and asked for Crackerjack in a very social voice. He was out, and her exit was as deft as her opening. Then she spoke, all business.

"He's at the club," she said. "I doubt he knows anything — he hears what Morris wants him to hear. Jill can read him, and I can read her. Normal day at the office."

I had an idea to try Durry then. The phone answered after one ring.

"Alain speaking. I am on extended leave of absence, but will be able to return calls of significance from time to time."

"Something's changed," I said. "Now he's announcing an extended absence."

Another disappeared scientist? That reminded me of Cambridge, and I called Mac. His fiancée Carol answered, her voice shaky, very quiet.

"You haven't heard," she said.

"What is it, Carol? Are you okay?"

"Sort of. Mac's dead, Rob."

My reaction was so compromised by selfish calculation that no words would come. For a moment I forgot that another human being was there, someone I'd always liked and respected.

"I'm truly sorry, Carol. How terrible for you — if I were anywhere near, I'd be there."

Stupid empty words, but the best I could do. She didn't mind.

"I'd want you to be, Rob. It's just been a nightmare the last month. I could see it coming, he was destroying himself. I found some cocaine one night in a shoe, a whole bag of it, and there was obviously some woman involved. He drove off the elevated part of the West Side highway, through the guard-rail. He was driving very fast and witnesses said the car suddenly went out of control and went over."

"What are you saying, Carol?"

"He was living in hell, Rob. First there were calls from some man who wouldn't identify himself, and then other calls — IRS, FBI, some woman with a foreign accent. They'd tapped his phone, I guess. God knows what he was up to. He was just going to pieces — he punched out a bartender who was going to sue, and his partners wanted him out. He didn't want to put me through it — he wanted to be sure I got the insurance."

"I saw him last week — what was going on, Carol?"

"He wouldn't say, he never would, you know how he was. He just loved it out on the edge. Anything not quite legal."

She was beginning to sound better, as if she'd been needing to talk to me about it. As if I'd been his really good friend, someone to be trusted. I hated myself.

"It was as if everything had finally linked up — his insider trading buddies and those Irish pals that never said anything and the tax people and then the FBI. It was like he was surrounded. I'd walk in the room and get a snatch of phone conversation and he'd be denying something and change the subject or hang up. It could have been anything, Rob. He loved a game."

No, I thought. It wouldn't be just anything, not with Mac. People liked him, and they bent situations for him, and he did it for them, that was how his life worked.

"You think someone did this to him, did something to his car?"

"Maybe. I think someone who knew a lot about him gave his name out in all directions and was watching him squirm. Waiting for him to talk, but he never would, of course. Irish *omerta*. Maybe it's better that it's over. It had been over between us for a while, but we didn't know how to end it. I — I just couldn't take it, Rob. I could take him, but not . . . that life."

232

Watching him squirm. That would be Eulenspiegel, giving his name out and hoping to flush a rogue courier. Carol said something else. Her voice didn't crack, just stayed quiet and sad. I hadn't realized how well she knew him.

"Nobody could take it, Carol. I'll call as soon as I'm back."

"You were his best friend. You were the only one who could get him to drop the mask. He respected you. Please call when you're in New York, Rob. I need to talk about it, and you're the only one I could talk to. I just keep trying to think who set him up, whether I know the person. Some woman who took him too seriously, I don't doubt."

It was hard to keep talking. I'd got Mac killed and all I could do was say I was sorry. A sorry excuse was more like it. The beast was up and turning on me, so I got off the phone. Then I stood there feeling Jennie's eyes on me across the silence.

"My friend Mac, who was helping me research BioTel — his fiancée. Drove his car off the West Side Highway, unassisted according to witnesses, maybe intentional. He started getting these phone calls. Morris probably, he'd know things about him from when I was vetted. Then it was other agencies. Never would have happened if I hadn't involved him."

I got it out in a dry, mechanical voice. She replied sharply from a distance.

"You know, Rob, this talent for self-criticism — "

I looked at her. I didn't care what she thought.

"It's *dangerous*," she said, calm and professional. "You're taking yourself apart, and you can't afford to do that."

The beast laughed. I felt a grimace pass over my face and looked off into the empty blue and tan California horizon for a few seconds. I'd been shut down since our disagreement about Zack, and talking to Carol had locked it in. All I could think was that I was alive and Mac was not. That he'd be alive except for me.

I got clear of my guts and called Keith back. "Hello?"

"Astrid?"

"Not in this life."

He said it with that little half-laugh in his voice again, and I was glad to have something to do. Keith was very relaxed, a phone man at heart, more at ease on a safe line than in person, at least with me.

"Hi Keith, what's new at the office?"

"Not much yet, except that I owe a consultant twelve hundred dollars for some computer work. A look-see. I'd like him to keep going, but his time is expensive."

And unlike me, Keith didn't have a stack of Swiss francs. I assumed he was hacking into BioTel and wanted me to ante up. My project, my expense. The cost was nothing, but I didn't want Keith to know how much ready money I had.

"If you paid him and put another five in his hand would it hold him for a while?"

"Long enough to see if we're going all the way."

"No problem except delivery. What about planting a virus to screw things up?"

"Absolutely *not*. Give us away and probably spill over into missile control. One more shot and I should know what's in there. The kid is very good. I'm not bad myself, but this is a specialist's game. Anything on your end?"

"Not much. If Epstein's alive he might be somewhere in the Caribbean. Where did you used to go down there?"

"St. Croix. I'd stay there, and the kind of boat they'd rent, they weren't going far. But this will interest you: Morris is keeping the lid on — he still hasn't told Jason anything about you."

"That phone tape is pretty incriminating. Anything else?"

"No, that's it. Call me tomorrow, but no messages, just try later. Around this time is good. And I need that write-up. Include the phone tape with it."

"Right. *Ciao.*"

I guessed that Clean Keith didn't go to St. Marcus for the same reason he wasn't in the SDI meeting Jennie attended — Project 38 wasn't TCC business. I turned to her.

"Well, Keith found someone to get him into the BioTel database. And Morris still isn't telling anyone about me."

"Morris wants you for himself, Rob. You know too much."

It didn't really hit me. *Mac's dead*, I was thinking. No more free drinks and bad jokes at the Pope. It could be FBI, or one of

Mrs. Thatcher's roving undercover units, but they wouldn't do it so artfully. That avalanche of phone calls Carol mentioned smelled like Eulenspiegel. I remembered how I'd drop into The Pope during my bad year, and how he'd stand me drinks and give me a new hair-dye for my birthday. It was still sinking in. I was under control, but I was ready to kill. Wanting to. Having made its point, the beast took a break.

An hour down the road we found a resort hotel and had an uncomfortable meal while looking out over the Pacific and drinking a lot of wine, two stubborn people losing contact at the wrong time. Later I lay awake beside her remembering Mac the Seal, who'd been my friend and trusted me. Thinking how truly bad it was to deceive a friend and use him, and then see him go down. I could blame BioTel or Morris or whoever, but it was me. And I wanted to be alone. After two divorces I was used to living alone and going inside myself to work things out on my own. Jennie slept, as she always could. I dozed a little, and eventually a cool foggy Monterey dawn came up.

I was in a foul, distant mood at breakfast, staring over the ocean, drinking water, my stomach rancid. It was agreed we'd drive to LA, return to New York and meet Keith.

"We should book flights now," said Jennie.

"That's crazy — our plastic's hot by now."

She gave me an unfucked look.

"They wouldn't move fast enough — "

Avoid credit cards whenever possible except to establish a trail.

"Really? You think it's beyond Morris to notify the airlines on — what's it called? A timely basis? With his connections? He's had two days."

Jennie looked at me the way women look at men they're getting tired of. I waved for the check.

"What is it, Rob?" she asked in a calm voice.

I stared at her, guts boiling.

"A person very dear to me has just recently left this world darling, and I fear I may have been involved." I said it in a cruel voice and kept going. "Tell you something else, lady — your security's pretty loose, and not just about the plastic. First time I came back from France I went into your files, that's how I knew who you worked for."

Okay, said her eyes, *you win, can we move on?* I looked down at my eggs. I was out of control, but the beast wasn't involved. I was just a crazed guilty sarcastic SOB, and it ended there. Above Jennie's Caucasian features were those patient Asian eyes, and the beast couldn't deal with that.

We walked to the car in silence, put our bags in the trunk, and looked for a phone booth, where Jennie called Boris-the-Butcher. I could hear Morris's voice: *Balding, Khrushchev face, nose like a potato.* Then I remembered something she'd said.

He wants you for himself. I'd lost it in the shock of Mac's death.

"'ullo!!" she cried into the phone. "Iss Tanya! They letting me out finally, you heard? The glasnost."

It was a pretty good accent, hoarse and crude.

"Really Boris? Dunt liking weather? Snow is beautiful you always saying."

A pause.

"You miss mama. Dunt drink too much wudka, Boris, just week-end. Okay, I see you, bubby."

Then she passed on the news.

"Boris says he can't stand the weather and my father would get sick from it. That's you with the gray hair. And he got off the line fast, also bad, because Boris wants to know me better."

"He knows we're together — "

"You got it," she said dryly. "Morris is leaking, but only to special friends."

We got back in the little Ford and drove in silence. Half an hour later Jennie took one of her rare cigarettes from the mother-of-pearl case. After a while she put it in her mouth. Eventually she lit it, smoked in silence, stubbed it out. Finally she said I'd been right about using our plastic. It almost killed her to say it. She turned on the radio and it was John Lennon sitting on his cornflake singing his guts out.

I am the Walrus . . . goo-goo-ga-joob!

I asked her to open the case, and watched from the corner of my eye. She looked at the crossbow without saying anything.

Then I told her how to take out the false bottom, and she saw the second Michaud.

"*Oh.*" Then she flipped through the stack of francs. "Some courier. You seem to have at least a hundred thousand dollars here. And I guess this envelope contains the document that's making everyone crazy."

"Only copy if Durry was telling the truth, and I think he was."

I never saw anyone do a one-eighty so quick and clean. Our argument was over, and she was pleased with me in a way that turned the page and changed everything. So she'd made a mistake about the plastic. I'd made a few myself.

"Fred sold me this contraption, by the way. Before I signed on, like a test."

"He's a master of the game, Federico." She paused. "Rob, I do understand about the boy. I didn't want to see it, but you're right, he was going to use this thing and get himself killed."

Another pause.

"That poor foolish woman and that boy she doesn't deserve."

"He'll be fine, he's not going to take it to school or show it to his girlfriend. His father was in touch, by the way. Unsigned postcards, but the cards stopped last month. Zack thinks he's dead, but he's decided not to tell his mother."

"He's been gone since November — what happened around then?"

"*Moi, cherie.* When Durry got back on line they needed poppa at the plant."

"Those cards he was sending — I wonder why they stopped." Her voice was calm and professional.

"Someone caught on, I suppose. Durry took a trip to the Caribbean, and Epstein talked about a trip there. He named St. Marcus, and let the boy know it was significant. And I'm sure this Kammler is Morris."

"*I know!* That's why I was so angry about the gun."

"Not much choice, he'd use whatever he has."

"If he shoots someone they'll trace the ballistics."

"I bought that one myself, and the Swiss don't help foreign

cops. Company like that stays in business by being discreet."

"Fred was right, you fit right in."

"I'm not real professional, Jen," I said after a while. "I wasn't too cool after Millie for sure. And Laura Epstein was all you, babe, she was never going to talk to me."

We were back in sync, but the blue was going out of the sky as we churned south toward the smog cloud over L.A. It was time for a next move, and I was tapped out. For the first time I seriously thought about coming in before I got us killed. If Jennie said it could be done, it could be done, but Olcott getting her back would be part of the deal. He wouldn't let it happen any other way. He was a vindictive man who didn't like me, and Oracle dressed up as Project 38 was big enough that he could authorize anything that came to mind once he had me. He'd make sure we paid, especially me. Jennie was too proud to think anyone could handle her that way, but I took it for fact and hated the man. Only woman I'd been willing to fight for in years. He'd probably fuck her around, too, because he was a selfish entitled old SOB. And if I said what I was thinking we'd have a really terrible fight, so I didn't.

Stay alive and try to be of some use to your daughter.

Jennie booked our flights at LAX while I sat in the car reading the papers and breathing air conditioned smog. Iran-Contra was still kicking around, but damage control was really excellent under the new administration, whitewash flowing from many hoses. Congress was the villain now, a collection of meddling fools, and everyone important was safe, including the adoptive Texan, spook emeritus and Saudi-buddy running the country. I moved on to the horoscopes. Sit tight, said the stars, Mercury is retrograde.

"I booked us on different flights," said Jennie, climbing in. "You're in first class."

"What's that about? You cutting me loose?"

"Don't make jokes like that, all right? And our little fight, I really didn't like that either. You can be right without the stink, okay? So anyway — separate flights because Morris will be looking for a couple. First class because you can stretch out and sleep. You need rest, I need clothes, and we both need haircuts. I know the right place.

The hair place was off Rodeo Drive, flossy, busy, and full of rich twits. Jennie hit like a shark with a winning smile. A hundred to the gatekeeper and we had priority. For another fifteen hundred plus tips we were different people — Jennie in dreadlocks, me with a punky-looking crest of blond hair that made me look ten years younger. I'd never have thought of it; I was too burnt even to know I was hungry, but Jennie got us to a deli. Eating blintzes in a big pink room full of lacquered ladies, I was thinking about Morris, waiting for the other shoe to fall.

"You don't look right," said Jennie.

"It's the hair. And I need a drink."

"No, that's what you don't need. You're losing weight, Cock Robin, you look like you're in training for a marathon."

"*Vuelta a España.* Fred and me, Team Geritol."

She lifted a neat section of blintz and placed it in her perfect mouth. She'd been flawless since our fight while I was lurching around like a disoriented civilian. She chewed, swallowed and looked me in the eye.

"Beyond meeting with Keith, what do you see, Rob?"

"*Belle dame sans merci* three feet from my nose."

"I'm serious, Rob. It's getting so tight we could run into Morris in an airport. He knows what you're up to and he knows he can't buy you, so one of you has to go. He has to kill you — do you see that?"

"Not if I kill him first, which is completely okay after the way he set you up."

But Morris hadn't intended Jennie to be harmed, much less killed. It was clear from the tape that he'd sent a psychopath and realized it too late. Smart man, slow about women. I stopped talking and found myself recalling the many Morrises. The stony face checking me out at Fred's and the Eulenspiegel with Crackerjacks in Washington Square. Mentor Morris at the steakhouse, kindly Father Morris opening up on the Atlanta flight. And in the end, the pro who lost it on the phone with Jennie and trapped himself on tape. Still a man and a half by any standard I knew of.

"What is it?" asked Jennie.

"Morris. Of all the people in this thing, he's the only one I respect. He's not some dirtbag mercenary, he's doing things for the right reasons. His own right reasons. I know, I can smell it. That's how he got to me. Morris is clean, he's not about money. He only regrets that he has but one life to give for his country. Doesn't happen to be my country, that's the problem. Even with Millie — he was afraid for you, gave himself away."

"I love how you're so smart and so dumb. I get it about Morris, but he had a reason to keep me alive, I was the bait. Don't you get it? *He'll kill you, Rob!* Me too."

"Probably has that double-X criminal chromosome, right? But in this bunch he stands out like a god. Israel needs more guys like him. Get rid of those racist shits."

This irritated her enough that her voice changed.

"We don't actually *know* he's Mossad, though, do we? Say he is, though — would that kosherize Millie? She was his asset."

She'd never pushed me like this. I took a slow breath and let it out.

"First of all, Keith thinks he's Mossad, and he's not just guessing. And as you say, Morris doesn't get it about women. He made a mistake, hired a psychopath."

"Just another career bitch, okay. What about Keith then? Does Keith measure up, or is it just Morris who qualifies?"

"Keith's a damn *lawyer*. Morris has scale, he's big. He's got the vision thing. Everything he does comes from that. I envy him, Jennie, we don't have that here any more. War hero who saw through Nam and walked away? Not many of those. It says something about us that he was born here and ended up there."

"Not proven, Rob," she said, her voice smooth as silk. "All we're sure of is that he'll do what he has to, and if you won't, you lose. It's the nature of the game, Rob."

"I'm buying Keith's take on Morris because of his access to FBI data. And I think I know the nature of the game by now. I just happen to like it that Morris isn't for sale."

She said nothing. I was sick of the game and what it was doing to us.

"Look," I said quietly. "Could we go somewhere else with

what we have? CIA is *dying* to bust TCC, they hate our guts."

Her face didn't change, and as the words came out I knew I was saying what she wanted to hear. Why she'd been riding me like that. We didn't pursue it further, and I was planning. I could afford a St. Marcus look-around, and I might find something there, like a missing scientist.

Bouncing along through purple-brown air in the airport jitney, we talked quietly about next steps, both of us very tired.

"No one knows about the Chelsea," I said. "I'll be Mr. Winters again."

She nodded, and then we just stopped talking. All I could think was that the cat was out of the bag. Morris knew enough from Fred that he'd kill me if he could find me. Keith was all we had, and who knew how he'd see things, being so close to Olcott. I closed my eyes, wondering what came next. I was so full of wonder that my bowels turned to water in the airport and I broke for the head. Then I rummaged around for the Kaopectate and had a big slug. Rinsing my face, I saw myself in the mirror. The new hair adjusted my features to jailhouse angles, and my suit hung loose. I was beyond the manual — what I needed was a whistle-blowers guide.

When I reappeared, Jennie looked in my eyes, kissed me, and was gone. I stood watching the crowd churn for a long time thinking about Mac. In my guts was a stubborn Yankee thing that said I ought to go for it, even if it didn't completely make sense, like finishing races when the break was gone and there was no catching them. It was the thing that had kept my father trying to teach history to kids whose parents' idea of the past was a for-profit fairy-tale. The longer I stood there the more came back to me about Malachai McVeigh. Little incidents and bad jokes and insults, and how he'd never judged me or let me go down all the way when it was there to happen. I owed it to Mac to finish this thing I'd involved him in, because I'd never have a better friend.

28

I slept on the plane and didn't wake up until I was checked into the Chelsea. I got a big room away from the street noise with an undersized green Naugahyde couch, a flowered easy chair, and a fine view of the frigid blue sky. When I had my bags in the room I went out and called Keith. No answer, so I tried every forty minutes, having a drink between calls. For variety, I asked for "Tom" when I got him, in a southern accent, which irritated him.

"No Toms here!" he said, clipping off the words, and I wondered if he knew it was me. I went for a cup of black coffee and read the *Post* while he went to a booth. Another dumpster baby, this one rescued by a homeless man who attempted to sell it. Baby doing well, homeless man attacked by fellow inmates at Rikers. I went back out into the cold.

"Tommy here," said Keith.

"We need to meet."

"Sure do," he said. "I'm in town. Do you have a car?"

"No. I'm at a hotel — "

"No good. You know the Williamsburg Bridge?"

"Yes."

"Start walking across from Delancey in forty-five minutes. Three o'clock."

I didn't have anything warm enough for a windy bridge in February, but I went with it. Not a nice guy, Keith. That edge kept coming back, as if he had to keep it sharp.

"Just walk toward Brooklyn and keep going."

Before I could ask for time to buy a parka he was gone.

There was a late afternoon sun, but you couldn't feel it. I climbed the stone steps to the bridge in my unlined trench coat, still irritated with how Keith had hung up on me. It was a long walk to Brooklyn and I was getting cold. On the far side was Domino Sugar, flanked by sooty factories, and down below were three tugs pushing a garbage scow through tiny whitecaps. I was alone on the bridge until I saw a figure at the far end, which turned into a boxer in hooded gray sweats getting in some roadwork. I saw him from a long way off, running, bouncing, backpedaling, throwing combinations. Finally he came by, bobbing and weaving. He was almost past me before I recognized him. He didn't say a word, and I kept walking. I was close to Brooklyn before I heard him behind me. He'd scouted the entire bridge.

"I haven't got anything in the mail from you yet," he said immediately, meaning the write-up I'd promised. I told him he would. He'd been running a long time and wasn't breathing very hard, pretty good for a chain smoker.

"Jennie okay?"

I nodded. He could see I was freezing, but strolled along as if it was midsummer. I acted as if Caucasians don't notice the cold.

"You guys are officially missing and wanted as of 0800 this morning."

"Have you talked to Morris?"

"No, he called Jason and Jason called me. I'm headed for Silver Spring as soon as we're finished here. Jason's pretty disturbed, Rob. He'd never mention it, but I think he's drawn the conclusion about you and Jennie. Morris described you as armed, dangerous, a thief, responsible for Al's death. Ops will have a picture of you but it's very poor — shot from above, could be anyone with bushy gray hair."

Responsible for Al's death. A nice touch, giving Morris even more latitude. I didn't take off my hat to show Keith my revised hair.

"And?" I said after another silence. The ghost of a smile passed over his features.

"Do you know you sound something like him?"

Zack Epstein had thought so, too.

"The good news is, we got all the way in. The bad news is, the computer knows it was molested. He blew it on the way out and a warning flashed on the screen."

"What did you find?"

"Too much. Lots of Pentagon data and budget projections

— SDI progress reports, Stealth paint specs, new-generation guided bombs. Mini-nukes, depleted uranium how-to. Enough to reveal Pentagon technical strategy for the rest of the century."

It got to him the way dope did, and I saw something. For lawyer Keith, loyal to TCC didn't mean allegiance to BioTel. It was leverage.

"Nothing on those nuke triggers or Marquardt's secret shipments?"

I asked mainly to stir things up.

"No krytrons," said Keith briskly. "Leads me to think there's something funny going on here — we ravished that mainframe, the kid was excellent. Stuff wasn't there. No Oracle, either."

"Nothing on BCCI or Menat Bagdosian?"

From his silent head-shake it was obvious that he didn't want to talk about bankers with White House connections.

"Your car nearby?"

"Yeah. You must be cold. Sorry, I don't notice it."

"Yes, quite cold. New topic. I'm not crazy about having a price on my head. What do you think about going to CIA?"

"With what, Rob? The computer knows what happened — everything will be gone. All we have is a dead Area Head who smelled bad and a lost document that doesn't seem to hook up with anything."

Then he lost it.

"CIA can't be *trusted*, Rob. They've been in the drug business since OSS and Chiang Kai-shek. Director Casey liked my specs, I could have gone with those cowboys any time I wanted, but they — look — this is the agency that was dosing people with lysergic acid and had guys jumping out of windows. They want to keep the lid on because it's just too close to the President. He was agency *head*, Rob."

Wind was gusting through my coat and I was walking faster, getting bored with Keith. I didn't doubt CIA was everything he said, but he hadn't hesitated to sign up with an outfit run by an old drag queen who blackmailed presidents.

"Couple of other interesting things," he said. "My friend at FBI found a cross-reference confirming the Walker Schultz I.D.

for Morris, and linking him with Laura Epstein and Lakam. The connection goes way back."

"What's Lakam?"

"Israeli military spook unit active with Diaspora, no Mossad connection — that's why we couldn't confirm Morris. You remember the Pollard case? Civilian analyst, sold information to Israel? That was Lakam. And by the way, the computer also links Morris with someone identified by the initial "S," which could be a work name, or stand for one. Ring a bell?"

"Not right off," I lied. My trust in Keith was limited, and I needed time to think about S. "This Lakam connection — what does that do to Morris and TCC?"

"Nothing. People move around, and Israel is a very close ally. Extremely. What are you thinking of doing now, Rob?"

"Caribbean vacation."

I was preoccupied and said it without thinking, then added something about needing some sun. Keith wasn't fooled.

"Bad idea, Rob," he said stiffly. "Dangerous. You could be made before you're out of the airport. And quite frankly, I can't think what you'll accomplish."

Very superior, but I let it go, not wanting to rile him further.

"Neither can I, actually," I said, "Anything about Fred in the computer?"

"Never on board, just a talent-spotter. Rob, I hate to cut this short, but I have to make a plane. I'll be back in a few days, but you can't call me because I'll be at The Briars with the Olcotts."

He couldn't conceal his delight. Morris's days were numbered, leaving him an open career path. It was distracting him, and our meeting wasn't finished. I was half-listening, thinking about loose ends until we were off the bridge, going through a tunnel full of swirling dust and grit. We got in his car and he held the rpms up to get the heater going. When he spoke next it was low key, and lubed with a self-deprecating modesty, but it was a statement I was meant to understand.

"I've had a lot on my plate since the trouble in France, Rob, and I've been assigned some of Morris's obligations."

He was happy at how things were going for him. I was still thinking.

"Initial S — what about someone named Snyder?" I said. "Worked with Durry, disappeared for no reason last summer."

"Not familiar. Could be a part-timer."

Snyder hadn't sounded like a part-timer on that one-word phone call. There was too much authority in his voice. Keith wasn't interested.

"Know this, Rob. Whatever's going on, Jason Olcott's not involved. Once there's something solid, he'll be the first to knock heads together."

"I'm sure," I said. Mine first and hardest. The car was warming up, and so was my brain. I had to get past my problem with Keith and tighten things up between us.

"Keith," I said, "Durry was working on an artificial intelligence breakthrough. Not silicon-based — no chips."

It stopped him dead.

"What are you talking about?" he asked abruptly, his civility slipping away to reveal the Ivy League cop.

"Carbon-based. The missing document has to do with a genetic technique whereby living cells are developed and accessed. Might be a lab down there."

He put the car in gear and drove toward a bridge ramp without a word, a half-smile on his face. Keith was amused. On the ramp he was offhand and superior.

"That's nonsense, it's not real. Organic cybernetics is a next-century dream. I know this field, Rob, it's my hobby, I have a math-science background — "

"This is from Durry," I said, cutting him off. "He designed the control apparatus for the French nuclear setup, and for him that was a boring job. And why would BioTel ever bother with Epstein unless he was onto something? His idea was a non-binary, true-verbal machine with human characteristics — human intelligence, but totally undistracted. Like those nine-year-old Japanese kids who play concertos."

I'd turned into a pumpkin for Keith.

"Don't believe it, Rob. He was playing with you, science breakthroughs invariably happen in several places at once — "

"People are getting killed over this, friend," I said. "Does Project 38 mean anything to you? TCC's Oracle is the

Pentagon's Project 38."

The river had become a rippling bronze sheet in the afternoon sun. I knew he'd shut down, and he did. When we hit a red light at the foot of the bridge he spoke.

"I can take you as far as Bowery, you can catch a cab there," he said in a more collegial voice. "I might be at Briarcliff several days, and I don't want messages on my machine. If you really feel you must go to the islands, there's a phone booth in the Bananas Bar, St. Croix. On Germaine. I'll try to call between one and two each day, backup time six to seven. If there's a problem, I'll say I have a cold. If I say I'm running a fever, get out by boat — the airport will be covered."

He didn't look at me.

"I don't like this, Rob. It's not just yourself you're putting in danger — "

I was out the door.

We were off the cobbles but it was still raining, and my fingers were too numb to feel the brakes. I was in my best form ever, but Alf was on my wheel, wearing full gloves. Not exactly on my wheel, but a little behind me on my right, his front wheel at my hip, out of the crosswind. Almost in the gutter, but Alf knew I wouldn't squeeze him. If I did, I'd pay for it all the ways a peloton full of Belgies could think of to remind an American asshole that he wasn't Greg LeMond.

Alf was comfortable, sheltered from the wind, sitting there like grim death with twenty klicks to go as the rain beat on my face. This break was going to stay away, and Alf was going to take the sprint, making sure I left Europe without a win. Felice was sitting in her Mini at the finish and I wanted the win bad enough to buy it, but Alf didn't do business with English-speakers. Not when they had a girl who wouldn't look twice at his leering snaggle-tooth grin. When I dropped back, he dropped back with me, and when I went to the front, there he was. He'd been racing since he was ten, and he knew the game asshole to eyeballs. He knew me, too, how I liked to go early, and had been getting stronger, staying off the front longer. He wasn't letting that happen, and with about five to go he came up alongside and gave me that grin. I'd never beaten him in a sprint.

I jumped up in bed and a sound came out of me, not loud but guttural, and scared. Alf de Vos was Morris and I was dead meat.

I smelled coffee and got hold of myself. It was the Chelsea, it was morning, and Jennie was doing something at the desk. Putting out food. She didn't say anything about the noise that came out of me, and I didn't move for a while.

"Okay," said Jennie, sitting on the couch looking at me. "What is it, Rob?"

"Bad dream," I said. "I saw Keith yesterday. Morris has Olcott thinking I killed Al. Which he has to, because he knows that tape implicates him."

"Yes, smart. If I came in with the tape before now and told about Millie, Morris was finished, but now it's like he was trying to save my life. Doesn't matter what I say. Now that I'm with you they discount my girly little testimony. Bad girl return, Bwana forgive. But *you* have no credibility, dude. *You* have to go."

She paused. "Keith's what you've got, Rob."

Lying back on a stack of pillows and drinking coffee, I tried to accept Keith and his new closeness to Olcott.

"He thinks Durry was misleading me on Oracle."

"He thinks he was setting you up?"

"Maybe not after I mentioned Project 38. But we're out of phase, Keith and I. Black guy out of a top law school and he goes into FBI? Ain't that peculiar?"

"He's risking a lot. For a guy like him. And he's not just some lawyer, he studied computer theory and went to MIT."

"Okay, qualified. But not on this. He's not a Durry or an Epstein, he just *isn't*. Y'know what gets him where he lives? He was really disturbed when he found a lot of secret Pentagon stuff in the BioTel computer."

"That's pretty normal. It's supposed to be secret, but you can get it if you're connected. At worst, BioTel would be fined. Slap on the wrist for naughty business partner. A home-boy Texas partner the administration probably gets along with.

I turned on the tube but it was commercial time, so I started to tell her about the mysterious Snyder when we heard a voice that jerked our heads around.

The voice and face of Zack Epstein. An angry, suddenly grown-up Zack Epstein in east coast jacket and tie, talking into microphones in front of a government building. Serious faces crowding around a boy-man with short, unstyled hair. Measured voice, frightened angry eyes. He was saying that for years his father had been afraid of the people who got his company and patents away from him, and that those same people had needed him back to complete his work. That the company was called BioTel, and that he'd shot this BioTel prowler, a Mr. Kammler, as instructed by his father, with his mother's gun. Very clear, hitting his points like a D.A. He finished by requesting the government open an investigation of BioTel to find out if his father was still alive. I felt weightless, sad, relieved, and strangely empty. And astounded that the boy had the prescience to name his mother, who'd known Morris, as the gun owner.

"He's dead," I said. "Morris is dead, missed us by a day."

I was torn between relief and respect. Next to Joe Kline he was the man I'd learned from and respected most.

"Yes," said Jennie in a slow voice.

Then came lovely space case Laura, incapable of speech, a disoriented celebrity-to-be surrounded by lawyers and an ACLU hustler who thought he was in show business. A local media-dildo spoke darkly of a "mystery within the mystery" and handed off to the anchor who finished with a hint that — *Shazam!* — National Security Might Be Involved.

Right, I thought, except they've got it backwards, and the real threat is old Ike's military-industrial complex. An ad came on and we looked at each other without saying anything. Zack was staying with me. The nightmare of being a kid, broke and scared, harassed by spooks, losing your father and dealing with a halfwit mom. Then General Motors was telling us that Today's Chevy Truck Is The Heartbeat of America. Maybe it is, I thought — maybe that's the problem. I turned it off and looked at Jennie, and there were tears in her eyes.

"You were right about Morris," she got out. There was bad

pain in her voice. "Everything you said. But I was just so afraid for you, Rob."

Then she started to cry. A moment later she stopped just as quickly and gave me a sad smile.

"Not a natural Op," she said. "This part was always too much. Hold me, Rob."

I did, and she was shaking. Then she kissed me, and in a minute we were naked, fucking like animals, half-on, half-off the little couch, then all over the room, groaning and gasping out the pain of the last week. The joy of sex, as they say. The joy of love, as people won't ever say. It was our Kaddish for the boss.

"What's wrong with me?" she asked after a while. "Am I just a crazy slut?"

The shake in her voice tore me apart, and for a moment I completely understood her. She could lose herself making love and feel safe.

"No," I said. "That's ridiculous. You're what I always wanted, I just didn't know where to look. You're to die for, lady."

"I've been very afraid for you," she said after a while, sitting on the green couch in a little black silk thing.

"Us."

"Not me. Not with Jason thinking so highly of me, and Keith and Fred there to agree with him."

"Me, too — I think very highly of you."

"I think you do, actually. I just wish things weren't such a mess."

"I'm going to have a cigarette," she added, and got one out of her little case. "You know, Rob, Zack gives us the option of waiting for things to develop. We could get out of the city and be human for a couple of days. I know you're dying to see what's on that island, but Keith could be right, maybe not the time."

"You think this might do it? Get them busted? With their lawyers?"

"The toothpaste is leaving the tube, Rob. People won't forget Zack."

"That was you, babe. He wasn't gonna talk to me till you got his mom relaxed."

"What I was trained for — Golden Girl out of Circe by

Midas. And you're my favorite swine."

Then she looked thoughtful.

"I guess the question now is, who got Morris into TCC? How that could happen."

I'd overlooked it completely.

When I woke up Jennie was naked in the middle of the room doing a kind of slow methodical dance with a big brown powder-puff in her hand. She was patting herself with it and turning an attractive mocha brown. Making us into a new-wave couple — aging white punk and cute well-spoken black girl.

"What you think, massa? I 'peal to you?"

"You always did. Tell me about this brown stuff."

"From the guy who did all that nice I.D. Sweatproof, lasts forever."

But on the evening news there were only passing references to Zack and what had happened in California. When cable news didn't jump all over it I felt the wind going out of our sails. The story wasn't going anywhere. Everything a journalist could hope for, and it was all going to disappear like Mr. Nir. Things wouldn't happen by themselves as the story came out, because it wasn't coming out.

"What's wrong with our fucking journalists?" I said.

"Oh, Rob, what do you think? CIA White House, wrong zeitgeist."

I was getting out of the shower the next morning when Jennie walked in with the papers. I skipped through them standing up, still damp. Cleavage shot of the bereaved Laura Epstein in the *Post*, plus some dish on her family, the irreproachable Graveses of Boston MA and Dublin NH. Nothing in the *Times*, which would have kept the story going. The *Washington Post* had two back-page paragraphs.

We went out for a quiet meal at a Cuban-Chinese restaurant, and after that Jennie got us to a Truffaut film that got me outside myself. But on the late news, the story was a soap opera centering on Zack's youthful courage and lovely Laura, potential victim of the unidentified prowler-rapist-drifter-thug.

Zack was a fine lad with an overactive imagination, and someone clever had planted the idea that he was expected to be away that night. The story was shriveling into nothing. The agencies would all know who "Kammler" was, but they'd never tell. Jennie had it right, national security was the King Kong of news killers.

"Goddamn," I said. "Back to square one."

Then I sat on the couch in silence trying to think past the news shutdown. Jennie waited, watching a man with an eye-patch talk his girlfriend to death on a soap.

"Won't happen by itself," I said after a while. "I've gotta go down there and see what I can find out, maybe luck into something to jump start some interest."

Jennie turned off the TV.

"No, you don't gotta, that's just you being how you are. Now that Morris is the villain, you could come in, Rob. You were seen as his man, his protégé, but that's over. With Keith and me to corroborate you, no problem."

It was true, and I was tired of the danger. I tried to see it her way but I still had a big problem with BioTel riding off into the sunset, saddlebags full of Pentagon secrets and cocaine. And I knew where coming in would leave Jennie and me when the smoke cleared, but that would be a sensitive topic, not something I was ready to talk about with her. I wanted to bust Jason Olcott out of our lives once and for all, but it couldn't be said. I felt like a roulette player in over his head, knowing he should quit but feeling a divine obligation to conquer all those sensible, practical, degrading fears just one time.

"I see," said Jennie after a while. "You're just gonna do what you're gonna do. You're an open book. It's kind of nice after all these professionals, but — well, you know what I think."

"I was feeling too good," I said. "It's like freezing to death. When you start to feel warm, that's the warning. I won't do anything foolish, Jennie. Except for Jason, the only company guys who got a look at me are dead. They're looking for gray hair, suit, heavy."

"Well you're not going alone," she said firmly. "I'm good, you'll see."

"I know you are. And I know your cool doesn't blow away, but there's something on my mind you may not want to talk about. I need to know more about TCC. Cellular separation isn't perfect but it was good enough to keep me in the dark about a lot."

"You know I can't talk about that, Rob. BioTel, fine, but not the company."

It was a deep, strong reaction, unlike anything I'd seen in her before, and I didn't understand it. I couldn't press her, but I needed to know more about my employers. She'd been on board from the start, Olcott's mistress, typed up the manual, but I knew not to push it. The conversation died, and I went back to thinking about St. Marcus.

"Okay," she said. "I've already broken so many rules it really doesn't matter. Okay, first of all, TCC is tiny. There are all kinds of operations like us out there, dozens and dozens. Most of them are CIA fronts, Director Casey loved them, but we're not. They want us gone because we're an uncontrolled information source. CIA and State have been scuffling since the sixties, and CIA is running scared since that Church Committee and Iran-Contra. We're trouble for them. If TCC got wind of some CIA scam and passed it on to State, congress might decide to look into it."

"Something like taking down a president by playing footsie with Iran behind his back?"

"Yes, that would do. Or just dropping the ball because nobody speaks Farsi."

"When you said 'tiny,' what did you mean?"

"Three offices, under a hundred employees. Closer to fifty. But very capable. No bureaucracy, we don't hire that way, it's more like a family business. No jerks. Al was whatever he was, I never knew, but he was excellent. Morris likewise. So anyway, TCC France is really all of Europe except for the UK which is the third office, plus a presence in Israel. Only four people know this much, Rob. Five with you."

About like Finlay Kline. Small enough that one man can know everything important. Then she told me where the offices were and a few more details. It went against all her training and instincts to give it up. She was loyal, and she was unhappy about doing it. I had no sense of where that loyalty came from, but it ran very deep.

"This won't go anywhere else, Jennie. No matter what."

It confirmed what Marquardt had said — TCC had begun as BioTel's security, and it seemed still to be basically that. The deal with State was a perfect fig leaf, but saying it would hurt Jennie, so I didn't. She was very upset at having spoken, and I couldn't see why, given all that had happened.

29

We landed soft as a kiss, runway shimmering in the heat, a plane full of happy fools looking for fun and sun. A few minutes later we taxied slowly past Big Blue, close enough for me to see a man in a tan suit and aviator shades standing thirty feet away in the shade of an old red and white Cessna, hands behind him, feet apart. His line of work couldn't be plainer. My chest tightened, and then I got calm. With my weird hair and no body fat, they'd need prints to ID me.

I stepped out into the tropic heat, very white arms and legs sticking out of halfwit tourist gear, eyes wide open behind fake glasses. Forty minutes later I was sitting by the pay phone at Bananas working on a giant piña colada. I'd made Keith's phone deadline and had time to kill, along with twenty-five or thirty happy-hour patrons, all silly-drunk in their vacation outfits like actors in a commercial, not a hard face to be seen. Bananas was an enormous thatch hut made of rough-cut four-by-fours, with a round bar in the middle, tables in the corners, and a light breeze blowing through. Sitting by the phone working on my bottomless drink, I imagined giant cockroaches going about their business in the thatch roof and waited for one of them to lose his footing and fall on the bar. Big Blue had blown a big hole in my confidence, and I was wondering if Jennie was right about pushing my luck. I ate plantain chips from a wooden bowl and waited, and when the phone rang I picked up.

"Bananas."

"Beach?"

It took just that one word to make me feel boxed in.

"*Yep*," I said, with attitude, in case Keith was planning to back me down.

"I'm here too," he said. "I have a car. Go out, turn left, and walk down the road. I'll pick you up in a yellow Ford. Ten minutes."

"White shorts, Prince T-shirt, bush hat, bags."

First Big Blue, now a keeper. I'd told him too much, and that had to stop.

Out in the street the sun was hot and blinding. I put on my shades, feeling tight as an admiral's bung. What did I actually know about Keith Alderman? Why was he here? Not just to talk me out of my plans. Big Blue wasn't here just so he could keep an eye on me. Something was going on.

I was breaking a sweat by the time I felt the car behind me. He passed and stopped, leaning over to open the door. Keith was wearing cut-offs and a purple flowered shirt, handsome as ever. I threw my gear in the back seat, and as soon as I climbed in he was bringing me up to speed on Zack, confident the story would come out in due course.

"I don't think so," I said. "Coverage was dying by the second day. Story had everything — sex, spooks, murder, teenage hero, beautiful socialite sexpot mom. They fingerprint bodies, they know it was Morris."

We rolled along in silence for a while as Keith digested that, and I saw that he didn't understand media at all. He lit a Marlboro and shifted gears.

"I don't propose to continue this game unless you take me into your confidence."

"Sounds like we're running a fever."

"Morris wasn't shot with a target pistol," he said coldly. "Three shots from a very unusual gun. It's in the computer that you were issued a Michaud. It was test-fired, and I've arranged to be copied on the ballistics report. Backchannel, as a courtesy."

"Thank you, Keith, but that's not my smoking gun. I still have mine. Maybe he gave Laura Epstein one, too, if she was his asset for Lakam, or whatever they're called. The boy probably knew where it was."

There was a pause while he digested this. After Al and Morris, Keith was easy.

"Yes, that's possible. I don't mean to sound accusatory, Rob, it's just that this is a difficult situation to . . . assess." He paused. "Lakam — pretty lame unit, but Pollard was big," he observed agreeably. "Huge score but crude, they didn't know when to stop."

"Well, at least they scored. What about us, Keith? TCC's the original spies who stepped on their dicks, we're totally infiltrated. The Israelis didn't just have Morris. Mossad was there, and they had Marquardt, and that girl in Belgium I told you about. And they were onto Durry — "

"Finished and done with. Jason's handed me Morris's responsibilities, lock, stock and barrel. Mandate to clean house. I need to know what your plans are, Rob. You were dodging Morris. Now that he's gone we can work from inside."

My fiction about the Michaud had brought him up short and he wasn't looking for trouble. We both wanted our conflict to be over, but I didn't see how to get there.

"We were also looking into illegal arms shipments, Keith — radars, guidance systems, krytrons. Stuff that could destabilize whole . . . 'theaters of operation' my dad would call them. Oracle's a mystery, but nuke fuses are not. There are some wild and crazy guys out around the Fertile Crescent, Keith. Couple of 'em might be close to nuclear capability. Remember that Israeli strike? They thought Iraq was getting close."

Keith just lit another Marlboro. I cracked my window and finished my thought.

"What can we do from inside? Tell your boss his boss is dirty?"

"He's his own boss," said Keith stiffly. "And those Iraqi missiles are Korean junk."

But Olcott wasn't his own boss, which even Keith had to suspect by now. I had him by the ethics, and we both knew it, but he couldn't admit that TCC was just a BioTel toy with government privileges. I left it alone and moved on to something else I'd seen in the shipping room after Zurich.

"Do the names 'Teak' or 'Juice' mean anything to you?"

"No. Maybe . . . there was a CIA Teak, but he's retired — "

"Or maybe not really? How about Alben?"

He hesitated and his timing changed, but he didn't shut down.

"Ex-CIA, involved with Gaddafi. He got Wilson out of Libya and turned him in. Getting off himself was his reward. Where does he fit?"

"Final contact name on the krytrons. Saddam Hussein has had a free pass since he attacked Iran, right? I really don't think that stuff should be out there, Keith."

"Nobody's going to thank you," said Keith, his voice almost inaudible. He didn't want to hear it, and he was getting cop-sullen. I let the silence develop.

"How does a lab on St. Marcus connect with that?" he asked. "The hardware's coming out of the US, Project 38 is another thing — "

"Keith, you came from a big organization. First rule for guerrilla ops is speed and surprise. We have to exploit the confusion caused by Morris's death. We're at a dead end in the computer, you said so yourself. There's a BioTel operation on St. Marcus — how do I get in?"

You don't.

He wouldn't say it, but he didn't have to. Keith was in a bind, ethics vs. career. He'd just been promoted by Olcott, but I'd tipped him to something he couldn't ignore. I reminded myself that even men of principle with Frigidaire vibes have friends and loyalties. Keith thought like an employee and needed someone to report to.

"You're going about this all wrong, Rob."

"Heresy is the unwed mother of progress."

A Durryism. It just sprang out at the wrong time, and Keith was steaming.

"I'm going there myself." He said it the same way he'd announced his visit with the Olcotts on our bridge walk, a proclamation of status.

"Probably Wednesday," he added.

I tamped down my irritation carefully, like a man working with unstable old dynamite. We were really fed up with each other.

"Ops are second-echelon in TCC. You'll see what they want you to see."

One of Keith's good points was that he didn't get noisy. He let it go, which gave me time to see that he wasn't just an op. Replacing Morris made him #2 behind Olcott.

"Does the name McVeigh mean anything to you?

Malachi McVeigh."

"It does," he said slowly. "He turned up on your background check and looked bad, so Morris tapped his phone. He was an IRA money-funnel and he didn't pay his taxes. We didn't do it, Rob."

No, Morris did, which you don't get.

"He was helping me research BioTel."

He went into another silence, so I changed the topic.

"Jennie thinks the big question is how Morris got inside to begin with."

"Done deed by the time Jason took over. There was nothing in the computer."

It didn't interest him at all. We were out in the countryside under a heavy sun, rich tropical green all around, Marlboro smoke swirling around the car. I wanted to say that with Al gone, BioTel France would be a safe place to hide purged data, but if Olcott got wind of it, that data would be gone.

"So how do I get into BioTel, Keith?"

Without a word he pulled over and parked. His voice was icy.

"This is the real world, Rob. You've been very lucky, but it can't last forever. Operations have time-frames, and I'm putting a cap on this thing. I'm not going to let you run wild showing off for your girlfriend."

I let it go.

"Something else to consider, Rob," he said. "Come in now and you're golden. Stay outside and the window closes."

Coming in meant putting myself in Olcott's big liver-spotted old hands after taking his girl. How dumb did Keith think I was? Or how dumb was he? Didn't he understand jealousy?

"What do you have in mind?" I asked.

"Two days. And that is a major risk for me personally."

"A week," I said.

"Out of the question."

He started the car, drove a little further, and turned around in a driveway. I took an envelope full of money out of my pocket and put it on the seat.

"For your hacker." I was angry and nervous, running out of civility.

"Three days," said Keith. "Starting noon today. Okay, St. Marcus: Kelsey Corners Road, mile and a half south of Lucian's Hotel. The hotel's a big white four story building on the south shore. There's one road around the island — look for a tall unpainted wood fence on the south side. You won't be able to see through it, but that's the compound, three buildings in the middle of a grass clearing a hundred yards back from the fence. Best to come in from the water, except you'd have to haul your boat up and hide it. The beach is Baffey's Cove. You'll know it from a big, hooked, rocky point. Huge stones."

"What about security?"

"Not super, but it won't be unprotected. Probably just dogs, but only Morris knew. I'm supervising an upgrade and tomorrow's meeting is about that. They want it done yesterday but I can probably slow it down a little."

Then he went back inside himself, at the end of his patience. He was reporting in two directions, totally conflicted. I sympathized, but it wasn't about him.

"Look out for a man named Jorge," he added. "Really big, about six-four. Long, black hair, soft voice. Korean-trained, not clever."

"Any indication Morris had part-timers down here?"

"*If I knew I'd have told you!*" His voice was really loud, a first. He was furious. "We don't *know* what Morris had going — that's why I'm here!"

We were approaching Bananas. He pulled over and faced me before I got out.

"Don't let anything happen to Jennie," he said.

I walked back into Bananas with that sticking in me like a poisoned dart. The place was filling up, everyone bombed on the big drinks and enjoying the afternoon breeze. I had another Colada and pondered Keith. Nothing was easy with Keith, and soon he'd have security beefed up to the point where I couldn't go in, and that window could close any time. I took out a pad and started a list of things I'd need, starting with a boat we could haul up a bluff. Before I was finished, the phone rang.

"Nice to hear your voice, I hate these separate flights. Anyway, I got us rooms."

"Good. Can you pick up some stuff while I rent a boat? I'd like to be out fishing at dawn."

"Sure," she said, not sounding surprised. "We're at the Horizon, between the beach and the airport. You're Richard Michaels, room 414, the key's at the desk."

I read her my list and she gave me the little platinum laugh.

"You don't mind if I add a few things on my own — "

"List isn't finished," I snapped. "Be my guest."

My voice told me where Keith had left me. I paid, overtipped the bartender, and had him call me a cab. Before I was through my drink a battered old blue Impala drove up, driven by a skinny kid who knew where to find whores, weed, blow, even a boat.

Jennie had a big cool room on the top floor with a giant bed, comfortable chairs and ceiling fan. I dropped my bags and changed into shorts and a loose white summer shirt while the Impala kid waited. Then I removed the Michaud from the case and stuck it into my shorts in the small of my back, letting the shirt hang over it. It was a small flat gun, but it kept poking me in the back, reminding me how crazy things were getting.

The kid dropped me at a tin shack on a narrow, unattractive stretch of beach about a mile from the Horizon. Outside the shack doing some primitive carpentry was a thin old man with short curly white hair and beard, all of it about half an inch long. Miguel. He looked me in the eye, though, and his battered sixteen-foot aluminum boat had an honest-looking old forty-horse Evinrude on the transom and a canvas spray shield that would be useful in rough water. Just about right. Like Marcel, he asked no questions and was easy to do business with. He let me kick over the motor, which started on the third pull and sounded good. I gave him a five hundred dollar deposit against seventy-five a day, fishing tackle included.

"Good weather tomorrow?"

He nodded, and I told him I'd come by at sunrise with cash. He nodded again, and I walked back through the tropical afternoon, stretching my legs and thinking about Keith, and how much I'd preferred Morris. To get past this mood I bought a bottle of over-proof rum on the way back, tapping it now and then, sweating it out as I walked. The sky was perfectly clear and nothing had gone wrong, but I hadn't relaxed since I spotted Big Blue. It was the same when I got back to the room, so I mixed a drink. In a while I was fairly drunk, in a lucid unpleasant way, trying to recall my last day without a few drinks. The TV had just confirmed Miguel's weather report when Jennie walked in carrying a string sack full of packages. She was wearing a pink dress that was perfect against her new mocha skin. I felt the rum as I stood up, but I went through the motions, kissing her and making her a Cuba Libre. She told me she'd taken a room for herself under separate ID so we wouldn't be seen as a couple. Good idea, but my mood didn't change. After I brought her up to speed on Keith I tried to explain our problem.

"Partly it is his being promoted. He's taking over for Morris, and he really likes it. In this dipshit agency, I report to him now — that's how he sees it. He's a company man, it's in his genes. Problem is, on Oracle he basically reports to me."

Jennie nodded.

"We're working together, but we don't really trust each other. He thinks he's at risk, but he's not, because whatever happens, he can just say he was picking my brain, giving me rope to hang myself with. Really he wants to back off — he can't help it, it's how he's wired. For him, Morris was the problem, and he's gone. For me BioTel is the problem, and I think there's a lab down here, and maybe that missing data. Which I can't tell Keith because I don't know what he'd do. If he tells Crackerjack, it's gone. Anyhow, he'd love to shut down my little sideshow. I'm talking nuke fuses and that Uniceptco deal, and he's talking — I don't know what the fuck he's talking. Covering his ass mainly, and watching out for you."

I was angry and slurring my words, and I couldn't look at her.

"God, do I miss Morris! He was a rock when you were on the same side. Keith — Keith is political. His . . . *ethical* thing isn't as strong as you think. He just wants me back in the fold."

And so do you, and it won't work, because Crackerjack wants you back.

It was getting old. I went to the big window to look out at a movie-quality early evening sky. I remembered standing alone at LAX feeling brave and thinking how it would be here. Drop in, loosen up with a swim, have a look around, no sweat.

Stupid drunk and a little crazed, I heard Jennie's voice, soft but determined.

"There's something I have to tell you for you to understand your Keith problem."

I turned to face her.

"Do tell."

"Oh please, don't be a bastard, Rob. I've been telling you I'm not in trouble unless I turn up with a smoking gun in my hand, but you don't know why — "

"Sure I do. Olcott's a herniated asshole hiding in a stuffed shirt off the original Betsy Ross pattern, but he's been your lover for a long time. Guy like that can be very loyal, especially if he's getting on in years and not very smart . . . "

She was bulletproof.

"I want to get through this without ruining everything, Rob. Do you?"

"Little confession here if I may. I'm not down here just to save the world. I also want to beat that old bastard at his own game. I want him out of my life. As long as he's bottom line the one who can save your ass, I am not a happy man."

I stopped, feeling ridiculous. I was very drunk, thinking it was the truth, and so what. I sat down on the bed. Jennie's voice was level and calm.

"It helps to have the backstory, Rob. Jason Olcott was a business associate of my father's and I wanted to stop being a virgin, but not with some kid. I led him into it. The physical part of my relationship with this man you hate so much just doesn't mean anything, it never really did, for me. And Keith — the problem you have with Keith is, you're afraid of each other. Keith is *gay*, Rob! He probably thinks you're a jerk for not picking up on it."

It totally deflated me, stopped me in mid-air, mid-gesture, mid-thought.

"Oh." I felt remarkably dumb.

"How can Keith be at ease with you, Rob? He's completely loyal to Jason. And he knows you're untrained. Unprofessional, which has to make him nervous. You've got him stretched pretty thin, Rob."

She'd explained a lot, starting with his amused distaste for me. My anger was gone and I wasn't hating anyone, just feeling foolish.

"Rob, the reason I'm safe is that I've been on board from the top. I know where the bodies are buried, and I'm close to everyone that matters. It's simple — everyone *likes* me, Rob, and I'm trusted because I've never screwed up. When I felt that coming, I dropped out of Ops."

And from a senior role, it felt like. She did what she wanted, like shacking up with a lowly rogue courier. Since I called her on using our plastic, she'd been perfect.

Was there more? We looked at each other.

"Okay, done," I said. Then I started up again like a drunken fool.

"Jason Olcott? Jennie, there's a certain kind of automatic liar I understand without trying. My father taught at one of those good New England schools, and hypocrisy is what you learn before anything else. Only reason he didn't fire me in Paris, I had half a step on the old fart . . . "

I heard my drunken ranting voice and stopped. Nausea hit me and I went to the bathroom to vomit. When it was over I washed up, apologized, and half-fell across the bed. I lay there for a long time with a case of the whirly-beds, pretending to be out and trying to think. I was planning something very high risk, and I couldn't seem to stop myself. And putting this really excellent woman at risk as well. I could hear Keith's voice: *Don't let anything happen to Jennie.*

I was awake and alert. It was still dark, and Jennie was on the couch, relaxed as a cat. I slipped into the shorts and shirt laid out for me, got a pack on each shoulder, and was gone. Trees were sighing in the breeze as I walked through the soft pre-dawn. When I got to Miguel's, he was awake and gave me a cup of coffee, but he saw the packs and felt my mood. As I'd requested, there were many containers of water and gas, half a boat-full. He knew I wasn't going fishing but didn't say anything. In the stillness I kicked over the Evinrude and listened to it while I stowed my packs. It sounded good.

Out in open water, I idled the motor and stood amidships to read the compass as far away as possible from metal. Then I looked back and took the radio tower for my reference. I figured I'd be out of sight of land for well over an hour, and the St. Marcus group was small. Small and flat. Things I'd said to Jennie were going around in my head, along with bloated hangover apologies that would pop like balloons at her glance. I'd been a shit, and I had no idea how to fix it. A pearl-colored dawn was coming up, and I was taking other bearings. Doing this alone was a loose cannon act — Keith was a company cop and I was a whistle-blower who might bring harm to his boss and benefactor. He could be waiting for me on that island, and take me in. Not totally unlikely — he didn't share my obsessions, and in his shoes I'd probably do it.

I stood to check the radio tower again, and it was almost gone. Watching the sun change the color of the sea and listening to the Evinrude, I knew I was totally entangled, and it wasn't only wanting Jennie and the idea of nuke fuses in Arab hands. All that was real, but I was obligated. I owed it to Mac. And the francs I'd skimmed. Seemed all right at the time, but my conscience was locked onto that like one of my Puritan ancestors on the trail of a sexy witch.

And I had to eat something before my blood sugar disappeared and I went mystical. Jennie had mentioned food, and I found foil-wrapped chicken and yams in her pack. Then I found a pair of Tilley hats and sun-block. I put on the larger one, tied the cord, smeared myself with sun-block, and ate. I kept checking my heading and thinking I'd been an idiot to leave Jennie behind. Squinting at the horizon, I felt booze-sweat coming out of my pores as I counted gas and water containers. Enough to get to Cuba. Time passed and odd thoughts came. My father told me that once when his convoy was under radio silence and being shadowed by U-boats, he found himself sitting at the wireless and hearing the Gettysburg Address. I couldn't remember it all, but then it came back. It cleared my mind. A war that had to happen, America before the big money hit.

I was getting more spray as time passed, and fear. The roll of the sea was stronger, and I had to brace myself when I stood to check the compass. By my very rough calculations I was nearly due. The sky was clear, but the sea had been driving me off course, and it was different from the Atlantic, which I had a feel for. At 0815 hours I was getting wet as the boat pitched, very worried, standing up often to scan the horizon and check my heading. At 0845 I saw nothing but water and figured I was overdue. Same thing five minutes later. I turned slowly in a full circle, carefully searching with the binoculars as the horizon dipped and rose, and the boat didn't wander, so I didn't sit down, just kept turning and looking, seeing only water. No Plan B. When I finally saw the St. Marcus group my legs were aching, and it was just a glimpse as the boat rolled. They were almost out of sight behind me — three tiny bumps. A little haze and I'd have missed them.

Having badly scared myself, I had a Plan B for St. Marcus. Get the hell out at the first sign of danger. Ditch the boat, take a plane, buy Miguel the boat of his dreams.

Lucian's was the first thing that came into view. St. Marcus was French, and it was a grand old European-style hotel, bright white in the morning sun, with dozens of big beautiful boats at anchor. I worked my way toward Baffey's Cove along a rocky shore with smooth pale patches of beach. Miguel's battered little boat didn't belong there, it was suspicious, a poor man's possession, and I wanted it out of sight. The cove was twenty minutes from Lucian's, easy to spot and completely unspoiled. White sand backed by deep green under a bright blue sky, and not so much as the cellophane from a pack of cigarettes to mar it. In a minute I was beached, loosening the transom bolts and running the motor up into the brush, racing back for gas, water and packs, and finally the boat itself. There was a big hump where the sea had eaten away the beach where the grass began.

Even ripping with adrenalin, I had to move it in lunges of a yard at a time. Then I sat there thinking I'd pulled a stomach muscle until the pain went away.

I got calm and broke a leafy branch off a tree to sweep away the track I'd gouged in the sand. Then I slid the boat further along the hummocky grass into the brush, and covered it with torn-off branches. After that I sat down and had a Coke from Miguel's cooler, still ice cold. There had been a sign for mopeds near Lucian's, and I thought I'd scout the island on one. Walking along the overgrown path up to the road, I was annoyed with myself for paying attention to Keith's remark about not letting anything happen to Jennie. She could take care of herself, and I'd made a bad mistake. And when I didn't answer the Bananas phone, he'd know where I was. If he caught me, he could do as he pleased. Jennie wouldn't forgive him, but his career would be safe.

I stepped onto the road twenty minutes later into a baking sun, smeared myself with sunscreen and walked to Lucian's on very white legs. Across from the hotel was the vehicle-rental shop, with a fat native owner. In the sandy yard were half a dozen Australian Moke mini-cars, and many mopeds. I rented a moped, bought two bottles of Red Stripe, and drove until I came to a shady patch beside the road. The sun was getting serious and my skin was warning me under the sun-block. A funny-looking old two-engine prop plane was coming into a field beyond the hotel and I stood up to watch it land. Then I sat back against a tree and pondered a move while sipping Red Stripe. Before I finished it, a Moke appeared, and the driver caught my eye. A face in profile, half-recognized — refined, sixtyish, white crew-cut, smiling under dark glasses. Not a company face, or a threatening one, but I thought I might have seen it before.

That ended my semi-siesta. I put on my hat and started off around the island, seeing many nice houses on big lots, two expensive watering holes, several small ones, and a number of open-air seafood places. I had a piece of fish at one of them and tried to relax, but I missed Jennie's presence and her experience. I was still thinking about the man in the Moke. Why did he look familiar?

30

Riding past the compound, I saw the fence and glimpsed two peaked roofs, set far back. Then I was at the path to the boat. I hid the moped in the brush, and walked slowly downhill to the boat thinking about electronic security. It could be there without Keith knowing, but I could observe from the brush with my binoculars and maybe spot dog-turds, cameras or black-box surveillance. I put on a camouflage shirt Jennie had picked up and started back up the path for what felt like a hundred yards, then headed left through the brush. The undergrowth was thick, and getting through it was work. Twenty minutes later I knew I was lost, and stopped to work things out by the sun. I'd left my compass and weapon behind, hadn't eaten enough, and my eyes were burning with sweat. I was irritated about getting myself lost and almost blundered out onto the perfectly tended lawn.

I backed away and looked around. Up the gradual slope to the road were two big old cottages and a long one-story brick building that looked new. It had a row of high windows with one-way glass, and it could be a lab. I swept the property with my binoculars very carefully. No cameras, black boxes or dog turds. No sound or movement, either, just three buildings baking quietly in heavy tropical sun. I backed further into the brush and worked my way uphill to repeat the process. Still no signs of security, but behind the brick building was a major helicopter that matched Big Blue. Keith was here ahead of schedule, probably in a meeting. I saw a neat gray crushed-rock driveway leading from the brick building to the road, but no signs of life.

I was sweaty and hungry, not thinking well. Back at the boat Durry's voice mocked me: *You must have a plan.*

I took another Coke from the cooler and went to my pack to get the Michaud. It was stuffed tight, and I had to empty it on the grass. Wrong pack. I emptied the other one, got the gun out, and sat there finishing the Coke before re-packing. By and by it was clear that I shouldn't enter that compound. It was time to bag it, and I changed into tourist gear before starting off for a meal. I was fresh out of ideas and half-starved, mission on hold. Mainly I was concerned with what I'd say to Jennie if she'd speak to me.

Lucian's was a fine old-fashioned colonial operation with a vast airy dining room and a scattering of quiet lunchers, all dressed island-style like me. Feeling safe, I ordered a vodka tonic and had a look at my fellow patrons. Good manners all around, no obvious spooks. I sipped my drink slowly until a waiter came over and I ordered. Red snapper and veg, and then talk to Jennie and hope she didn't hang up on me. How to call without leaving a phone record? Not possible. I tried again to think about coming in, but Jason Olcott wasn't going away.

It was a really excellent meal, and I ate slowly, hoping for an idea. As I was finishing, someone stopped in front of my table. I looked up expecting the waiter and the dessert menu. It was Alain Durry in a spectacular cream silk tropical suit.

"You are such a thinker for an American."

I pretended to be pleased rather than blown away, and invited him to join me. Then I told him that on his recommendation of his island I'd brought a girl, then lost her to a rich guy with a seaplane.

"Or perhaps you are planning something you prefer not to discuss, eh?" he said. "Still, you have good taste in restaurants. This is the only adult food on the entire island. Your hair is good, I must admit. Inventive."

There was no fooling him, and he'd always been on my side. I shrugged.

"Look," he said, "you are no professional like these people here. Whatever you have in mind, reconsider, Beach. What is happening here . . . "

He hesitated.

" . . . is very dangerous for outsiders. Extremely."

"Why don't you tell me what you know?"

"I know that your employer — the employers of your employer — are looking for you. Because of your disappearance with the document, they are retaining my services, for which I am still further indebted to you. I suspect there has been further violence; I thought you might be its object."

"Not yet. How's work going?"

He got the unhappy look I'd noticed in the Olympia bar.

"Yes, Oracle. I am duplicating in practice something I had solved as a theoretical problem and which no longer has interest. For me, I mean, not them. But you, *ami* — what else have you done? Why are you here? I will not violate your confidence, I am only curious. You are a friend who has been patient and brought me much luck. I would not forget that. Work is what it is, but this place is a sexual paradise."

He made a French gesture of acceptance. I had questions he could answer, but the waiter appeared with a little silver tray. In an envelope with my work name on it was a note on TCC stationary.

Pay check and leave by main entrance. Five minutes.

"Is there a reply?" asked the waiter.

"No. But I'm called away and will pay the check now."

I shook my head as Durry started to speak and looked at the note again. It was neatly printed in pencil, folded once. I guessed I'd been pointed out by someone in the bar and assumed that he'd cover the door to the beach while someone else waited in front. The best I could hope for was that if I followed directions I might be able to come in and stay alive, because Keith would be handling it, and he thought there were documents in the hands of my lawyer.

"You have been spotted, I assume," said Durry. "Possibly I can intercede. I have influence — they depend on me totally, and seem to fear me a little. I hope you will believe I had nothing to do with this and that I am still a friend to be trusted."

"I know."

"I think you must cooperate completely. I will help if I can. They know I am impulsive, and this creates leverage."

"You recognized me," I said. "You sat down to join me for a drink, we talked about Mme. Gauthier's, you have no idea why I'm here."

I started across the white sand of the parking lot waiting for contact and searching my peripheral vision. Nothing but Mokes

270

and mopeds. I'd almost reached mine when someone behind me wiggled the Michaud in the small of my back but didn't lift my shirt.

"It shows with the wind on your back," said Jennie.

I turned to face her feeling relieved and ashamed. Her face was unreadable.

"I just didn't want to drag you in anyfurther. Keith said —"

"I don't care what Keith said, I can run rings around Keith. I'm *good*. Morris called me Slick — that was my work-name, in case you're interested."

Her voice was cold, and she was really angry.

"Okay," I said, then ran out of words. I tried again. "Last night — I'm really sorry, It was stupid. I couldn't face you — "

"So you run off like some amateur to get yourself caught? What about *me*?"

She stopped and stood there, eyes hard, looking undecided about Robin Price. Before she could say any more I put my arm around her. She didn't move, just stood there like a piece of spring steel. I started to say something but she slipped away and started walking toward the shade of some trees along the road.

"I picked you, you bastard!" she burst out. "A lot of men wanted me. I thought you were different. You're just arrogant."

Then she stopped and glanced back at my moped.

"If that's yours, let's go."

I mounted, and she got on behind me.

"No, wait — I want my own. Wait for me up the road."

At the boat her anger was gone. When I started to say something she shrugged.

"Your first operation," she said. "But not mine. I've burgled homes and broken bones and been shot at and all that crap. I gave it up, but I made an exception for you."

"What happened last night, Jennie — I'm ashamed of it. It was just fear. "I remember every stupid thing I said. I've been drinking too much and it caught up with me. Your friends are your friends, none of my business."

Nothing else to say, so I shook my head. She fluttered her eyes at me.

"Thanks, Rob," she said. Then she smiled. "Anyone can freak out. You're sweet, must be why I like fucking you so much. But you're a real bastard when you think someone's not leveling," she added. "Very civilian. Anyhow, I had a look at the compound. I saw two old residential buildings and one big new one, and a big helicopter with a radar bump."

"You've been in?"

"No."

"I didn't see anything but two roofs when I went by."

"Cause you didn't go up the hill 'cross the road with your binoculars, Massa Bond."

"True, but I found Durry."

"You exposed yourself, you mean. He could set us up, Rob."

"He won't do that, Jen. We're friends. We both froze when your note arrived, so I didn't learn anything about Oracle except that he's bored with it. Except for the money. He thought my hair was very inventive, which is Durry-speak for brilliant."

She didn't quite smile.

"I'm thinking about stopping in the pubs later and keeping my ears open. Maybe ask about property around Baffey's Cove. Say I'm looking for a place with a few buildings on it. To send screenwriters or something."

"For your studio? Guy next to you might own one for real."

"Whereas?"

"Whereas I've become an attractive, affluent and available beginner-brown lady with a good accent who enjoys hearing powerful men brag. Not too dangerous the way we look now if we go solo," she continued. "That's what this work is about, right? Being alone and looking for trouble. When did you have in mind?"

"Soon. Happy hour, then meet here at seven. Dinner time, people go out."

"And we go in?"

"While security is still light. Keith said it's probably just dogs and a big karate guy, but he's installing new security. Maybe as soon as tomorrow. No black boxes or dog dung, by the way. I checked it out carefully from inside the brush."

"On this island they'd have turd service. I don't think the flimsy security is accidental. That was up to Morris, and I think he left it loose so he could get a team in without problems. Do you mind if I carry your Michaud? I'm used to it, not as good with the Glock."

"Which you brought on the fucking *plane*?"

"Custom. More composite, less metal. You carry it in pieces. Didn't Al tell you anything at all?"

"Not really, nothing hands on. He kind of worked around my limitations."

"Like me. I brought some stuff I picked up."

In her bag were the Glock with suppressor and clips, black silk pajamas, gloves, belly-bags, charcoal paste, and a small blue cardboard box.

"Where'd all this come from?"

"Standard stuff. Those are tranquillizer darts in the blue box. How are you thinking of going in?"

"You're trained for this — what do you think?"

"We could get fancy, or we could just go point and cover, which is what I'd do with someone inexperienced."

"Okay. I'm thinking about dogs. I didn't see any, but Keith said so."

"Yeah — I'm glad we have the darts."

I looked away, thinking what a Dobie could do before a dart could work.

"Look," I said, "I know all about the great southern horse-and-dog tradition, but we're not using tranquillizers on an attack dog. They won't be normal dogs."

"*Okay-okay*," she said, displeased.

I looked at the darts again and remembered dragging Millie across the roof. I didn't want to kill anyone else.

"How do these work on people?"

"That's what they're for. One is regulation, but Al said it takes two to do the job. Not dangerous unless you have a bad heart, and we don't hire people like that."

I had a vodka at each place, keeping to myself and dumping them, which was easy. They were all rustic, with dim lighting and rough board floors that soaked it up. I smiled, listened, and went with my screenwriter's-retreat tale when queried. It was a waste of time until I met Daryl ("one R, one L"), a friendly young bartender who wanted me to look at a screenplay.

I said I wasn't up to talking business then, but maybe later. I could see almost everyone from my end of the bar, and by turning my head I could see the dining area, which had two elderly couples. I was finishing my half-drink when a large swarthy man came in, followed by the man in the Moke who'd caught my eye that afternoon. The big one would be Jorge, exactly as described by Keith. He was all of six-four, beef clear down to the heel, totally out of place. The older man was around sixty, bright-eyed and youthful in his white crew-cut, fit and lean. Walking through, Jorge took in all the men, and his master didn't miss any women. The old boy's eyes moved here and there, a smile on his face that was finally awarded to a pair of buxom Swedes around the corner of the bar, both around thirty.

"Most incredibly spaced human being," said Daryl very quietly. He had a good bartender's sense of decorum but was willing to bend rules to get to Hollywood.

"Tough-looking friend."

"Right? They hang together. Showed up around Thanksgiving and never left. The old guy loves the ladies, still got a handle on that."

Then he went to serve them while I glanced briefly at the older man, but I still couldn't place him. He was all charm, and in no time he was chatting up the two blondes, and they were laughing. Soon it was a little party.

I looked away, taking tiny sips of vodka. Who was he? I needed to get back but I gave it another five minutes. I glanced back and saw Jorge was surveilling the dining room, head turning like a gun turret. The older man had a refined bearing not usually associated with military-style hair. Maybe a tiddly English eccentric; I couldn't hear his voice. He turned, and a coin-sized pinkish spot under the crew cut caught my eye. I made myself look away, glanced at my watch, and saw it was time to go. No way did I plan to irritate Jorge or get anywhere near him.

The moped didn't want to start, so I let it roll down the hill leading to the road. It caught when I popped the clutch and I putt-putted away thinking I could really enjoy relaxing with Jennie at that little place. A civilized drink, and then some fresh-caught grouper from the still clean waters of the very rich. And that nice local white wine from Mme. Gauthier's cellar. It was the end of the day, and the sun had finally cooled down. The sky to my left was a rich purple, and to the right it was a deep blazing red-orange, throwing long shadows across the blacktop. It sucked me right out of my facts and fears and speculations. All my tight little thinking and plotting slipped away, and I cruised mindless through the creamy air. It ripped my soul out of its crummy cave and left it trembling naked in endless time and space. Down the road a mile or so it was over, and my mind was back fresh and clear. A Moke passed me going the other way with a standard-issue spook driving and Olcott alongside. In the back was a guy with rimless glasses and a bent-wire smile — Alain Durry, chatting away, driving Keith crazy. I wondered what BioTel was paying him to reinvent what I had in the yellow envelope. He'd stretch out that consultancy forever, laughing all the way to the bank.

I laid out what we'd be needing in two neat stacks with a gun on top of each, then lay on my back waiting for Jennie. She came up silent as a doe in hunting season.

"Sorry I'm late. I did all the bars, talked to people, didn't learn a thing."

I remembered where I'd seen the white-haired crew-cut man.

"I got lucky," I said slowly. "I saw Jorge-the-Humongous. He was with the very distinguished Richardson Smith-Davies, scientist of the mind, missing since October. Cut his hair, which totally changed him. And we should get going, because I saw a Moke full of company men headed away from here about twenty-five minutes ago on their way to dinner."

We stripped and put on the black pajamas, then rubbed blacking on faces and hands. Finally Jennie handed me a belly bag and a pair of black gloves.

"I want one clip of mercury tips and one of Teflons."

"Teflon? Are you expecting body armor, Rob?"

"Better for locks, it's in the manual."

Then I put four darts on top of the Teflon clip because I really didn't want to take anyone's life. When we were ready, we loaded the boat and dragged it to the water and I re-attached the motor.

31

"Dogs," whispered Jennie, barely audible through the insect buzz. We were at the edge of the clearing under a bright moon, but the dogs were barely visible, two Dobermans coming in far apart, running patterns like wide receivers. They were completely silent. I fired at the one on my side when it got close, the Glock jumped and the dog jumped. I shot again and it went down. I felt Jennie turn and heard a single squirting *pop!* from the Michaud, but her dog was still coming. I swung to aim, but not in time, the dog was in mid-air aimed at her throat. I had an endless second of crazed desperation but with her incredible coordination, she stepped aside and swung the barrel down on its muzzle. It leaped again, and she shot it dead.

I was switching clips, and we both missed the Rottweiler skirting the brush on my side of the clearing. It was fifteen or twenty feet away, coming like a train. Too close, and I was rattled, firing one-handed as it launched itself. I twisted, fell and rolled, but it got my inner thigh. I tried to get the Glock around, but before I could, there were two more *Pop!s* from the Michaud. I could feel the animal spasm, jaws relaxing. It was dead.

"Oh shit!" muttered Jennie. "How bad?"

"Don't know, let's see."

"My bad," said Jennie. "Damn."

We backed into the woods and she looked at the wound with the light from her bag while I stood looking out at the compound.

"Not too bad. Good piece of meat, artery's okay. You were born lucky, Rob."

"I had the fucking dart clip in."

"Well, keep it in, unless you want to take out Jorge for keeps. Hold still."

I did, and she took off her pajama-top and ripped away an arm. Binding the wound, she had a change of heart.

"That's nasty," she said. "We abort now."

"It's not that bad, Jennie, no worse than a bad cut or a hand-tool accident. I'm fine, and I really want to see what's going on here. Just a quick look."

"I don't like this, Rob."

"I'm okay," I said. "Really. It's our only shot."

"Okay then, I'm point. And we're out when I say so."

I agreed, and she started across the lawn while I waited at the edge of the clearing for her to signal me. The dead Rottweiler was lying in front of me. It was a huge bitch, almost as big as Jennie. Then I watched her. In ten seconds she was at the brick building, flat against the wall, then waving me forward. When I got there she touched her nose, but I didn't smell anything. Then she pointed to the ground to hold me back, lay down and snaked her way along the foundation to where she could see around the corner while I aimed over her. Then she backed away and waved me forward again. I smelled weed as I peered around, and there was Jorge. He was sitting on the steps, big as an ox, working on a ganja cigar. I could see a cloud of smoke in the light of the yellow insect bulb. Jennie came up and touched my leg, and I backed away.

"He'll miss the dogs," she whispered.

I didn't say anything, just got down on my belly and crawled back while she covered. Then I squirmed around and took careful aim. As I aimed, he put his hands in his mouth and whistled for the dogs, a big shrill sound that cut through night. Sitting there stoned, he was the perfect target, big and close. I fired with a careful squeeze, then fired again. The Glock farted twice, and from the way he jerked I knew I had both darts in him. He was too stoned to react sharply, but as I backed around the corner, a loud *kackata-kackata* shattered the silence, a wild preemptive sweep from an assault rifle. Bits of chewed-up cabin flew through the air over my head and came down in front of me while I held the Glock ready, aimed up. Jennie was backed around the corner, ready to shoot over me when he came into view, and I was still lying on the ground jammed against the foundation. Then came rapid, heavy, thudding steps. He'd be coming around the corner and we'd all fire, and at that range, someone would be hit.

Didn't happen. Jorge ran off at an angle, away from the

house and up the driveway, heavy steps crunching in the crushed-rock. Then he slowed down like a battery toy running out of juice, stopped to look around, and fell forward. I ran up and stuck the Glock under his ear, but he was out. I pulled his gun out from under him and flung it into the brush. A rattling snore came from his open mouth, but I thought he'd be all right with all that body mass to soak up the shots. As I was frisking him, Jennie came up, and we rolled him out of the driveway. I felt sure we'd be okay for a while, because he wouldn't have been smoking like that if his employers were expected back soon.

The door to the brick building had a standard lock, which I shot out. Jennie pulled the flash from her bag and we saw a long conference room that matched the interior of Big Blue down to the Recaro seats, with a massive table running the length of the room. There were windows along three sides, and a wall with a door at one end.

"I'll be outside," she said. There's a flash in your pouch. If they show up I'll fire through a window and we'll go into the woods where we came in."

The door at the end of the big room wasn't locked, but when I got inside there was only a big glass-top desk with a work-station, and a plant in a corner. Small rug, no file cabinets, and nothing useful in the drawers. But there was a door to another space. Jennie called from the door.

"Two minutes, Rob. If there's an alarm — "

"We'll be gone before they can get back. He didn't have a beeper."

The other room was unfinished storage space with shelving full of boxes. The only window faced toward the water, so I turned on the light. Then I ripped open a couple of boxes and found electronic equipment I didn't recognize. Nothing else but a rug on the floor that matched the one in the office. After a few seconds it didn't make sense having a rug in a storeroom, and I jerked it away. Underneath was a locked trapdoor. A metal fragment ricocheted past my temple when I shot out the lock and woke me up, but I was too pumped to think about it, just yanked the door open. In the dim green half-light below was a large space. I couldn't see much at first, but I knew I was there, and I was startled by the size of the space. It was much larger than the building, and in the center was a huge round object almost filling the space, domed by a giant plastic tent. The light was too poor for me to see much, but then I saw a second plastic tent inside the first. My breath caught in my chest as I went down the stairs and saw the equipment along the walls. There was no end to it, and I had no idea what any of it was, except for the Cray, a computer so rare I'd only seen a picture of one once.

As my eyes adjusted, I saw a large gray-pink thing floating in a pool of dark liquid inside the tents. I was looking at Epstein's Pancake. Time seemed slow down. Closer to it, I saw ripples of liquid flowing from the pool's perimeter that kept it from touching the edge. A fine spray kept the top wet. Durry's accomplishment had been to grow brain tissue as a giant *crêpe*, twelve or fifteen feet across. On it were hundreds of dark little button-like growths like tumors. Hanging above these were dozens of little black boxes gathering a huge filament-skein of wires that cabled up from the button-growths through the plastic tents and across the ceiling to the kind of machine used to monitor brain activity in hospitals. Pulsing lights and a wave on a screen indicated electrical activity, and presumably life.

I was running out of time, but there was another light source on the far side, and I went around the tent. Framed in the doorway of a room and back-lit by a night-light was a man. The Glock came around by itself. He had to have seen the shaft of light from the storeroom, but he didn't move, just kept leaning forward awkwardly, staring at the pool. I couldn't see his expression, but his body language was that of total concentration. He was wearing shorts and a tee shirt, and his hair was big dark unkempt tangle, and he looked like a dog straining at the leash. I moved forward with the Glock aimed at him, but he didn't give me a glance, just stood there in the doorway leaning forward. When I got closer I saw that his ankles were shackled, tethered to something in the room behind him. He was a prisoner, and that was as far as he could go. When I got within a few yards of him I saw the face of a skinny toad, and I smelled him.

"Excuse me — "

"Get upstairs where you belong, can't you see I'm busy?"

I didn't try any harder than that, just came back up through the storeroom to the office and turned out the light. More than two minutes had passed. There was no time to free Jake Epstein, and I guessed they'd move him when they saw that we'd been in. That rattled me and my mind was a blank going back into the office. I needed some tangible evidence of what I'd seen, but had no idea what it could be. Then my flashlight picked up the workstation and my brain unlocked. *Where there's a keyboard there's a CPU.*

Under the desk was a cable going into the flagstone floor. It could be the Cray, but I doubted BioTel would have business and scientific data cohabiting. I remembered how TCC France was built into a space that appeared not to exist, and started smashing panels with the butt of the Glock. Nothing. I went back into the storeroom and noticed the faint hum of an AC, though the space was warm enough that I was sweating. There was a window in the outside wall which left only one place it could be. I threw some boxes off shelves on that wall and smashed at the panel behind it with the Glock. I punched a hole in it, but couldn't do any more. I yanked violently on the end of a shelf out of frustration, and the whole thing fell on me, sheetrock and shelving, knocking me down, dumping boxes and parts all over. Inside was a twin to the Paris IBM, in its own air-conditioned space. I ripped out the cassette, then noticed several more in a box. I was stuffing my pockets when Jennie came in.

"*We're out of time!*" she snapped. She reached into her belly-bag, pulled out a plastic bag, holding it open for the cassettes.

Outside was a velvety moonlit night and the heavy tropical insect-buzz.

"Smith-Davies should be here, they were together," I said. I was in total focus.

"He's throwing a little party in the small bungalow, but Jorge will be coming out of it in a few minutes Rob, those darts don't last long."

"He's unarmed now."

"And you don't have his weapon." She was irritated, but she didn't mention the time, just waited next to the lab building while I sprinted to the small bungalow.

Smith-Davies didn't lock doors, and I walked in to see one of the restaurant blondes giving him head as he lay there with the other one sitting on his face. From the giggles it sounded lighthearted, and I walked into the room unnoticed until the girl on his face spotted me and scurried to a corner, big breasts jiggling. And I had an idea.

"You're coming with me, doctor. If you don't resist, no one gets hurt. If you do, you will — all of you."

The girls got it right away, and stood obediently in the corner talking Swedish fast. Smith-Davies didn't take it seriously, just sat up with a tolerant expression.

"Well I'll be damned. But it won't work. See this button I'm pushing? In a minute or so, one of the most dangerous men you can imagine will be here. When he sees that gun he's liable to kill you. If I were you, I'd get out that window while you can."

"Jorge's out of the game," I said. "Get dressed. Stay where you are, girls."

He gave me an odd look, then slipped into khaki shorts and a blue golf shirt while the women stood naked against the wall, one with her hands behind her back, one hands-on-hips, calmly staring. A good witness, but I had blacking on my face and it was dark.

"May I bring just a little bag?" asked Smith-Davies, putting on his sneakers. "It's already packed."

I nodded. One girl started giggling and the other one barked at her. I was thinking it was time well spent. For my purposes, Smith-Davies was better than the lab. BioTel lawyers could routinely forestall investigation forever, but a smoking-gun celebrity would change everything.

"Ready to go," he said, bag in hand.

I walked him out at gunpoint, but there was no need. His composure was spooky. As far as he was concerned, it was all a lark. Jennie slipped out of the shadows and he found time for an appreciative glance as we started across the endless lawn.

Almost immediately, we heard tires on crushed rock and there were headlights cutting off our escape route. Jennie switched off her flash and we moved behind the lab building while Smith-Davies looked amused.

"You're dead if you try anything," said Jennie as I pulled him back, and I couldn't be sure if she meant it or not.

"Mum's the word," he said, and I could just about hear the marbles rolling around his head. We moved to the shadow of the other cabin, waiting for them to cut the lights so we could get across to the brush. It was close to a hundred feet, still brightly lit.

Then a shout from the truck at the top of the knoll.

"*Jorge!* Come over here — we need you."

We stayed in the dark, keeping behind the cabin as they called again for Jorge. The lights went off and the sound of feet on crushed rock.

"*Something's wrong — weapons out!*"

By then the three of us were running for the brush.

A searchlight came on and the insect-hum was shattered by *kackata-kackatas* but the light missed us, and we were out of sight in the brush.

"Big on preemptive," said Jennie when we were in the brush. She was third in line, keeping an eye on Smith Davies.

"*Motherfuck!*" shouted an angry voice. "*They got Jorge!*"

More *kackata-kackata.*

Get Down! bellowed Keith. Second time I'd ever heard him raise his voice. It was big, and rang with authority. Intentionally or not, he was making it easier for us. Then came a pause, and feet were pounding the crushed rock again, but not in our direction. Then nothing but the sound of our bodies moving through the brush. I remembered getting lost that afternoon and stopped. Smith-Davies read me.

"Water's down to our right," he said. Jennie didn't contradict him, so I took his word for it. In a few minutes I had second thoughts, but said nothing and kept going. Then I started to lose it.

"You'd better be right," I said in an ugly voice.

"Not far," he said, as if not noticing. "I swim every

morning."

"Faster without you, doctor," observed Jennie, as if discussing the weather.

"We'll be at the water in ten minutes," replied Smith Davies, equally cool. I trusted her instincts and said nothing, and no one spoke for a while. I was questioning my kidnapping idea when I saw black water shining through the trees. We were there, but on the wrong side of the breakwater, and jogged back to where the boat was sitting on the beach, ready to go. It moved down along the sand easily with Smith-Davies helping but I was unsure about the next move. I'd planned to go to the next island and wait for dawn, but it felt like a bad idea with TCC so close.

The two of them got in at the stern and Jennie kept an eye on our prize while I waded in body-temperature water halfway up my thighs before they pulled me aboard. Then I crouched in the stern over the motor pulling the starter cord as we drifted in the moonlight listening for Keith's people. We were sitting ducks under that moon if they figured it out. Everything was riding on me, and the old Evinrude wouldn't start. I pulled the cord over and over and tinkered with it.

"Less choke," suggested Smith-Davies. There was something very strange in the way he'd come over to us, but I didn't doubt him. He seemed okay with it all somehow — it was beyond strange, but I went with it. The Evinrude finally started, but it sounded tired, as if the run from St. Croix had taken something out of it, and I guessed Miguel used cheap dirty gas. Time stretched out while I fiddled with it, and then it died. I was starting to feel my leg, but it was the sick motor I was concerned about. I told our new member to row for the lights on the next island while I crouched by the motor and Jennie watched. Finally the motor caught again, and for lack of an alternative we headed for the other island, about a mile away. I was bonked, so I split a coke and sandwich with Jennie. We didn't say much.

When the motor died again, Smith-Davies started rowing. My leg was throbbing as I tried everything I could remember, but it didn't give even the dull puffs of a flooded motor, so I went at the plug with a vise-grip from Miguel's pathetic tool kit. It was stuck, and when I did get it out it was fouled. I cleaned it, but looking at it with a flashlight I had no faith in it. It looked old enough to be original equipment.

"I'm rather good with motors," offered Smith-Davies.

I got the spooky feeling again. Whatever happened was fine with him — he seemed to have no trepidation, no concern about the future. No sense of the world as ordinary people see and fear it. It was Durry's antic confidence to the cube, except that he was so good-natured. Jennie and I looked at each other and she nodded.

"The plug's about dead," I said. "Might be leaking past the porcelain, and there's no spare." I was looking him in the eye as I spoke, our faces quite close. His look was straight and solid.

"Might be able to bring that plug back to life," he said. It occurred to me that he might be kind of prisoner too, a different kind from Epstein, on a longer leash.

I glanced at Jennie and she nodded again. I felt the same way, so I handed it to him and hoped he wouldn't toss it in the water. Then I sat watching, thinking while Jennie was spraying the Michaud with a tiny can of WD-40.

"That chopper," I blurted out.

"Not going anywhere," she said. "I put some Teflons in the tail rotor drive while you were inside. Not fixable."

32

I rowed mechanically through the calm sea and watched Smith-Davies as he worked over the motor. He was checking it out the way experienced sailors do, Jennie sitting next to him, making herself quiet and small and watching every move. He was into it with the focus of an Asperger case.

"God, what a dirty motor!" he exclaimed cheerfully in his gentle voice.

Jennie pulled a handkerchief from somewhere and soaked it in gas from a spare container. Then she produced a plastic bag to put parts in, causing Smith-Davies to think she was awfully keen. I couldn't see what he was doing, just kept rowing, not very hard. I was getting worried as the adrenalin fell away, feeling a chill along with the leg. I let the boat drift while I went through the packs for more clothes, as many layers as I could find. The chill set in anyway, so I opened Jennie's bottle of rum and had a long slug, partly for the calories, knowing I should have eaten more. Jennie saw what was happening, and we switched posts, me holding flashlight and pistol as Smith-Davies proceeded. It was very methodical, and watching him work was like watching a child do something enjoyable. The plug came last. As I was envying him his remarkable freedom from stress, I remembered the pink circle that showed through his crew-cut in the bar. It had to be the entrance for a brain-scraping. I remembered Durry at Madame Gauthier's.

Not from the brain of Alain Durry at any price.

Had Smith-Davies volunteered, been selected by committee, or just fed a turbo-martini and left to draw his conclusions when he woke up? Whatever — they'd apparently accomplished what lobotomies never did. Nobel Candidate Richardson Smith-Davies was untroubled by anything, and was quite operational. Very spaced, but no problem functioning. I wondered if the rules were different for super-smart people, and they could move brain functions around to zones of unused gray matter at will. Then I remembered Epstein. Would Zack be better off thinking him dead, which he might soon be.

The plug, announced Smith-Davies, was *sad* — electrodes burned, gap way off. The porcelain seemed okay, but he needed some sort of file. Jennie produced an emery board and he went at it, checking his progress from time to time. How he figured the gap was anyone's guess, but I could see that he'd grown up around boats. Then came assembly, several pulls at the starter, then choke and spark adjustment. And success. I'd been having a wild and crazy idea as he worked, not wanting to bivouac on the neighboring island any more. It was tiny, and for a small reward TCC could have everyone on it looking for us. The calm night and my sense of Smith-Davies nautical savvy made my idea a little less wild. If he knew the stars, which I thought he might.

"I made it over from St. Croix at three-quarter throttle in about three hours," I said. "It's past eleven, and the sun will come up a little after four. The stars are different down here, but do you think we could find a heading and come out about right if we went with less throttle and used the stars to navigate?"

He smiled and thought about it.

"I familiarized myself with the constellations here to pass time while waiting for Dr. Durry. Probably could, yes, I think so," he said, as if we were old acquaintances. "I'd say chances are pretty good, and at dawn there'll be boats coming out all over the place, lots of traffic. Weather's the thing, Caribbean blows up like nothing. But you've got to take chances at this point, of course."

His face was wide open, with the trust and vulnerability of a child.

"Weather's supposed to be fine through tomorrow."

"How are we for fuel?"

"Half again what I needed for the trip here. Double."

He thought about it for a minute.

"Then we'd probably be fine if we take it a little slower, as you suggested. Avoid overshooting, that would be the big danger. No guarantee of course, but I don't sense any weather coming. I'm sensitive to it, spent half my childhood on the water."

Jennie and I nodded, and he set the throttle. He selected a

star and I went to the bow with the compass and checked our heading, thinking there had really been no choice. We had to be back before they got a search organized. When we were on course to Smith-Davies' satisfaction, we cruised, sipping the rum now and then like the well-mannered people we were, given the choice. I was cleaning the Glock when our guest queried me.

"Whatever is this all about? You don't seem the type."

I was toward the rear on one gunwale, himself on the other, Jennie in the bow to trim the boat. I had a hunch that he would smell a lie better than most.

"Don't really know yet," I replied. "I was employed by a division of the outfit you're working for, and I came across indications that suggested a possible national security threat."

"Don't believe it. Can't believe it — good people, spending a fortune on research the government should be funding. Wonderful, challenging project. Real science."

But his irritation disappeared when I said something conciliatory. I had no doubt he'd yielded the bit of tissue Durry would not allow, and I wondered if he was on some drug as well. He seemed to be on the ever-positive trip that people thought life could be back in the sixties. The sea was calm as a pond, the wind light and steady, almost directly astern, and the moon let us see each other. Smith-Davies taped a dead branch that had fallen into the boat to the tiller, which let us sit together amidships with the boat trimmed. We were having a good time, a little party. Maybe the last party. Whatever else, Smith-Davies had great *joie de vivre* and not much standing in the way.

"What about this Epstein?" I asked after the next round.

"Yes, Jake. Can't separate himself from his ideas at all. Had the luck to come upon one that looked like leading somewhere, and he kept at it. A number of us were speculating in the same direction, but Jake's the one who took it on, you see. Problem is, he's impossible to deal with. Can't get over himself, get in bed with the Devil for money. He has that style people pick up in those government labs. Push your idea, never let up, sell your mother. Thing is, what we're doing is too interesting to walk away from. A bit like Manhattan, which I had a taste of as a student. Still in my teens, dogsbody to someone important because I had some German and a friend in court. But the scale of it — never forget that. Just throbbing with excitement, all those brilliant temperamental Europeans. Speaking in tongues someone joked. What a *time!* Nothing like it ever. Well, if Oracle speaks, it will be close to that scale. Enormously important, change everything."

"Work much with Dr. Durry? I know him from France."

"Yes, but not directly. Alain's in charge of — care and feeding, I suppose you'd call it. Getting tissue to survive and develop under control. Early ones all went wrong at a certain point. Crib-death we called it. Alain solved that, but apparently his only copy of the new procedure was lost, or so he says. Very peculiar. Got himself hired on to re-develop it and supervise. I pick up from there. Half my job's helping Jake over the rough spots. Very headstrong man. He's quite insecure in some areas, and touchy about it. High-strung, always pressing, can't step back, lives in that lab under the main building."

"People in Cambridge seemed to think Jake was an ass, Dr. Smith-Davies," said Jennie, as if she'd lived there all her life and knew anyone that mattered. Smith-Davies allowed himself a gentle laugh.

"Do please call me Dick, both of you. And about Jake, it's true. Abrasive, after any woman, married or not, sloppy scientist. Bad businessman too, couldn't hang onto his company or the people he needed. Alain plays with him, finds ways to send him up. Wife must be going through hell. Jake's, I mean. Laura's not very clever . . .

"Might as well say it," he added, as if speaking of the dead. "Jake's quite mad. Doesn't come out often, locked up much of the time. Totally unpredictable, reminds me of that orgone fellow, Reich. A bit violent lately, too. Might've taken the wrong bit of tissue. I can still talk to him, but I'm the only one, and he can't keep his mind on process any more — what we're doing day to day. He's still re-inventing it, theorizing, theorizing. Thinks people are poisoning him, talking about him, stealing his ideas — case right out of the books, and worse after Durry showed up. Alain was here around the holidays, announced he'd solved the main problems and snobbed Epstein while he was about it. The French do that to everyone, of course. Better than bombing people, I always say."

"There was trouble between them in Cambridge," I said, thinking what a force Jakob Epstein had been in so many lives, and what had been done to him. I hoped his son would never find out.

"Alain was settling a score I suppose, and Jake's just strung too tight. Took a poke at Durry at one point, and of course he doesn't know how — nice Jewish boy, got his exercise in bed. Lord, I'm sounding like Alain! He stepped aside, took Jake's arm as it went by as if dealing with a child, and down he went. Worse than just striking him back."

"And?"

"And the girls like Alain. I think he goes for anything at all. Mad about the good-looking black fellow, Keith. Well, there was this woman Jake had his eye on, a young waitress, but waitresses like the French type, I think. Endless dinner, all of us around the table drinking lots of wine, Alain playing to the crowd and the girl non-stop — the new man who solves everything, y'know. Jake just eating the girl up with his eyes, very obvious. Withdraw from combat's what you do there, my view. Well of course he didn't. And finally Alain turned to him, with the girl just behind them. Jake had just said something foolish about some next-century application as if it were a real-time possibility. Talking at the girl, looking for attention.

"'There are not many stupid Jews,' says Alain, 'But you must surely be one of them, Epstein.' Says it just for the three of them, except that everyone's riveted and he knows it. Jake went white, stood up, took his swing and found himself sitting on the floor. Totally reduced, not worth a thing after that. Smashed ego, you could see him sliding. Useless. I never told them, I couldn't. Doesn't shave, thinks in circles. Then they found he'd got hold of a knife somewhere, and it was obvious who he'd be using it on."

Smith-Davies paused again and spoke for the record.

"Thing is, though, Jake took the bull by the horns. Hands-on, like Marconi or Tesla or the Wrights — he went and did it. Alain has a problem with that, knows damn well that education's only half of it. Jealous. Jealous of each other, really."

"I saw Laura recently, and she's really having a bad time," said Jennie, opening her cigarette case and offering them.

"Frankly, he ruined that girl," said Smith-Davies, taking one. "We all, well — we took care of Laura. She's terribly limited in some ways, can't think at all, go to bed with the mailman. Jake Epstein gets her to run away from Sonny Turnbull, perfectly nice man, great sailor, and then he can't afford her, or even go easy on her. Bastard, crazy or sane. You two are a couple, I suppose?"

"More than less," I said, still thinking about the prophet Epstein and his son.

"Oh yes, we'll be married in June!" warbled Jennie ingénue. Then she went forward to leave us alone.

"You must know Spiegel, too?" I asked after the next round.

"Oh, yes. Tough customer. Fierce sense of humor. I expect he'll be after you."

"I don't think so," I said, and caught Jennie looking at me.

"Your field?" said Smith-Davies. "You don't seem quite right for this, Beach."

"History. Languages."

"Lucky man. I'm lost in a foreign country, quite literally sometimes. You'll like Jane, my wife. Natural linguist, does translations, knows how to find a good restaurant anywhere. I'm absolutely not allowed to contact her on penalty of forfeiting my job and bonus, but if you could drop by and ease her mind without giving me away I'd greatly appreciate it."

"I'd be glad to, but she'll want to know when to expect you, you know."

"Yes. Well . . . months. Say half a year."

"I got the impression from Alain that the project was only just starting to happen."

"The French are conservative, known for it. One reason their nuclear situation is better than ours. Still have their farms, too, careful about chemicals. What we've got now — well, it's certainly not failure. With Alain's techniques we've been able to develop and sustain the tissue. The breakthrough was getting it to develop as a flat sheet — it floats in a pool of nutrients. And we're able to access it using biologically generated electrical current which we pick up from symbiotic life-forms. Well, somewhat parasitic, it turns out — another problem for Alain. But in itself that's quite an achievement. It's at a point where it can play checkers, not very well I must add. But access is a long slow near-random process. It's delicate, you see, not much more than a thick film floating there raw. Very, very difficult. Government project, rightfully — "

"I think that's the plan," I said, but my mind was elsewhere. A coolness had cut through the rum, a sudden perspective shift, like seeing a chess position through someone else's eyes. Smith-Davies was optimistic, but I'd sensed Durry's doubts more than once, and he still had his entire brain. Maybe the real reason for Epstein's breakdown wasn't Durry, but knowing that he'd failed. Honorable failure, like Professor Langley's flightless aircraft that couldn't do what the Wright brother's bike-shop contraption did. But BioTel was very committed to this thing that could barely play checkers, and had invested God only knew how much. But those Texans were no fools. Project 38 would get funded to make the world safe for democracy and a fortune for Biotel. Cost being no object in support of SDI, it could go on indefinitely.

Smith-Davies spoke again.

"Now that Alain's here, everything's in high gear of course, moving right along."

Alain, who'd made a joke about Oracle and Descartes' delusions about the pineal gland. But his arrogant presence and government credentials would add business credibility. We talked and drank and ate plantain chips that Jennie had picked up. I began to drift, and went into my pack for a stimulant pill. Then I found myself dropping out of the conversation, working out what to do in St. Croix. I'd been generous with Miguel and I doubted he'd volunteer information, but I hadn't paid for any more than that. I had an extra-long slug of rum and excused it on the grounds I was wounded. My crew laughed politely and Jennie told me I looked cold, to lie down under the foil blanket in her pack.

"She's right, Beach, you look a bit peaked. Wound like that drains you."

"Not 'til the rum's gone, Dick," I said, but then I did it. As soon as I closed my eyes I was asleep and dreaming. McVeigh's voice, solid and clear on the drive to Cambridge. *There's something about an operation.* The wisdom of courage, Mac's ace in the hole until he got involved with Leni Hartt. For the moment I had a little of that courage. I felt calm as old Aldous Huxley at death's door, dropping a load of mescaline to enhance the experience. Then I was at the Chelsea with Jennie, her voice calm and logical.

I guess the question now is, how did Morris get on board?

Right. I woke up part way. When did Eulenspiegel happen? Before Olcott, Keith said. And who preceded him, if anyone?

Smith-Davies was chatting on about bio-feedback and a friend who could fly his plane without touching the controls. Even as we were carrying him off, he didn't connect us with the idea of the project being disrupted. I slid back down into a happy dream about Layla as a child.

It was first light, not yet dawn, and I had a major headache. Jennie and Smith-Davies were talking about restaurants, and the Evinrude was cut back close to idle. My mind was clear, but I was cold, worried about the leg. My immune system would be down from lack of rest, and the wound would probably get infected unless I could get warm and sleep for a day or so. I sat up and flexed the leg, which was functional but not happy. Everyone smiled, and Jennie passed me the rum. I had a swallow, smiled back, and started coming to life. First light wasn't looking very good. Fog and silence.

When had he lost the stars? I didn't dare ask. The jug came back and I killed it, thinking that I'd put my faith in a man who'd lost part of his brain. I had no confidence that Smith-Davies knew where we were, but tried not to show it. As they talked, the fog began lifting off the sea here and there. I sipped a warm Coke in silence, looking at fuel containers, thinking about how to best use that fuel, wondering how the two of them could keep chattering. I still wasn't ready to ask when the stars had disappeared, and my watch told me we might have gone past St. Croix. Jennie opened her pack and pulled out a pair of roast beef sandwiches. Eating them brought on a silence, and it continued when we were finished. I settled myself and rehearsed my calm.

"What do you think, Dick? Shut down and save fuel until visibility improves?"

"Well you see, the wind's shifted and there's the beginning of a chop, so I'm really just holding her in place."

It was obvious when he said it, and he didn't sound crazy at all.

"It's been compass and dead reckoning for almost an hour," he continued. "I don't think we'll be too far off, though. This wind coming up will blow the mist away."

We understood each other. There would be lots of boats out normally, but if the wind kept building, most of them would be gone. If a blow was coming, they might not come out at all. I closed my eyes and tried to plan ahead. Then Smith-Davies tapped my shoulder and pointed behind me. I turned and saw a fishing boat twenty yards away. I put a finger to my lips and he nodded. In a few minutes another one came from the same direction, and we headed where they'd come from. I considered hailing the next boat, but its crew wouldn't forget our little group, and I thought I smelled land. In a few minutes Smith-Davies pointed again, and there was the tip of the radio tower.

33

It was 0540 hours when I found Miguel's dock. He stepped out of the tin shack at the sound of his motor and walked to the tiny pier in a gimpy old-man's morning gait. He was wearing a serious face, and I shot Jennie a look as I climbed out, wanting a word with him alone. Jennie picked it up and kept Smith-Davies occupied unloading the boat.

"Police ask 'round," said Miguel, just loud enough for me to hear.

"About what?"

"Who rents boats. Wake us at night, say to call when boats return."

"Oh? What did you tell them?"

"American boy with girl and beer." His weathered face was as hard to read as Fred's. I nodded, reached into my billfold and handed him ten fifties. He took them, unsmiling, money earned at risk. With the unclaimed deposit, it was a major bribe in his world, but he was a poor old man with local ties, and he'd have to talk if they pressed him. But would anyone believe that night voyage in his little tin coracle? Jennie and Smith-Davies were finished unloading, and she fussed with the packs, giving me another few seconds. The wind was steady and seemed to be rising.

"What kind of police ask such questions?"

"Just police," he said, meaning local.

Then Jennie was beside me nodding earnestly, brown and friendly, looking about seventeen. The old man took her in and a fleeting look passed over his leather features, as if remembering a dream from his youth. Who would give such a beautiful creature to the police?

"Go now," he said in a very quiet voice. "Quiet — people sleep."

Walking up the dirt road I saw it had been stupid to return with my crew, which he could describe. Just returning the boat was stupid. Miguel needed his boat, but I'd have bought him another. Terrible mistakes, like spilling my guts to Fred. We needed to disappear before the cops visited him again. Before people started waking up.

"We can't go to the hotel, Jennie."

"I know. I checked us out. I've been down here before, Rob. I know the island and have a place in mind. We'll have to walk."

To avoid being seen as a group, we split up, Jennie ahead with Smith-Davies, me following thirty or forty yards behind. I kept them just in sight, struggling through the damp foggy morning along quiet back streets, dazed but reasonably functional. People were waking up and cooking food. My leg didn't hurt much, but the pack weighed a ton, and we were on a long gradual uphill. Then it gradually leveled off to a very poor section where the houses lacked paint and there were fewer of them. Some buildings had old ads painted on their sides. A faded ghostly WWII ad covered the side of an abandoned shed.

LUCKY STRIKE GREEN HAS GONE TO WAR

In my grin I felt the edgy crash-hangover of the stimulant chip. I had no blood sugar and followed like a zombie, a line of poetry going round and round in my head:

> anyone lived in a pretty how town
> with up so floating many bells down . . .

Who wrote that? It carried me as I trudged through the gray morning in a feverish half-daze, smelling fried food and coffee. The wind was relentless on my chest, and I kept telling myself how lucky we were to have made it. I was out of gas, insanely thirsty, my mouth paper-dry, wondering how long I could go. The weakness and desperation that had caught me in Milan was back. I told myself I was among friends and could beat it if I just kept walking.

I woke up standing with the two of them in the empty road. I'd lost it completely, walked myself into a trance. We decided it was okay to walk together now that we were out of town, and I continued my dazed march until we came to a crossroads hamlet where we stopped under a big tree. The wind was really coming up, and I could see the undersides of the leaves. Across the road by itself was a big yellow three-story wood-frame rooming house for locals. My leg was throbbing and I needed to lie down and get warm. Smith-Davies and I sat quietly under the tree like a pair of lost fools while Jennie disappeared into the house. As my fear was starting up again, she came back out and told us we had rooms.

"*Excellent!*" said Smith-Davies. "Absolutely dying for sleep, I've been all-in for hours. I thought Jorge would help out with those girls but he wandered off. I'll never understand Indians."

Jennie had taken the top floor, three rooms, of which we used two. They were as bare as my Saint Denis garret but had decent beds. She left to arrange food as soon as we were installed, and I lay on a bed in the biggest room, still cold under three blankets. Before I fell asleep, a tall, dignified black woman named Miralda brought fruit, tea, and home-made bread, but I'd lost my hunger and just drank a lot of tea. Smith-Davies lay down in the next room and fell asleep after eating. Before I did the same, I had a thought.

"Keith might call Bananas between noon and one. That was our standing arrangement. I'm not ready to deal, but how would you feel about waiting for a call? No one answers the pay phone."

"Good idea," said Jennie. "I'll be fine after a nap. What about this leg, Rob?"

"Not good. My resistance is down and I really need sleep, but I think I'll be okay. What about Dick?"

"He won't leave; we've replaced Jorge for him. What's wrong with him, Rob? Have you noticed the pink spot on his skull that he touches every once in a while?"

"I'm sure that's from a brain scraping for that goddamned Project 38. That was a requirement for it. You're stuck with a pair of crazies, lady. And there's more you need to know — I never told you what else I found. There's a lab under that building, a huge operation, and I saw it. Big round pool under a plastic tent and this live thing floating in it — Durry's hydroponic brain.

Epstein's down there with it, crazy as a — "

"Shithouse rat?"

"They'll kill him, Jennie. They'll have to, he's literally shackled to the wall, and he's not the kind to shut up, we know that about him." I paused. "Maybe for the best. Poor Zack — that idiot mom, and this on top of it. Those fuckers could care less."

She nodded slowly and handed me a slice of pear. I was exhausted from talking, not ready for a meal, and she kept passing me slices of pear. When it was gone she gave me a long slow calm look that went so deep that I felt as if a big spring in my back had been released. Then she washed my wound very thoroughly while I lay on the bed, re-opening it and smearing in antibiotic salve from her kit. She didn't spare me and it hurt like hell. While she was bandaging it I fell asleep.

I heard Jennie moving around and tried to wake up. She came over with a mug of tea and sat on the bed while I tried to focus. The whisper of a string quartet was coming from somewhere — Smith-Davies listening to his Sony in the other room. It was afternoon, the wind had died, and the sky was blue, but I was still cold.

"We're all right so far," she said quietly. "I talked to Keith, and they're in total confusion. He came back to take charge here, so information about boat rentals goes through him. Jorge covered himself by reporting a force of four to six, and Keith bought it. I let him think we started to go in but got out when a dog bit you. He thinks we were lucky not to run into this other team, which is presumed Israeli because of Morris. They think this gang of five and Dr. Dick are already halfway to Tel Aviv in their James Bond submersible aircraft and he'll show up as a bargaining chip on some deal down the road."

She paused and gave me time to react. It was what I wanted to hear, but I didn't feel any relief.

"What is Keith not buying?" I asked after a while.

"Going public immediately, which I'd say is code for going public on —"

I snapped out of it and words started jumping out of my mouth like hot rivets.

298

"No. Now that we've got Dick, we don't hold back, it doesn't work that way. Media's the only way to get at them, and we need it all — Arvin Telemann and his BCCI brother in law, krytrons, Lakam, the Epsteins, arms shipments, *everything*. The story has to compete with Monday Night Football, schoolyard shootings, gang-rapes, crack wars, blowjob priests, sci-fi movies — gotta jump all over your couch-potato cretin like '*Check this fuckin' movie, dude!*'"

I stopped. There it was, exactly what had to happen. I hadn't really seen it until the words came out of my mouth.

Jennie waited and I started over, quietly.

"Look," I said. "It's like a jigsaw puzzle — it's nothing until you've got most of the pieces in place, then suddenly it's there. Like Watergate — No Pentagon Papers, no outcry. No Deep Throat, no John Dean. No John Dean and Nixon gets off. Well, they learned from that. This time the attorney general gave North and his girlfriend time to shred the documents, and they offed that big-mouth Israeli. People at the top stood clear. Then the Prez pardoned North. People never had a chance to know."

"And nobody *wants* to, darling, you always leave out that part."

She dropped it in politely, a patient and knowledgeable woman lighting her designer cigarette. A signal to back off.

"Yeah," I said, thick and stubborn. "Well I'm going with what I know — America likes good TV as much as sex."

"We're clear, Rob — aren't you a little bit pleased?" she asked in a hurt voice. I said something about needing to finish the job.

"How about settling for a minor masterpiece like staying alive, Mr. Price?" she snapped. "Are you above that? I need to know that much."

I shut up and she continued.

"Keith says those cassettes have everything. That's where BioTel stored anything they didn't want in the US — illegal arms transactions, financials, tax scams, off-shore accounts. St. Marcus is French, no jurisdiction — "

Hairs all over my body came to attention.

"Right. Keith is sure about this?"

"So sure he's scared to death. And they're completely up the wall about Dick. Keith says any doctor will see what happened. Worst case, *mega*-scandal. Dick's super high-profile and his wife's an ACLU lawyer."

"They must be fucking *praying* it was Israelis. Anyone but Americans. They know Dick is incapable of lying."

Jennie nodded and got her professional look, as if she had more when I was ready. I waited and she looked at me.

"Keith is getting shaky, Rob. He's worried about Jason taking the hit — "

"*Fuck* Jason Olcott, he's just another rich bastard, he knew what was going on."

Stupid. I apologized and took a deep breath. She felt my forehead and said I needed an antibiotic.

I'll make it up to her, I thought, and fell asleep in the middle of the conversation.

It was night when I woke up, and I was feverish, the entire leg aching knee to groin. Jennie was in the rocking chair, waiting for me.

"We've got penicillin, are you allergic?" I wished I deserved her.

"Not allergic," I said, trying to wake up and think straight. "I think it's a developed allergy — you're okay, and then one day you're allergic after using it."

"Miralda got her pharmacist to give it to her for her daughter."

"Bribe her?"

"No," said Jennie. "I told her I was pregnant and you had to stay alive and make me an honest woman. Dick's your rich but goofy uncle, and he wants us to get married. Keep you alive and she gets a wedding present."

"Dick wants me gone so he can get in your pants."

She snickered, then went to the other room and woke Smith-Davies, who appeared in a pair of bright red pajamas. He stretched his skinny arms, accepted a cup of tea, and chatted us up on penicillin. He thought it would be safe to test me with a tiny bit.

"Big thing is anaphylactic shock, the throat closes up," he said cheerfully. "I've seen a tracheotomy done — simple procedure, really, just need everything clean . . . "

As he offered his medical services my new uncle sat on a chair in his scarlet pajamas. He was wearing the same expression he'd had working over the Evinrude.

"I'd start with a very small test shot, just a tiny bit. If all's well in twenty minutes, I'd feel safe about the full dose," he continued. "Certainly in the high eighties, percentage-wise. At least we know those beasts weren't rabid. Lived better than the natives. No larynxes, completely silent, that's how they surprised you."

I rolled on my side and Jennie gave me a touch of penicillin in my butt. Then I lay back looking at a spot on the ceiling and got sleepy. Then I was back. I nodded and rolled over, and Jennie squeezed the rest into me. I closed my eyes and started slipping away.

"I'm not a doctor," said Smith-Davies quietly, "but he doesn't look like going into shock. Sleep's what he needs."

Then I slept long and solid, and the penicillin smote the infection like the T-34s routing the Panzers at the battle of Kursk.

34

It was early afternoon with a breeze blowing through the room, and I heard a kettle whistling as I woke up. Smith-Davies was brewing tea, cheerful as always.

"Get some tea in you," he said. "Feeling better?"

"God bless those women," I said.

"Yes, yes, put you right on course. Jennie's out shopping, due back any time. Need to talk a bit if you don't mind."

I wasn't awake yet, but I drank tea and listened.

"Jennie's told me about the both of you, why you've been doing what you have. I pressed her a bit. Keen sense of ethics, that girl. Big project makes you lose perspective — fall in love with it, you have to. She's right though. Making it a profiteer's game is all wrong. And SDI's a fraud, that's hardly a secret. Like the Maginot line — stupid, all graft, infamous. Before your time."

"My mother was French."

"Then you'd know. Star Wars of its day — myth of invulnerability, never works. Insanely expensive. Problem is, we're inherently porous, it's obvious, that's how we have the drug trade and all these immigrants. Make a nuclear device the size of a suitcase these days. You and I and some friends could bring enough of them in on Cessnas and Chris Crafts to destroy half our cities and kill everything downwind . . . "

He stopped to gather his thoughts.

"Los Alamos wasn't like that," he said with nostalgic assurance. "I was hardly more than a boy, but my eyes were open. It was terribly pure, dedicated. Highly political at times, but never foul. Not about money, we felt the world hanging in the balance and didn't know how far along the other side might be. Germans started out ahead, you know — if they'd been sensible about their Jews, they'd have beaten us to it. No Jews, no bomb. We were *so* lucky. And we still don't really know what the Bomb is over here, or war on our own soil for that matter. Still think war's about feeling powerful and boom times and perhaps your cousin doesn't come home, and then a parade. The Russians know — scorched earth and they rape your mother while you're out hunting for turnips. My daughter married a Russian. After Chernobyl they know what radiation is, too. Dead farms, and what does grow, you can't eat. I'm glad Jennie talked to me, got me thinking."

I wasn't so glad. His bright blue eyes were troubled when he came over with my tea. Before he was a scientist or well-born or a hopeless womanizer, Smith-Davies was a decent man, and there was humiliation in his voice. He was seeing himself as used, a mini-Speer to a corporate Hitler. He couldn't let it alone.

"Hardly ever notice the world, typical scientist. World of our own, ignore things we don't want to be bothered with. Governed by fools, country going to hell in a hand-basket. Vote left and hope for the best, Durry's hilarious on the subject. All I knew was a quarter million tax free in an offshore bank for half a year in the Caribbean, expenses paid. Not much money in science, hard on wives. You just hope to be on the cutting edge, make a bit of history. If it flies, they put a plaque on your old dorm, if it hasn't been turned into a mall. Letter from the President thanking you."

I was hard at work on my report when Jennie breezed through the door, a totally composed rich girl who happened to be mocha-brown. She was followed by Miralda carrying a tray with fish stew, greens and yams. She looked me over, peered into my eyes, examined my tongue, poked my leg hard and asked after my testicles.

"You all right now, just 'bout," pronounced Miralda. "'nother two days."

"With your help," I said, thinking of the penicillin.

She gave me a nod and left, followed by Smith-Davies. When the door closed, Jennie and I looked at each other.

"We're still okay, Rob. But Keith's wound very tight — he looks worse than you. He's afraid of what will happen to Jason if everything comes out."

"Things he really never knew about."

Jennie ignored my sarcasm and nodded — she was that

303

eager for peace. We let it ride and sat down to eat. Keith's price for total cooperation was Olcott getting off — no surprise. That wasn't going to happen, but I didn't say so.

"He's purged all records on Morris," said Jennie. "But before he did, he learned that Laura Epstein went to Israel with her dentist after her divorce and spent the summer on a kibbutz. That's when Morris got hold of her. Her assignment was Epstein, which was easy, since she was already in Boston and connected."

"Must've thought he'd died and gone to heaven."

"Shut up. So, good plan, but then she fell in love with Epstein, became his total slave while still reporting to Morris. For years."

"Poor Morris. No luck with women."

"You need to meet with Keith," she said in the professional voice. "Since our little raid, you're running him, Rob. He's your asset — he knows it, and he needs contact."

Her look demanded my full attention.

"What Morris did for you on that plane ride you told me about — you've got to do that for Keith. Pick him up and pull him together. Could you do it later today?"

"Yes, sure, I understand. I'll be fine if I sleep some more and have some coffee."

We went on with lunch, me eating slowly and methodically to get back my strength, drinking lots of tea. What was going on in Keith Alderman's head? How could he imagine I'd let Jason Olcott walk away? Didn't he know I wanted Crackerjack hoist on his own petard, blown sky-high for all to see, along with BioTel?

"Keith could just bring me in, you know. With Morris gone, he's in charge."

"Not with those documents in the hands of your attorneys, stuff he's never even seen because you're so clever. All ready for media and Congress, copies safe offshore."

I chuckled. The tension went away and everything was peaceful. Outside an endless vista of deep green tree tops baked quietly in the mid-day sun.

"So how do we do it?"

"He'll call Bananas after five. I have a place in mind if you can walk a mile."

"I'll be fine."

"Good. I can't talk any more, I need some rest myself."

She lay on the bed while I stood up and began some easy stretching. A hamstring stretch from back in cross-country days at school. It hurt, but it felt okay, so I stretched some more and started planning exactly how to out BioTel. I said something to Jennie, but she was sound asleep.

Toward sunset I was sitting under a big tree back in a brush clearing — Jennie's safe spot, near a footpath that branched off a dirt road. I was reading a two-day-old L.A. Times in the dying light, hoping some local editor might keep the Epstein-BioTel-Prowler story alive, but it was gone. I was bothered, but mainly I was afraid. Keith was Olcott's man, and could do as he saw fit, no questions asked. If Jennie was wrong, I was gone. My backup was the Michaud, which I'd concealed in a little scooped-out hollow in easy reach under some leaves. I'd stand, shake hands, and sit down in the same place.

Keith came down the path through the trees, very colonial in khaki shorts and bush jacket. When he got close I saw that his skin was drawn and lifeless, gray with fatigue. I smiled and made my greeting as real as possible. Then I sat down and told him I was full of penicillin.

"Jennie told me. Looks like it's working."

"I'll be fine. Just rather sit."

"I've got twenty minutes," said Keith, balancing in a crouch, knees bent, letting me see more of him than he did of me. He got down to it quickly.

"Our immediate problem is Dr. Smith-Davies, acting project director. He disappeared that night, taken by whoever came in later — assumed Mossad. He's on medication, incapable of discretion."

Discretion. Keith's impossible dream.

"They'll keep him out of sight and pump him," I improvised. "Does he have his medication?"

"Good question. Probably yes, his kit was gone. You also need to know that CIA has a team here. They're taking the

Epstein boy seriously because of Marquardt's death — both stories connect with TCC and BioTel, which is why CIA blacked them out."

He paused.

"Al was theirs."

He squeezed these words out against his will, not looking at me.

I was too stunned to say anything, just stared. When I could speak the words came out like bullets.

"Al was CIA?! And Morris knew?"

Keith nodded. He wasn't forgiving himself. I wasn't either.

"Sheepdipped," he said.

I looked at him.

"Turned loose with prejudice to make him look clean. They do that sometimes. To get inside somewhere."

"Al Marquardt," I said slowly. "He was strung out, Keith. For real, I saw it."

"You mentioned. Probably CIA found out and fired him, then offered him the option of working off the books. *Agent provocateur*, mission to screw TCC. Screw the State Department. But he apparently didn't tell them much."

"If he told them about Oracle he couldn't steal it. They're talking to you?"

"On a limited basis."

And he'd be talking to them. But I had confidence in Keith when it came to dealing with standard spooks. They'd get name, rank, serial number and a smart lawyer.

"Anything on how Morris got into TCC?"

"I checked. The computer had nothing on his hiring, just a couple of references to someone work-name Snyder and someone identified by the initial "S" — probably the same person."

He'd forgotten discussing Snyder and "S." with me on the Williamsburg Bridge, but I said nothing. He was maxed out and fragile.

"Snyder's a current reference, Keith. He preceded me as the Durry contact, then disappeared. Durry said he was very good. He thought someone had offed him."

And he's back. I didn't mention that.

"Just a work-name," said Keith, his voice back to normal. "Rob, CIA still know very little, and I cleaned our computer thoroughly. The question is, what version of the story do we reveal?"

The real one, warts and all. But I just nodded.

"Jason Olcott could be destroyed," said Keith slowly. "He had no real idea what was going on — "

"Keith," I said, "I'm not sure that's completely true."

He gave me a look of distraught resentment and fear.

"But Rob, really — the man invested in a company and they gave him a job. He thought he was doing something patriotic, but his operation was infiltrated by an experienced man that he accepted and relied on. He knows that now. Full disclosure would break him."

"Negotiable. He tried to break me, you know. In Paris. When I told him CIA was on our case, he backed off."

He gave me a harried glance. I was running him, alright, and doing it all wrong.

"It's history," I said, "Doesn't matter. Next time we meet, you tell me how you'd like it handled. What you want to hold back. We'll work it out."

A very cold lie that I couldn't avoid. Keith's exhausted face showed relief as plainly as he ever showed anything.

"What was the bug up his ass about me?" I asked, to move things along.

"It was that Hartt woman. Loose cannon — walked into BioTel demanding to speak to you. You were connected with her through your friend McVeigh. It looked like you'd talked. She's gone — found in a hotel room, beaten to death."

Millie's work for sure, but I said nothing.

"So you see why Jason was on your case."

"Agreed. The organization failed him when it let Morris in, however that happened. We should find out how he got in and plug the hole."

He bypassed that and mellowed his voice.

"Something else, Rob. I've checked out Uniceptco. We weren't involved — that was Al."

And BioTel. But he wouldn't want to go there. I tried to look convinced, but I couldn't lift the rock without exposing Olcott. I went on lying, and saw that Keith was believing me. He wanted to, the way I'd wanted to believe Morris. Time was short, and we'd covered everything we were willing to talk about, so I stood up to end the meeting. We shook hands old-style and Keith walked away leaving me to think about Alvin Marquardt, CIA pro. His mission had been the same as the guy at the Tic-Tic — get TCC. He'd done it perfectly, got me to doubt TCC with spilled information, blew me away with his revelations in that piano bar, and confirmed all my suspicions. Al was gone and I was still chasing TCC as he'd planned. No wonder everyone respected him. And no wonder I never felt anything bad from him — he'd had to use me, no choice, but otherwise he'd liked me fine. Maybe because I got along with his son. Had he salted anything away for his family? I stood still for a minute, listening to the insect orchestra, but I couldn't get him out of my head.

Il n'est pas serieux, my mother would have said, and been wrong. Al had been a great bunch of guys, none of them dumb.

I was fading by the time I got myself up the stairs, but one look at Smith-Davies snapped me out of it. He was alone in his room with the door open, pacing and quietly talking to himself. He was in a fog, but he nodded at me.

" . . . application," he said, in a weak, hollow voice. "Curious about application. No question how Los Alamos applied, eh? But at times I wonder what Epstein really sees. What is this 'special kind of thinking' required for recognition and response without adequate information? How do you make premature choices correctly . . . ?"

I could feel his mind spinning on and on, out of control.

"Guessing's what it is!" he concluded brightly. "Isolating major elements and acting before full data is available. How most things get done in life, really. But Durry says it's like the chess that comes from a great player compared to what comes out of a machine. The machine eventually will overcome, yes, but given time — "

His mood dropped suddenly and he fell back into the

hollow tired voice. I was remembering what Keith said about medication. He was going on two days without it.

"We're so far from success — just beginning to get useful responses. Still completely experimental."

"Like SDI," I said, wondering how to bring up his medication.

"Yes," he said, in a dull old voice.

We looked at each other. It was a rough moment, because part of him understood.

"Are you all right, Dick? I have tranquillizers — "

"No, that won't do it. I've got another of these damned headaches. Can't see. Look in my bag for me, would you? Blue box, hypo and bottle. Three cc intramuscular. You'll have to help."

His voice was mechanical, as if struggling to get out the information while he still could. He stopped talking and I saw tremors in his hands. I opened the bag and started rummaging through it, then realized Jennie should be back. I tapped hard on the wall, and she was there by the time I found the box.

"Dick needs his medication. Three cc intramuscular."

She opened the box without a word, broke open a disposable hypodermic and drew the fluid into it. The tremors were getting worse and I was afraid for him.

"Muscle back of upper arm," he muttered.

I sat him down and grabbed him hard to stop the shaking, and Jennie injected whatever it was. It took forever before he started to relax.

"Thank you, nurse," he said then. He had no idea where he was.

Jennie looked at me, then at the bed. Smith-Davies eyes were empty and far away.

"We'll talk SDI later," I said, watching his reaction.

"Manhattan wasn't like that . . . . Durry's absolutely hilarious about it . . . . just a big man's dogsbody, but my eyes were open . . . . problem is, we're inherently porous, it's obvious, that's how you have the drug trade . . . . Evinrudes are good . . . ."

It was like hearing scrambled bits of a tape recording.

"Time for some bed-rest, I'd say."

"If you think so, doctor."

Jennie guided him to the bed and he closed his eyes. She put a blanket over him, and in minutes a rattling snore came from his mouth. Bone-weary and shaken, I sat down. After a while Jennie spoke.

"I've been resisting you, Rob, but the way I feel now, I don't mind anything that happens to the bastards who did this."

We lay down on the bed and I thought she was going to cry. When she really liked someone she didn't hold back, and Smith-Davies had got to her. I had a sense of life rolling on like the cart of Juggernaut, throwing people together, tearing them apart, chewing them up and spitting them out.

35

I woke up late with the sun in my face and saw Jennie sitting at the table with a stack of newspapers. She came over and handed me her cup of coffee.

"Are you ready to talk? she asked, in a quiet, urgent voice.

"Slowly."

"Okay. I had breakfast at the airport and overheard some journalists. I flirted them up, and they were excited. CIA is everywhere, they said. Lots of them. There was a big leak, and they thought it was intentional, that CIA wanted a buzz going down here."

"So just stay put until we see more?"

She nodded. I went to the table in my shorts and looked through the newspapers while drinking Jennie's coffee. Zack's case was back, but on a company script. Lawyers, mother, prosecutor, and journalists were agreed: BioTel was not involved and no such employee as Kammler had ever existed. Zack had heroically and appropriately shot and killed an armed prowler, and the rest was an adolescent conflation of factoids. Protecting his photogenic well-born mother was apple pie, of course, no one would ever indict, etc.

I was beyond strong feelings about it. What I had was a marketing problem. How to get what I knew out there in a way that the whole thing couldn't be fixed by a tame attorney general working for a patriotic CIA President knee-deep in Iran/Contra. I kept thinking about it as I stood under the cold-water shower in the hall. The leg was okay, but the scar was a dramatic purple-red, three or four inches long. I'd look scary in a bathing suit, but it was healing fine. I was working on my report a couple of hours later when Miralda's voice got my attention. She was on the ground floor, but it carried.

"Sergeant Hauten, how long I knowing you? You come in my house you upset everything! Bad for my business, and you know that. You know I don't lie to you 'bout no police business!"

"Just formal'ty, one quick look. Or Captain have to come, Mirald'."

The Sergeant was polite, but with a tough bullfrog voice. Miralda was equal to it when she opened her pipes, and smart. In a few seconds the whole house knew about Sergeant Hauten.

"You just *tell* him you look! Damn if I want you upsetting my house, Louis, and you know I have my ways!"

"Miralda, got to look whatever you say — "

I smelled reward money in his determination. He was violating an established relationship in a small close-knit community, and not comfortable with it.

"How come you out of your uniform on official business, Sergeant Hauten?"

"Undercover today."

"You got legal warrant come in my house?"

I looked at the room. It was spotless, and the bags were in the closet. There was no sign of habitation except for my case. While they bickered, I put my papers in it and went to the other room. Smith-Davies was in the easy-chair listening to Bach on Jennie's Walkman loud enough that I could hear it through the headphones. I turned it off and put my finger over my lips. This room was empty too, except for his bag.

"The police are downstairs."

Headphones off, he could hear Miralda delaying Sergeant Hauten. Smith-Davies nodded, followed my eyes to the window, and headed for it. Outside the window was a narrow section of roof. The voices were moving along the lower hallways, Miralda loudly informing Sgt. Hauten what she'd have to say to his mother and wife for his own good, and the Sergeant telling her that a man's gotta do what his boss says. I passed Smith-Davies' the case and his bag out the window and followed him onto the roof with his teacup. We were crouched with our backs to the wall when they came in. Down below, a lost tourist couple passed, cameras dangling, too busy quarrelling to see anything. Then the door to the room opened to Miralda's announcement:

"See? No one!" she said in that powerful voice. "You are satisfied, Sergeant?"

"Yes, yes, no one occupying this room. Two more."

He was very eager to get away from that voice. The door slammed and the one leading into other room opened briefly, then shut. A big red dog in the yard was looking up at us, ready to start barking. Smith-Davies looked back at it, smiling faintly and shaking his head. The dog believed him, and a minute later we climbed back in. Then we stood back from the window to watch the Sergeant continue down the dirt road to his car.

Smith-Davies made a little gesture of disbelief with his hands and I went into the other room with my case, thinking that Miralda was up for a major bonus if she didn't throw us out. I put two hundred francs in an envelope, but she didn't appear, so I got out my papers and went back to reconstructing my TCC initiation — Durry at the Velodrome, Millie at the Tic-Toc. Morris and Olcott at the steak house and Al painting a target on me at the Marquis.

I was working when a young local male voice broke into the music on the radio with hot news — CIA was now on St. Marcus, said the voice gleefully, investigating some *peculiar activities*. Someone had sent a witty Fax about this to the media, which he read. St. Marcus being a rich and resented neighbor, this was all very gratifying. *What had those naughty Marcusians done?!*

And how far would CIA get on a French island full of rich and private people?

The weather was changing, and there was a hard wind was gusting hard through the trees. The afternoon went dark, and in a few minutes the creaky old house felt like it might take off and fly away, trees groaning in the wind and tropical rain slapping the leaves. I closed the windows and was back to the narrative when Jennie burst in, soaking wet and irritable, dreads sopping. As she stripped her ruined yellow dress, an envelope slipped under the door behind her. I got to it and slipped it in with my papers while she toweled off, then asked if she'd heard the CIA story on the radio.

"No, but some comedian nominated St. Marcus as our next regime change."

She sat down wearing my robe and looking at me. I asked

her what else she'd heard and she shook her head.

"Let's see what's in the envelope first, Rob."

There was no fooling her. In the envelope were two pictures left by Sergeant Hauten. One from the hidden camera that Marquardt had announced on my first visit — myself in a suit entering TCC France, still heavy, lots of gray hair, face unclear, distorted by the angle. The other shot was Jennie as a teenager out in the country with two big mutts, her black hair long and straight. When I looked up, she had her no-bullshit-please expression.

"Yeah, they almost got us," I said. "Local cop. Miralda did a number on him and he never really checked. I was going to tell you when you settled down."

"Pretty close, Rob, but it's probably the last shot. CIA's leaking wholesale — the Morris-Zack-TCC connection is out now, but nothing on BioTel. It's like we were this rogue midget operation that went crazy. I ran into one of those journalists at Bananas and he told me they've leaked Jason's name. He had a picture of him and asked me to call if I happened to spot him, so now Jason's bait. About the only thing that's still secret is Dick. And BioTel, of course — "

The words were just pouring out of her. I got her down on the bed under a blanket and gave her a shot of rum. She couldn't stop talking about Keith's concern for Jason.

"Keith was so fucked up, Rob. He didn't know whether to shit or go blind, so I took Jason off his hands and stashed him in a rooming house like this one."

Where he's getting some field experience. I couldn't say it, but I liked the idea.

"And we should get out," I said.

She hesitated.

"You're out as soon as the airport's clean. I may have to stay behind a couple of days. Jason can't be alone, so I told Keith I'd get him through this. Stop in and spend time with him each day. I'm the only one who can calm him down. He's too old for this."

Her voice fluttered nervously as she spoke, and she didn't look at me. I took time to think.

"I'm not in love with this," I said.

"Do you think I am? But we can't just leave him on Keith's hands, it's just too dangerous. Keith isn't Morris, this is too much for him to handle. Jason trusts me, they both do. We've got to play team. And Keith is with you, Rob, it's solid."

"I know he is, Jennie. I just don't like it — you at risk here while I get on a plane."

She felt she had my assent now, and her face relaxed.

"We can't be together if it blows up, Rob. Alone, I can talk my way out of anything, you know that. And you can't do what you have to do down here. I'll touch up your hair and buy a guitar for you to carry on. CIA has never seen you except for that guy in Paris, so there isn't much risk. This will blow over in a couple of days and I'll get out."

I couldn't come up with an argument. Slick was the name for her, Morris had that right.

"I'm just so *pissed,*" she said, getting out her cigarette case and extracting the last Sobranie. "But I said I'd do it. I have to, Rob — if Keith caves, we all go down. The up-side is that there are BioTel-Pentagon meetings coming up that blow away this little agency feud like nothing. Bush will make CIA disappear and it'll be business as usual."

She stopped and looked at me. I waited a couple of beats, and found myself seeing it. Hating it, but not seeing what else to do.

"You've been right all along, Jennie. I'll live with it. And I'll do what I can to spare Jason. But any games and he's gone. All I have to do is tell who hired me and Crackerjack is a hands-on spook — "

"*Okay-okay*! she said, furious. "Enough Cotton Mather! The hell with this, I'm sick of it! I don't *get* it, Rob — why does Jason have to pay? For fucking me? Is that it? Are you that dumb?"

It was cold, and it rocked me. After a silence I decided I wasn't that dumb after all. Jason Olcott was finished.

"Don't be angry, Jennie," I said. "It's not just him, it's what people like him did to us once they had the Kennedys out of the way. How they kept getting us deeper and deeper into Nam. They made fortunes, and it ruined us, it just *ruined* us. This country has never been the same. My people had been doing

Navy time for a hundred years, but I shouldn't have gone. After a while I knew it, but I stayed. It soiled us, that fucking war, it took our self-respect. The people that *died*, Jennie! Civilians, women and children, hundreds of thousands, half a million. Then we lied about it, and lied, and lied. Lied to ourselves, and still do. I'm ashamed of it all, and my part in it, small as it was. I'm still angry, it still drives me."

I stopped and she looked at me.

"And that money I skimmed. I knew Jason would be getting rid of me one way or another. I was thinking severance pay, but what it did was obligate me."

"God, I love it when you talk liberal. I can't help it, it's like a revival meeting. Anyway, present time. It could be a lot worse, Rob. Project 38 *über alles*. Works for me."

As she spoke she took her lighter out of her bag, tore up the pictures of us, and burned them in the fruit bowl by an open window, tossing the burning pieces like a salad. I went to my case and got the envelope I'd filled for Miralda.

"Two hundred Swiss. You handle it, you're the one she wants to deal with."

"Too much, a hundred is more than she'd expect, and we don't want to look too rich. But let's finish: Keith really trusts you — "

"So did McVeigh," I said, more to myself than her.

"You can be such a fool," she said, not raising her voice. "No one ever gets it right enough for you, do they? I tell you good news, you turn it into bad. Why don't you get the fuck out of my life?"

She put her face down on her fists the way she had in her car on our way out of New York after the Fred debacle and I apologized for not appreciating what she'd accomplished. After a while she looked up and gave me a slow, searching gaze, as if I might not mean it. Then she picked up where she'd left off.

"So CIA is on it's way out, the BioTel brass are here, and Keith says they're meeting with the Pentagon people tomorrow. Then everyone goes to Washington for more meetings."

Something else hooked up in my head.

"Right," I said. "And by the time Arvin Telemann and his

BCCI banker-buddy are through wining and dining and blackmailing everyone, the Pentagon will see it has no choice but to carry on. And it's a *fraud*, Jennie. Alain joked about it, compared it to Descartes' pineal gland, which turned out to be religious nonsense. Dick said almost the same thing — barely plays checkers. And he's an optimist, if you haven't noticed."

Jennie looked at me thoughtfully.

"That story about Durry and Epstein and the waitress," I said. "I'm sure it happened, but I think maybe Epstein really flipped because Alain let him know it won't work. He's a nut case now, but he might just be honest enough to tell the truth. Everyone says he's a dick, but no one doubts his integrity. Worst thing in the world for BioTel, they'd lock him up and throw away the key, concrete galoshes, whatever.

Her expression hadn't changed.

"BioTel has the *data*, Jennie, they *know* it's not remotely close to working. They had Jason flat-out lying at those Project 38 meetings. They lied to him and he passed it on. With so much invested, they have to sell the thing any way they can. Who's to stop it? Dick's a basket case, Epstein's out of sight, and Alain will move on to consulting for the Pentagon. BioTel gets some lab-whores to fake results and away we go. Everyone does it these days, it's in all the science journals — "

"That's right, honey," said Jennie in a devastating drawl. "And y'know what? Once Arvin T. sells them on Oracle, they'll forgive anything BioTel ever did, TCC included."

"Not those nuke triggers, babe — "

"*Yes those nuke triggers!*" Her voice was a screaming hiss. "Iraq is the enemy of our enemy, that's what's called a *friendly power*. The damn shuttle blew up and no one swung for it, did they, Rob? National Security covers *anything*. No one talks, that's it. Get yourself disappeared if you do, like that Israeli you keep talking about."

"You're one smart lady. I keep forgetting."

"For someone who doesn't read. My father told me Lenny Bruce was dyslexic, too, did you know that?"

She smiled and yawned before speaking again.

"Would you mind if I throw the bolt now? Do y'all think

you could find time to love me a little between crusades Cock Robin? I'm just not feeling very political this afternoon. Recuperative sex, easy on your wounds. Little brainwash, help you forget."

36

It was two in the afternoon at the Soho Sound Studios, a tired old lower Broadway space layered with the grunge of ten thousand recording sessions. They were just starting up for the day, and I sat waiting in a control room full of bad air and electronic gear while bleary engineers drifted through with reels of tape. My guy was a big fat balding audio-paparazzo in his thirties eating Chinese takeout. He had a brain under his fringe of greasy black curls, and saw through my prop guitar right away. I told him it was tapes of a bootleg session and handed him the bag of cassettes. He gave me a look.

"Computer tapes, huh?"

"Two copies. What's it going to cost?"

"I dunno if we can do it," he said, and hit the intercom.

"Hey Rudi, come on in here, we got an interesting problem."

Rudi was different, a Hitler Youth type with thick rimless glasses and a prim rocket-scientist presence.

"RDATS or Exebytes," said Rudi. "Chu would know."

Chu was a small Asian with a very quiet voice. He pronounced on the mystery tapes without hesitation.

"Gonna be WangDAT, same as RDAT," he said. Then he peered up at me curiously, all innocence. "Hey man, you're not, like a spook under that hair?"

"Just a thief," I said.

This drew smiles and caused them to think I was okay, and they had a technical séance. From behind my *Times* I kept an eye on the tapes, and followed them up to the back office of a financial shop in the building that had appropriate equipment.

It took forever before I found what I was looking for in the *Times*. The paper of record had covered itself on rumors from the Caribbean by back-paging two tiny paragraphs on a "possible link" between the Epstein case and allegations of offshore hanky-panky by the BioTel Corporation. It was a meticulous tiptoe through the tulips of national security. Not much, but

BioTel's name had finally appeared in the Gray Lady, which might open the door for bolder publications. Or maybe the *Washington Post* would trump them again with a second coming of Woodward and Bernstein.

It cost a lot more to copy the tapes than I paid Miguel, but it was all TCC money. I was getting optimistic, wondering if the media might be letting Laura Epstein's legs carry the story until someone came up with red meat.

I took a green and orange motel room that smelled of plastic out near LaGuardia, then stood in a hot shower for a long time worrying about Jennie. By the time I was warm, it was call-in time at Bananas. I called from the unsheltered outside payphone, freezing in the wind. Jennie picked up on the second ring, and I forgot the weather.

"I've got your wedding present," she said, and I knew from her voice that she wanted me to think everything was fine when it wasn't.

"Oh? I'm a two-time loser, you know."

"This time you're a winner," she said, with a kind of twist in her voice. "Jason's decided to tell all and you get the first shot. The only condition is that Keith is left free and clear to fulfill his role in life as Senator from wherever and lead his people to the promised land. I got it on cassette and expressed a copy to your P.O. Box. And take it easy on Jason when we get together, Rob? There's not much left of him."

For once there was something like fear in her voice. There would be dangerous stuff on that cassette, and I wanted her off that island so badly I could barely think.

"That's fine," I said. "Perfect, but when do you get out?"

"Day after tomorrow. And get some rest, because I need some debriefing myself. Four-fifteen, Island Express 381. Get your questions ready, Rob, and keep it simple. Jason won't hold up very long."

"What about Keith?"

"Doing better. The Pentagon meetings put CIA on hold and the pressure's off. Are we still in love, Rob?"

"I hope you're kidding," I said. "At this point I don't care what happens to these people anymore, I'm really just trying to make an impression on this woman I know — "

"Oh, you are, you're doing fine," she said. "Stay warm, round-eye."

I stood there in the wind wondering just what could be on that cassette that would bother her so much. The computer tapes had the purged data. Could it be personal? How?

I put it aside and called my daughter. A proudly correct girl at the dorm desk informed me that the students of Finch Hall had, on their very own volition, democratically instituted a policy that calls were not taken from men after six PM during exams. No men at all, because men could pose as relatives, even as fathers. And would we all please just die — that was clearly implicit. Cold with rage, I went back to my plastic room, laid out my notes on the bed, and sat at the tiny desk writing up my final meetings with Durry and Mac. The trip with Mac did me in. I was all right while I was working, but when I took a break I went negative fast and wanted a drink. I flicked on the TV and got the news. Another big air-traffic day — one plane overshooting a runway into the water, while its cousin blew an engine over Topeka.

Then the *Intifada*. A previously quiescent Palestinian group, Hamas, had changed course and got behind the resistance movement. Exasperated Israeli troops had shot up some stone-throwing kids with plastic bullets, killing one and inspiring others. Then a rock-bimbo tried to sell me jeans, a guy tried to sell me a truck, and *Bingo* — Zack Epstein. The network had exhumed the original footage, and hooked it up with the St. Croix/CIA farce. It was hot enough that a tiny-mouthed moon-faced Arvin Telemann appeared briefly, deplaning Big Blue with a suave half-smile to grease his denials. He was replaced by Laura Graves-Epstein looking ten years younger, all tits and tears, and that was new footage. In the manner of beautiful women through the ages, Epstein's wife had daintily reversed her field and was offering morsels of truth. The prime tidbit was her Tel Aviv introduction to that unspeakable master of chicanery, Mr. J. Burton Spiegelman, spy-monster. No date, of course — a date might suggest her age.

An apparently far-reaching affair, opined the anchor, his dreary eyes dancing in his skull.

I lay on the bed with my hands behind my head. BioTel had run into the unpredictable. Not only had the Israelis killed one of those rock-throwing teenagers, they'd chased away the sacred TV cameras, and that was *really* unforgivable. The Intifada was suddenly in, and the BioTel-Mossad-Epstein saga fit the new agenda. My lucky day if they kept it going, but I didn't feel lucky with Jennie still on that island. Lucky would be a lake in Idaho with no TV. Concorde to Paris, rent a Porsche. Dinner at Madame Gauthier's.

In a little while I saw how to use it, and was standing in the wind at the phone. Eventually I got a sullen female gatekeeper at the channel I'd been watching. She sounded like a cross between my greasy-haired audio engineer and the girl at the desk of Layla's dorm, and she wouldn't pass me to anyone else until I authenticated myself. But she wasn't dumb. When I described the gun Zack had shot Morris with, she got me to someone named Jed with better manners, who played games for a minute or two trying to figure me out. I told him my outside phone was very cold and again described the gun that killed Morris, adding the serial number. This got him very interested, and then I gave him a detailed account of the murder near Le Mans, France, of a BioTel exec named Alvin Marquardt who moonlighted for a dirty-tricks BioTel operation called TelcomCo. I thought that was plenty for starters. He waited a second or two to see if I might blurt out some more.

"Do you have anything else you could tell us on this to give more substance to the story? he asked politely. "Perhaps we could meet."

"Not now, and I'd say you had quite a lot, all verifiable and exclusive. But yes, I have much more. Documents and tapes."

He gave me his name again, along with a direct number, and asked if it would be possible to retain my services. Then he asked for a meeting again.

"Let's see how this goes, Jed. You'll hear from me soon, and I won't release what I gave you to anyone else until I see what you do with it. Twenty four hours."

Back in the room, I lay on the bed looking at the ceiling. It was a plan. Feed Jed enough to get him barking. He had to bark loud enough to rouse the others, so I'd give him some more next time. But did exclusivity guarantee that they'd go whole hog and use it to ream the competition? Or would a sampling to the other networks set a giant troika rolling? Deep Throat had kept faith with Woodward and Bernstein, but all I had was a well bred media cupcake who wanted to buy me.

What to release, and when, and to whom? I tried to get my ducks in a row but I was tired and the ducks were splashing around, bumping into each other — tapes, krytrons, radars, Durry the Frog, Crazy Jake, the thing in the pool, and poor, damaged Richardson Smith-Davies. A Smith-Davies appearance would blow Arvin Telemann all the way to Doonesbury, but that duck was grounded. He'd never survive the vultures. Maybe later, with his ACLU lawyer-wife present. I wanted to call her, but I didn't know what that might set off. And I'd told Carol I'd call — another call I couldn't make, because Morris had tapped Mac's lines, and that might be ongoing.

That sent me into pre-history — Morris stealthing his way into TCC. Somehow, very early, when TCC was looking for squeaky-cleans like Keith, the funky and ambiguous Morris had been hired. And had taken over, because Jason Olcott was a fool. BioTel was the big game, but for me it wouldn't be over until I cleared up that mystery. As Morris's protégé, I felt I owed it to him, and I had a feeling that the mysterious Snyder might shed light on that. Snyder the invisible. I still remembered that one-word call to Al. Just one clue: an accent that reminded Durry of a friend from the Pyrenees. I knew it from following the Tour.

The next morning I stepped out into the freezing gray pre-dawn half awake and feeling like a Picasso, head on backwards, hair inside out, ear where my nose belonged. I stood there a few minutes half asleep and watched a jet come in, letting the cold wake me up before going into the lounge. Then back to the little desk with some junk food and phony coffee, filling in details and keeping an eye on my chosen channel. It was local news, but included a reference to the breaking Epstein/BioTel story that would be on the evening news.

I took no satisfaction in it. When I tried Layla again, I was informed that she'd taken a weekend in Boston, which made sense if she was through exams. Hooked up with some lucky book-bag boy probably, but I was uneasy. It was not impossible that someone was back-tracking Beachcomber, and there was no way to know. I got back to work and listened to jets that reminded me of Al Marquardt at the Aerodrome. And the very different Al in the piano bar telling me about 1983 and open silos. Of course he knew — he'd been CIA.

I finished writing at noon, and with the narrative and tapes I had a very live bomb. To cover myself, I chose George Billings, attorney, of West Hartford, Connecticut. We'd gone to school together but Felice hadn't liked his wife and we'd been out of touch for years. It was obvious from his unguarded surprise that no one from TCC had discovered him. He was glad to hear from me, and we found ourselves talking kids and divorces. Then I told him about the arrangements I wanted to make.

"No problem, Robbie. Do you want to tell me what this is about?"

"Industrial stuff. I also want a copy in the hands of a European firm."

"We have a relationship with a Swiss outfit," he said in a slightly different voice. "They'll want to be in touch with you."

"Fine. I'll send two copies."

We said goodbye and I turned on the tube hoping for a cop-show. I got libidinous talk-shows offering a choice of women-married-to-cross-dressers and men-who-have-raped. I turned it off and had myself a little epiphany: what was so crucially important about my little crusade? Why did I think it sane and appropriate to take such risks and involve others in them? How could I think journalists who'd been buying the Emperor's new clothes would turn into Woodward and Bernstein? Nothing new, nothing I could do about it. I was pissing in the wind, but I was going to finish the job.

Food and people, I thought, I need human contact. Someone like Tom Terrific. It would be safe to meet Tom somewhere. Feed him, lend him some money, drink beer and let him bring me up to speed on the Del Psychos' endless search for another hit. If anyone had come by to ask about me, he'd mention it. He picked up on the third ring.

"Yeah-hey!" he said, too loudly. Just my voice had made him uncomfortable. "How ya doing Robbo? How you doin' over there?"

I lied automatically.

"Great job. A little bored sometimes. I thought maybe someone might have tried to get in touch."

"Yeah," he said carefully. "Dude looking for you knocked on my door last night and I told him you were in France. Older guy, European. Didn't get his name — "

"Oh yeah, Gesualdo. Forget him, I had more like women in mind. Any mail?"

"I looked through it, just junk. Hey, I'd like to talk but we've got an audition."

Out-of-the-Loop Fred again. He'd made Tom nervous, which wasn't easy. He'd come looking for me because he'd know where my TV channel was getting information. What would he do if he found me? Pretty much anything, I guessed. But not on impulse.

37

I went into Manhattan for breakfast and had some real food at the Asia de Cuba. A good safe restaurant, and my first actual meal in a while, a big one. Washing down my shrimp and rice with a Dos Equis I was re-thinking the elusive Snyder. Something was trying to fall into place, something in his timeline: Snyder dropped out shortly before I was hired, then re-appeared when I was in Milan. What happened in between? There definitely wouldn't be any vacations while Oracle was coming to a boil. Something had come up for Snyder, something big enough for me to have to replace him. Medical emergency, death in the family, nervous breakdown. It had to be there, but I didn't know anything about Snyder, and I couldn't hook it up.

Jennie's cassette was more immediate, and that was why I was in Manhattan. Visiting my box at the 34th Street Post Office felt risky, but if I Fedexed the tape and my document to George first, I'd be as covered as I could be. Two copies mailed separately, just in case. I found a shop, made copies, and sent them. No one was waiting for me at the P.O., just a pile of junk mail and Jennie's cassette in a padded envelope. I got it all into my case and walked through a bitter-cold afternoon to an electronics store to buy a cassette player. Then I listened to the tape through headphones while walking down 8th Avenue in a freezing wind off the Hudson. I was feeling guilty about leaving Jennie behind, and her danger.

I was very distracted and missed a lot, and what I did get was grim. As usual, Crackerjack didn't get what was going down and didn't sense that the conversation was being directed. He'd been cooped up with a bottle of bourbon and felt like talking, and he was used to doing what he felt like. His situation was aging him fast, and he was trying to talk his way out of depression. I guessed he'd be spending the rest of his life lubed on good bourbon and going on about the good old days. He talked a lot about the golden age of TCC, and his talk was full of sentimental references to Jennie's father and Fred, and others from that time. *Such wonderful men — how could things have gone so wrong?* He talked long and openly, and I saw him as a person for the first time. The fair-haired young clothes horse without any brains, carried along through good schools as a legacy student, forever sucking hind tit in a family dedicated to power. Easy to read, easily used by people like Morris. The periodic references to his love for Jennie were wrenching, but she kept re-directing the conversation until there were plenty of detailed admissions about TCC's activities. It was the smoking gun, but something was missing. It was almost there but she wasn't going after it — just how that golden age *began*. TCC was kaput, my mind knew that, but I wanted the big bang — TCC being born, going from BioTel's security to government agency, maybe with Morris Pell already on board. *How did the Eulenspiegel get inside?* I had to know, it was personal.

I bought the day's papers, walked into a Blarney Stone, and sat down among the rummies to put away some of the house Irish. I was in knots worrying about Jennie, barely able to read, but I read enough to see that everyone now had some version of what was going on with BioTel and the Epsteins. No one had Oracle or Menat Bagdosian and the BCCI connection. Nothing on Morris-Kammler, nothing on TCC, and nothing tied together. That was fine — Jed and his channel would clarify all that. I opened my case to put the newspapers in before my second drink, and it was stuffed with junk mail. No room for my papers, and I wanted to go through them again carefully, and get reporters' names. The *Times* or the *Washington Post* could blow it wide open.

What was I doing in a Blarney Stone drinking lunch? I needed to be alone and calm, so caught a cab.

I lay on my back for a while on my motel bed sorting out my business. There was my mail, the cassette, and the timeline issue with Snyder. I'd met Morris in mid-October, and in November I was working with Durry, my company paperwork still in process.

I started with the Jennie/Olcott tape and knew I was right

about her skirting the deep history. She was also avoiding her own question about how Morris got in? Olcott had been ready to talk about anything, and she never brought it up. She pressed him on everything else, but nothing about how Morris hooked up with TCC. Olcott was putty in her hands — why didn't she ask?

I put it on hold and went to the lounge for some imitation coffee and drank it at my desk while going through my mail. In it was a letter from Layla, written after we met. An apology for having avoided me so long, and an invitation to come up whenever I could. It gave me a brief, warm moment that almost brought tears to my eyes. Then I went on filling my trash basket with junk mail until the next surprise — a note from Mac, who rarely wrote things down. Done with a computer and dot-matrix printer, no signature or date, but it had to be after Cambridge.

Where in hell you might be I've got no idea but like I said, that deal was just some good old boys doing a corporate shuffle and picking up some intellectual property. I think I mentioned they were hooked up with something called Chenco. Turns out that's a security outfit with Nam connections. CEO JP Chen. Sounds to me like one of these little spook operations and I smell a rat. If it's you, don't ever show your face again, I run a bar these days, period.

Chenco. The deep history in one word. When he mentioned it on the phone I thought he was saying Chinko, as in Pinko as in me. And on the Street it *would* be Chinko, being headed by a half-Chink. Chenco had hooked up with State and morphed into TelcomCo. Simple as that. Jennie had said TCC had no bureaucracy, like a family business. She'd just about spelled it out the night I was so drunk in St. Croix.

The reason I'm safe is that I've been on board from the top, and I'm close to everyone that matters.

Right. She was the boss's daughter. The mysteriously dead boss who'd hired the funky street-smart Morris to run it, and Olcott to hook up at State and front for them. But old Chen must have uncovered who Morris really was and who else he reported to, about which he would have raised hell. Which had probably got him killed, leaving Olcott in charge as titular head with Morris running the show. Very neat. Lakam didn't impress Keith, but here they were leading the State Department around by the nose.

But how had Morris fooled Chen to begin with? Experienced with references wouldn't be enough. Someone solid had vouched for him — someone knowledgeable and trusted, and experienced. It had to be that way with an old hand like Chen. I pictured Jennie there through it all, loving her father, suffering his death, grieving and lost, leaning on Olcott. Not dumb, just missing some facts. She was her father's daughter, and she gutted it out, and I didn't think less of her for keeping it to herself.

Which left Snyder, and I could think of only one person who might shed some light on that. It would be a conversation that needed careful managing, and surprise would help. And another drink would help with the Nam-beast. I could feel it getting restless in there, and I'd be on a hair trigger if I wasn't careful. I opened the case and carefully cleaned it, starting with the Michaud, clip and mercury loads one by one. Then I took a cab into Manhattan. I was early, so I went back to the same Blarney Stone for my drink. The liquor worked, the beast dozed, and I turned into Robot Rob. At five-thirty I left some money on the bar and put on my gloves. So far so good. My coordination and adrenalin were about right, and I walked fifteen blocks, immune to the cold, watching the light die over Jersey. How would Mac handle it? Quietly, like a civilian. Slow and easy, put on the poor mouth and blow some booze-breath for diversion. Tell a story to break the ice.

At six I was standing at the door, listening. No voices. I rang the bell. No answer. I felt myself sagging, turning human and afraid. The door opened, and there was Fred, tweed jacket as usual, fresh handkerchief in his pocket. He shook his head like a broken man, and his eyes had the weary look they'd had the night Morris recruited me, as if he really and truly wanted to retire.

"It is dangerous for you to be here, Rob. You should have called as I asked — now I must say you were here, you understand."

"You came looking for me last time."

"No, no — very different. Lock the door, we will go to my rooms."

I just wanted the truth, whatever it was. That was my thought as we walked through the dark racks of clothes to the room with period furniture and small light bulbs. He asked me to take off my coat, then went to the cupboard-bar and poured brandies. I placed my coat over the back of a chair and we sat down before Fred spoke. After a light remark about my hair, his voice was gentle but firm.

"I don't need to tell you the extent of your difficulties, but I must tell you that I have some of my own, too, now. Let us see what can be salvaged."

Collegial and encouraging, but I wasn't going to spill my guts again, just nodded earnestly and didn't reply. Fred gave me two beats, saw that I wasn't making that mistake again and smiled.

"Things go badly but you look well. You have good color."

"A walk in the cold and a few drinks."

Having spotted the sun on my skin, would he suspect I'd been in the Caribbean? Or would he know already?

"You are aware that this man the Epstein boy killed in California was Morris?"

"I suspected."

"Are you aware that a couple visited the Epstein house before Morris was killed?"

"No, I wasn't." I paused. "They're not blaming Morris on *me*?! That's ridiculous!"

"That depends who you mean by 'they.' The gun — you gave it to the boy . . . ?"

I gave him an exasperated look.

"Of course not, I was never there. If they knew each other from before, which the boy suggested on TV, Morris may have given Epstein or his wife a similar gun."

He nodded slowly. It was possible. We had another sip of brandy. He wasn't quite himself, and I remembered his remark when selling me the case.

I am not eager to sell it, but my wife requires to be in hospital.

Right! So right that I couldn't think for a couple of seconds. Then his voice focused me.

"You did not go to California, then?"

I'd already denied it twice, so I gave him a mild exasperated look. Then I slowed my voice to serious and patient, and puzzled. Confused, and a little disoriented.

"Fred — who was Morris? What's been going on? You introduced me to him, you said you knew him well — "

"Within limits. Morris was never indiscreet. Tell me — do you have any idea what happened down there on that island we are reading about?"

"Not really, just TV and what I see in the papers."

"And Jennie is all right?"

"I don't know, I think so. She got tired of living in a ski cabin. She got tired of me, really. It was over, she was bored."

Very possible, and he couldn't quite conceal his satisfaction.

"So why are you here, Rob?"

"I'm afraid people will think I know more than I do, and they'll want me dead, like Al and Morris. I'm going to have to start over under a new name. Somewhere I'm not known. Quebec maybe. I had some ID made up, but I could use a loan, Fred."

A flicker of amazement went through the eyes of Jennie's old family friend. I couldn't tell if he believed me at all, aside from Jennie getting bored with me.

"I'm curious about something," I continued as he sat there looking bored with me. "A man named Snyder preceded me in France — I don't think I mentioned him. All I know about him is that he spoke French with a southern accent. Does the name mean anything to you?"

No reaction. He shook his head and gave me a look as if to ask why I'd expect him to reveal anything to me, of all people. Then he picked up his glass and took mine, which still had a little brandy in it. It caught my attention. He stood there a moment and I spoke again.

"I just had the feeling I'd been set up, and that this Snyder might be involved."

He waited, glasses in hand, and I repeated what I'd said about starting over and being broke, adding something about how hard it had been to lose Jennie. He looked concerned, as if he was trying to figure out what to say to me. I bluffed.

"Something about a man known by the initial 'S' came up with Crackerjack the last time we spoke. I thought it might be the same person — Snyder."

Which was often an Anglicized Schneider, which happened to mean tailor. A tailor who needed some time off because his wife was going in hospital to die right around the time I was hired. Thank you Morris, for your trick names.

Time slowed down. I'd shot my bolt and could only watch for some reaction, however slight. Nothing. Fred just shook his head silently, with a kind of stuffy empty expression. Not an expression at all, it wasn't him. He turned and put the glasses on the bar, then leaned forward to reach for the bottle as I digested that expression. It was a fake.

He reached past the bottle, his body shielding his hand from view. Then he turned away. The turn melted into a spin. It was too fast, it gave him away. A bad mistake, and perfect proof of everything I'd guessed.

I was ready, but he was quick as a snake. When he finished his spin there was a big old automatic in his hand. I was firing before I saw it, and if I hadn't released the safety and put the Michaud on auto, I'd have been gone. I fired without thinking about it, and it saved my life. The first round threw him off, and his Walther went off with a deafening crash when I hit him. It didn't stop him. I kept the trigger down, the case jumping in my hand. He kept turning in a spastic nightmare pirouette, but I was ducking away as he fired again with another huge crash. A wild shot over my head. The Michaud's phlegmatic little auto-fire *pop-squirts* continued and Fred was hopping and staggering around until finally he fell backward across the rug. By the time he went down, he was stitched from crotch to throat, blood coming through his shirt. The clip was empty, so I couldn't put one in his brain, but there was no need. He was definitely dead, flung back on the beautiful Persian rug, the old Walther lying in front of him, his mouth open, a blind stare in his eyes.

It was cold-blooded premeditation. No question of saving another life or anything like that. Self-defense, but only technically. I'd goaded him into it. But really I'd just settled a score for someone who couldn't do it herself, and would never know about this.

I finally had the deep history: Fred introducing old friend Morris to old friend Chen, and vouching for him. Perfect man for the job. And when J.P. got onto Morris, Fred had done the old man himself so Morris would have an alibi. After which he'd comforted the daughter. Cool Fred.

I stood there rooted for a couple of seconds before realizing I'd been hit. His first shot had taken a slice from the upper arm of my jacket, and a shallow groove of upper bicep meat was bleeding through. I took off my jacket and was about to pull off my tie to wrap around it, then stopped. The tie gave me a look I needed. I leaned over and removed Fred's fresh white handkerchief. Factory product, no monogram. I wrapped it around the wound and dressed, glad that my coat was intact, and thinking all the while how crazy it was for Fred to fire an un-silenced gun. Pure desperation — I'd had him dead to rights and he knew it. It meant I couldn't use the front door, but it was locked, and very solid, which gave me some time. I started down the hall where Jennie had appeared last time. The hall led to stairs, the stairs to the roof. I was okay until I opened the bulkhead door, when the whoosh of warm air reminded me of Millie. Then I stepped out onto another icy roof and looked around. Three bulkheads leading down into other buildings. It was almost dark, with a wind driving off the river.

I went to each bulkhead, calm and deliberate, seeing that I might be trapped. They were all locked, and the Michaud was empty, so I couldn't shoot one out. If I'd brought the Walther, no problem, but I was running out of time. I guessed I had two or three minutes to get to the street without being noticed. No one would investigate gunshots, but someone would make a call, and it was a well-policed neighborhood. I stood there for a long moment wondering. Could I go back down into Fred's building? No.

I walked the perimeter of the roofs in a kind of trance.

Nothing. I was out of time when I saw a rusty fire-escape. It had a chain across it and an old sign warning that it was unsafe. I stepped over the chain and went down as lightly as I could, rust crunching under my shoes, praying no one would spot me passing a window. All the way down I was waiting for the fire escape to fall off and land on top of me. At the bottom I dropped the case into the filthy alley. The swing-down ladder was missing, so I hung from the edge and let go. It was about fifteen feet, and I hit hard, spraining my ankle, banging my elbow and falling forward, smearing my hands on some ripe old garbage under the slush. There were sirens in the distance, but in Manhattan there are always sirens. I was wiping my hands into my coat pockets when I heard them getting close, so I stepped into the street, case in hand, shoes still covered with muck and snow that I stamped off. Seconds later two blue-and-whites from opposite directions converged thirty feet away with a screech. I'd barely made it, but people were gathering to see what had happened, and I lost myself among them. I stood there with them, my hands soiled, but looking respectable in my trench coat with attaché case. I shifted with the gathering crowd, looking at the cops and the doorway like everyone else, waiting for a cue to leave. Another cop car arrived and three cops went in while one stayed in the doorway, glaring us but not looking at faces. Their cars were blocking traffic and the crowd was getting bigger. The cop in the doorway didn't like it.

"G'wan home, nothin' t'see."

A young man in a leather jacket took the suggestion and was followed by a teenage girl. I followed them, then turned a corner and was walking alone. Alone every way I knew of. I couldn't feel my ankle or my wounded arm. I couldn't feel anything, I was numb.

Down at the river I stood facing the wind. New Jersey was faraway lights across metal-colored water. I looked back to make sure I was alone, then wiped down the case with a Kleenex and placed it at my feet lying flat. It was clean inside already, so there was nothing to connect me with it, and I'd put on my gloves. I cleaned my shoes with the remains of the Kleenex and looked out at the river, its rough water catching what light there was.

For half a minute or so I was in a kind of trance. When I came out of it, I pushed the case off the pier with my foot. It floated for a few seconds, one end up, then slid below the surface while releasing some air-bubbles. After that I uttered a very simple prayer that I be forgiven if it were possible. When I turned around I was still alone.

At the motel I washed my hands first, then my coat pockets. After that I showered, cleaned the wound, and smeared it with antibiotic cream before re-wrapping it. After that I sipped Jameson for an hour or so, listening to the jets and watching a movie about patriotic spies. When the news came on, I switched to my channel and caught a few words from the kinder-gentler president. Mr. Bush was going to stop the drug trade in its tracks by fixing Panama and his old CIA buddy, Señor Noriega, an unworthy man who knew too much and was being disrespectful. Time to test some weapons and install a new puppet. I hated the president as much as his father had hated FDR. But Jed's network was going for it. BioTel-Epstein had ratcheted up and had a sidebar — Alvin Marquardt, man of many faces and CIA connection. The commercials came on and I surfed channels. The others were going with scraps, filling in with Laura. She was planning a book, which Zack could write for her. If he didn't have a girl, he'd have his choice tomorrow. And maybe a damaged father that he cared about. I hoped not. Like Mr. Nir, Jake Epstein had outlived his usefulness, and I guessed BioTel would disappear him.

To avoid using the motel pay phone, I hopped a jitney to the airport for my Jed call. I avoided using his direct number, and his blown-out groveling assistant got me through in seconds.

"*Very* glad you called. It would be an understatement to say we're pleased. Your material is invaluable — we want to continue the relationship and compensate you."

"I have a Swiss account. Let's talk numbers."

"We should really sit down to discuss it — "

"That's what we should really *not* do. As it stands, you might be harassed and your notes taken, but you've never seen me, which is to your benefit. Recording me is a natural thing to do, but a very bad idea. You can take my word on that. Lose your tapes. Physically destroy them all and toss them in someone else's dumpster. If you're recording now, stop."

"Our attorneys — "

" — they won't really know much about national security situations like this. I do — stop recording. Trust me. What matters is that the facts are demonstrably correct, based on information from anonymous calls."

"Okay, and I'll dump the tape I started when we get off. Both tapes."

"Erase first, then physically destroy, Jed. You don't want what comes with them. Think about Dan Rather."

"Got it. Could you give me a general idea of what else you have?"

"For tonight, the location of a secret BioTel lab engaged in research on carbon-based artificial intelligence with application to SDI." I paused so he could write it down. "I also have something that your local news should have by now, but without background. A man known as Federico D'Andrade was killed at about six-thirty. West 17th Street near Eighth Avenue. He ran a tailor shop and was also known by the name Snyder." Another pause. "He was an associate of the man killed by the Epstein boy in California. That man's name was Pell, Morris Pell. Also known as Arnault, and he may have had dual citizenship, US/ Israel — "

"Would you hold for a few seconds?"

He dispatched his assistant to check out the precinct and we resumed.

"The lab project is organic cybernetics," I continued. "Known in the Pentagon as Project 38, known within BioTel as Oracle. Project director is Jakob Epstein, father of Zack, the boy who shot that intruder in California. He's prominent and easily researched. He's being held on a Caribbean island against his will. Alvin Marquardt was killed in connection with this project, by the way, and they both worked for that BioTel subsidiary, TelcomCo, that I told you about." I paused again. "The man killed in the Epstein house, Morris Pell, was theirs, too. He also worked for Lakam, Israeli military intelligence agency that ran

Jonathan Pollard, spy who was convicted last year — "

"I know the case. Can we verify all of that?"

"Not without my help. They'll fight you every step of the way, nobody wants this out. The lab is on St. Marcus, which is French. It's two kilometers south of Lucian's restaurant on the coast road. That's why CIA was down in the islands. If you can get in there quickly you may save Epstein's life. And there's a Frenchman, Dr. Alain Durry, who can verify Marquardt's role. He isn't subject to US law, and he can be bought. He knows as much as anyone about Project 38."

There was a pause, and a little grunt away from the phone.

"I just got confirmation of the D'Andrade shooting," said Jed. "We really need to discuss further arrangements now that we're committed. I take it that's what you want."

I gave him a two beat pause.

"Yes. The story and the money both. I also have possession of BioTel computer tapes detailing illegal arms sales involving a prominent banker with Iran-Contra and BCCI connections. Adoptive Italian citizen, you'll know him."

"Really. Can we get the details and discuss numbers soon?"

"One hundred thousand for everything."

"I can't say yes to that on my own, without seeing what there is — "

"Maybe not, but that's — what? Year's salary for a mid-level exec? Research fee? One-time expense, once in a decade story. Someone on staff can figure it out, Jed. No one else has the material, and if it comes to negotiating, I'm going to test the market. There's plenty of material. That Frenchman alone would be plenty. And the tapes, of course. Talk it over, but quickly. Decide tomorrow and be ready to transfer the money by end of the business day. There's nothing more until that's done, and I'll shop it around if I have to."

"Oh no, really, it won't come to that."

Then I called lawyer George in West Hartford and told him to expect two packages the next day, and to be sure to get one off to Switzerland directly. It bothered him. I wasn't an imposter, but I wasn't the guy he remembered, or a client he really wanted. It didn't bother me; knowing I was covered was what mattered.

I walked outside and stood watching an airport jitney, wanting it all to be over. Oracle would have its day, then Jed would have the krytrons and the illegal routings, and Arvin Telemann's brother-in-law from BCCI hell. All I had to do was dole it out and stand clear. Pass Go and collect my hundred thousand. But in the middle of these thoughts I remembered Fred wheeling on me, and the pop-squirts from my case and that big bang from the Walther, with Fred staggering around like a spastic puppet, still trying to shoot me.

I went back inside and sat on the edge of the bed thinking about George's reaction and what I had turned into showing off for my girlfriend as Keith put it. All I could think was that I wanted that girlfriend, wanted to know she was safe. While I was fearing for her, the phone rang. I froze, thought, composed myself, picked it up with a quiet *hello*.

"Daddy . . . ?"

A great weight lifted.

"I was in the country and I thought I'd call. It's great to hear your voice."

"Are you — okay, dad? You don't sound right, do you have the flu or something?"

"I was napping, I'm just waking up."

"I'm glad you called. Since we had dinner I keep thinking about you, about not talking to you for three years."

"Layla, you were a kid. I'm just glad to be talking to you now, I missed you."

From her voice I knew that no one had contacted her.

"So are you going to come and see me again?"

There was such unsureness in her voice that it just froze me.

"Sure, definitely. Like maybe a week or two?"

"Whenever you can. Can we talk about math? Seriously, I mean. I'm doing fine except for math."

"It's genetic, Layla. No one in your mother's family can count, they hire people like me to do it for them."

She laughed in spite of herself and told me to back off her mom, and we started talking about things that are important at school. She was taking a music course and learning harmony. What a pain it was missing out on the math gene, the greatness of Dylan Thomas.

When I was off the phone I started putting myself together. Where I was, what to do, what not to do, what to think, how to think. It was like going through a mine-field.

38

LaGuardia was a metastasizing third-world bus terminal, businessmen and tourists and families in endless lines, delayed flyers parked around the edges. I found a screen that told me Jennie's plane was late, so I picked up the morning papers, and tried to eat a cardboard roll with fake coffee while I read them. The story was coming alive like Frankenstein, and a woman at the *Washington Post* was giving BioTel their Who-Are-These-Bozos? treatment. She'd dug up the fact that Arvin Telemann and his bag-man brother-in-law were unindicted Iran-Contra co-conspirators, up to their necks in tax games, re which prosecution had been mysteriously lax. An old picture showed the pair of them, plump as Marquardt, with that same seal-like smoothness, surrounded by pretty women and politicians. It didn't matter, I didn't really care. I didn't even care about Olcott; all I wanted was to see Jennie coming off a plane.

Time passed, Flight 381 was fifty minutes overdue, and my stomach was a sour knot. I tried a paperback, but even Elmore Leonard couldn't distract me, so I worked my way through the crowd to the Island Express counter. My face must have said something to the kid on the other side, and he made a call.

"Still nothing new," he said frankly. "They left late, that seems to be it."

I thanked him and went to the bar, where I had a double Jameson straight up in memory of Mac. Had there been something in that kid's face? In a little while I was getting drunk and sad. It's rare, but I know the symptoms. Time gets slippery and I'm careful about dismounting bar stools. It was happening on one drink, and I wanted a lot more of them, and I thought I knew why. I had killed two people, and I didn't know what to do with it. Never had the Ops brainwash that makes it okay. And Jennie was out there somewhere in the Bermuda Triangle. Courier Rob ordered a black coffee and reminded himself not to do anything stupid.

"*Oh God!*" said the man next to me, his voice cutting through my thoughts along with other voices. Muttered *Oh!*s and wordless sighing gut sounds. A woman started sobbing quietly. I came back out from wherever I was and felt a terrible affirmation of the air-fear I get whenever someone close is on a plane. A message was printing itself at the bottom of the screen during a chatty little talk show.

" . . . *reports of unidentified commercial aircraft lost in the Caribbean on St. Croix-New York route confirmed by Mayday signal* . . ."

And watch for floating bodies on the evening news.

A black man sitting alone at a little table was crying. Without thinking I went over and put my hand on his shoulder. He didn't mind.

"My wife," he said, "my little boy."

I walked away lightheaded with pain and hate. I'd sacrificed Jennie to a herd of warlike sheep that worshipped a movie actor and thought patriotism was flags and nukes and cheap oil. After a while I realized I was crying, but it was New York and no one noticed. I got a cab back to the motel, and when we got there the driver gave me a funny look when I paid him. I realized that my face was still wet, and I couldn't stop the tears. It had never happened before. Forty years worth all at once.

In my room I sat on the edge of the bed with my head in my hands, shaking all over, a thin keening sound rising from my chest, tears still pouring down my face. Then I walked around the little room to see if that might stop it. I noticed the call-return light flashing, but my guts were fluttering like trapped birds and I couldn't talk. When it let up I called the desk. The girl gave me two St. Croix numbers for calls that had come in about an hour apart. The second one was around Flight 381's departure time.

She called from the airport, I thought. About the delay. For a moment it was as if she was back. Then it thickened my dull, dazed feeling until I was almost paralyzed.

The girl said there'd been another call, from a man I'd never heard of, a Mr. Bamford. A Washington number. It should have made me nervous, but all it meant to me now was that I should get out. Life as a series of motels. It was coming at me — no visible means of support, fake ID, using my skills the way spooks do when they become expendable. Nature of the game. I remembered Jennie trying to warn me about that in L.A., and I knew that almost anything I did or thought for a long, long time was going to bring her back, like with my father when my mother died.

Gone, I thought. All of it — Jennie, the love she'd pulled from my bitter guts, the demented crusader I'd become, the decent father I'd been trying to become. Even my shabby underemployed loft-dweller existence was gone. I never wanted to get close to another human being again, or another cause. And there wasn't going to be anyone else. I was too far gone for anyone else. Death, I was thinking. I'd asked for it. I'd been playing with it, and it had called my bluff.

The phone rang. It would be the SOB from Washington, Bamford, Banford, Bumfuck, whatever. I felt okay to answer it now, having nothing significant to lose. All I had was some black money, a Swiss account, and an inclination to suicide that ran in the family. When you're useless to yourself and everyone else, the option becomes obvious. I let myself think about that for a minute. How to do it right and not hurt anyone. That was what it took to get my mind off Jennie for a moment.

The phone was still ringing, so I answered it.

"Broome here," I said in a quiet businesslike voice.

"We have a message from a Lily — Lily von Schtupp, I think it is. Please call . . . "

Jennie, giving me a St. Croix number. I was weightless, afraid to breathe.

"Okay," I said, like a normal person getting some normal information. "Could I have that number again?"

She read it off and hung up, and I got professional. Out of the room, no checkout; there was another motel I could get to by crossing the freeway. I grabbed my bags and started overland toward an endless six-foot spume of dirty gray ice-water flying up off the traffic. I watched for an opening and got myself to the divider, and then the other half, narrowly avoiding death by tractor-trailer. When I got to the other motel, I called St. Croix. Jennie said my name and then broke down. When she could talk again her voice was small and childlike, like after Millie had nearly killed her.

"I felt it coming, Rob. In my stomach. I started thinking how badly they wanted Jason, and how he sticks out in a crowd. I knew we'd be picked up. First I couldn't go through the airport with him. Then I watched him board and just didn't get on the plane."

"I want you here, Jennie — can you come soon? I need to know you're here."

"Yes, I think it's safe. I paid Miralda to take care of Dick for two months, so he'll be okay, she knows about his medicine. I'll call his wife when it's safe."

"Good. I'm going to the Chelsea and watch some TV. Should I tell them you're due the day after tomorrow?"

"Yes. Tell me you love me, Rob."

"You're the best thing that ever happened to me. I just spent two hours in hell."

"Am I really the best? In your whole life? I won't ask you again for a while."

"I don't qualify to kiss your ass, Miss. By the way, someone in Washington traced me to the motel, some guy named Bamford — they're onto the Broome I.D., so I'll register under . . . I've got the second ID you had made. Jeffrey Jackson. I'm thinking about returning that guy's call, though. I can't be on the run forever. But as far as they know, you're gone — is that what you want?"

"I'm gone, all right — some poor tourist kid lost her ticket and I gave her mine. I'm gone, and I think I'm staying gone, Rob. But listen — do *not* call that Bummer guy till we have a chance to talk. Don't do it — promise me that, Rob."

"Okay, I won't. I got the narrative and tapes to a lawyer, a guy I can trust, and he sent a copy to a Swiss outfit. I think I can cut a deal with Big Brother on some kind of terms where I can go home after they debrief me."

"Not until we talk — *promise* me, Rob!"

"I just did."

"Shit, I'm afraid I'm gonna to lose it again, and there's a woman with about ten kids who needs the phone. Let's take our vacation up north, okay? Go skiing."

I agreed. I would have agreed to anything.

Also by Bjarne Rostaing: BREEDERS a crime novel

When tough, self-made thoroughbred owner Pat McGoohey hires African American Len Thomas as his trainer, he breaks with ancient protocol, taking Len across the color line, setting off a rapidly accelerating adventure of crime, racing and race.

Len Thomas likes being the only black thoroughbred trainer anyone ever heard of, but Pat McGoohey is one rough, tough, unethical owner. Lacking good ponies, he's obsessed with having his top mare bred with a champion stud owned by Kentucky blue-blood Dixie Dixon, whose weakness is her clever Creole confidante and lover, Holly St. Cyr. Len falls hard for Holly and breaks some rules to win in Saratoga, impressing oil billionaire Sheikh Lakham.

When McGoohey approaches Dixie for her stud's services, she humiliates and insults him, enraging the impulsive, dangerous owner, who presses Len to get hold of that super-sperm however he can. It all blows up, with Len in jail and wingman Paco on the lam with the juice and one jump ahead of the law. When Holly leaves Dixie for Len and springs him from jail, it leads to a showdown in Mexico, complete with Sheikh, a bent *Federale*, true love, and a huge bluff that works.

Bjarne Rostaing delivers the goods. He knows horse racing — and, more importantly, he knows people. From the racetrack to the back streets of L.A., BREEDERS zings with flavor and flair. A strong debut novel from a writer who we should be hearing a lot more from.
— **C.E. LAWRENCE**
author of *Silent Slaughter*

America is a country in which the complexity of the truth runs so contradictory to clichés that it can seem revolutionary just by being itself. What Bjarne Rostaing has achieved here is something so free of clichés about minorities, women, and privileged men that we are continually startled by his authority and insight. In the process, he reinvents the heist tale as a commentary on contemporary life as it is actually lived.
— **STANLEY CROUCH**
author of *Kansas City Lightning,*
Syndicated columnist, cultural critic

BREEDERS

A CRIME NOVEL

BY BJARNE ROSTAING

#

Trainer Len Thomas glanced up in the direction of the boxes hanging over the grandstand at the Santa Anita track, enjoying the heavy sun. His mahogany skin would have made his presence in his employer's box awkward, but that was fine with him. He understood the thoroughbred racing caste system and was happy to be a trainer, it being mid-summer 2002 and training still very white turf. Len was the most generally respected member of the McGoohey camp among true horse people, but he was happier and more relaxed in the stands than he would have been in the box with owner Pat McGoohey reigning in tacky splendor. Cool, reserved, with a straight, distinctive nose, Len was anything but tacky in his lightweight navy blazer, yellow turtleneck and gray slacks. The parched track favored his horse, Popsicle, a big, nasty bay owned by McGoohey. He badly wanted this overdue win but it didn't show in any way.

The McGoohey box was a kind of share or sublet, filled with people who served various purposes. He'd have preferred others, but this was a social occasion and a paying of debts, so it had to be his wife Jasmine, of course, boobs hanging out of her latest drop-dead outfit, a kind of bathing-suit-with-tutu in aqua. Next to her was the tweedy Public Works Commissioner Big Jim Bullitt, a fine figure of a man at six-four despite the sloping gut. He loved racing, and had the power to deliver major contracts to McGoohey's construction company. Jasmine's assignment was making nice with the Commish, and her snuggly smiles suggested that but for the presence of others she'd be doffing her designer dress for him then and there. On Bullitt's other side was his skinny well-born wife, who didn't like McGoohey.

Behind them with his plump pink wife sat Uncle Fred in

an ancient blue seersucker suit. Well into Alzheimer's, Fred couldn't remember that McGoohey had a horse in the race, but back when he'd had his wits about him he'd staked his wayward nephew on a hunch, and he was now richer than he would ever understand. McGoohey was bored, dreaming of a world where you could have your trainer, your bookie, a lap-dancer, and maybe your Hispanic horse-whisperer in your box without everyone getting pissed off. He stopped talking as his horse approached the gate and watched the animal intently. Popsicle, a.k.a. Crazy Horse, had speed to burn and hated the world. He was behaving himself, though, and entered the gate quietly. Jockey Jimmy Broughton's pinched face showed nothing at all. To McGoohey he looked like a man at prayer.

Ten seconds out of the gate, Popsicle was lying fourth of nine, right behind big Decks Above, a one-speed animal who ran hard and steady but had no finish. Dust was kicking up off the bone-dry track, which was just how Popsicle liked it. In the lead was Beppo, a pure speed horse, unbeatable up to a mile, followed by Atomic Fireball, an unknown. With any luck, the race would end with Popsicle chasing down Beppo, and Popsicle was right where he belonged. McGoohey's emotions as he rose from his seat were primitive and powerful, more intense and complex than any he'd ever experienced with his trophy wife. The track was right, the distance was right, and his horse was right, running easily, a little off the rail, but with no other horse squeezing in there, because all the jockeys knew he was trouble. After the first turn, the horses behind him were gradually falling back and the Fireball was faltering, letting little Beppo slip away as Decks Above kept hammering along. Fireball flamed out, and it was three horses, Beppo still going well and Decks Above not quite keeping up.

"*Now!*" bellowed McGoohey through the howling crowd. "*NOW!!*"

He trained his glasses on Jimmy Broughton, who was making a fierce effort to get his horse around Decks Above and chase down Beppo before it was too late. Popsicle was on cruise control, thinking about it. Beppo was still pulling away, but there was a good furlong to go, and Popsicle was a real closer. When he started his move, the crowd felt nervous wonder. Instead of going around Decks Above, he was closing with the rail, stubbornly edging himself into a trap. The crowd went quiet at this bizarre and very dangerous maneuver. Broughton's crop whacked his horse's left ear hard, but the rail beckoned and Popsicle didn't flinch. The jockey whacked the ear again, but Popsicle was doing it his way, through an imaginary hole between Decks Above and the rail, nosing into it as if blind, his head edging toward Deck's hindquarters as the jockey fought him.

Len Thomas understood instantly. He'd seen Popsicle get ideas like this before, like maiming some groom or kicking in a particular section of barn wall, and these ideas would take possession of him. Crowding the rail was an old favorite. A higher power was commanding Crazy Horse to squeeze into a hole that didn't exist. Len froze as he saw Jimmy battling the horse, a few seconds lasting as long as a presidential address.

McGoohey was livid, standing in the front of his box, leaning forward and bellowing savagely at his horse in a penetrating blue-collar voice, a brutal, industrial-grade voice developed to cut through the roar of pneumatic drills, cement mixers, pile-drivers, truck rumblings, and electrical tools. No one within fifty feet missed a word.

He picked Jimmy up again in the binoculars and went silent. Decks was still on the rail, and Jimmy had to be fearing for his life as he fought his horse. Horses sometimes flipped over the rail, and big Decks Above wasn't moving over. McGoohey was sick with fear, knowing the animal was crazy. Then, for no apparent reason, Popsicle lost interest in the rail and started moving out where he belonged. As he made his move Beppo ran out of gas, forcing him further out. Then he was flying, and at the wire it was anybody's race. After the lull it was announced: Decks Above, winner by a nose, Popsicle second.

McGoohey recovered slowly, still standing as the Commissioner seated himself with dignified composure beside his shocked wife. The owner was oblivious as people in other boxes and the stands watched from the corners of their eyes. Deeply relieved that Jimmy was safe, McGoohey noted that his wife had engaged the Commissioner closely enough to anger his wife. Thinks fast, he thought. Drives me crazy but she doesn't miss a trick.

He was accepting defeat, but talk was out of the question and no one dared approach him. He wanted to be somewhere else. Some place where he could break something, terrorize an employee, start a bar fight, beat his head against a wall. Decks Above a winner at last! What a joke! All thanks to Crazy Horse, who'd kept his losing streak alive after all. In two years he'd won just once, but had been disqualified with good reason. And Popsicle could not pass on that wonderful natural speed. Like the rest of the string, he lacked something, in his case, testicles. As the owner came out of it, the crowd was buzzing about the next race, except for those in his box, who shrank from him. Others within earshot would be avoiding the McGooheys for a while, if they weren't already.

"That one horse must be crazy," said Uncle Fred, causing a taut grimace to pass McGoohey's face. Jasmine nearly exploded in laughter but managed to convert it to a smile for the Commissioner, who was ready to explode with lust while his wife stared straight ahead.

Eat your heart out Fatso, thought McGoohey. At least he would not have to see any of them for a while. He was developing a fine headache as his thoughts moved to excavation problems out at the canyon site. As he put thumb and forefinger to the bridge of his nose and slightly lowered his head, his wife recognized the symptoms and felt guilty relief. She didn't know exactly what would happen if one of his horses ever actually won, but she knew it would involve a lot of drinking and herself being on call for many victory laps.

Len Thomas was limp. By some miracle Jimmy was all right. But Popsicle had to go, because Jimmy would keep taking the rides, and the animal was just too dangerous. His cell phone rang.

"Just glad Jimmy's still with us," said McGoohey in a calm voice. "You were right about Popsicle, gotta get rid of him, and I'm gonna do that."

"Glad to hear it, Pat, I was thinking the same thing. See you in the morning?"

"No, you take it. I've gotta get on that canyon crew. I'll be in touch."

His calm was not convincing, and Len expected a difficult week, along with a New Plan, which might be anything other than investing in a sound horse with some real potential. Pat was going to do it his way, buying animals like Popsicle for cheap. But no matter what the man came up with, Len knew he had to keep a firm grip on his relations with this owner, because there was no replacing him. No one else would hire a black trainer, but McGoo had no use for racing protocol and Len was the only trainer he could get along with.

Give him credit for that, he mused soberly. *It's not just that I come cheap. Man loves his horses and he trusts me with them, knows I can do the job. Gotta keep that in mind all times.*

He leveled himself off by reflecting on the totemic Jimmy Winkfield, a.k.a. The Black Maestro, the last great African American figure in the sport. He was Len Thomas's model. A hundred years ago when Southern aristocrats controlled racing, Winkfield had won everything, including back-to-back Kentucky Derbies. When a Jim Crow cabal squeezed blacks out, it was over. Stable hand, hot walker, groom, exercise boy — that was it for black people now.

Stay cool and you can beat it; that was Len's mantra. But you might have to be a little creative. Winkfield had beat it by going to Russia, winning as usual, and marrying an aristocrat. Caught in the Revolution, he'd moved south to further victories in Poland and France. He was Len's idol, and his picture hung on the living-room wall alongside Secretariat's. A smooth, calm face with large thoughtful eyes.

www.ingramcontent.com/pod-product-compliance
Lightning Source LLC
Chambersburg PA
CBHW050913250626
47155CB00001B/211